Penny Benjamin was born and raised in central Alberta. Surviving a serious car accident when hit by a drunk driver, she came out of the coma to find herself on her own at the age of sixteen, until meeting her partner, when at eighteen, together they rebuilt their lives. Eventually Penny balanced a successful career in real estate with a loving relationship and family which included their two sons and numerous animal rescues. Throughout it all, Penny found peace in writing and an escape in dreaming. With her first full length novel *Linked* she invites us all to take a journey with her.

I would like to dedicate this book to my mother, who always urged me to be creative, my partner for daring me to dream and my kids, who gave me the courage to seek out a way to get this novel published.

Penny Benjamin

LINKED

AUSTIN MACAULEY PUBLISHERS™

LONDON ∗ CAMBRIDGE ∗ NEW YORK ∗ SHARJAH

Ordering Information
Quantity sales: Special discounts are available on quantity purchases by corporations, associations, and others. For details, contact the publisher at the address below.

Publisher's Cataloging-in-Publication data
Benjamin, Penny
Linked

ISBN 9781647506780 (Paperback)
ISBN 9781647506797 (ePub e-book)

Library of Congress Control Number: 2021923474

www.austinmacauley.com/us

First Published 2022
Austin Macauley Publishers LLC
40 Wall Street, 33rd Floor, Suite 3302
New York, NY 10005
USA

mail-usa@austinmacauley.com
+1 (646) 5125767

I would like to thank everyone at Austin Macauley Publishers for their faith in me and their guidance and expertise in getting *Linked* published.

Prologue

The key chain rattled as Emma pushed it into the lock. Damn! It never failed, just when matters couldn't possibly get any worse…

Trying desperately to balance purse, briefcase and various shopping bags, not a hard feat for someone with an ounce of dexterity, she laughed hysterically. Damn! The phone was ringing, probably the office; Christ, she had just left the bloody place. Why is it, keys never friggin' work well? Taking a deep breath, she worked it back and forth and up and down. Finally, the door swung open and everything she had wedged in between simultaneously dropped in a cluttered heap on the floor. Hurdling the pile while the door stood open, Emma ran in a marathon attempt to catch the phone before her answering machine did. She'd made it! She had won!

"Hello…hello…oh damn! Oops…Mother, Mom, you still there…? Sorry; I dropped the bloody phone. Yes, I know I shouldn't swear Mother, but I shouldn't try running a god damned marathon throughout…oh never mind. To what do I owe this call?" Emma said quickly revising her thoughts about 'winning' the race with the answering machine. Mom only called if she was planning a famous family get together or something as equally time consuming and tedious. Shaking her head, Emma anticipated and listened patiently waiting for the sky to fall. It didn't take long.

"Well that was quite a hello I must say. Maybe we should start again; it will give you time to catch your breath. Hi, dear, I was afraid I had missed you, I almost hung up. I am so glad I didn't. It was imperative I speak with you as soon as possible. What's this about a marathon dear? I would have listened closer, but I didn't quite know when the appropriate language would begin. You know I never did hold much use for swearing."

"I do, Mother, but to make a long story short, I heard the phone thinking it may be work, I ran. It's been very busy lately. As a matter of fact, you only caught me because I came home for a bite to eat."

9

"Well then," there was a slight pause, "you will be glad to know that you can take a breather. I have been planning a family vacation to the Islands. I have all the tickets; everything has been looked after. An early Christmas present to all my lovely children if you will. We never get together as much as we should. Lately you have all had so much to do at Christmas time, well I thought…anyway…Surprise! We all leave in four days. You can join us at the airport; the flight is at nine so be there by seven at the latest. Okay?"

Okay? Okay? No, it was not bloody well okay! The voice in Emma's head was shrill. She was thunderstruck; no one mentioned this before! To call her now, expecting her to drop everything, it was now only four days away for Christ sakes. There was no possible way she could make all the arrangements in time. Not that she would anyway; at least it provided her with a reasonable excuse. It galled her though. Just how long had they been planning this she wondered?

"Mother, when was all this planned? What do you mean everyone is going?"

"I mean everyone, Emmy dear. Your father, your brother, the twins, me…and you of course. It's a family vacation silly. Who else would you expect to attend?"

Who else indeed? It all sounded so final. So definite. Emma felt her temperature rising. Her mother continued babbling about how everyone managed to get time off, even Andre, whose business was going 'gang busters' now, the seat sales were terrific, it was the holiday of a lifetime. Better prices could not be found anywhere.

"Mother, please…whoa, just holdup a minute…Mother! I can't possibly go for three weeks right now. The office is very busy, I'm swamped; I can't leave. I'm sorry." There was silence on the other end of the line. Emma waited anxiously to see if her mother would send her on an all-famous guilt trip. She wasn't to be disappointed.

"Well, dear," her mother said at last. "I guess if you can't manage a little time away, for the sake of the family." Letting the sentence drop she continued, "I guess I might be able to find someone else to give your ticket to." Trying not to let her mother's words phase her, and as far as guilt trips went this one was mild to say the least; she could handle it. But even she knew better then to let it continue any longer. *End the conversation, Emma, count yourself lucky and just get her off the phone. Give yourself time, calm down and then call her back.* Yep. That was the way to handle all situations like this one. Breathing space, that's what she needed. They both needed.

"Yes, please do, Mother. I am sorry. I hope you all have a wonderful time. I will be thinking of you all kicking up your heels on the beach, sunning yourselves, while I am plugging away at the office."

"Well, dear, we will miss having you along." Before she could say any more Emma cut her off.

"Maybe next time, Mom, please give my love to all. I really do have to get back to work; Beatrice is waiting for me. I will call you later, I promise." There was another long pause; Emma could picture her mother's elegant face showing signs of stress from the loss of the battle. Emma had no fear she'd re-group and plan another attack, and it wouldn't be long; Emma thought affectionately. Not long at all.

"All right, Emma; good-bye, dear. Don't work too hard."

"I won't, Mother. Bye."

Emma hung up the phone, smiling. She really did love her mother, but sometimes the woman's timing was way off kilter. She laughed and went back to the door gathered her things and closed it. It was a good thing nobody came by. They'd probably thought she'd been mugged. Oh well, they would have found her safely inside the apartment. She smiled at the thought. Nothing that bad could possibly happen. She was on a roll. Yes, things were really going her way lately. Sure, she was over worked but that was the way she liked it. Quickly she grabbed a shower and changed into some more casual clothes. After making a sandwich, she headed for the door. She gave herself a mental reminder to call her mother and wish everyone a safe and happy flight. It was the least she could do and if she left it right until they jumped on the plane, then there would be no time for another round of 'make Emma regret staying behind'.

Catching the elevator to the under-ground parking garage, Emma shook her head in astonishment as she replayed the phone conversation with her mother. Cheerfully, she got into the car. Mother will never change; bless her generous heart. She truly is a wonderful woman. Emma pulled her silver Toyota out of the garage, into the heat of a Washington summer night, smiling. Feeling at peace with everything around her, she let the sun wash away the strain of a hectic schedule, she steered the car toward her downtown office and the mountain of work she had left on her desk.

Emma fell into bed exhausted. It had been a very hard week. Covering her workload and that of two others currently on vacation had almost driven her to lunacy. She was so tired, so very tired. Her last thought that night being that she had to call her mother. She would reach someone tomorrow. Yawning, closing her eyes she fell into an exhausted sleep.

…Tossing and turning, pitching violently this way and that, bright lights, sparks flying, so bright, so hot, so very hot, people screaming…so much screaming. Emma bolted upright in bed.

Screaming, she was screaming.

Sweat ran off her forehead.

She was trapped.

Fighting an entity that held her too tightly, "God-Oh-God, help me! Please help me!" Twisting and turning; Emma managed to free herself from the blankets that trapped her. A nightmare, she breathed under her breath, just a nightmare.

So different from the earlier dreams that plagued her; so terrifyingly different, so intense.

Lying back, she let her breathing, still labored and ragged, calm down. She wiped the sweat from her brow with the covers.

The sun streamed in through the blinds. The sun! Shit! What time is it? Emma looked at the Big Ben clock, she had gotten for Christmas last year. The chimes which normally went off, that is when she remembered to set it, sounded like long ago church bells, a sound Emma found welcome and soothing…her eyes focused on the little gold hands.

Eleven!

Damn! She'd slept in and now it was too late to call her mother. They'd be in the air, cell phones turned off, if they even had their cell phones with them. She would try later and if she couldn't reach them by cell, she'd try to find the name of the resort they were going to; she had written it down somewhere at the office the other day when she was doodling. She'd find the paper again and then locate the number through information if she had to. It was a good thing it was Saturday, at least she wasn't late for work too.

Emma felt more than a little guilty; her mother had called a couple of times, but her schedule had been so busy, and it had been so late when she fell into bed, she hadn't returned any of the calls. She'd do it first thing tonight. By then they should be settled, drinks in hand.

Dragging herself out of bed she headed for the shower. Maybe she would get out of the house and not think about work. A jog would be an excellent way to clear any lingering effects of the nightmare she had just experienced.

Chapter One

"Emily. Em darling, come. It is time. Em, answer me! This isn't funny, young lady! Oh, Em, where are you?"

Emily heard her beloved mother calling while she seemed so distant. Her voice was fading farther and farther, beyond her reach. And yet, the constant clanging of church bells grew louder and louder. She snuggled down in her favorite spot. Eyes clamped shut she tried her hardest to block the sound. She pictured the lush green fields, the blue sky and could hear the soothing sounds of the oceans waves as they crashed against the rocky shoals below. It was fading. Everything was fading. Except the damn church bells, ringing, clanging louder than ever. The pain would come soon; she gripped her head between her small hands and lowered it to her knees.

Emma reached up covering her ears attempting to block out the deafening sound. Her head thrummed, sending vibrations clear to her toes. Her skin prickled with the force of a thousand acupuncture needles. With the damn acupuncturist constantly flicking the bloody rods while they pierced her skin. She flung her arms about to protect herself.

Then silence, right before all went black.

Gradually Emma opened her eyes. Propping herself with her elbows she rose cautiously. Carefully she assessed her surroundings, each piece of furniture, her bed, her mirror, her vanity. It happened again. It was getting harder to return from the peaceful place she resided when the lights dimmed.

Emma rubbed her eyes. Her alarm clock lay upturned on the floor, her eyes barely able to focus on the read out. Eight o'clock. Damn!

Damn! She was going to be late. And this her first day back. Flinging back the covers, she thought, God, I didn't know cotton could be so noisy. Forcing herself out of bed and on stiff legs she wobbled to the bathroom. She needed a shower.

She stood there, letting the steaming hot water thoroughly wash away any of the lingering effects of the night before; too bad it couldn't rid her body of the dirt she felt clinging to her very soul.

Opening her mouth, she let the water fill it, then swished and spit several times trying to rid herself of the dreadful morning after which clung to the side and roof of her mouth. Closing her eyes, she drifted back as the hot water coursed over her skin.

It was strange. She could picture a field of wildflowers, the sky so blue, and the smell? Where was it? Why was it familiar, yet different, changing? She felt as though she belonged more than she'd ever belonged anywhere. Wherever here or there was.

Oh hell! Thinking about it only aggravated her already pounding headache. An all too familiar after effect from the night before. She couldn't think about it, at least not right now.

Forcing herself back to reality, Emma sighed as she turned off the water. Her head was still pounding, and her body ached, from lack of food, possibly, or maybe if she were honest, too much alcohol. A sign, at least that she was in the right place, a place where pain ruled. She needed the pain; to suffer just as they had. If she added a little of her own mix, then so be it. She deserved whatever life dished out.

The day, as the morning it followed, was hell. Computer problems had seriously exhausted all possibility of getting any work done. Emma warily sat behind her beautiful Victorian style desk, the mahogany polished to a shine that she felt was decidedly hard on the eyes. Leaning back, in her not so comfortable but practical office chair she stretched, trying to ease some of the tension in her limbs.

Closing her eyes and rubbing her aching temples, Emma took a deep calming breath. Unexpectedly, like a breath of fresh air, the smell of wildflowers and spring grass attacked her senses.

A thought, no, a feeling, yes, a feeling. What was it? The aroma triggered a sense of simplicity, of peace, something she'd not let herself experience in a long time. There was a loneliness, a lingering forlorn feeling. Emma shucked it off. It was a part of her everyday world, a part that would forever surround her. She reached for the serenity.

It was not the first time she'd had this feeling. However, it was the first time, in a long time that Emma hadn't been too drunk to notice it was somehow linked to the dream world she visited when she closed her eyes. Could it be the same place? No, that was crazy! Dreams cannot pause, rewind and play at will. Yet there was such a sense of déjà vu. Emma fought hard to think back, years and years. Her head throbbed. No ! It had been a dream. Conjured up by a teenager who needed to escape the present? Escape. No! She would not start thinking of that. It was in the past, where it belonged.

"Jesus!" Emma screamed.

"I am going crazy!"

Sitting up she stared at the mountain of paperwork waiting to be input into a dinosaur of a computer. She glared at the piece of crap technology currently the source of her woes. "You god damned Devil incarnate!" she yelled. "Why in the hell can't you work right?"

She brought her fist down on the keyboard. The screen answered back with a couple quick flashes of blue before going black again.

"Bloody government bureaucrats, it's not as though they couldn't afford to have decent equipment in here!"

When no one answered, Emma glowered at the wall, wishing the whole room would explode before her eyes.

They knew she would be returning today. The computers and their viruses were problems before she left over a month ago. She'd filed a complaint with maintenance. According to Beatrice, her receptionist, the virus was gone. Still here she was trying to play catch-up on a flooded infield and there wasn't a dry mound to be had. She hadn't even gotten past first base. Life was throwing her nothing but curve balls.

Emma cursed her thoughts. What was she? An announcer for the Orioles? Too much bar room TV. Not that she'd had any better way to spend her time these days. She was feeling sorry for herself. Yes. Damn right! And she didn't care one lick.

It was not like Emma needed assistance with the workload or her flagging social life, but it would have been nice to reach out, grab the phone and call someone, anyone. Caring shoulders to cry on, someone to vent to or talk of old times until she managed to get her murky mind back on her work.

Not that she would but she no longer had the option. Everything was gone. Everyone. An old familiar burning in the pit of her stomach erupted; like the strongest back alley garbage it made her throat burn, her eyes water and her chest ache.

Two months. Had it been two months?

No, fifty-eight days since the crash; her whole family. Mother. Father. Her brother and sisters; Andre, Amanda and Christine. Dead.

All dead!

The crash took many lives, not just those of her family, but it was so hard to consider what others had lost. Right now, she couldn't cope with her own.

Life wasn't fair, she thought bitterly.

Hovering on the edge of her seat, elbows pressed into the desktop, face buried deep in her hands Emma wondered when it all went wrong. How could her life go from good too bad in such a short period of time? Two months before Emma had everything going for her. All was right with the world. Her world at least.

She survived many obstacles in the past; wrapped in the knowledge that there would always be someone there should she stumble and fall. Now there was no one. Not one single soul left in this dreary world would miss her if something happened to her. She swallowed trying to ease the pressure in her throat.

Numb, Emma's mind drifted back, the tears she'd held in for so long silently ran down her cheeks and filling the palms of her hands. All the family get-togethers she'd been too busy to attend. Or at least that is what she claimed. The too few she attended played like old movies on fast forward through her mind.

She should have taken the time off!

She should have been on that plane!

She should have died with the rest of her family!

She'd been there, or at least some part of her, she thought back to the nightmare she had the morning of the accident. Somehow, she knew. She called the airlines shortly after she awoke. At first, they denied anything was wrong. Then Emma heard chaos and she knew. They questioned her motives. Even the investigators they sent the next day couldn't provide a link.

"…I'm sure you understand Miss St. Claire, we had no choice. With so many terrorist attacks, well I am sure you understand how difficult it is for us to believe you knew flight 714 was in trouble. Let's start again, shall we…?"

How could she know before hand? It was in those dreadful seconds after her call that Emma felt utterly helpless; it hadn't happened yet and yet, there was no way to stop it before it did. She would never admit how she knew. They hadn't been able to prove a connection and eventually she was left alone. Now she forced herself to remember. She deserved every painful memory and all that went with them.

So, what happened? She ended up having to take a forced vacation. A mandatory Leave of Absence they called it; time to mourn the deaths of her family. Gone, all gone. Some vacation. A crisp, choked, hysterical laugh escaped her.

She hadn't wanted to go because there would be too much paperwork to return to when she finally made it back to her office. Emma let loose with a stream of raw curses. A vicious stroke of her hand sent the papers swirling about and onto the floor.

Grabbing her purse, she headed for the door not bothering to look back. She had to get out of here. A drink! She needed a drink. Needed to get so mind numbing drunk she could no longer feel.

Emma hollered to Beatrice as she passed through the outer office, "I'm gone. The damn computer isn't working, and the bloody guy hasn't come down to fix it! I can't do anything here except sit and stare at a fucking mountain of work that can't get done. See you tomorrow." Like a hurricane, Emma left the office short of leaving devastation in her wake.

Beatrice sat back shaking her head. Should Emma have come back to work so soon after losing her family? Sometimes after the initial shock, jumping back into life was the only way. No, no one said it would be easy. Perhaps, it was better for her than being locked away in her apartment where no one could see her.

Beatrice thought of Dexter's accident; she would have withered if she'd not been forced to stay busy. Things were different when one found themselves alone, time, as she could attest to, could stretch on forever.

When Emma took over Rodman's position in Exports, three years ago, Beatrice felt obligated to take the younger woman under her wing. Since then, their relationship had grown. Although not much older than Emma protected her like a daughter, loved her like a younger sister. It was a perk that Beatrice was not ready to forfeit any time soon. Although, she had never confided her life outside of the office to anyone, if she ever did, Emma would be the first to know. But until then the risk of Dexter's family finding them was too great. She'd come too far for too long to risk it all. She still wasn't clear on the legalities of what she'd done, but with a father so high in the judicial system;

Beatrice felt her chances were not good. No doubt he'd try to declare her incompetent for actions toward her husband's family. What some people would do for the sake of money.

All would get better. It had to. Emma would never completely heal, for the scar of survival would always be there, survivors guilt they called it. Though Emma had not been diagnosed as far as Beatrice knew the girl's actions spoke volumes. Eventually she would learn to cope. Until then, she would continue guiding her as gently as she could, toward the path of peace. Yes, all would be well. It would just take time.

Emma stormed through the front doors of the building and stomped across the street, without a care for the buzzing traffic, to where she'd parked her car. Normally she would have parked below, but today she could not bring herself to enter the dark underground garage. Pressing the fob's buttons, the locks clicked open and the car engine roared to life before she was even behind the wheel.

All she could think about was how much she needed a shot of tequila, possibly two. Tequila had become her drink of choice over the past months. She could feel the cold glass in her hand; see it sparkle in the glow from the fire, clear and gorgeous. Potent! Ice cubes danced with the cool wet liquid; harsh but bitterly smooth, she could already taste it.

She'd savor it, like a fine wine letting each tingle caress her mouth. Swallowing, she closed her eyes as it scorched the path from her throat to her belly. Soon now, it would dull the ache in her heart and the pain in her head.

Companion and friend; unlike everything else, it would only leave if she chose to leave it first. A doctor something-or-other had given her Ambien. She snorted at the thought. They didn't work. They knocked her out, froze her mind. Her mind didn't need to be frozen; it was the rest of her body.

Pulling out of the parking lot, she headed toward her apartment building. Although she needed a drink, she'd leave the car at the apartment, walking rather than risking an accident. If she did go out of this world it would be because of God's plan not because she was too much of a coward to face life. She laughed at the irony of that thought; one would think hiding in a bottle of tequila was in fact running away, maybe one day she'd leave it, but not today.

She parked the car, pressed a button and headed down the street on foot. Glancing at the building, she decided there was nothing in her apartment she needed. She didn't care how she was dressed. As for food, the thought alone made her stomach toss like she'd swallowed a cyclone.

She'd lost so much weight recently; she could write a book on the worst ways to lose thirty pounds in a month. The Tequila Diet. How many others made money off the tragedies of others? It was fast becoming the American way.

'Fred's Bar was close to Emma's apartment and it didn't take long to walk there. A quiet place; it was never busy at this time of day. The dark atmosphere offered quiet solitude; it was the perfect accompaniment for her black cloud.

The last thing Emma wanted was to see anyone. She'd never liked being around a lot of people. Being the center of attention had always disagreed with her. She'd tried it once and had failed miserably.

She'd just as soon not talk to the bartender but that was impossible. Fred seemed overly interested in making conversation every time she walked into the damn building. She should consider going elsewhere. No. It was entirely too much trouble. Fred's was close to home, and she didn't want to be far from bed when her senses finally deadened. Emma walked in and glanced about. Sure enough, only one other person was there. The TV was tuned to the Sports Channel. Highlights of last night's baseball games flicked by on the side of the screen while an overzealous announcer covered the latest bloopers.

Sanctuary!

She was almost there. Quickly she made her way to a small out of the way table next to the fireplace.

Fred stood behind the bar wiping the counter as Emma crossed the floor. He watched in the mirror as she seated herself at a table for two next to the fire, she didn't know it, but Fred himself, had specifically redesigned the layout for her shortly after she started coming in. She looked worse today. Her clothes were a sight better, he noticed, as if she'd taken pains to make sure they were clean and ironed. Still miles too big, they hung off her like a rag doll. What was her story?

She had the look of someone, he knew from experience, who'd had more than her fair share of problems. In his thirty-five years as bar owner, he'd seen the signs in others, and through diligence had learned their tales. After all wasn't that his role in life? To listen even when there were no words. In many ways the little lady didn't fit the mold. But in others…? What would possess a young woman with such an obviously good background, to frequent this place day in and day out? Where had she come from?

She looked as though the weight of the entire world rested upon her delicate shoulders. He tried many times to break the shell that surrounded her, feeling if he could get her to speak, some of her troubles would lessen if not go away altogether. Still, after two months of trying she said no more than, "Tequila straight up. Thanks," in such a distant voice it damned near broke his heart.

Fred tossed the rag aside, filled a glass of tequila and headed toward her table. Each day was a new day holding a shitload of new possibilities.

Emma nodded to Fred, took the glass and tossed it back, handing it back empty, "Another," she said.

"Today must have been a real bummer; you downed that rather fast. Even for you. Want to talk about it? I find it helps and I am an excellent listener. Had lots of practice," Fred said gently.

"If I wanted to talk, I wouldn't be here! Just bring me another!" Emma snapped. Immediately self-chastised, she added, "Please." She knew in her heart the man was only trying to help but help was one thing she didn't need right now. Not from him or anyone else for that matter. Two months ago, she could have used a little help but where in the hell were the good Samaritans then? Where were they when her family bought tickets? Where were they when the plane…Oh hell!!!

Fred returned with another drink. Her head was bowed in her hands; she looked even more defeated. She didn't belong here. But where exactly did she belong? He set the glass on the napkin and quietly backed away. Maybe tomorrow, he thought, knowing she would be back like clockwork.

At closing time Emma could barely stand. Just the way she liked it. She eased herself out of her chair tipsily navigating her way through the other tables and chairs. There, she thought with a grim smile of satisfaction. She was getting better at this. Not once did she run into anything this time.

After five misses, the key finally connected and entered the lock.

Emma headed straight for the bedroom. Turned on the alarm and fell forward onto the bed.

"Here you are, Poppet. I have been looking all over for you." Emily giggled as she looked up from her hiding spot to find her mother standing over her. Hands on her hips but smile on her face.

"I was thinking," Emily said. Her bright green eyes sparkling in the sunlight.

"Thinking? Child you didn't come when I called, where did your thoughts take you that your ears no longer worked. I was getting worried. Besides you are getting much too old to play these games Em. You're practically a young lady. It is time you started acting like one. Did you not hear the church bells? It is time for the service."

"Sorry, Mama, I didn't mean to worry you. It was such a lovely day; I simply felt the need to be alone. I honestly didn't hear you. I was not playing games."

"It's all right, child. In these times, no matter your age, it is always best to retain a bit of the inner child. May we proceed to the services now?"

Emily and her mother walked arm in arm toward the small village chapel. Lately it seemed Emily clung to the closeness. She knew she was protected and loved. Yet there was still the undeniable need for re-assurance, to hold on and never let go.

Church was the reasoning for a weekly town get-together; after the minister gave his sermon, all gathered behind the chapel for a picnic. While mothers and fathers conversed, Emily would fool around with Kendra until it was time to eat.

Emily was a pretty girl; emerald green eyes and long wavy golden hued hair. A long plait reaching past her waist, a nice if slightly under-developed figure; a fact causing much irritation, as she got older. Still she was quite popular, and she liked that. She would be fourteen soon, a young lady. Often, she daydreamed about getting married and having children of her own. Other times, like today, something called to her. Pulling her away, demanding her attention, it was in those times, times more frequent of late, that she sought her special place.

Sometimes she would come back feeling the need to remain a little girl smothered in her mother's bosom.

Soon she would have to find a way to cope with these spells; a young woman could hardly sneak off under the bushes whenever the fancy struck her. Whatever would Daniel think if he knew?

Daniel, the boy Emily liked, was five years her senior. He was always polite, talking to her, helping her. She feared he saw her as nothing more than a child. No doubt because of her non-existent breasts. Emily would often see him with the older girls holding hands or dancing at the church socials. How she wished it were she on his arm.

He was more than handsome. His raven black hair hung well below the collar of his shirt; in the sunlight, it glinted with streaks of deep blue. His eyes were blue as well and as stormy as the sea after a heavy squall. He was tall, almost six feet. Already his muscles seemed to have been chiseled by the finest sculptor. He was a breath-taking sight indeed. She guessed it had something to do with the work he did on the ships with his papa. Emma hugged herself, lost in the wonder of turbulent emotions coursing through her. One day she silently swore, one day he would be hers. She would be the one to allow him stolen kisses and she would relish it.

The minister finished his sermon, telling the congregation that he would see them at the picnic. Her head snapped up. She hadn't heard a word of his lectures, so lost had she been in her own little world. Outside, kids ran wildly to the swing while the parents, chatting away, readied the picnic ground.

The children took turns on the swing; Emily sat off to one side watching everyone, waiting her turn. Finally, when a chance came for her to take her place in the swing; Daniel lifted her on, placing his large hands on her waist he gently set her down on the seat telling her to hold on tight.

Lord, why must he treat me like a child? She felt the swing lift higher and higher. Daniel's hands tenderly pushed on the small of her back causing little thunderbolts in her stomach warming her clear to her toes. She stared at the blue skies overhead comparing them to Daniel's eyes and daydreaming once again.

Suddenly she was falling. Falling faster. Faster. The ground below rushed upward.

Connecting with the hard surface forced the air out of her lungs. All went black. She struggled to open her eyes. Why wasn't someone coming to help her? Where was her mother, her father, Kendra, Daniel? There he is. His deep blue eyes stared into hers. What was he saying? Why didn't he just speak up? Her eyes closed.

Emily rolled back and forth urging her mind to make her eyes open. She needed to see Daniel. Did she hit her head? She forced her arm to move, to reach up, and feel the back of her head for any sign of a lump, there wasn't one. She noticed something, was it the grass? It felt strange. It didn't feel as it should. Not cool and moist. Instead it was bumpy and warm to the touch. Still soft but…

Emma felt like a jackhammer was inside her head; her body was stiff and sore all over. Slowly she came back to her surroundings. She reached over; touching her hand to the night table she gingerly hoisted her body from the floor and onto the bed. More sleep, a little more sleep and she would be fine. As she lay down the alarm went off.

"Fuck!" she yelled, wincing at the sound of her own voice. Just my freakin' luck; the alarm continued ringing. She reached over and smacked its top knocking the obnoxious black box to the floor.

Chapter Two

Beatrice looked carefully at Emma as she strolled into the office ten minutes late. If her pink mohair sweater sagged anymore at the neck it would be indecent. Her black designer slacks stayed in place only with the use of a belt, her hair was wild, but pulled back with a scrunchy and there were dark circles under her eyes.

Beatrice handed Emma her morning coffee then decided against giving her the phone messages until she was seated at her desk. The way the girl's hands were shaking, it was a miracle she could hold the cup.

Beatrice silently followed Emma into her office and placed the messages on her desk. Sadly, she left without saying a word pondering what her next step should be. Anyone could tell from one look at the girl she'd been drinking. No, flooding. She'd gone to Emma's apartment, as soon as the office closed. There was no one home, she even stayed for a while talking to the doorman seeing if he'd any idea when she might return. The doorman hadn't seen her come in since she left this morning, where in blazes had she gone? Each day shed no further light. The doorman had seen her, though Beatrice had to practically drag the words from his mouth; still when he buzzed her suite no one answered. Beatrice knew all signs pointed to abuse, and that must stop.

After staying an hour yesterday Beatrice left, she'd had other commitments. At the institution, Beatrice sat with Dexter, worrying about the most important person in her life. He seemed dormant, taking one small step forward and two back. Yet this wasn't a dance and the music ended long ago.

Much of that week remained the same; computers weren't fixed until Thursday, although Emma came to work each morning, she sat isolated in that damn office of hers, speaking only when she had to. Beatrice tried several times to get the girl to come out for lunch, but she refused to eat. What to do?

It had come to her in those silence filled hours. What Emma needed was a companion, someone, of the male persuasion to take her mind off her troubles, help her take the next step toward a future. Yes, that's it! The only question was who? Tapping her finger against her bottom lip she contemplated. It would have to be someone kind and generous. Patient enough to win Emma's heart, brave enough to go the distance, for it would not be easy, and the stamina to survive the future.

She could never remember Emma dating, even casually. She was young and beautiful, with so much to offer the right person, and right now the right person could give the world back to her, urging her back to the land of the living. She would have to mull the idea over for a while. Beatrice felt, in her heart, the possibility had a great deal of merit. She knew enough about great loves; to know that if the right person came along, there was nothing you couldn't overcome, for you were sheltered once you were loved.

Emma sat down at her desk switching on the computer. All the files from last week still lay scattered about the floor; she'd been in no mood back then to even think about picking them up, and what would have been the point. She let the tantrum run its course. Feeling the way, she did, she left work early Thursday and headed for her favorite hangout. Friday, she hadn't bothered coming in at all; she'd called Beatrice and told she was not feeling well. Hung over more likely but she would not think about that. And last night the dream was back.

Apparently, Beatrice told the cleaning crew to stay away from the office. That at least, was good. Imagining the rumors that would be flying about the water cooler if anyone had seen the mess, gave her the chills. Leaving her desk, she bent down to pick up a file then quickly decided it would be best to kneel. She'd try to reorganize her desk along with her thoughts.

Hopefully the repairperson hadn't said anything about her office being in such turmoil. And if there was a God, he never would. Emma had just finished organizing the files in piles on her desk when Beatrice rang over the intercom, "Emma, dear, there is a gentleman here to see you. He's from out of town. No appointment."

Emma pressed a button and stated, "Send him in."

She was sitting at her desk by the time the door opened. Daniel? Emma shook the cobwebs from her head as the man stalked toward her desk. He was far too intense; it didn't bode well, and Emma could feel her stomach beginning to knot. It wasn't a pleasant feeling. God she could use a drink. He was tall, with wavy hair as black as midnight. He had a false smile pasted on his face. His blue eyes sparked with the very same anger that filled his entire structure. Emma swallowed nervously as he approached, fighting to resist the urge to wipe her hands on her slacks. She was sweating; she could feel little droplets running between her breasts. Her breathing was labored, oh God it was so hard to breathe.

She could have sworn she knew this man. He was so familiar, and she knew that if she were her old self, he never would have bothered her for a moment, angry or not. She'd never laid eyes on him before except maybe in a dream. And that was downright ludicrous!

Gathering her backbone, she held her hand surprised that it didn't shake more than it did. "I am Emma St. Clair; can I help you?"

He studied her features slowly as if she were some anomaly under a microscope. The process made her more nervous with each passing second. Her recent lifestyle, the ever-present devil of a headache, combined with tons of work, set her on edge. Her eyes flitted briefly over the files that lined her desk as she frustratingly waited for him to speak. Slowly she lowered her hand.

"I'm Dan O'Brien. I filed a complaint with your office two months ago and no one has had the decency to call me back; forcing me to travel down here!"

"Oh dear, Mr. O'Brien I am dreadfully sorry, I've been away. We had a few minor problems my first week back, I'm afraid your file may be somewhere in there." She grimaced while she pointed to the files lining the top of her desk. Thank the good Lord she'd managed to get them arranged neatly before Beatrice announced his arrival.

Mr. O'Brien raised an arrogant brow at the pile, "So how long I'm I to wait before my issue will be addressed? I have a business to run. And I do not have the luxury of the government to take my sweet time doing so. My complaint concerns only one order still it is crucial to my company that this matter be resolved…immediately. I want my ship!" He hadn't raised his voice, but Emma was sure he would have been less daunting if he had.

"Ship?" Oh, damn! It would be something big. Emma swallowed hard and pressed on. "I truly am sorry, sir. If you would give me the company name, I will go over the file immediately. Maybe you can make an appointment with Miss Rolands, my receptionist, for first thing tomorrow morning." Emma held her breath waiting for a reply; her heart was pounding wildly. She really wasn't ready for this. Maybe if she could get rid of him long enough to stop the world from spinning and her knees knocking, she'd be able to handle this matter more efficiently.

A great deal of her job was customer service; pacifying irate clients. Normally she was quite good at it. At least she used to be. Now, her hands were clammy as she fought to keep the anxiety from her voice. She jumped when he spoke, though he didn't seem to notice.

Eyes of blue steel bored into her. "Fine, if tomorrow is the best you can do, tomorrow it is. The company is O'Brien's Shipping Imports and Exports. I will see you in the morning, Miss. St. Claire."

With that he stormed back out of the office. Emma heaved a great sigh of relief as she fell back into her chair. Spreading her palms on the desktop she stopped them from trembling before starting to wade through the files on her desk. Finally, she found O'Brien's Shipping in a pile she'd set aside for later. Good God it could have been next week before she even got around to opening it.

She scanned the file, someone had obviously taken his phone calls, but never relayed the information verbally, there was a list of catalogued phone calls, and a letter outlining said calls and comments pertaining to the handling of his account. They were not good. Figures! A letter from the Custom's Officer, manifests, charges and fines. Sure enough, they were holding one of his ships.

Why hadn't Belinda or Francine handled this while she was away? When they had been on holiday, she'd covered for them. She'd stayed late almost every night to do so, but at least nothing fell behind. She was one person. They should have been able to handle her caseload even if they had to split it. She'd talk to Henry about this. It was bullshit. Pure and simple.

The ship contained a cargo of imitation ivory from China to Boston Harbor. According to the paperwork, the person in charge of checking the load was new and could not tell the difference between fake or real. One of which of course was illegal and carried a stiff sentence. Not something her office would sit on. Warning bells went off in her head. The idiot! Not knowing any better, the clerk immediately had ship and cargo impounded. Shaking her head at the shear naivety of the officer, Emma read everything again trying to find a loophole.

The documents briefly outlined why the clerk thought he'd had something more than just a shipment of man-made ivory, including his reasons for having the ship impounded. Trying to climb the imperial ladder two missteps at a time, he neglected to say anything to his superiors until such time as the paperwork made it way slowly to their desks through the proper channels. Hoping to be acknowledged for his find. Not!

A week later the load was inspected again, nothing was found wrong with the cargo, but since the paperwork had been processed to impound the ship, the trail of red tape that must be completed was as thick as a meatloaf sandwich. And of course, that part of the process hadn't even started.

No wonder the guy was pissed.

Emma took a moment calculating dates and times in her head. Jesus that would mean that the ship and all its contents, had been in the impound yard about two days before she'd taken her leave. It wasn't Emma's mistake and the chances of something of the magnitude happening had to be at least a million to one and yet it did happen, and Emma couldn't help feeling responsible.

It was a stupid mistake, one that could have been easily rectified with an apology and a suggestion that the captain maintain a more detailed manifest. But now? Now over two months had gone by. The client was within his rights to sue for damages, loss of wages for his crew and much, much, more. The Customs officer would have to go back in for retraining or be dismissed from his position. It would be hard enforcing the regulation now, after two months had passed, but like all other aspects of this case the time lapse could not be helped. Deal with what you can, when you can, and leave the rest. That's all anyone could do.

Emma had to think, tapping her pen on the desk her mind began to run through the possibilities. How could she make the client happy enough to simply take his ship, and cargo, without lodging a suit?

She had until tomorrow. Time was on her side. Picking up the phone, Emma started dialing. A few calls would release the ship and contents. Then she would see about the impound charges. Accounting will not be impressed. They would have already logged the fines and sent the paperwork. Well she was not the only one having a party they might as well join in. The guy had done nothing wrong. No wonder he was pissed, he'd done nothing illegal.

Beatrice smiled as Dan O'Brien came out of Emma's office, stopping at her desk, he requested the first appointment for the following morning. Nodding, Beatrice penciled him in; and wrote the information on one of

Emma's cards all the while mentally calculating his age and attributes as a likely candidate for Emma. Handing the card over, she decided he maybe more than a little alarming, and still he seemed an excellent prospect. So strikingly handsome he made her heart pound. Excitement? There was something to be said for men in suits, men like her Dexter. Such a formidable presence it would have made a delicious shiver course through anyone's body. She would never have been cut out for the life of a nun.

Dan wondered what was taking the woman so long to write down a damned time. Finally, she was handing him the card. After placing it in his shirt pocket, he sauntered to the elevator.

Miss. Emma St. Claire. He'd never met her before. He would have remembered the long wavy blonde hair, and those eyes…what shade were they? He'd be certain to check tomorrow. She calmed him, she did something else to him to, but he wasn't quite ready to admit that; her words reached out to him. Felt familiar, like those of a…Friend? Doubtful! It certainly couldn't have been sexual attraction. No way! Her clothes draped over her, pale visage and yet she wore no make-up, had her hair been combed? Well he couldn't remember, and that said a lot. He had always been partial to strays, maybe that was it. Of course, part of her duties in Customer Service was to make people feel more at ease, more satisfied. Yes, that was all it was. It had to be. He was sure he would see her true colors tomorrow. When she came back to him with all sorts of excuses for the Customs officer's incompetence and the departmental delays.

Dan exited the elevator feeling better for the fact that someone was finally going to address the problems. He had other ships. True. And there were other incoming loads, yet he was losing time, money and manpower. An enormous waste, all of it, and it fueled both his anger and determination. Not to mention the crew members unable to collect a check because they were forced to sit in dry dock waiting for their ship. His poor captain had been detained like some criminal for hours while the ship had been boarded and taken to the impound yard. Some of the men he'd managed to relocate onto other ships, so at least they wouldn't lose an income; but there wasn't room to reposition them all.

He hoped they would come back even if they had to search out other companies for work in the meantime. He headed for his SUV. Find a room, that would be the first order of business. Then he'd prepare arguments for his morning get-together with Miss. St. Claire. Although, he'd been so angry for so long over the whole ordeal, he already countered every possible development in his mind at least a hundred times over. If they didn't work, then he'd take the matter through legal channels and sue their pants off. Media attention, whatever it took to make them sit up and take notice. Satisfied, Dan jumped into his vehicle and left.

Emma set down the telephone receiver. This was not good; maybe she was losing her touch; maybe she didn't try hard enough. She felt so damn accountable for what this client was going through. She should've looked at the file before today but, there had been so much to do. She was handling everything in the order in which it had landed on her desk, before she knew it, the weekend had hit and with it, all hell broke loose.

She'd meant to call her family that Saturday but after her jog she got called back into the office. She'd worked late that day and part of Sunday. It was Monday morning when she received a call back from the airline. There were no survivors. No survivors!!!

Emma brought her fist down on the file. Why should she feel guilty? It was partly his fault for not hiring someone capable of keeping concise documentation of his cargo.

It was reaching.

She knew it and she didn't care one bit!

She'd done all she could for the day, at least as far as O'Brien's Shipping was concerned. She had made some headway, so it wasn't a total loss. Accounts was willing, in their timely fashion, to delete the account. Copies of fines if issued were to be rescinded; she called the dockside Customs office and enforced regulation 34-B requiring retaining or dismissal of the officer involved. Still she could not get the release for the ship and cargo signed until the person in charge came back from holidays. That would mean Mr. O'Brien's ship would be detained for at least another week. Exactly how angry would he be about this little development she hadn't a clue.

His body, mannerisms, movements…everything about the blasted man, exuded ultimate power. Emma shuddered. A drink; if she didn't get one soon her body would refuse to function altogether. She looked back over her desk. She had managed to go through a couple other files today; still there were so many waiting. At what point in time would other irate business owners come stomping into her office?

Should she stay late? She was supposed to be the best in her field handling more cases than anyone. Always with satisfactory results. Shrugging, then with a final sigh she switched off her computer grabbed her purse and headed for the door. She was neither as strong nor as dedicated as she should be. At least…not anymore, and that fact rankled her almost as much as she needed a drink. Almost!

"See you in the morning, Beatrice," she said on her way to the elevator.

Beatrice smiled one of her sunny smiles telling her to have a good night. As an afterthought she added, "Try to get some rest. You look like a linebacker for the Red Skins. Oh, don't forget dear, you have a 9 a.m. appointment with Mr. O'Brien, he is such a handsome man don't you think?"

Emma shook her head paying little heed to the last of Beatrice's declaration, assuring her she'd try to get some much needed sleep. She was lying through her teeth. Sleep. Hell, she was always more tired when she woke up. It didn't seem to matter how long she'd closed her eyes.

Emma's stomach grumbled. She was caught in traffic, when it finally clued in. She actually felt hungry. Not wanting to jinx it by over thinking, she quickly pulled into an empty parking stall outside a little Italian bistro. Running inside she ordered spaghetti for one, to go.

The sauce would be rich with garlic, oregano and basil; her mouth watered. Remarkably her stomach didn't seem to churn as it had many times in the past. Maybe things were finally getting back on track.

The television was tuned to TSN; 'The Redskins at home to the Ravens'. There was loud pre-game coaching from the pool tables, as construction workers told the big screen rather stridently what the Redskins needed to do to pull off a win against a team, they had not Beaten in five years. Would it help? Emma could have cared less. Football had only been fun when Andre had been here to enjoy it with.

Sitting at her favorite table, picked up the drink already waiting, and looked around. The loudmouth in soiled checkered-flannel attire chugging a Coors didn't bother her today. His pal was dressed similar, obviously just off shift. To the right there was a table of five, dressed semi-casually, conversing with another group the next table over; there must be a convention. At such times Fred's took on the over-flow from the hotel down the street. She heard mention of the Renaud hosting a seminar. What was it now? Oh, yeah. 'Night Journeys'! She gave a brittle laugh. She wondered what they would have to say about her nighttime excursions. With another laugh, she sat back, sipped her drink, and let her mind ease her body out of this world.

"Emily, come on! This is not funny! Get up! I know you're not hurt. The ground is covered with soft moss. Come quit teasing!"

Emily peeked up to find Kendra staring down at her. She smiled at the look of distress on her friend's face.

"What's the matter, Kenny? Have ye never seen anyone fall 'efore?"

Kendra could not help but answer with a smile. Emily was her very best friend, doing many things just to be noticed; she emitted enough sunshine to brighten anyone's day.

"Come on, you are a big fraud. We must be getting back; our parents will be sending out search parties soon enough I imagine."

Emily hoisted herself up and looked around. She loved this time of day. The waters glowed with the force of a thousand fires as it swallowed the sun's last rays; a true sight to behold. Too bad most locals no longer took the time to admire the little miracles

She could feel the soft wind from the ocean on her face as Kendra began pulling her along heading for home. She knew too that their parents would be worried, but they should be used to her disappearing acts by now. Emily had a love of nature, a love for life. It was as though she would never be able to get enough of the little miracles.

Yet there was so much more she wanted to experience; things, which piqued her curiosity, demanding answers. Scores of things she wanted to try. She used to only, think of what it would be like to settle down, have a family. That seemed so long ago. It was easy to think of a husband, a family when Daniel was here, and she could see him every day. Dream of a life spent with him, pleasuring him.

Daniel left shortly after being given one of his father's ships, Emily no longer saw him on a daily basis. She still thought of Daniel; more than anything she wanted to become his bride. It irked that he could go out into the world, finding adventure, when she was stuck here on this tiny rock. Women should be allowed more freedom. Instead they were supposed to wait for a man to court. Wait for a man to ask for her hand. Wait for a man to come home. Wait, wait!

Well, when Daniel married her, she'd not wait at home for him to return again. No. She'd make sure he took her with him, at least until they had children. He would protect her, and she could experience all life's adventures firsthand. If all of God and sundry expected her to wait, then wait for him she would, but after the wedding she'd be doing her waiting aboard The Maiden. Mind made up, she walked on, determination in her gait.

Emily walked into the cottage to greet her scowling parents' faces. Going to them at once she hugged them while hiding a smug smile.

"Emily you really must spend more time learning the skills one needs to please a husband. You're always frolicking about the countryside like some low born waif," her father said.

"Yes, Papa, I know except it was such a lovely day. My chores were all done before I left. Weren't they Mama? I am sorry, please forgive me."

Looking at her mother, he noticed the smile she tried to cover and failed. Emily had gotten off lucky. Again! He didn't have the heart to discipline his only daughter. They both knew it. A sigh indicated his surrender to a losing battle. With that he motioned to the table where dinner was waiting.

Following supper Emily helped her mother clear the table while listening to her father play. Emily loved these peaceful evenings with her family. When the time came to embark on her adventure, she knew down in her very soul she would miss the simple times.

Saying good night, Emily donned her night rail before combing and plaiting her hair. This was the time when she thought of Daniel the most. She could almost imagine him there on the bed waiting for her to come to him. His blue eyes glazed, growing darker with desire for her with each passing moment. She longed for the moment when he would raise her gown over her head, kiss her, touch her, and claim her as his own. Forever!

When would he come home? When would his ship finally reach shore? She wanted him to see the lovely woman she'd become; to walk beside him, hear of his adventures. Would her breasts brush against his arm as they walked? Emily reached up running her hands over her breasts trying to appease the ache that gripped her every time she thought of Daniel. She knew it was wrong; a proper young lady should never touch herself in this way.

A proper young lady would not ache for it desperately as she did. Emily didn't give a fig about being a proper young lady. Not in her bedroom or in their bedroom when the time came. She could act the lady better than most girls she knew, and she would…when she had to. The warmth spiraled through her, making her smile as it eased the tension. She pulled down the covers, climbed in as she closed her eyes letting her dreams take her body to new heights.

Emma came back to her surroundings slowly. Her cheeks were hot, and she was not entirely sure it was from the fire. She looked down at the drink in her hand. No, not the drink either. She noticed that with each passing dream the girl's contentment flowed over into her. Lasting longer! It was nice, to be able to look about the bar without it being a blurry haze. She felt a sense of triumph.

Fred stood at the table, looking at Emma, weighing the possible reactions should he speak. She normally drank between five and six glasses of tequila; tonight, she was only on her second one. "I came to check on your drink. I see you still have it." He couldn't help himself. He winked. "Could I get you anything?"

To his astonishment she smiled and winked back. He was struck speechless, mouth agape. He must look like a guppy. Getting control of senses stalled with her reply.

"Thanks, Fred, I think I'll have a Pepsi, if it's not too much trouble, then I'll call it a night." Fred continued like a fish out of water gasping for air, he simply turned back toward the bar to fill the little lady's request.

Behind the counter Fred thought about miracles. For this was one. She smiled. Damn she was beautiful when she smiled like that. She spoke. She winked. She said more than two or three words and by Christ she even sounded pleasant. He felt like jumping and clicking his heels together. A Pepsi! Things were looking up.

Cursing for acting the jackass, a mute jackass to-boot, Fred added a cherry and swizzle stick to the glass. He'd make sure to speak this time. On that note he headed to the table with a drink in hand and hoped he would be blessed with another of her radiant smiles.

Emma finished the drink and handed the empty glass to Fred. She was feeling a buzz, as she sipped the Pepsi; the sweet taste cleared the flavor of the tequila.

Washington at night, when one was not too drunk to notice, was breathtaking. The lights reminded Emma of a lit Christmas tree, some on some off, but all a part of life. Feeling an ache in her chest she hurried for home; she didn't know if it would cause her tears to flow but she was not about to be caught on the street crying.

Instead of tumbling into her bed fully clothed, reeking of alcohol, Emma decided to take a page from the young girl in her dreams. The girl always seemed to be there for her. She had been a source of strength; coming when Emma needed it the most. Staying with her, and never leaving her. With Emily, Emma was not so frightfully alone.

Emma showered, brushed and gargled. Pulling on a nightshirt, she sat on the edge of her bed combing her hair. "Sorry, Emily, I'm not one for braids," she joked, setting the brush aside and switching off the lamp. Would she be able to find the girl again? She liked her immensely. Felt a connection. Emma sighed and closing her eyes promptly went to sleep.

Chapter Three

Emma awoke to the sound of ringing. Reaching over she tapped the top of the alarm clock. The ringing continued. She opened her eyes. Bright sunshine slanted into her room through the blinds. Emma blinked a few times; the phone rang again before she registered the sound.

"Hello?"

"Emma? Dear, it's Beatrice. Your nine o'clock appointment is here wearing a hole in the carpet the size of a damn crater. He's quite put out. Now where on earth are you?"

"Well, Beatrice, if you called me at home and I answered then the powers that be should tell you home is where I am at."

"Emma, as much I love your sense of humor, I'd like it a lot better if you would drag your little patootie out of bed and get down here PDQ. That Mr. O'Brien is like a caged animal."

"Pa-toot-e?"

"Your ass, Em, your ass, get it down here, now, before he starts doing your job for you!"

"Shit. Beatrice, why the hell did you let him into my office? I have files, papers…things, everywhere! Beatrice you get into that office. I am on my way."

Emma threw back the covers. Running full tilt, she grabbed a pair of navy-blue slacks, the color of his eyes, she thought as she pulled them up then shook her head in disgust. She pulled her cream-colored satin camisole over her head followed it with her navy-blue blazer. Stuffing her hair in a scrunchy, she jammed her feet into her pumps and ran for the door.

Waking up after a full night of drinking and a drugging dream was better than this, she thought. What a day for the alarm clock to not go off. She probably forgot to set it. Last night Emma had been more relaxed than she'd been in a long time, taking advantage of the brief feeling of inner tranquility. She had collapsed completely and went to sleep. Sleep, she thought. She actually slept. That was a miracle in itself. In the past whenever she woke, she remembered her dreams very vividly but last night was a blank. Nothing! Did that mean then that she didn't dream?

Her mind was so full of thoughts it was a good thing she was running on autopilot. Before Emma realized she was pulling her car into her parking stall. Getting out and setting the locks she headed to the elevator on a dead run. What the hell time was it? When did Beatrice call? Did she say? How much time since? Emma felt frazzled. She tried to keep her thoughts from venturing to the man she was meeting. He made her nervous enough, without being an hour late. Her body gave an involuntary quiver, a sure sign of her frazzled state, as she stepped off the elevator into the outer office.

Beatrice's desk was empty. Good. Beatrice was probably in her office chatting with Mr. O'Brien. Hopefully! Emma stopped looked at the clock on Beatrice's desk it was worse than she'd anticipated. Ten Thirty-Five. Damn. Straightening her spine, she took a deep breath while pasting what she hopes was a pleasant and eager smile on her face she opened the door.

"Mr. O'Brien, please forgive me. I am so sorry to have kept you waiting." She walked toward him hand outstretched. Silence! Beatrice, the rat, immediately excused herself. Fine!

Mr. O'Brien took her hand. The only indication he acknowledged her was a lift of that damnably handsome, arrogant eyebrow and a look toward the clock on the wall. Emma swallowed. She felt like a bird kissing a lion. Wonder if he'd had breakfast? God, I hope so, she silently answered. Doesn't the man ever blink? God his eyes were so blue. So intense! Emma felt herself sinking. She opened her mouth, but nothing came out. She cleared her throat.

"I…I am sorry for being late, Mr. O'Brien. I made quite a bit of progress yesterday. I would be glad to go over it with you if you would be so kind as to give me back my hand."

A little crusty perhaps but it was the best she could do when her innards were trying to climb out her throat. At least, she thought, she didn't come across sounding like a croaking frog or a lusty teen. Lusty she was, teen she was not. Now where on earth did that thought come from; she hadn't lusted after a man…in well…Ever! Before releasing her hand, his thumb ran delicately across her knuckles. Her cheeks pinkened. Emma stepped over to the window her back to the client, allowing her face to return its normal shade. Giving him wide berth Emma made her way to her seat.

Still uncomfortable under his unwavering gaze, Emma reached for the file on O'Brien Shipping. When he spoke, her eyes darted upward meeting his sneer.

"Miss. St. Claire, they say nervousness is caused by covering a lie. You won't be doing that. I hope. You're not about to open that file and tell me that my crew is to blame for this?" He raised his brow again. Even higher, Emma found herself trying to contain a chuckle at the idea that his eyebrow might just reach his hairline and become stuck if he was not careful. It felt good.

As she listened to his tirade, her joking humor was quickly replaced. She found herself getting downright angrier by the second. What right did this man have to talk to her in this way? Before she could vent, he rattled on.

"…I find your office to have been lax. I filed my complaint over two months ago! I come here because I received not so much as a letter from your office and when I get to the God forsaken city you tell me you need time. More bloody time! I give that to you! Setting up an appointment with you for a time you stipulated, and you don't even have the decency and consideration to be here! *I find you incompetent Miss St. Claire! Very incompetent!"*

He obviously hadn't eaten breakfast before coming and decided to make a meal out of her. Well, she wouldn't have it! If he said 'you' one more time, like it was some disease, she'd feed him a knuckle sandwich, job or no job. Egotistical! Overbearing! Son of a.

Emma sat arms crossed over her chest, feet linked with the chair legs keeping her from lunging across the desk; she stared at the file, the clock, the paperweight. Yes, the paperweight. *No Emma not now,* she scolded quietly. Her hands were shaking. She was torn. She could almost have sympathized with the man. Almost! Subsequently he called her incompetent and anger won out yet again. She bit the inside of her cheek. Breathe, just breathe. Managing to get a rein on her temper she looked up into eyes as sharp and deadly as shards of blue glass. Her own, now blazing emeralds spit fire.

Their gazes locked and held. Emma knowing what she wanted to say; and knowing she couldn't, cleared her throat banking the rage that burned. It was a different rage from what she'd previously felt. This rage felt good. Still she could not act upon it. Not and keep her job. Taking a deep breath, she calmed herself before speaking.

"Mr. O'Brien, Dan. I can understand your being upset and I am truly sorry. Now if we could please continue, I am confident we can get this mess wrapped up and then you will not have to be in my presence nor my incompetence any longer." She paused briefly noting his eyes flickered with…with what? Admiration? Was this a test she wondered? Well she hoped to God she passed because she wanted him out of her office and out of her life for good.

"Now then, I took time yesterday to read your file. I can see why you are upset. I can only say I am sorry I never got to the file before my leave. If I had I can assure you would not have waited very long for results." He still didn't deign to give her an answer but the look of piqued interest on his face gave her the confidence to continue.

"First of all, I'd like to apologize for the incompetence of the Customs official you encountered. Let me assure that this mistake will not be repeated. The Customs officers are trained very well, aside from misreading manifests that are not filled out correctly, they know their jobs."

She seen he was about to comment holding up her hand she forged on never allowing his mouth to open. God forbid he'd never shut it again.

"Most of the time companies' ships, which are impounded, are guilty of importing illegal substances. In this case however; your case it was not the fact that you imported an illegal substance, but that your manifests were inaccurate. If you will look at this document you will find that the contents of the shipment were not documented to be imitation ivory, just ivory. Had your captain made sure the loading manifest or customer invoices stated imitation I am quite sure this mess would have been avoided. By right he should not have left dock without clarification."

Dan took the manifest, reading it over. He admired the lady's spunk and although he was irritated at the way she'd put him in his place, he was however more intrigued with the why then the how. She'd seemed such a timid creature when he met her yesterday, shaky, jumpy. Usually a sign for lack of confidence, which was strange in someone so beautiful; usually those types tended to let their vanity take over. Yet even though he said otherwise she gave him a sense of peace knowing his problem was being addressed by someone who knew what she was doing; so why so nervous?

Today, after arriving, finding her office empty and her apparently nowhere in sight his temper flared. He was being put off again. For her to come strolling in like nothing of consequence happened made him lash out. The smile she'd on her face as she entered came rushing back. She was gorgeous. Did she know? Not likely, she didn't strike him as the type to use feminine wiles to advance her job.

It wasn't her he was angry at. Still he couldn't help his need to vent. Then she came at him. Not with foul words but with enough emphasis on the right words to let him know he'd pushed her too far. God she was amazing; the way her eyes spit fire changing them from green to amber. The way she chose her words to give just the right effect. He found himself thinking she was not as timid as he first believed. She was passionate but for some reason she held that part of herself at bay. Why?

If nothing else, he promised himself…he would find out. Later, it would have to be later. First, he'd to get his ship. "I see, Miss St. Claire, perhaps I misjudged. I concur with your observations regarding my captain and he will be reprimanded. Thank you for bringing this matter to my attention. Now as it was not illegal cargo when will I get my ship back? And compensation?" He paused waiting to see acknowledgement in her eyes. He'd hit a nerve. Good. Score one for him. Just as he thought, her eyes told him like hell and her lips…her lips were lush, free of lipstick. Ripe strawberries plump and juicy; waiting to be tasted, nibbled, savored.

They parted slightly, an unconscious invitation to slip his tongue inside. Open, lips moving. Oh Christ, she's talking. And he hadn't heard a word. Nothing registered. His errant thoughts wouldn't bode well in his favor. Shifting his weight slightly tried to relieve the tension building in his tailored pants. He forced his mind to what she was saying before she realized what he was thinking.

"And so, I was unable to get your ship released yet, but I did manage to have all impounded charges and fines waived. Your ship should be able to be released next week sometime. I am sure. Only I must wait for Mr. Harding to get back from holidays to sign the release papers. I also have a call in to the Government bureaucrats you love so much, requesting damages for loss of wages. If you are able to let me know a reasonable amount, I may be able to handle this by the time in which you retrieve your ship." Not likely but he would be gone and that was all that mattered.

Emma waited for a response; when it came it was not what she'd anticipated. She expected him to be angry, to rant like a lunatic. Act the ferocious lion. Stalking and devouring, like he had when she first arrived. She was stunned when his voice drifted clear and soft. Almost…husky, she thought. Confused. She was very confused, by the feeling that coursed through her lower abdomen clear down to her toes. Never having felt this way she couldn't decide if she liked it or not.

"Well, I guess if that is the best that can be done, I will call the office, get the quotes you require and clear my schedule. I'll stay in Washington a little longer to await the paperwork. I will be back in a couple of days to see how you are making out with those release papers." He stood and extended his hand.

Emma reached out for it, but her mind kept replaying his last words. He was staying. He was coming back to her office. She forced a smile to her face absently telling him to see Beatrice at the front desk; she would help him with anything else he required.

Dan left the office withholding his smile. Not only had he resolved company matters he now had a reason to stay closer to Emma. Judging her reaction, it would prove interesting. Closing the office door securely behind him he allowed his smile to take hold as he sauntered to reception. She had said Beatrice would help him with any of needs. He couldn't help the small chuckle escaped him.

Emma sat at her desk; she felt afraid, yet it was not fear. The feelings this man stirred in her were new and she didn't totally understand them. Her stomach fluttered, sweat pooled in her palms. Love? No, what did she know of love? Lust? Hell no! She didn't even like the man, right? She knew there was something; she only had to figure out what, then she could stop it.

Emma had never been popular, spending most of her time alone, committed to her books. She never went out. Dated once. Disaster. The nightmare had taken years to get over. Since then, she'd never met anyone who affected her in that way. Seven years. Keeping her distance, focus on work and nothing else. Until now, it had worked. Was she getting upset over nothing? She could have misjudged her feelings, his subtle looks, the softening of his voice. He was probably not even interested in her. She certainly had given him no reason to be interested. Yet his heated gaze bothered her, leaving her wishing she knew more about these things.

Forcing thoughts of that disturbing man and his actions from her mind, Emma picked up the next file. Damn! There was so much to do; the last thing she needed, was to be distracted.

Dan went back to his hotel after making reservations for the week; he sat on the queen-sized bed in his room, thinking about Emma. A nice name; it suggested closeness and friendship. Especially closeness. Oh yes. He could hear himself uttering it, in the middle of the night, while he was buried deep inside her. She had such a nice body, petite yet shapely. Proportioned just right, so that her legs seemed a mile long. He usually liked his women taller, but from the first time he noticed, she just seemed—right. Just looking her stirred him, made him rock hard. Thinking of her legs, made him wonder how they'd feel wrapped around him as he stroked in and out of her. Her breasts looked as though they would fit nicely into the palm of his hand. It would be the first thing he discovered before leaving town.

Stripping off his business suit as he walked to the bathroom Dan's mind still whirled with thoughts of Emma. Turning on the shower he stepped under the spray. Such passion, he could sense it. It was focused on her work; he assumed it had been for a long time. Why keep such fire locked inside? How long had she hidden it away and why? It'd be his mission to find out. He loved a good mystery and it would be a waste to allow her to go on this way. It would be his pleasure to show her where to focus that passion.

Emma managed to put a dent in her workload. Each time she stamped a file closed she soared. It was the strongest medicine; each file was a step, bringing her closer to controlling her life. It had been ages since she felt confident. And Emma liked the feeling.

Her chair tilted as she stretched to massage the tense muscles in her neck. Glancing at the clock, the red 5:30 p.m. told her it was time to go home. She had stayed later today; the need for a drink not surpassing all else. But now it was time for a little supper. To be brutally honest a drink would not be amiss either. One day, she hoped to be strong enough to say good-bye to the bottle. For now, not letting it control her was a very big step and all she was willing to take.

Switching off the computer she looked around. Three years ago, she re-decorated. Everything was a piece of herself; the pictures adorning the walls were quiet scenes, sunsets and sunrises over the ocean, lush green valleys with wildflowers so vibrant you could pick them. Looking anew, Emma was coming to realize that her dreams had been a solid influence of who she now was. Why had it taken her so long to see?

The lovely mahogany desk contained delicate intricate artful swirls and other little carvings that to her looked like mountains and cliffs but to anyone else it could be totally different; handmade, designed and paid for by her.

The office of course, would have provided her with the same claptrap everyone else had. Emma wanted extra; knowing she would be dedicating more of herself to this room than anywhere; she wanted peace. This décor; simple and old-fashioned, maybe even silly to some, represented her serenity. When she first came back, she hadn't been able to see her office for what it was. A second home; a place of refuge from the world outside. A final glance before shutting the door lifted the remaining weight from her shoulders.

Beatrice was at her desk, which was unusual; normally she was one of the first people out of the office. Where she went in such a hurry; Emma didn't know and had never asked. It was after hours; she was off the clock. Yet Emma wondered why she rushed home to an empty apartment. In the past three years they had become closer, but the past seemed an off-limits topic. She still had no idea who Beatrice was before. Strange, especially since she was the closest thing to family, she had left.

"What are you still doing here, logging brownie points?" The kindly receptionist looked up smiling.

"I have no need of brownie points; you'd never find someone better if you looked a thousand years."

"Pretty confident," Emma said, with a chuckle.

Beatrice's eyes sparkled. Overjoyed at the sight of Emma acting more like her old self. She was young still with so much to look forward to. If only she could let, go of the past. "I just stayed to make sure there was nothing you needed. Alarm clock? A wake-up call?"

Emma laughed. Beatrice missed that sound. Looking at Emma innocently, she waited for the laughter to die.

"My old clock is just fine, never fear. I forgot to turn it on and unless you have the infinite wisdom or mechanics, to correct that minor defect then you're not much help. As for clients, I know my schedule, I have none." I hope, she finished silently.

Beatrice sat back with a cocky smirk. Thinking over her conversation with Mr. O'Brien. Did he have anything to do with Emma's escalating moods. She hoped so. While he was in town, she would see that they spent more time together. If this man had her smiling after only two days just think what he could accomplish in a week. It was obvious to her that Emma felt something for him, even though she would probably never admit to such a thing.

Beatrice finished cleaning her desk, her mind reeling with possibilities. Could she trust him to use this time to his advantage? What would it be like to ride around in his pocket for a while? To see firsthand what he had in mind. She had filled him in as to a few of Emma's likes and dislikes. A small hint here and there; it would give him a slight advantage. Could he be the man she'd pictured for Emma? It was a little soon to tell. She would let things coast for a while until she could get his full measure. If the relationship was good and needed another push, or if the worst happened and it turned out to be bad; she would be there to help steer. Humming, she pictured them together; it felt right. Just like her and her beloved, Dex. Either way it would be a challenge and that, would have Emma's thoughts turning in another direction. Yes. Anything was better than the current status quo.

There she was; he couldn't believe his eyes. Blinking, Dan made sure his runaway imagination wasn't playing tricks. Of late his visions of Emma were so vivid that just this afternoon he damn near kissed the shower stall before he gained control of his senses. Yep, it was her. He had passed the pub earlier on his walk. After speaking to Beatrice, he realized that his hotel was close to Emma's apartment, so he did a little reconnaissance. He never imagined getting this lucky. She looked lost, he thought as he approached a bar stool.

Without pausing or looking up, the bartender said, "That little lady has had quite a time. I made sure she always had a peaceful place. I don't let anyone bother her. She does not need you making eyes at her from afar either. The name's Fred, what can I get you to drink?" Looking up, he lay aside the wet cloth, and stared into a stunned face; he noticed the direction of the man's gaze. It had lasted only seconds, but Fred had the senses of a bloodhound.

Dan had been caught off guard and it took a moment to collect himself. "I'll take a Brandy. Sorry if I gave the wrong impression, I have no designs on anyone. Merely checking the place out. Nice place. I'm not into big cities myself. Whenever possible I am on the ocean, captaining one of my ships. So, this quiet place seems like a nice refuge."

"A captain of a ship? Wow. Sounds like you are a might out of your league." Fred chuckled letting the pun lighten the mood, "What brings you to Washington? You own a ship? More than one? Here's your drink, sir?"

"Sir is my father, I'm Dan."

"Here's your drink, Dan. What brings you in seeking refuge? You're not with that convention, are you? Thought they wrapped up Sunday."

Dan held the drink to his lips savoring the taste. God it was good to have a drink after a day like today. The solitude was even better. He didn't mind the questions. Fred was the type of man one instantly liked, a wise owl, brimming with answers. Taking another sip, he tried to put an order to Fred's questions. He had a knack for asking the kinds of questions that solicited a lot of information without making the person feel interrogated. Dan liked that.

Setting the glass on the bar he returned Fred's scrutiny. He resembled an older version of the Radar character from MASH. Big round-rimmed glasses sat upon his face. He was short, with a rounded paunch. His thinning hair held a bluish-gray tint indicating it used to be black. His eyes were big and brown behind those glasses and he seemed to blink more than the average person. Looking at him right now, Fred really could have been mistaken for an owl.

"I'm in Washington on business. Hadn't heard about a convention. Anything interesting?"

"Not unless you're interested in dreams."

"Dreams?" Dan smiled and shook his head.

"Yeah." Fred smiled back.

"Nothing wrong with that. Everybody needs a dream."

"You don't say?"

"I do. I may not have your years my friend, but I know enough about success to know you have to start with a dream."

"Right you are my friend."

Dan took another sip. "I hadn't planned on an extended stay. My business couldn't be concluded, so here I am. Guess I'll be here for a week, so I might as well make a holiday out of it."

Fred didn't fire more questions but waited patiently for him to finish his drink and his answers. Although this was a man who cherished peace, he didn't like to be alone.

Not like the young lady by the fire. She came here to escape, and he would see that she was afforded the solitude she desired. He liked her even though she had never said much. She was not looking as lost or tired of late. Still her loneliness seemed enforced. Penance? Possibly, but for the life of him he could not figure out why. At least she was smiling more. Still not talkative, but since her small breakthrough the other day she was for the time being speaking in full sentences. That was a step in the right direction. She would take a bigger one when she was ready. Regardless of the obvious she didn't seem to be the type to wallow in booze. Although he may never learn the why of it, he did intend to make sure she stayed on the fast track to getting herself well again. Each day he watered her drinks a little more, soon the alcoholic haze would wear off completely, he hoped. He was certain she wouldn't realize the extent he helped her with the little nudges he gave, a word here and delicately formed question there and as for the drink, he would bet his life, she didn't relish the taste. He glanced again to the man at his counter as he began speaking.

"I own nine cargo ships; none are passenger ships. You said the lady had a rough time of it. What did you mean? Another drink please Fred. I am sure this one will last longer than the first."

Fred took Dan's glass, in a fluid motion, set it on a tray with other dirty glasses then turned back to the counter and filled a new glass. Setting it on the napkin, he studied Dan with new eyes. The man was direct. Even though he'd masked the important question amongst ones of a lower value, the tactic didn't escape Fred's notice, but it didn't bother him; he liked how his brain worked.

Dan was beginning to think he over played his hand when Fred finally spoke. His eyes took on an intense light. Bracing his elbow on the counter, chin in his hand; posture screaming confidence.

"She started coming in here for the first time a couple months ago. Never spoke and didn't want anything except to be left alone. She drank; Tequila, downed them like water. She'd find a faraway table to sit at and drink until her blonde head damned near fell into it. The first time she came, there was no table by the fire. The area had been set up for darts however most play billiards now. I set it up hoping to draw a comment. Nothing. She homed in on the table like a beacon. It was hers and hers alone. In a way, it was. She'd get so liquored she had problems maneuvering around the furniture to the door. The reorganization allowed her a clear path, although I don't think she noticed. She's never so much as told me her name, where she lives or what had happened to her to make her seek oblivion. She seems to be doing a little better lately. Smiles now whereas she didn't before. Starting to look more her age too; I'd say around twenty-five. I swear when she first came in, she looked like a wraith. All white and pasty with huge black rings under her eyes. Outwardly she's gorgeous but I am guessing a whole lot nicer than that on the inside. She didn't seem to belong to this world; I used to try to drag a conversation out of her. Stubbornly she refused to be pushed so I took on the role of a guardian." He smiled sadly. "I watched out for her and tried to let her know there was someone here if she needed." Fred scratched his balding head. "Why am I telling you this? Others have been intrigued, yet I told them nothing. There's just something about you."

"Although most would see your hard exterior letting it go at that, I see you have softness in your heart, a kindness. Not that I am sanctioning hunting season on the little lady. For what it's worth, I do not think you'd hurt her like many others would, if given a chance."

"She does not belong to the world she's adopted; just not a drunk. Sometimes it is a dark world, where the sorrows of misfits are drowned in a bottle. I think she is beginning to mend and for that I am extremely grateful. You would not do anything to stop her from healing now would you?" Fred looked into Dan's eyes then glanced toward Emma. "I'll be right back," he said as he headed for the table at the far end of the bar.

Dan watched in the mirror behind the bar. He could see Emma sitting at the table holding the glass but not drinking from it. Like it was giving her power. It appeared to be warming her more than the fire. Although it was autumn here the weather was warm even in the evenings. One could tell just by looking that she was cold. Not an outer cold. More like a deep freezing of the soul. What happened to her? It would have to be something big. Two months ago, would have coincided with the time he filed his complaint. He remembered her saying she had just gotten back. He had assumed a holiday or vacation. In hindsight two months is an awfully long time for anyone to be on break. Even a government employee. Frankly he'd been so angry about government bureaucracy that he hadn't paid attention to much else.

Had she wanted sympathy she could have told him anything to make him go away then took her time getting to his file, it was what he expected but it was not what happened. Instead, she immediately reassured him that something would be done and did it. He remembered her being shaky but thought it nerves.

She had been so outraged when he needled her about incompetence, he should have known there was something more behind it. Looking at her here he could see her pain. Either she masked it better at the office or he had been a blind jerk. And he was sure it was the latter. He found himself admiring her even more.

One thing was for certain; something happened to her. It would be wise to find out what before approaching again. Finishing his drink, he set the glass back on the napkin. At least he was working with more information than poor Fred. He at least knew her name and where she worked. Grabbing a pen from the counter he quickly scribbled on the napkin before fishing out a twenty and tossing it on the bar.

He took his time walking back to his hotel silently listing possibilities that would make a person fall so far, so hard and so fast. She wasn't an alcoholic, but she was spending the better part of her days in an alcohol induced haze. By the time he reached his room he had a couple of ideas. He'd go to the library tomorrow, read through the newspapers from two months back. He hoped he would find a clue to confirm at least one of his theories. If not, maybe he could entice Beatrice to be more forthcoming with the information.

Sliding into bed Dan closed his eyes. He could feel the sway of the ship beneath his feet; smell of the salty sea air. The sea, he sighed as he sunk deeper into his pillow.

It was not Dan at the helm but a young lad. He felt he was watching a scene from a movie. Being there, but at the same time not. This had happened before. Numerous times, as far back as he could remember. The lad was the same. A younger smaller version of himself with the same wavy black hair and intense blue eyes; somehow, they were linked. It used to bother him, jolting him awake, always remembering everything he'd seen and felt, intensely. It disturbed him to the point where he'd looked up every piece of information he could on dreams. Briefly he thought about seeking professional help. That wasn't his way. Then finally, an old sea dog changed his way of looking at the dilemma. In a scratchy cigarette voice, he said, "Son, you're lucky; to have a life away from the everyday; it's a second chance to correct the mistakes you made the first-time round. Don't fear or scorn it. It cannot hurt you. It is a gift. Few would be so lucky." It took time but eventually Dan realized he was in control; and if need be, he could alter the outcome. No longer did he awake exhausted from fighting the enemy that attacked when he closed his eyes. He reveled in it. It made him a better person, a better businessman and a better captain; of that he was sure.

Emma looked up to see Fred standing beside her. Smiling. "Is there something wrong with the drink little lady? I see you've been nursing it for quite some time. Not that I mind. Never thought you were doing any good zapping them back one after another. Something on your mind? More than usual I mean? Want to talk about it? Would it have anything to do with that fella over at the counter? I saw you sneaking peaks in his direction. Don't worry." Fred chuckled. "I don't think he knows you saw him. He seen you though. Appeared a might interested I must say. I don't think he is dangerous. Seems like a right nice lad to me…"

Emma stared at him wondering if he would ever stop talking. Yes, she'd seen Mr. O'Brien, Dan, sitting at the bar. Truth was she felt him the moment he entered. That bothered her more than the fact he may have seen her drinking. What should she care if he saw her drinking; it was after work? She didn't have to answer to anyone on her own time. No sir. She didn't care one wit, what he thought. Clearing her mind enough she offered Fred a big smile. That stopped him. She knew it would. He seemed to live for her smile. Not that he got one very often, but he never stopped trying. He had never given up on her.

"No, Fred, there is nothing wrong. I do know the man at the counter; he's a client. I'm working on a complaint of his. I didn't expect him to walk into a bar so close to where I live. I was kind of hoping he'd left to go back home to Baltimore, check on his shipping business. I guess he has decided to stay on in Washington instead. I can't fathom why. He does not strike me as someone who likes the city life. Not that Baltimore is small, but I figured maybe he lived out of the city. Somewhere quiet. Sorry, Fred, I'm rambling." She shook her head. "I can tell by the shocked look on your face I have never said so much before. I am sorry for that. You have been very kind. Have I told you that? No, probably not. I apologize. The drink is fine. I guess I am just getting to the point where I am strong enough without it. Thanks though."

Fred was stunned. He couldn't believe the little lady was turning around quite so quickly. He found himself wondering if Dan had anything to do with it. She appeared interested, beyond business. She was intent on running away before he could ask her though. Glancing back at the counter he found only the empty bar stools. Oh hell. He left. Disappointed, he would have to let his curiosity rest. He looked back at Emma.

"You're a strong one. You just remember that missy and you'll do fine. Glad you are getting your wits back. You have a good night." Fred hid the knowledge he'd caught her blushing.

She knew he was looking for Dan, the warmth she felt on her cheeks probably betrayed her feelings. Emma gave him another quick smile. Sliding her chair back and standing up she headed easily to the door.

Fred was a good matchmaker. He'd see what he could do. Tomorrow. Walking back to the counter he picked up Dan's glass, noticing the napkin, he read it. "Emma," was all it said. He placed Dan's and Emma's glass on the tray; whistling a tune he began cleaning the counter.

Emma's mind was occupied; her body filled with so many feelings it was like a shark during a feeding frenzy, at the forefront was the way her pulse sped whenever she thought of Dan. The blasted man didn't have to be anywhere near, and her thoughts were still infused with a great deal more lust then should be healthy.

Trying to clear her head, she readied for bed. Wondering what the little girl would do. They were so much alike and so different too. Emily seemed so brave where boys were concerned. She took enjoyment from the same type of feelings that Emma was shying away from. She wished Emily were here to give her advice. She wished anyone were here to give her advice. That was impossible. One was all too real and the other was make-believe. Emma lay back on the pillow closing her eyes as a tear slipped and ran down her cheek. It still hurt. It probably always would.

Chapter Four

The sun slanted in through the window; its rays playing brightly on the desktop, when the office door creaked open. Emma glanced at the clock; it was time for lunch. Beatrice, forever worrying about Emma's eating habits of late, had probably come in to guilt her into eating. Emma didn't want to stop. She had managed to get a lot done today. The pile of files was diminishing, and now, only a few remained; Emma felt a surge of pride at a job well done.

"Yes, Beatrice?"

"Time for lunch. I was going to go to the deli on the lower level. Do you want to come?"

"No thanks, I'd like to keep working. Everything seems to be going well now and sure as rain, as soon as I leave all hell will break loose, the computer will blow up or some smart ass without a conscience and a twisted sense of humor will be dumping another shit load of files on my desk." She waved her finger at the offending files, but a smile played about her lips. "Rain check?"

"Sure thing; don't work too hard. You're doing fine considering all the things you had to cope with since coming back." Beatrice didn't think it prudent to mention the days Emma had been too hung over to come in. That was in the past. "I am certain you'll have everything back under control in no time. Rome wasn't built in a day. Can I bring you something back?"

Emma decided to order, or chance being dragged downstairs. "How about a Rueben; I haven't had one in a long time. I can almost taste it now." After placing her order, hunger struck and now she couldn't wait for Beatrice to be gone just so she could get back.

"Be back in a jiff, Rueben in hand. That's a promise." With that the door closed.

Emma sat enjoying her office. It was a peaceful place to be. Her home away from home. Or at least it used to be. She waited for the overwhelming sense of guilt and loss to flood forth, but instead of engulfing her in pain as usual, she felt only a dull ache. Not letting her conscience question her lack of agony, as she should, she tossed back her head, staring at the ceiling until the thoughts fled her mind. Getting up and walking to the window, Emma laid her forehead on the smooth cool surface, and sighed. Her office had a spectacular view. When her supervisor showed her the office she would be working in, the first thing she did was look out the window.

She'd agonized over starting at the bottom in a big government office, imagining a little office and no window. She'd remembered how scared she was at the thought of feeling trapped.

To her relief the office was roomy, and the window was almost full length. She was so high; she could see clear across the city. From her chair she had only to lift her gaze and she would be refreshed by simply looking at the skyline. DC had lovely sunrises and even better sunsets; from here nothing interfered with the magic. She was lucky they did not place her on the other side where the other buildings were higher. Staring into the windows of another office across the street wasn't her cup of tea. It would take away the privacy factor, which she valued almost as much as the scenery. Stretching, pushing her palms into the small of her back, Emma walked back to the desk and picked up another file. No more breaks for today. Time to get back to work; the thought brought forth a smile.

It didn't seem very long before the door opened. Emma didn't look up from the computer "Just set it on the desk Beatrice I'll eat it in a bit. Promise. Thanks again."

"Well I was kind of hoping you'd be able to take a little break and eat it now, I did go to all the trouble of getting it to you." Came a deep voice.

Much too deep to be her secretary. Where in the hell was her special radar where he was concerned? Emma tensed, lifting her head she stared straight into the deep cobalt blue eyes of non-other than the delectable one himself. Before she could help herself, she smiled. Her heart slammed in her chest with enough force to bring down a barge. The smile disappeared. She did not want this! She did not need this! Her voice, when it came, was ice cold.

"Mr. O'Brien. What are you doing in my office? I was not aware we had an appointment today. I am sorry to disappoint you, but Mr. Harding is not back so the documents are not signed therefore we have nothing to discuss." She hoped she'd managed to counter whatever it was her first impression gave away. Why the hell was the dratted man standing there with a smile on his face? A look of combined confidence and devilry twinkled in his blue eyes;

surely, she'd put the right emphases on the right words, any other man would be sputtering and storming out of her office right now. So why wasn't he?

Dan couldn't help smiling; the furrow between her brows told him just how badly she felt about her plan backfiring. It was comical.

"Miss St. Claire I was coming to your office to give Ms. Roland's another number I could be reached at when, as luck would have it, I ran into the lovely lady in the courtyard. She had just finished purchasing the much needed nourishment for you. She asked that I take it up, maybe have lunch with you. She had remembered somewhere she had to go, and she didn't like the thought of you locked up here all alone. I do believe she was worried you were spending too much of your time working since you have been back. You really should slow down a bit from what I hear. You can't solve the problems of the world in one day you know. She made me promise in fact. Wouldn't like to break a promise. Not good for future business."

That did it! How dare the ass come in here and tell her what to do. Just what did he know anyway? How the hell would he know anything about what happened before. Did Beatrice tell him anything, she wondered? Over working herself. Of all the pompous, arrogant jack assed things to say!

Dan looked into eyes, the amber flecks appeared like dancing flames, and God she was beautiful when she was mad. Barely managing to contain a chuckle; he allowed himself the pleasure of a small smile. He'd gotten to her that time. He liked to see her skin take on a heated blush. At least in her anger would it in passion? That thought pleasured him even more.

"Mr. O'Brien. What a tremendous change in attitude from just a couple days ago. You were the one coming in here telling me of my incompetence. Do you remember that? Of course, you do. How silly of me. Someone without any faults of his own finds it difficult to overlook the faults of others. Well as it so happens, I am trying to rectify that right now and contrary to what everyone may or may not believe I will not fall apart from having put in an honest day's hard work. I do not want or need you or Beatrice to tell me I am working too hard." She stopped and dragged in a breath.

"I am a big girl and I can make those choices myself. Out of my many faults I assure you making decisions is not one of them! Now, if you would be so kind as to leave my office, I will have my lunch while I work. I just find my competence before it is time to go home for the day!"

Dan stood in front of her desk, unphased by her outburst if anything; it cemented his resolve. In a soft lilting voice, he whispered, "Have supper with me…" He paused watching her face display more changes than Mozart's symphony. He wondered if she knew how well he could read her just by watching. "Look it is either supper or lunch; your choice. But it is the only choice in which I am willing to let you make."

Emma could not believe her ears; this guy was giving her an ultimatum. How dare he? Well a choice. She had a choice she would take and be damned if she was going to choose lunch with him here right now when her guard was down. No bloody way! "I could call security, and have you thrown out, Mr. O'Brien."

"You could," he said smiling. "But you won't."

The ass. Damned if he wasn't right. Fine. She'd choose supper and by that time she'd have an excuse.

"Dinner. Good day Mr. O'Brien."

He smiled not looking the least little bit taken aback by her tone. He picked up the bottle of wine telling her he would collect her at eight o'clock and with that he left. Collect her, would he? What the hell was she? A piece of luggage? Oh God, what if she couldn't get out of it? What had she done?

Emma listened to his footsteps fade away. She would have a talk with Beatrice when she got back. How dare she send that lion stalking her!

Emma reached for the sandwich, hands shaking. She had to calm herself. She stared at the sandwich as though it was the offending Mr. O'Brien, opened her mouth wide and tore off a chunk. How could that man affect her senses so? It seemed every time she was around him, she lost it one way or another. She could normally keep a good rein on her temper, but she'd blown it this time. Swallowing, she took another bite letting her tongue savor the combined flavors of sauerkraut and corned beef. Mmmm…delicious. Food.

Suddenly Emma stopped chewing. She set the sandwich back on the wrapper and sat back, astounded. He told her he would pick her up. How? How, in blue blazes, did he know where she lived? She was still sitting there replaying their conversation over in her mind when the door opened again. He was back, what the hell could he want? No matter, this time she was ready. "Get the hell out! I'm trying to work here!"

"I'm sorry, did I startle you?"

It was Beatrice. She'd come back from lunch.

"Sorry, Beatrice, I thought you were someone else."

"Obviously," Beatrice said, knowing the reason for Emma's loss of temper and not caring one Iota. Still she gave Emma a thoroughly confused smile.

"Could you come in here for a moment?"

Beatrice nodded. They'd need privacy, for this conversation no doubt; she closed the door.

Dan left the office; his heart, lighter than it had been in a long time. She was becoming addictive. He'd known all along she'd pick dinner. Now all he had to do was finalize the arrangements to ensure this was the best night she had ever had. Walking back to the library, he made plans for tonight. Beatrice had given him a list of Emma's favorite foods; she even went so far as to make reservations at a little restaurant she thought Emma would enjoy. Beatrice was turning out to be one hell of an asset.

At the library, he asked the librarian where he could find old newspaper articles. She pointed to the microfilm machine. He sat down, began going through newspaper clippings from the end of July. He only knew the approximate time frame, end of July to middle of August, not wanting to miss anything he made sure to cover a wide range. Beatrice had said that Emma grew up in St. Charles. So, he should be able to find something in the Times or the Post. It was sure to be something big; it had to be for Emma to suffer from the type of guilt she carried. Considering he'd been at sea about that time it wasn't any wonder he'd missed it.

News was usually depressing, filling pages upon pages of murders, thefts and the like. He only looked at the sections he had to in order to keep his business running smooth. And that was left up to his manager allowing him to avoid wading through the mire. If the books remained solid there was no need for him to look. But now? Now he had an incentive. Besides he certainly didn't have anything better to do. At least…not until tonight; his heart beat faster. Then if all went well, he could find himself very busy soon. A smile spread over his face as the pictures played through his mind. Oh yes, he thought wickedly, very busy.

Shaking his head to clear away his lusty thoughts, he looked at the screen and began reading. If he could find something to go on, some hint behind the mysteries that make up Emma St. Claire then maybe, just maybe, he would have a chance with her. At first, truth be told, he was only interested in getting her in bed, but the more he watched her that night at the bar the more the mystery that surrounded her, obsessed him. It was a quest. One he wouldn't give up.

Dan continued scanning the articles; some were just a flash, he felt sure that when he came to the right piece somehow, he'd know. Wait! What's this? Plane crash. The Pan America jet left the Washington's Ronald Reagan airport bound for the Caribbean. It never made it. Unforeseen complications caused the deaths of all 307 passengers and six crew. No names were listed; that was all. It said nothing further; all reports hinged on finding the black box before the investigation could get underway.

Dan felt he'd been punched in the gut; it could be caused by reading about the loss of so many lives. However, he was sure there was more to it, still he had nothing to go on. Just a hunch. Dan started looking for more articles about the crash. When and where the black box was located. The investigation concluded that something went wrong with the engines, probably electrical. And yes, St. Charles was listed, but no mention of names. He could be way off base; he didn't think so. His gut told him the problems surrounding Emma had something to do with that crash.

Aside from the fact that the crash had taken precedence, over anything else considered newsworthy, at least in his opinion; sure, there was the everyday stuff, murders being one but that wouldn't explain the kind of behavior Fred explained. Those types of things, although tragic, would not cause survivor's guilt, a hardened society, one reared in the modern age, was better equipped to cope with these events. Emma did not strike him, as someone who would be weakened by the loss of one individual. No, it had to be personal and it had to be astronomical.

Dan swore he'd find out as he left the library and headed back to his hotel to change. Smiling once more at the look on Emma's face, sweet Emma's delectable heart shaped face. He chuckled; he'd been able to read her like a book and manipulate her as easily as turning a page. Would he be able to get her to open-up, succeeding where others had failed? Maybe not; not yet, anyway.

St. Charles was not far from Washington. A field trip was required. In a small town he should be able to find out more. Someone there would be willing to talk even to a stranger. In his experience, people looked upon big news, good or bad, to bring their world into the limelight.

Whistling Abracadabra, a hit from way back, Dan left the hotel eagerly making his way to Emma's apartment. Did she realize she hadn't told him where she lived? He wondered if she found out where he got his information. Probably, for if it was one thing Emma wasn't, it was dumb. He'd bet his company, she figured it out before he reached the elevator. Beatrice would need an extra big bouquet for braving Emma's temper.

Emma was a bundle of nerves. Her feet ached from pacing. She thought of canceling so many times she had a headache. Because of this date…no…she refused to call it that. Because of this night she missed her chance to go to Fred's. The fortification from a glass of tequila would have been welcome.

Well. If he thought he would have a good time, he had another think coming. Emma was bound and determined not to enjoy herself. For that reason, hell would freeze over before she allowed him to have a good time either. This was war and she fully intended to treat it as such.

The phone rang, startling Emma, she grabbed it. "Yes, Donnelly. Yes. Thanks." She hung up just as his knock vibrated against the door. She glared at the door. O'Brien must have taken the stairs. Not even the elevator was that fast. Sweet Jesus he was going to break the effing thing. Emma eased the chain from its casing and pulled the door open.

"Do you mind? That racket is going to get me evicted!"

Maybe, a slight exaggeration on her part, but he didn't know that. If she made a bad enough impression he'd leave. Hopefully. And then she wouldn't be force into this farce of a date.

Dan stood at the door smiling, listening to Emma holler. The thought of his knock being loud enough to arouse the neighbors was humorous considering the door was open, he was in the hall and her voice was as loud as firecrackers on the Fourth of July.

Dan took a step toward Emma' instinctively she backed up. For every one of his steps forward she took one backward until her back was pressed up against the closet doors. Dan closed the door with one well-placed kick of his boot. Not moving he stood staring and smiling into Emma's anger-reddened face. Grabbing Emma's fisted hand, he carefully uncurled her fingers and placed them around a small bouquet of orchids. It was the only flower he could find that matched her passion and her fire.

He could tell by the look on her face she was about to switch topics in midstream and berate him for the flowers she now held. Dan was, as always, one

58

step ahead and before she could utter a single word his mouth came down meeting hers with the softest brush. The gentleness shocked her to the core. Then his tongue traced the outline of her lips and her heart stopped as suddenly as her words had. Her hands shook, bouquet forgotten, it dropped to the floor. Her hands slowly glided inch by heated inch until they wrapped around his neck. He was hard and smooth and soft and warm. She leaned closer.

After what seemed like hours, his head lifted. Dan gazed down into desire-darkened green eyes. She was so quiet. He feared awkwardness would take over any minute; shrugging nonchalantly he retrieved the flowers and placed them into her hands; a cocky smile played about his lips, "Hush," he said, "I wouldn't want you to get evicted." He tapped his finger to her nose and smiled. Emma's face glowed red as she stomped into the kitchen looking for a vase. In the background, she heard the smart-ass chuckle.

In the restaurant, Emma sat across the table listening to Dan's one-sided conversation. She wasn't inclined to give anything more than necessary. Aside from answering obvious questions she stayed quiet. If this bothered him, he gave no sign, and while he talked Emma looked about the Italian Restaurant. A quaint place authenticated by the décor. In the background, music played soothing the soul, conjuring thoughts of warm summer nights and faraway places. The atmosphere made it difficult to stay angry and damned if he didn't know it. Sitting there all superior, he knew she would love a place like this. Beatrice. The whole damned setup had Beatrice written all over it.

That afternoon, looking for an outlet for her anger, Emma's rage zeroed in on her receptionist not realizing until too late that she had made the woman cry. Feeling like shit, she apologized but it hadn't improved her temperament. Beatrice of course quickly accepted the apology, dried her tears and went back to work. Emma still felt like a heel. The gentle woman would never hold it against her; for that she was lucky. Beatrice said she was sorry for meddling; she was only trying to help. She never would have given out information if she'd known. Something struck Emma as odd, but with her earlier outburst she didn't dare voice her opinion. Beatrice honestly thought there was chemistry between them. Emma couldn't fathom where she got such an idea.

Her mind flitted back to the kiss. If she were honest there had been something from the very first, but she wasn't into feeling honest right now. She was still annoyed at herself for welcoming the kiss. Welcoming? Relished more like. It affected her to the core. And he'd brushed it aside like it was one of the most natural things he done. Probably was. The bloody Casanova! What he would say if he found out he was the fifth man to kiss her. Not that she'd tell him of course.

Emma sat picking at her Chicken Scaloppini, watching Dan eat Stuffed Chicken like it was going out of style. He was a very handsome man; it was undeniable he held a certain power over her. Not being able to control it, was what scared her. Forcing her feelings was dangerous. To love was to lose. To get close was just asking for trouble. She couldn't afford to lose anyone else. To open her heart. She was just adjusting to the loss of her family.

Dan looked up and Emma found herself pulled in. His blue eyes held her mesmerized. Her cheeks flushed pink before she forced her eyes back to her plate. "This," she said, motioning with her hand, "is very good, did Beatrice tell you about this place?"

"Actually, yes. She's been very enlightening. It helps to know what one likes when trying to impress. Don't you agree?"

"I wouldn't know. I spend most of my time trying only to please myself. I've never worried about pleasing others. Life's easier that way."

"You don't get out much, do you. Why is that? You're pretty, pleasurable at times; I'm sure you must receive hundreds of invitations." Dan watched her closely.

"I wanted to wage war. You, forcing me to dinner; was not well done. I do not normally go out with clients, it's bad business." Her words were rewarded with a flash of uncertainty before he quickly covered it with his usual stubborn glance.

"You needed to get out Emma; I was forced to stay in town. It is kind of your fault I am here. Besides I like you. Is there anything wrong with two people who like each other going out for dinner?" Emma heard the innuendo but let it pass.

"What makes you think I like you?"

He chuckled.

He did have a point. This really didn't have to be any more than a dinner between acquaintances; so why in the hell did it feel like more? She looked up. "Since you put it that way. Just know there will be nothing more between us. I wouldn't like to give you the wrong impression. I am alone. It's the way I like it; less complicated."

That's what she thought. She was a great actress. Aside from the hesitation in her voice he almost believed her. She may not want anybody, but she couldn't handle being alone. Her stint with the bottle proved that. Dan knew if he pushed, all would be lost. Biding time seemed to be his best option. Watch, listen, wait and then react. It worked in business. His Emma was a contradiction. There was more to her; layers upon layers more. Dan loved a good mystery. He steered the conversation down another path, determined to drag the evening out longer.

"Thank you for the dinner," Emma said, when they reached her apartment. "You don't have to see me up."

Dan smiled widely; he knew what she was doing. He'd let it go. Leaning forward hovering just above her mouth he whispered, "Good night." Then left her standing, staring, confused.

Hours later, Emma couldn't stop replaying the night over and over in her mind. It was a good time. Maybe if she just admitted it, she could get some sleep. She had gone, determined for the date to fail. It hadn't. There was verbal sparring but instead of fueling her anger; she liked it. It sharpened her wits giving her great joy when she won. If she could complain about anything tonight, not that it was a complaint worth noting, it was that Dan hadn't kissed her good night. She'd been prepared for him to try, then his head lowered and forgot all about stopping him, and then nothing happened.

She shouldn't be disappointed, yet she'd spent the night staring into his blue eyes and his handsomely chiseled face; how was she not to notice his mouth as well. The way it moved when he talked or smiled. Such nice lips; not hard or cruel. As a matter of fact, Dan didn't seem cruel in anyway at all. But then, neither had her high school idol Travis; he seemed nice too. At first. His charm ended prior to their first date.

Sighing Emma climbed into bed still thinking of Dan's soft lips and moist tongue. Her body was betraying her, from the flutters in her lower abdomen to the aching of her nipples. Closing her eyes, she groaned; she could smell the salty sea air knowing the dream would take her.

Standing at the edge of the cliffs shielding her eyes from the sun, Emily stared out over the sea. Still nothing. Emily looked every day, hoping, to spot 'The Maiden'. Daniel had been gone so long. Too long, yet she never gave up hope. Surely if something bad happened his family would receive word. There had been none. One day, he would return hale and hearty.

Emily slowly walked back.

"Any sign yet, dear?" Emily's mother asked.

"No, but I shall not lose faith. He is the man I want, and so, I must wait."

Emily's mother had known for years her daughter loved young Daniel. She hoped upon his return, he would notice the gorgeous young woman before her. And she was praying he would accept the precious gift of her love. Her daughter was special; sunshine, loyalty and commitment. Once Emily gave herself there would never be another. She would always be there for him. Tiny as she was, she would protect him and any children that came with her life. Her little girl was a lioness, always had been. Please God, grant them the chance.

Emily sat rocking, sewing yet another dress designed to show Daniel the woman she'd become rather than the little girl he left behind, she knew with each stitch her daughter sewed, she thought of Daniel; his interpretation of her in it. She was lovely. Her long blonde hair hung well below her waist and shone like spun gold. Tiny but curvaceous. The boy didn't stand a chance. He will be stunned when he sees her. She hoped that Em's efforts weren't for nothing that the boy would come home unharmed; but over the course of a year or two anything could happen.

"Don't worry mama, he'll come. He is well. I know he is. Surely, I would feel differently had he come to harm. I love him." Looking down at the lace collar she stitched Emily ran her fingers over the soft fabric. She missed him. Wanted him to come home. Home to her; to tell him she loves him. And always had.

Her mother walked away pretending not to notice the tear silently slipping down her daughter's lovely cheek. "Please, God," she prayed.

Dan was still whistling when he hopped out of the shower. He was very pleased with himself. He wanted to kiss her good night, desperately. Reining himself in had been the hardest thing he'd faced in a very long time. He'd wager his nine ships she was left wanting for the kiss she had never received. When was the last time Emma had been kissed? Had she enjoyed it? Had she melted with desire as she had tonight? He didn't think so. It was one of the reasons he held back. The last thing he wanted to do was scare her off.

Opting for a taxi, allowed him a closeness he could not have had while driving. Coming home he practically sat on her, draping his arm across the back of the seat; pressing against her every time they turned a corner. If she had tried not to notice; she failed. Her shudders betrayed she felt the same electrical current go through. He touched her hand, by accident of course, slowly running his finger over the pad of her thumb then apologizing and pulling away. His father used to say, "The best way to catch a fish is to play with it." Emma was no fish, but she was the catch of a lifetime.

Beatrice let slip, that in the three years of working with Emma; she'd never known her to go out with anyone. Emma had never spoken of being asked out except in fun. That surprised him. She was beautiful; although she could come across as an ice queen, he didn't believe that persona would stop a determined man from trying. The odd thing was, not one of them succeeded. Astounding. More questions bubbled to the surface. What could have happened and why avoid relationships?

The cause went beyond whatever happened two months ago; Beatrice had known her for three years. A workaholic prior to her leave; what could it be? What made Emma shun togetherness when he could tell she hated being alone? Solitude; privacy possibly, but never ever alone. She was made for togetherness, closeness and love; one way or another he would make her see that.

Dan climbed into bed; he needed a plan of attack in place before seeing Miss St. Claire again. Once settled, he closed his eyes sighing as he felt the rhythmic sway of the ship's deck under his feet.

Daniel was going home at last. This trip had taken longer than he'd planned. There had been much to do. The cargo he brought back on his first voyage had to be better than those that had gone before. He left twenty-six months ago, long enough to become a man in his own right. He hoped his father would see him as such.

As the ship moved toward the horizon Daniel mentally catalogued his wares. Silks, spices, tea and coffee would bring great returns. Traveling great distances had brought the advantage of a buyer's market. All it had cost him was time. The voyage had procured twice as much as any other captain and for the same price. Even with the crew's promised percentages, the trip was a success. He hoped his father would see it the same way. It amazed him; often the ideas were not premeditated, they just came to him. Like an angel watching over him showing him which route to take, which goods to purchase or where to begin bargaining. He thanked the Gods for sending him a supporter.

He loved the sea and feeling its power beneath his feet. Restlessness had set in weeks ago; it was time to go home. He yearned for the church socials, the Sunday gatherings. The picnics. He was too old now to romp with the children; he'd been too old before. In any case, he would not let it stop him. All the children had grown up together; it was no longer a matter of age but of friendship. You were neither too old nor too young to have fun with a friend.

Another day, just twenty-four hours, with fair winds then he would dock. Handing the wheel over to his second mate he gave a longing look toward the horizon before heading below decks.

The captain's quarters had been decorated by his dad, for he was usually in command. Daniel added pieces found on his journey to make the place his. He would be taking over so why shouldn't he feel comfortable in his cabin? Going to the desk, he took a bottle of French brandy from the drawer. Pouring himself a healthy portion he toasted his good fortune. In another year he'd have enough to add another ship to the fleet.

Downing the brandy, he opened the captain's log recording the events of the day.

Chapter Five

Dan was in shock. To lose a family. An entire family was un-fucking believable. The waitress, at White Bull Diner, talked about it as though it were the best tidbit she'd heard in years. Frankly the whole thing made him sick. Managing to thank Maude for the information he left; he followed the direction she gave and viewed Emma's home. Sitting, staring at the neglected lawns, he couldn't help noticing what a special place it must have been. What impact did it have on St. Charles? Were people devastated, were they in awe, overwhelmed? He could only imagine what Emma went through. Will have to go through for the rest of her life. Holy Mother! Was it any wonder the girl turned to the bottle?

Dan was an only child, longing for brothers and sisters. However, his parents and he enjoyed a close relationship, still did. What would it be like to have all that and lose everything in millisecond? Devastating. He had to help her. The question was how? He could no longer say good-bye to Emma. Even knowing the mystery that surrounded her wouldn't free him of her hold. The truth was he had felt connected from the first meeting. The need was new to him. She was like a magnet pulling him, even as she was pushing him away.

Even before he could admit it to himself, he knew she was the one. There was just no turning back. He wanted that strength beside him. Forever. Heading home, Dan pulled into the underground parking across the street from the hotel. It was a good thing they were able to extend his reservation another week. After their dinner the other night, Dan had decided to stay until he knew more about Emma.

He intended making an appointment for tomorrow. Now that he was back, with what he knew, he had to see her. He'd like nothing better than to take her in his arms. Discretion was a must he reminded himself. He may know, but she didn't know he knew. Dan exited the park-aide's side entrance, without looking he crossed the alley, his mind in turmoil. In his heart he couldn't leave until she was his. Until they came to an agreement and agreed on a future. Dating, living together, marrying; anything so long as they were together.

Everything happened so fast. Dan spotted the bright yellow flash. A horn blared. People shouted. The sounds faded, distant. In a second impact a hard punch to his mid-section sent him hurtling through space, five maybe ten feet from the van. The pavement rushing to meet him; his head connected…Then nothing.

Emma was just getting ready to leave when Beatrice rang. "Hon, there's a call on line two. You need to take it."

Emma pressed the flashing line.

"Emma St. Claire, may I help you? My card? Oh my God, yes, yes! I know him. Is he okay? Yes. Don't worry we'll be right there."

Emma disconnected shaking. She was having a hard time focusing. Jesus, oh Dan, Jesus. Those bastards. They never look. Always in a hurry, always assuming they have the right of way. The more fares they get the more money they make that's all they think about.

"Beatrice!!! Beatrice!!! Damn it, Beatrice!!!" Beatrice came running into Emma's office; she was sitting behind her desk as white as a sheet and shaking. Oh God she was shaking so bad you'd think there was an earthquake.

"What's wrong?" Beatrice said kneeling, taking Emma's ice-cold hands in hers.

"What is it?"

Emma looked up. There were no tears, but her eyes were glazed over like a person possessed.

"Dan, Dan…ah Mr. O'Brien, he's…"

"Em, spit it out. What's a matter with Mr. O'Brien?"

"Oh, Beatrice. He's in the hospital. Hit by a minivan. I must go. He's unconscious. He had my card in his wallet. Can you take me? Help me get to DC General."

Beatrice knew now wasn't the time to fall apart, nor think of herself or the same tragic phone call she'd gotten years ago. No! Angrily, she pushed it from her mind. Not now!

"Of course, Hon. Come on, I'll get the lights you grab your purse and we will head over there right now."

Running through the doors of admitting Emma yelled "They brought a Dan in earlier, hit by a van, they called; please take me to him."

The nurse stared. The poor thing looked about to pass out. "Are you alright Miss?"

"Yes, I am fine I need to see Dan. Now!"

Beatrice came up putting a hand on Emma's shoulder. She looked at the nurse's name tag.

"Sorry Mary. This is Miss St. Claire; she's a little distraught. Not making much sense right now. Please, let me explain."

Emma cast Beatrice a withering look but said nothing as her friend explained.

"We received a call about 40 minutes ago. A friend was brought in. Dan O'Brien. Apparently, the staff here had no other contact. I know usual procedure only allows family members, but I am assuming they wouldn't have called if Emma couldn't go in. Can you tell us what room he's in?"

Emma could not seem to get her mind or mouth working properly. She needed to see Dan, assure herself he was okay. "Please, God," she prayed. "Please let him be all right, please."

Beatrice led the way; Room 526. Funny she hadn't heard the nurse. Inspecting the room, Emma wasn't sure what she was looking for. There were four beds only one was occupied. Other than that, it was like any other hospital room rank with the smell of medicine and disinfectant. Depressing. Slowly she walked to the bed. Dan lay on his back. A big white bandage covered his head, a little of his jet-black poked out the bottom. His face looked gray instead of tanned with the possibility or blue, green and purple arriving in the days to come, but he didn't look as though he was in pain.

Beatrice pulled a stool over for Emma to sit on and then left the room to find a doctor and hopefully an update on Dan's condition.

Emma straightened his covers, which were perfectly fine but made use of her restless energy. and then sat on the stool next to him. His shoulders were bare and although she would have liked to check him for other injuries, Emma resisted the urge to look beneath the blankets.

"Oh Dan. I'm so sorry. I'm a plague. Anyone who gets close pays the price. I only hope you can forgive me."

Emma kept talking. She had a myriad of topics. Coming to Washington, meeting her, taking her to dinner, being on the road. Anything she could think of. She told him of her family; why it was her fault. She kept talking, rambling. She really didn't know what else to do.

Emma didn't know how long Beatrice was gone; in truth she didn't even notice her leaving, nevertheless she was glad she was back.

"Where did you go?"

"I went to see if I could find a doctor and get an update on our patient."

She patted the covers in a familial gesture so suited to her personality, if Emma's thoughts had been a touch clearer, she may have perceived how strange it was for Beatrice to remain single, she so loved mothering people about.

"And, did you find one? Did he say what was wrong with him? Will he be alright?"

"I didn't find a doctor, Em; I guess they went to supper. Ida, the nurse on this floor, said they should be around at about six." She glanced at her watch.

"Another 30 minutes. So, I guess we'll just have to wait. Has he moved?"

"No. I've been talking to him, but Oh God, I don't know what else to do. Why does everyone close to me suffer?"

"Don't be silly. I am close to you, and nothing but good things have happened to me since the day we met. Now, stop this nonsense. It is not your fault. Do you hear? Besides you can hardly say you're close to Mr. O'Brien you only just met. Or is there something going on I don't know about?"

Emma didn't reply then again, she didn't need to. As pale as she was the blush glowed like a lighthouse beacon out over a stormy sea. Emma leaned forward trying to hide her heated face and brushed her hand up and down Dan's covered arm. She jumped. A moment later her hand was back on his arm.

"Beatrice, I think I felt his muscles tense. That's good, don't you think?"

"Yes, I think he knows you're here. Keep doing that. He needs to feel a connection. Here." Beatrice took Dan's hand from under the covers and placed it firmly in Emma's. "Hold his hand; brush your thumb over the knuckles. That's right. Good. Just like that. I am going to find you a cup of coffee. I will be right back."

Beatrice left Emma holding Dan's hand. They needed time alone. She'd hunt down some coffee so she wouldn't be caught in a lie. Should take at least thirty minutes if not more to find a decent cup. Beatrice smiled; Emma was like a student cramming for finals, biting her lower lip and brows furrowed in concentration. This was not how she planned to bring the two together nevertheless if destiny was going to lend a helping hand who was she to spurn it? If in the end she got what she wanted. This should bring the couple together.

They both had feelings for one another. The stronger, more intense they get ensured success for their future. It had been the same with her. They were meant for one another; she was sure of it.

Emma watched her fingers glide back and forth across Dan's knuckles. She opened his hand; traced the lines. They were blurring she knew then; she was crying. One tear then another slipped down her cheek and landed on Dan's palm quickly she dried them but refused to let go of his hand. Beatrice said it would help. Tear after tear dropped from Emma's face onto Dan's hand and although she could hardly see she just kept wiping them away.

"Hey. Sweetheart. Don't cry, come on baby…please don't cry."

Emma looked up to see Dan's eyes opening slowly. She tried letting go of his hand and felt his fingers tighten. "Please," was all he said, and she knew he couldn't let her go right now. And that was just fine by Emma. She needed his touch. To know he was here, and he was okay. Damn her treacherous soul, she knew better then to get attached to someone. Getting attached was dangerous.

Shaking away her errant thoughts before Dan read them, she asked, "What happened? They called me at the office, said a taxi driver brought you in. You had been hit."

"I don't know, I am sure I will remember but right now…I just don't know."

She looked at Dan. The tense lines around his face told her he was feeling the pain deeply. How selfish she'd been only a few moments earlier, thinking only of herself. Would she ever learn? Clearing the lump that formed in her throat she said, "Let me go and get a nurse, she can give you something for the pain."

"No Em, don't leave. I don't think they will give me anything right now anyway. Not until a doctor has checked me out. How long have you been here? Has the doctor come?"

Nervously, Emma started picking at the blanket with her free hand. She was not used to this sort of closeness. What does one say? It had been so much easier when he was unconscious.

"Right. How silly of me. I never thought. Sorry. No, it seems they go to supper around this time. The duty nurse assured Beatrice the Admitting doctor would be back in shortly."

There was an uncomfortable silence. Emma blurted, "Beatrice went out to get a cup of coffee for me. Did you want one?"

Dan almost expected her to jump up and run out the door to fetch him a cup of coffee. And though a strong dose of caffeine would be a blessing he doubted very much if he would be allowed it at this precise moment. He tightened the grip on her hand in case she decided to bolt. She remained silent but watched intently as Dan's stroked his thumb across her knuckles. The touch seemed to comfort her.

"You look like you lost your best friend sweetheart, how about you, are you okay?"

Emma ignored the endearment; something in his touch made it okay; she pushed the thought aside. Really, she didn't care what he called her or how he touched her if he was awake and talking.

"I am fine. It was a bit of a shock getting the call earlier at the office. I guess it took more out of me than I thought."

Dan said no more as he continued stroking her hand, it calmed her, and she seemed to like it. He looked at Emma; so pale. He cursed the fates; he was thankful to have her here with him, holding his hand, accepting his touches, but he was angry at how it happened. She was still adjusting to the plane crash and here he was lying in a hospital bed. He hoped she could cope; he didn't want to be her reason for turning to the bottle harder than before.

He would use this time Providence gave him. No matter how badly done, it enabled him to achieve his goal. She was his destiny. Words echoed through his head, a soft voice he shouldn't recognize yet did… "Throughout all time." They sat quietly feeding off the silent connection flowing between them.

The sound of footsteps drawing close had Emma looking expectantly at the doorway. Beatrice had been gone a long time. Where on earth, did she go for the coffee? Still the person belonging to the footsteps was not Beatrice. A short fifty-something with a shiny bald head and white coat bustled in, clipboard in hand.

"Hello. Mrs. O'Brien, I'm Dr. Hansen. How is our patient doing?"

Emma stared at the extended hand.

"Dr. Hansen, I am Emma St. Claire, a friend and business associate of Mr. O'Brien; he awoke just a short while ago. He's been talking but looks like he is in pain. Can we have something for that?" she said, completely business-like.

"No. I am afraid I cannot prescribe anything for that condition right now. Let me check him then we'll see." He turned toward Dan. "So, how are you? I imagine your head hurts like the devil, but other than that, how do you feel? Can you see okay? No blurriness? No dark spots?"

"Aside from an ache in my head and ribs, I feel okay. No problems seeing. Though I can't seem to remember what happened."

Dr. Hansen looked at the chart.

"Three cracked ribs, lucky that, concussion, abrasions to the right temporal lobe and left side. Nothing too serious; though it probably doesn't feel that way right now. Does it? Maybe next time you'll pick on something more your size. As to the memory, that's normal, it may or may not return, but so long as you remember everything else, you'll be dandy. You do know who you are? Right?" Dr. Hansen smiled.

"Sure, I'm Dan St. Claire." he said, chuckling, holding his ribs, at the look of pure terror he had seen on Emma's face.

"Glad to see you have a sense of humor. Though I don't know if your friend here appreciates it. As for your head, because of the concussion, it'll hurt for some time. You required some stitches but other than that your head is just fine. You'll have to come back in and have those stitches checked in about a week. They will dissolve on their own, but I'd like a doctor to check and make sure all is okay. If you have any problems at all, I want you to see me or your own physician right away. Is that clear?"

"I'll see my doctor when I get back home to Baltimore. Right now, I am staying at a hotel downtown waiting to finalize some business matters. Can I be released now?"

"Do you have someone you can stay with? You are not to be spending any time alone for the next seventy-two hours. I won't release you otherwise."

Dan looked puzzled. He didn't have anyone that he could call to come and stay with him; he knew who he would like to stay with, but he didn't think that was an option. Before Dan finished that thought he heard Emma's voice low and unsure.

"Doctor I live not too far away from Dan's hotel I would be able to check on him occasionally. Would that do?"

"Although I am sure you'd check periodically, I won't release him until I know he has someone to watch him round the clock. Anything could happen over the next seventy-two, including convulsions, possible chance of him not waking that sort of thing. Head injuries are always a touchy subject. It is crucial that he has someone right there in case something develops."

"Emma, dear, you could have Dan stay with you. You have an extra bedroom at your apartment after all. I could help you link your computer with the office so you can work from home. No one will ever know you're not right there."

Beatrice's perfect or imperfect timing in this case was very suspicious as she entered the room. Emma looked at Beatrice. She would have liked to choke her. How could she possibly say no now? She couldn't; it would appear heartless.

"Yes. That's right. Thank you, Beatrice." Emma said through barely noticeable clenched teeth. "Doctor could he be released into my care?"

Dan had trouble covering the smile. Beatrice. The sly old dog. A box of chocolates was in order, a huge box, when he got back on his feet. Emma was furious, but was hiding it well, but he could feel the waves running through her as if they were pumping through his very own veins. She was a firecracker. He laughed. Covering his mouth with his hand he managed, barely, to turn it into a cough. Beatrice glanced his way. She knew. Emma looked at him as well, he could see the lines of worry that creased her forehead.

"Are you okay?" she asked.

"Maybe you shouldn't be released just yet."

Dan got himself under control and smiled.

"Emma, I am fine. There is no need for me to stay taking a bed from someone who may need it more."

The doctor stood there nodding his shiny head in agreement.

Dan said, "I'd simply like to get my clothes and get out of here if that's okay?"

Emma looked toward the doctor; he seemed to find something amusing but right now she just didn't care what it was. "I will take care of the paperwork then. When you're ready, you both can meet me out front." Emma followed the doctor out of the room.

Dan's eyes followed her out of the room then turned to Beatrice, he winked. "Nice going."

"I'll run your wallet over to Emma while you get dressed; she'll need some of your information I'm sure. Unless of course?" Beatrice eyed Dan beneath the covers; Dan shook his head and chuckled, turning red. It had been a long time since anyone had made him blush. Shooing Beatrice out, Dan slid his legs off the side of the bed.

Emma was waiting out front when a wheelchair pushed by a big chested redhead in a cream-colored uniform complete with little white hat, came up. Emma couldn't help thinking, she was far too big chested to work in a hospital; good thing Dan was going home. The way her shirt clung could be classed X rated…well indecent to say the least. Emma gave her head a shake and realized the bimbo was speaking. "So, I thought we would give him the farewell treatment," she purred as she placed her hand on his shoulder.

Emma was immediately struck with the urge to break every one of those long fingernails and possibly the fingers right along with them. She was being ridiculous. Jealousy wasn't for her. She didn't even like the man; had no designs on him and never would. But she stood there glaring just the same. The woman should not be working around injured men.

"Are we ready then?" Beatrice said, pulling Emma to the moment.

Emma turned around in time to see Beatrice and the bimbo hold out their elbows to Dan. He grabbed Beatrice's but before he'd a chance to get the Bimbo's, Emma gently hip checked her out of the way and suggested that she get the door. Beatrice and Dan smothered smiles as Emma fussed and struggled getting the injured party out of the room and into the car.

At the apartment, they helped Dan out of the car. With him in the middle for their support they walked him slowly to the elevator. Dan really didn't need the assistance but having Emma put her arms around him voluntarily was magic and he was not about the break the spell. Inside the apartment Beatrice went to the computer clicking it on. She was busy entering in something that would link the computer to the office terminals while Emma helped Dan to the kitchen and into a chair.

Dan surveyed the apartment, everywhere he looked he saw family portraits, sketches and paintings of seascapes as well as landscapes, same as in her office but what got him, was the stuffed animals; teddy bears, raccoons, bunny rabbits, whales, dolphins piled high on decorative pillow shams and crocheted throws. A child's refuge. How had he missed all this? Goes to show where his mind was and where it wasn't only a short time ago. Then she had been a conquest, but now she was so much more.

He had the impression, that aside from her family and possibly Beatrice, no one else had ever disrupted this little paradise. Well, except for his all too brief visit when he picked her up for dinner. The memory still brought a smile to his face and heat to his loins, too bad he was in no condition to act on it.

She'd been roped into having him there, so he would make sure she didn't regret it.

Emma was busy tiding the kitchen, more as a delay to the inevitable; the place was clean except for the morning dishes. Finally, she said, "It isn't much but it's mine. I bought it shortly after I got out of college."

"It is very charming. I like it. Thanks for letting me stay. I promise I'll not be much bother."

She blushed. "The spare bedroom's right across the hall from mine; I should be able to hear you; if you need anything just call. Are you hungry? I can make some soup and sandwiches if you like. Then you should lie down. You can't have any medication until after midnight. Are you in much pain?"

"I'm fine." Noting the look of disbelief on her face he retracted. "Okay I hurt a little. Well, maybe more than a little but don't worry. I'm not some simpering prep schoolboy who can't tolerate a little pain. I can take it, honest. I would like that soup though. Sandwiches sound like they will hit the spot too. If it's not too much trouble?" Dan's stomach growled and Emma smiled.

"No trouble at all. I haven't eaten yet either so I could use a bite. Hey Beatrice! You hungry? Want some soup and sandwiches?"

Beatrice came into the kitchen. "No thanks I have to be going; the computer is all set. Call me in the morning and we'll make sure you can access the system. I'll even courier some files over; that should keep you out of trouble. Although…" Beatrice's eyebrows waggled as her eyes darted from one to the other.

"Don't, Beatrice Rolands. Don't you dare! Do you hear me?"

Beatrice chuckled. "Good night guys, I'll talk to you tomorrow." Looking at Dan she smiled. "You take care of yourself; be a good boy and listen to Emma. She'll take real good care of you. Won't you?"

"I will." Emma smiled shooed the beloved busybody out before closing the door behind her.

"What would you like to drink? I have orange juice, milk. …No, scratch that, I don't think it's safe anymore. You can't have anything alcoholic so that about covers what's in my fridge. Would you sooner coffee or tea; I might be able to find some." Setting everything down on the table in front of Dan, as she started to back away, he snatched her hand. Startled she looked up; their eyes met. Without saying a word, he lifted it to his lips and kissed it. A silent thank you. Just that simple touch, rattled Emma. No one had kissed her so gently or sweetly. Never. She got herself together and looked at him questioningly.

Dan ignored the question in her eyes and said, "Coffee would be nice Emma." He dunked the sandwich into the soup lifting it to his mouth he took a bite. It was heaven. Roast beef sandwiches and mushroom soup; he let the flavors come together in his mouth. It felt like he hadn't eaten in days. He would always remember this meal, it wasn't much. Just simple Campbell's soup and deli roast beef but it was special because Emma had made it for him. The first of many he swore.

Coffee perked loudly in the background, while Emma's attention remained on her bowl. That kiss wasn't even a peck, really, but wow. She felt like she'd been hit with a thousand volts of electricity. The current charged the air and Emma could feel tingles right to her toes.

After dinner Dan placed his dishes in the sink. "Should I wash?"

Emma jumped. "That's okay I've got it. Why don't you, um, take your coffee into the living room. Watch TV." Dan smiled as he went into the living room.

Emma used the time to get a grip on herself. For God sakes what was she, some teenager on her first date? She winced. Well maybe a normal first date for a normal teenager. She slowly sipped her coffee as she loaded the dishwasher. Three years in this apartment and she'd only used the dishwasher six times. It was easier to wash the dishes immediately instead of waiting a week for a load. How long it would take to fill with company here?

Emma walked hesitantly from the kitchen. It was a short distance, a small place, but seeing Dan on the couch Emma felt like she was that guy in the commercial where the hallway kept growing as he was walking. The sofa loomed big in the distance, all of three feet away, enormous. Having planned on living alone, she'd never seen any reason to fill the space with a lot of furniture. However, now, there was a problem. Nowhere else to sit, just the couch, which was more of a love seat. Chewing it over, she contemplated what to do.

"I don't bite. You're as dead on your feet as I am. Now come and sit."

Emma would have liked to argue, but damn it all; the man was right. How did he interpret her thoughts, feelings, and body language like a book? No one had ever been able to do that. Not even Andre. She learned long ago how to hide her emotions. Mastered it. No one ever knew. Except Andre and she swore him to secrecy. If she convinced him she was coping, he promised to never tell.

Dan noticed Emma wasn't with him. Eyes shadowed by ghosts so deeply entrenched they couldn't have been caused by her current set of circumstances. They melted away. With practiced calculation. That was his Emma, the shadows disappeared leaving no trace.

Shrugging, she sat down exuding more confidence than she felt. "What are you watching?" she asked.

"Nothing really, just surfing. The channels are different than in Baltimore. I used the guide in the hotel room anytime I wanted to locate something."

Glad for something to do, Emma reached under the coffee table locating the TV Guide. It was a good thing she'd been sober enough lately to indulge in watching TV. She had even purchased an updated Guide yesterday. "Let's see? What do you like, news, sitcom, oh wait here's a Mel Gibson movie? You interested?"

"Sure. Which one?"

"*Lethal Weapon 2,* it looks like there's another one after. Must be a movie marathon."

Emma snatched the remote from Dan and switched the channel. During the commercial she went into the kitchen rummaging for munchies. In five minutes, she was back with popcorn. She set the bowl between them. Dan smiled. Protection by popcorn; well, it might work until the bowl was empty.

Toward the end Dan was not laughing as often as he was in the beginning. Emma knew he must be in pain. The clock on the wall read eleven-fifty. Close enough. Getting up she went to the kitchen returning with a glass of water and a couple capsules. "Open up." Emma placed the pills on his tongue then handed him the glass. Dan wondered if it occurred to her how intimate that gesture was and figured, she probably hadn't.

"Come on I'll show you your room. Shoot. We didn't bring anything from your hotel. We will have to go there tomorrow to get you some clothes and toiletries, but for tonight." Dan squeezed her shoulder softly, "It's okay. Really, I don't sleep in anything anyway. I won't need to shave or shower until tomorrow." Emma's mouth opened then closed as her face burned Dan bit back a smile. He'd bet she never even heard anything he said past, "don't sleep in anything," he managed to contain his amusement until after she left his room, but it was difficult. Closing the door, he laughed. His arms gripped his sides. Damn ribs.

Emma switched off the lights and locked the door before retiring. Why did he have to say that? The fiend. Now she would have a hell of a time sleeping. He was across the hall. In her spare bed, soft cotton sheets pulled up over his naked body. Curses! She climbed into bed. Tonight, was nice. Not that she'd tell him. It was nice not being alone. For however long it was to be, she would cherish it. And God, yes, she'd miss him when he returned to Baltimore.

Emma heard a moaning. What was…oh, Dan? Probably the pain; she focusses on the clock, three, time for more medication. Emma threw back the covers and walked quietly to the kitchen. Getting a glass of water and couple more pills from the container she went to Dan's room. She padded to the bed, switching on the lamp; she stared dumbstruck as she realized in his pain, he'd managed to shake the blankets free. They were in a hump at the bottom of the bed. She blinked her eyes hoping it was a trick of an overly active imagination, but no such luck. No surprise there. She hurried trying to untangle the blankets and get them in place before he awoke found her drooling over his much too naked, handsomely sculpted body.

Finally, the blanket freed, Emma slid it up and tucked it around him securely. As she reached for his shoulder to awaken him, her fingers froze. Her cheeks flushed. She felt hot all over as the jerk lay staring up at her smiling. How long had he been awake? "You…ah…you were moaning. Time for your medicine. Here." She thrust the pills in his direction, hand trembling. Dan swallowed the pills and placed the glass on the nightstand. "Thank you."

Emma wanted to leave. Before she could he grabbed her hand. First reaction, she yanked. He pulled. Emma teetered. She tried to stop herself, didn't want to hurt him; she came down on top of him, hard. "Oomph." She struggled to get back up, but his arm came around her. Holding her. She gave him her best ice queen look. Most people would have run the other direction but not Dan. He didn't look like he was going to run, even if he could. Frickin' man! It would serve the tricky bastard right if he got hurt.

Dan knew she was angry, but he also sensed she was intrigued and maybe even a little scared. Angry, yes, he could see. He'd after all pulled her on top of him. Intrigued, yes, she was that too, not understanding the undeniable currents that flowed every time they touched. But scared, why in the hell would she be scared? Dan let go of her hand but kept his arm firmly around her waist.

His hand slowly cupped her face before running a fingertip from cheek to jaw. "So beautiful," he said in a gravelly voice as he ran his fingers sloppily over her lips.

Lifting his head hurt, he ignored the pain. Tenderly he placed a kiss upon her lips. Slowly, gently he worked his lips over hers enticing her to let go of her fear. Feeling the tension leaving her, Dan ran his tongue over her bottom lip. She hesitated not knowing what to do. He nibbled. With her gasp, his roamed the inside of her mouth. Just as he remembered she tasted of cinnamon and heaven all rolled into one.

Emma's circuits overloaded. A hundred different emotions coursed through her. The last time he kissed her, it had been different; controlling yet tantalizing. This time the kiss was designed to lure; employ her participation. And, it was working. She wanted to participate. Neither kiss was anything like what Travis had introduced her to. She liked it and that shocked her pulling her back. Dan released her body but held her in place with his eyes.

Running his thumb over her cheek he smiled and closed his eyes. Emma stared unbelieving. He kissed her. Like…like what? A lover? No…a lover would have stayed awake and done more…wouldn't he? Then he fell asleep. He left her senses whirling. Emma contemplated whether she should be angry or relieved. Gently so as not to wake or injure him further, she pushed away from his sleeping form. She felt like running from the room, but no, she was not a coward. She didn't think she'd be able to sleep for the rest of the night but she had to try.

Dan heard the door close, then smiled. He knew if he were awake Emma would have seen a need to voice her outrage. That would not further his cause. This way she would stew over 'the problem' letting mind run wild. While he did the same. The feel of her lips was better than he'd remembered and her taste…addictive. She smelled of flowers. He was the first to admit he struggled for control. His senses charged and he reacted. Waiting for the next one, would be hell. He'd make sure he wouldn't have to wait long.

Taking advantage of his banged-up head may not be the most honest way of getting what he wanted, but that had never stopped him before. And it certainly would not stop him now, when he was so close to getting something so important.

Chapter Six

Emma was sitting at the computer when Dan strolled into the living room. She could feel him as he stood watching her; although she could not bring herself to look up. Not yet.

Dan walked to Emma placed his hands on her shoulders ignoring the stiffness, he leaned forward kissing her cheek. "I am sorry I slept so late. Is it time for more medicine? Babe Ruth is using my head for a battering ram."

Emma looked up. He looked in pain, his color was better than yesterday, but his taut face brought lines to his eyes and mouth. She really should scold him for being so forward, but she couldn't berate him, he was hurt after all. Reprimands could wait. Oddly enough she knew he would not force her too far or wound her like Travis. It surprised her to realize she trusted him.

"Alright, come into the kitchen I will get you some breakfast and give you another pill. The doctor said you shouldn't take them on an empty stomach if you didn't have to. I forgot about that last night, guess I should have made you some toast. Is cereal okay? I haven't been a diligent shopper of late. I'll go to the store and pick up a few things. Shit! No milk. Cereal is out. I guess I had better go now. I have a bit of time. Just waiting for Beatrice to courier over some files. The system seems to be working fine…"

Dan knew she was uncomfortable; rattling on to beat the band. She probably hadn't realized it, but it was hard to miss the fact that she was not giving him an opportunity to respond.

"So, we'll do that if you are feeling up to it."

Before she got off on another tangent Dan said, "It is okay you know. You don't have to fill every waking moment with conversation. I will not jump on you as soon as you stop."

Emma looked at him. Her eyes told him what she was too afraid to say. Without another word she grabbed her purse and headed for the door.

Bloody man, Emma thought. If his frickin' head hadn't already been bashed, she was more than willing to pick up a bat and have a go. Pompous, arrogant, smart-ass, she wanted to strike him, hold him, and kiss him---preferably all at once. How could he do this to her? Tie her up in knots, make her so nervous she could barely function and at the same time she longed for him to hold her and kiss her again. It was wrong! She was spoiled for any man sexually. Wasn't she? Of course she was, she had tried a couple of times in college. It was always the same. She'd freak out; there would be name-calling and anger. She just couldn't do it. Not even something as simple as a kiss, she just couldn't. The boys had all thought she was a tease, a prude and nut case. So, after third unsuccessful attempt she just gave up. But you kissed him back. It was different you said so. You felt something. Still feel something. Yesterday she would have laughed had anyone told her she would be having this conversation with herself in the middle of her damn foyer, but she wasn't laughing now. She was…Oh God she didn't know what she was, but she wanted this. Wanted it more than anything. Could she do it? She knew she should not allow anything more to happen and yet…oh hell!!!! It was just so hard.

Emma looked up and saw Dan standing there; he smiled but wisely said nothing as he followed her out into the hall.

Emma put away the groceries while Dan headed for the shower. He offered to help; she declined. Her kitchen was too small, he'd be too close, and she was unsure. She finished putting the cans away each in an orderly line. At least something in her life could be orderly; then she checked the computer. A courier had dropped off a package while she was out. Hopefully Beatrice had sent her enough to keep her thoughts off Dan.

She started inputting, triggered by the sound of running water; Emma's overactive imagination kicked into high gear. She groaned picturing Dan in all his glory. Seeing him last night, his muscles looking scalped, his arms, shoulders and even his chest. Black hair covered it, tapered downward into a single line to his groin then surrounded his penis. She remembered fighting the urge to touch him while she untangled the blanket. She would have touched him; how had he felt? Warm? Soft? Hard? Why couldn't she remember?

Heat gathered in her abdomen, then lower. Dan entered; towel secured about his lean hips. He asked something, she pointed automatically; and the next she knew he was walking out of the living room with the cordless in his hand. Emma closed her mouth and tried shaking the fog out of her brain. God

Emma, what are you sex starved? Well, yes, she was but that was beside the point. This couldn't be healthy.

Dan sat on the edge of the bed; he'd let her wicked thoughts soar. They suited his purposes. The more wicked the thoughts, the more chance he had. He dialed the office and waited for Porter to pick up. He filled Porter in on what had happened with the meeting and with the accident. Porter enlightened him as to what had been happening at the office then asked further about the ship.

"A week at most, no, I'll not be able to take her out," he said, thinking of Emma's sweet lips as he touched his briefly. "I have unfinished business in Washington. It may take a while. Can you handle things? That ship will need a full cargo bay by Friday next. She's lost enough money these past two months. I want her and her crew at sea as soon as the ship is released and loaded. Have Captain Henderson pilot her." Porter, efficient as always, assured Dan everything would be handled before hanging up.

Dan, having taken pity on Emma, dressed before going back into the living room. Glancing at Emma, who seemed to be typing faster than a stenographer and just as absorbed, he chuckled as he placed the phone on the base.

"What's so funny?"

"Nothing, just something Porter said," he lied.

"Porter?"

"My business manager; I just checked in to see what was happening."

Emma's face fell. "When are you leaving then?"

Shrugging, Dan headed toward the kitchen. Soon the sounds, cupboard doors the fridge doors and the counter drawers opening, and closing could be heard. What on earth was he doing? Getting up she ventured after him. The bandages that wrapped his head were gone; from the back you could see no sign of his injury. He stood there, no shirt and no socks just jeans hanging much too low on his hips. She cleared her throat. When he turned, she saw a small butterfly band-aid placed directly over the stitches.

"What are you doing?"

He stepped closer; she stepped back. The kitchen was so small it was comical. Where was she going? Soon she was back against the table. Tilting her chin defiantly Emma looked him in the eyes. Instantly she was lost. Her pulse hammered. Could he hear it? In slow motion, he came closer until they were touching chest-to-chest, thigh-to-thigh. Closing her eyes she waited for his lips to touch hers, instead they touched the rapidly beating pulse in her neck, his thumbs held her head, so her neck was extended; he nibbled. Her eyes flew open; she couldn't stop the small moan from escaping, her knees were jelly; his breath trailed upward finally connecting with her lips. He was a patient teacher, playing with her, toying with her. She reciprocated and it was heaven. Dan waited until the desire clouded her eyes turning them a deeper shade of green. Taking her arms, he linked them about his neck. Moving closer still, he rubbed his full erection against her. Letting her feel his desire for her, letting her know exactly what he wanted and what he meant to have.

Releasing her mouth and resting his head upon hers, he sighed.

"Ah Emma, sweet Emma, how I want you. It scares you, it shouldn't. I won't press but listen well. I will have you. You will be mine. Soon."

She didn't answer him, her breathing was labored he knew before she turned that she was going to try and bolt, he had seen the panic in her eyes. He released her to make good her escape.

He'd give her some time, a little space something caused the panicked look, maybe a little time alone would give him a chance to figure out the puzzle that was Emma St. Claire. He used to think it was the accident, that she needed time, but now? Was she battling him, or herself? Either way he'd find out. He started preparing supper; the work would help him concentrate. Eventually, he'd call if she hadn't emerged from her hiding place when it was ready. He'd give her time but be damned if he would let her hide away forever.

"Time to face the world Emma," he vowed silently.

"Time to face it with me."

Emma could think of only one thing to do. She would tell him. It would turn him off completely. Then he would leave, and Emma could be alone once again. In her safe and sheltered little world; she couldn't take the chance. Sexual oh God yes, she finally felt something. She would even consider it good. And it was those feelings she would cherish always. But she could not take the chance of getting close to him, having him hurt. Again. Just like her family she'd lose him as well. That would be unbelievable; she'd sooner let him go than have him hurt further. She couldn't, protect her family but she could protect him. Laying her head on her pillow she cried. For Dan, for her, for a love they'd never know.

Dan knocked. Supper was finished, the table was set, soft candlelight lit the kitchen. A perfect setting for seduction. Even the meal, finger foods, he would place each morsel into her mouth sealing it with a kiss as she chewed. He envisioned little else. There was no answer and Dan knocked again. "Emma, dinner's ready come and eat. You haven't eaten anything unless it was before I woke up in which case it has been much too long. Emma, come now open the door." He heard movement; the door opened. She'd been crying, but he made no comment.

Bowing, and extending his arm like a gallant knight of old, he waited until she placed her hand then began escorting her to the kitchen.

It was dark; the lights were off still there should have been light coming in from the balcony window. He must have pulled the curtain. Emma's eyes gradually adjusted to the semi-darkness. The kitchen table was set elegantly complete with folded paper towel in the shapes of little boats sitting each of their plates and candles in the center emitting the only light. He leaned down and kissing her ear, said, "For you, your throne awaits, Princess." Guiding her into the chair he kissed the top of her head before sliding into his own.

It was all so lovely; such a nice gesture and it tore Emma completely through. Although she tried not to, she began to cry. Dan slipped to the floor and knelt in front of her. Placing his fingers under her chin he lifted her face until he could look into her eyes. "What's wrong? Emma, please talk to me."

Emma strived for control. "It's lovely." Dan slowly wiped her cheeks dry. Waiting.

"No one has ever done something like this for me. I am being silly; I am sorry I'll be fine. Please let's eat."

Dan nodded knowingly there would be time enough for that later. Skewering a cube of beef tenderloin and dipped it into the sauce in the fondue pot. Twirling the thick sauce, he brought it to Emma's lips. "Open," he said.

Emma did as she was instructed, the sauce was some sort of sweet and sour, and God did it taste wonderful. She was savoring each flavor when Dan kissed her mouth his tongue licking away the sauce from her lips. One by one Emma let him feed her. She wanted this memory. Becoming bolder Emma dipped the meat into the pot and offered it to Dan. She watched his tongue come out and swipe away the excess, allowing her to breathe easier. She wasn't ready to be that bold.

After dinner, Dan led Emma to the loveseat, placing an arm around her shoulders he pulled her closer. They sat in comfortable silence, letting the currents flow. Dan prayed the closeness would give her strength enough to open up. He knew she felt something for him, sex would not be a problem as he originally feared, so why was she so intent on fighting it. She snuggled closer, remaining silent.

An hour later, his patience ran out. "Emma, talk to me. What's bothering you sweetheart? I thought, no, I know you feel something for me. So, what's wrong? Why are you holding back?"

This was the perfect opportunity to tell him. To watch his face fill with scorn, before he said good-bye. Tilting her head without looking directly at him, Emma tried to speak the words that would send him running. And keep him safe.

Dan knew by her averted gaze what she was trying to do. He wouldn't allow it. Repositioning himself he forced her to look into his eyes. He was real damn it, a person she cared about on some level and he would not let her pretend otherwise!

Looking into Dan's blue eyes punctured her will like a pin in a balloon. The words she planned to say wouldn't form. She was a selfish bitch, but she didn't want him to go like that. Hating her or worse. There had to be another way. Coward! He was waiting; she had to say something. "Oh, Dan." Emma shook her head sadly; "I have a lousy track record. People close to me; they, they get hurt. I can't let it happen. Dan. You have to let this go, let me go. Please."

Dan was quiet for the longest time. "I can't. I won't. What we have is special. It can be the greatest thing either of us has ever had. I won't let you push me away. The answer is no, Emma...no!" He grabbed her forcing her mouth to comply with his in a sensual dance he knew she could not deny.

It started forceful but as soon as Emma gave herself, no longer fighting him, the pressure eased. Dan's hands ran over her, his fingertips caressed with each move of his lips. His hand came to rest on her breast; his finger moving over her tightened nipple. She pushed against his hand. It was sweet torture. Her nipple burned as it peaked hard as a pebble. This is what she'd missed, what she longed for since the night they dined together, Emma now knew what her body had been denied.

Gliding his hand to the bottom of her shirt, his mouth on hers he felt the sigh of disappointment. "Shhh...patience, my love." His hand began its climb upward beneath the material. Finding the front clasp of her soft satin bra, he worked it open. He toyed with the already erect nipple until Emma's breathing became erratic. She was moaning and arching toward him. Surrendering. He lowered his mouth running his tongue over the nipple. She shivered, as desire flamed; taking the nipple into his mouth, he did what he'd dreamed of doing for so long.

Emma's head fell back as she moaned. "Yessss." She had never imagined it could be this way. This wonderful. The best part, she was not scared. In the back of her mind she knew she shouldn't be doing this; she couldn't ask him to stop. She was intrigued, forever she'd wondered. Reading about such things was not the same. No, not the same. There was not an ounce of pain. But somehow, she knew with Dan it would be different. He was neither mean nor evil; he would not relish hearing her scream in pain.

Dan moved onto the other breast. Emma leaned back over the arm of the loveseat even as she reveled in the feel of his mouth upon her breast, she missed his lips on hers. Reaching down she pulled his head up, careful of the stitches. She didn't know how else to ask. Emma had tears in her eyes, not from sorrow but from joy. Something told her this is what it should have felt like with the right partner.

Dan wanted to give her everything; still he was not in any condition to carry this out properly tonight. It would have to wait. A series of soft kisses brought her down from the high he had induced. "It's late Em, and I am afraid that even though this is heaven, I am dead on my feet. Maybe, we can finish this lesson tomorrow." Cautiously she smiled. Standing Dan reached down and pulled her up. At her bedroom door, he gave her a brief kiss wished her pleasant dreams, then walked across the hall letting himself into his bedroom.

Emma's body was still on fire, staring at her bed with longing she slipped under the sheets hoping they would cool her.

Emily could not believe it. Daniel's ship! It had to be!

Standing poised on the cliff, hand shielding her eyes from the late afternoon sun, Emily jumped up and down with excitement. He was home! At last he was here! Picking up her skirt, knowing it was unladylike and not caring one wit she ran for home.

"Mama, Mama, he's here; he has come home! The ship, his ship, the Maiden. Oh, Mama he will be in here in a matter of hours, what shall I wear?"

"Dear, calm down. You have hours maybe more. He will want to see his family first. And right now, Darling, that doesn't include you. Calm down now;

come have a cup of tea. We will decide what you should wear and exactly how you will get to see him. Together we will think of something."

Emily walked to the table gaining composure each step of the way. She was so excited she fidgeted as her mother prepared the tea. "Well daughter, the time has come to see if your wish will come true. Poor Daniel will not stand a chance. One look at you and he will fall head over heels in love."

Emily beamed in the face of her mother's praise. She really hoped that Daniel would fall so hard he would insist on marrying her before he had to set out again. If she were lucky, he would take her with him. A honeymoon trip filled with adventures. She couldn't wait!

"So why does ye look like a cat whose captured the fattest fish, Emily my love," her father said, as he walked through the door. "It wouldn't be because of a certain ship they have been talking about in harbor. Heard tell The Maiden ha' been spotted to the west. Betcha ye didn't even know, sittin' 'ere sippin' tea like an old woman?" The twinkling in his eyes belied his words; nothing escaped his daughter, especially if that something involved a certain young man.

Afraid he would pressure his daughter into marrying one of the many gentlemen who had asked for her hand, his wife stated in no uncertain terms that Emily's heart was already taken. One would have to be daft not to see how his daughter felt about Daniel. He never would have pressed her anyway; even if she would have complied which was not bloody likely to happen, he had faith in her own choosin'. He'd lay odds she planned her life with young Daniel when she was still in nappies.

Hearing her father chuckle, Emily eyed him sternly. "And just what is so funny Papa? Do ye not think I have what it takes to win the heart of my beloved?"

"Child," her father started to say then decided he best switch tactics. "Emily, my love, you will always be, the light of my life. I've seen ye overcome many obstacles already and I 'pect I'll see you overcome at least one more."

"Father."

Chuckling he held up his hand. "Ye'll not have a fight to win his heart. He has been gone for a long-time love; he'd have to come back deaf, dumb and blind not to notice the treasure that awaits him on this here shore."

"Oh, Papa," Emily said, jumping out of her chair and hugging him fiercely. "I will miss you when I am married." Emily's father hugged her close and kissed the top of her golden head.

"Counting chickens before they're hatched child is not the way of the wise."

"Oh, Papa," Emily huffed playfully punching him in the arm. Tilting her chin, sparkle in her eye, with a ladylike flounce not given to her nature she walked back to the table and finished her tea.

She watched as Papa enfolded her mother in a loving embrace, a nightly ritual; he kissed her cheek and patted her behind before taking off to wash up.

"Any ideas, Mama?"

"I'm thinkin' child. Give an old woman a bit of time. I promise I shall think of a way."

Wiping his face her father smiled. "We wouldn't be trying to find a way to see young Daniel, now would we. A way, perhaps, that doesn't scare the poor blighter off? I could always have some men jump him at the docks, once the ball and chain are on, he is yours, let's say about dinnertime. Would that be soon enough for you daughter?"

Emily knew immediately he had something up his sleeve. "Papa?"

He took his time, toying with everyone's emotions until her mother was ready to beat him over the head. "Alright, alright," he said, "I may just know of a way."

"Well?" Emily said, impatience showing through. Laughingly he told them of the arrangements. "We have been invited to dinner. As a matter of fact, we are to be there at seven o'clock so you slow pokes had best get ready." Upon saying this he went to his favorite chair, sat down, picked up his mandolin and started playing as though nothing out of the ordinary was about to happen in the next sixty minutes.

Emily and her mother managed to close their gaping mouths as they made their way to the bedrooms. "The royal blue, Emily," was all her mother said before closing her door.

Emily ran to the chest taking out the royal blue gown her mother suggested. It was cut low, and clung, showcasing her small waist while enhancing her breasts. Every delicate stitch had been lovingly sewed for this purpose. To lure Daniel. Showing him, she was a woman. His woman.

Arriving at seven sharp, Daniel's mom, Annabelle, welcomed them warmly. They had been friends for an eternity it seemed. Daniel was one of the first topics brought into the conversation, even before their coats were hung; Annabelle informed them he was home and freshening up. She hadn't told him there would be company, knowing he would enjoy the surprise.

Looking at Emily, Annabelle couldn't help guessing Daniel's reaction. They had always been friends though both families hoped one day their relationship would blossom into something more. The timing had never been right, Emily was a late bloomer and when Daniel left, if he thought of her at all, she doubted it was in those terms. Emily was no longer a little girl. She'd make a dutiful and loving wife for her son.

Showing the guests into the parlor, Emily's father clasped his friend's shoulder, before taking a seat. Emily's mother followed Annabelle into the kitchen. With nothing to do but wait, Emily went to the fireplace sitting elegantly on a stool she dreamed of Daniel.

"Emily looks lovely tonight," Annabelle said. "I think Daniel is in for quite a shock. He always thought of her as a little girl. She certainly does not look that way tonight. I suspect she will have him eating out of her hand in no time at all."

"I hope so." Emily's mother sighed. "She has loved him for so long. Five years is not much between a man and a wife but when as children it can be like crossing a great ocean without a ship." They both agreed and moved onto other subjects.

Daniel stood at the end of the hall. His heart lurched. He didn't see his father talking in the corner nor did he investigate the kitchen. Saw nothing but the vision of an angel sitting before the fire. Who was she? By God, she was divine. He'd seen many women on his travels some more pretty than others but never in all his days had met someone who could so completely stop his heart with one look.

Her hair shone in the firelight like spun gold, yet in the shimmering light a hundred different muted tones danced as she moved gently. Although he had yet to see her face, he imagined it would be heart shaped, delicate and beautiful; Emily's face. He hoped once she stood, he would see the swell of her breasts and a small indentation where her waist would be. Walking into the room he spotted Mr. Claremore sitting talking with his father. Damn! He wanted to go to the woman by the fire but knew he couldn't. Walking to Mr.

Claremore, Daniel held out his hand in greeting. "It has been a while sir. How are you, your wife? Emily? Everyone is fine I trust."

Emily's father took Daniel's proffered hand. "Yes, Daniel you have been gone for a long time. Your father is very proud. Your first journey was more successful than he'd ever dreamed." Letting go of Daniel's hand, he smiled at Robert, Daniel's father. "The wife and I have been well. We were very happy when your mother extended us this invitation. You have been in our thoughts regularly since your departure. As to Emily, she is fine, I gather, though one never quite knows what frequents the minds of young women these days. Maybe you'd best turn around and ask her yourself."

Daniel's face went ashen before he slowly he turned toward the fireplace. He could faintly hear the chuckles of the men, in background, as he stood once again rooted in spot. Emily rose and walked toward him. Graceful and elegant. Her blue dress picked up hues from the firelight; he watched the material hugging her hips as every step she took brought her closer toward him.

Daniel swallowed hard when Emily extended her hand. Clasping it, he bowed slightly bringing it his lips. Lifting his eyes ever so slightly he could see the soft swells of her breasts above the neckline. With each breath they were emphasized at least in his mind. He swallowed again, placed a kiss on her knuckles then reluctantly relinquished her hand.

Emily watched the different stages of shock play about his handsome face, she smiled, a smile she'd practiced in the mirror every day since the day he left; a smile constructed to ensnare his heart, and he acted just as she'd hoped. He was undone. He smiled back but remained silent. Funny, he had a million things running around in his head, things he could have conversed with the old Emily about on many an occasion. Yet standing here two years later looking at this extraordinary creature, he could not think of a single thing to say. Sure, there was much that needed to be said, given his reaction to her. However now was not the time for such conversations.

"You are looking well Daniel. People feared something might be amiss. You were gone so long. I never lost hope. I knew in my heart you were okay. I went to the cliffs everyday glancing out over the horizon for a sign of The Maiden. I am so pleased you have returned safe and sound."

Daniel cleared his throat knowing exactly what the other men must be thinking but needing to do it anyway. "It was a long trip Em, but all was well. I learned so very much. Next time I will learn even more." On that comment their mothers entered and announced dinner. Daniel offered Emily his arm and walked her into the kitchen.

He would have ignored the smiles of satisfaction on the face of each parent, if he'd noticed, as it was, he had eyes only for Emily. Egads, she'd grown up into one hell of a woman.

Chapter Seven

Picnic basket in hand, Daniel made his way to Emily's just before noon. They decided the night before to go walking. He wanted this time to reacquaint himself with the enchanting creature his friend had become. Emily would love a picnic. It was an excuse to spend more time in each other's company without people becoming suspicious. His father generously gave him two days off for relaxation after his journey. His mother, ever so helpful, woke him with a smile on her face and basket in her hand. Leftovers from last night that she needed to get out of the way although Daniel knew they had the same thoughts as he.

All hoped for a union between the two families. Before there was always an age gap, he found difficult to surpass. Now, Emily no longer looked like the child he left behind. Daniel knew there was a conspiracy at foot. He didn't care. He'd known Emily all her life; played with her, as he'd done countless times with other children from the village. Once he carried her home after she'd gotten hurt, running wild and playing hard, she fell and rolled a considerable distance down the hill. Smiling at the recollection of her running full tilt, pigtails streaming behind her in the wind; seeing her slip, and the memory of his heart climbing into his throat. Even after rolling to the bottom she was laughing her fool head off. She'd sprained her ankle so bad she could not stand, let alone walk. He had carried her home. "The designated chauffeur," she dubbed him.. She chattered and laughed not once complaining although her ankle must have pained her.

She'd always been the most unladylike creature, hose in tatters, dresses marred with dirt hair plaited but never put up. Never contained. Not in hundred years did he anticipate the sight of an elegant, graceful enchantress in a gown of royal blue velvet, enhancing her many charms; even her hair was styled in a neat chignon. Truth be told, he liked both; the devil may care fun loving girl he left behind and thought of often as well as the woman he'd encountered and dreamt of last night.

Emily's mother answered the door, "Come in Daniel. Emily is just freshening up. Tea?"

"Thank you, Madam, if you are sure it is not too much trouble."

"I'd be delighted, Em will be a while and please, it's Irene."

As Daniel drank his tea, he told Irene of his plans for the day. She was as accommodating as his mother had been. He smiled, so it did go both ways.

Appearing just as Daniel finished his tea. Emily looked lovely dressed in a simple yellow cambric day dress. The high waisted tie boasted a darker satin ribbon. The scooped neck and clean lines held him entranced. Emily smiled as her mother cleared her throat. Emily offered him her hand; instead of kissing it he placed it in the crook of his arm as they said goodbye.

Why had he not kissed her hand? In her mind, her entrance went as planned until she held out her hand, then he was supposed to place a kiss on her knuckles as he did the night before. His breath would be warm, his lips soft and he would hold his mouth to her longer than was appropriate. But he didn't. What did that mean? Daniel's thoughts were of the same order. He should have kissed her, broken the ice, the tension. But Daniel hadn't dreamt of kissing her hand, he wanted more. Fearing he would lose control, right there in front of Mrs. Claremore held him in check. There would be time for kisses, his kind of kisses, shortly.

Veering close, letting her skirts brush against him as she'd done many times in her dreams, Emily voiced her many questions; Daniel answered patiently in storybook fashion. To Emily, it all sounded like one great big adventure. He spoke of people and places, new crewmembers he commissioned at various ports. Some had the most unusual habits as Daniel explained, she laughed.

Reaching the cliffs Daniel left Emily looking out over the sea, she seemed to enjoy the sight, looked at it with wonder as he did. Taking the blanket his mother put inside the basket, he flipped it out over the soft lush grass. Even in fall the grass was high and soft here. He'd missed the grass. Silly he knew. Nevertheless, when the majority ports boasted only dirt, sand or muddy streets, grass was a highly valued commodity.

Sitting, he wondered whether he should take the food out. Deciding he would let Emily do it he sat back engrossed in the vision before him. What had he thought? That she would never become the woman he felt he could marry?

She was a little girl when he left; his feelings ran more to the brotherly side, now they were the farthest thing, from brotherly one could imagine.

Always around him he considered her a friend; their families were close and wished for more yet at the time she was too young. But this change in her, hell he'd only been gone for a little over two years, in that time, she aged years. The little girl full of mischief had been replaced, or was she? The way she crowded close when they walked, the sparkle in her eyes when she listened to him talk, subtle things, reminding him of days gone by, times when she was up to no good. How old was she now? Turning she smiled and sashayed to the blanket; should she know how to sashay? Raising a shapely burnished gold brow in question, he nodded toward the blanket.

Emily began taking the food from the hamper. Placing them one by one in the center of the blanket she murmured softly, "You must have questions. I've asked so many of you this day. Is there nothing you wish to know about what whilst you were away?" Needlessly leaning over him she placed the chicken on the coverlet.

Daniel tried not to look at the alabaster skin peeking above the neckline. Swallowing hard, he said the first thing that came to him. "How. Old. Are. You?" The question dragged out; each word pronounced through gritted teeth. Emily gave him a winning smile. She knew the effect she was having on him and was enjoying it immensely. So long had she waited for this day. And now that this day had arrived, she swore she'd not waste one second of it. He would be eating out of her hand before he returned her home. She was no longer the diminutive little girl he knew.

"Almost seventeen. In case you're wondering, I was fourteen when you left. Not a child but you always treated me as such. It was quite annoying. I was not as well-endowed as the strumpets you had clinging to you at the socials." She ran a hand in front of her emphasizing her figure. "Several times I wanted to scream. 'Other girls my age were already spoken for; soon to be married'." She sighed, "I forgave you one week after I started wishing you were back. Wine?"

His question had not been the best to start off with, but Emily answered in the same blunt fashion reminiscent of her younger days. He was stunned. Had she really been fourteen? She was right, he hadn't seen her, as anything but a little girl, perhaps he should have. Back then he'd been anxious to set sail; prove his worth. Marrying, anyone had been the furthest thing from his mind.

He courted many girls, mainly one's other fellows wanted just to ruffle their feathers, but not once had they been the type of woman, he would consider for himself. They were just too different. He needed someone more like him. Someone with a love of life combined with a craving for adventure, someone, he realized, like Emily. Daniel grasped Emily's hand; he admired her long dainty fingers. "The others, they meant nothing, I was a boy trying my wings."

Emily listened, heart overflowing with love as Daniel tried to explain. Over time, she'd realized the truth on her own. Taking pity on him she placed the fingers of her other hand against his lips halting his words. A confused look came to his sapphire eyes.

"I knew, or at least I understood in time. It doesn't matter. You are back. No worse for wear from your adventure. I now have the chance to fulfill a promise made. Every day, when I glanced out over the sea, I vowed if God returned you safely, I would tell you what is in my heart." He looked astonished. "Have you not wondered why I have not married?"

Daniel cleared his throat. He hadn't had time to contemplate that specifically but now that she broached the question, he found himself wondering. Had he taken the time to wonder he wouldn't have asked; it would have been most awkward. Tempting fate. She was offering him the answer; he'd be a fool not to take it. "Yes, I have."

"I gave my heart long ago to a boy who would become a man. A boy who laughed at me and tousled my straggly hair while gently picking out the embedded grass; the boy who so effortlessly picked me up and carried me home, scolding me all if memory serves me correct." She giggled.

It was a carefree yet sensual sound that shot heat through his body zeroing in on his loins, as if there weren't enough tension in that spot already. She loved him. Good God he'd been a damned lucky fool. "Please tell me I was that boy."

She laughed leaning forward Emily kissed him. "Yes Daniel, I don't fall for just anyone after all." Together they laughed. Emily was the first to sober. "I have waited five years to tell you what was in my heart. Now, sir, do shut up and kiss me."

He needed no more encouragement. Placing his hands about her slender waist Daniel pulled her onto his lap, looking into her ever-changing bright green eyes, he watched them deepen. His eyes drifted to her dampened lips and lingered momentarily before his mouth dropped to hers.

Emily had no idea what to expect when Daniel's lips met hers. His gentle guidance enflamed as his lips moved over her mouth. His tongue swept over her bottom lip. "Open your mouth for me Emily, I want to taste you." She complied at once. His hand tightened on the back of her neck as his tongue swept into her mouth. Every touch of his hands, every soft caress of his lips pulled her deeper and deeper into his web. The kiss was beyond anything she imagined. The flutters in her stomach, the heat, her racing heart; felt glorious. Images whizzed in and out of her fogged brain. Her lips moved questing, learning, memorizing the lessons he taught. Her natural thrill for adventure soon had her tongue battling with his. Tasting him as he was her. She was moaning. Or was it him? She couldn't tell; she didn't care. She wished they could go on forever. Daniel apparently thought otherwise, for as the thought entered her head, he released her.

"We should eat, Em, and then I should get you home before your father comes after me."

Emily chuckled, low and husky, at the image conjured by his comment. Nodding, she picked up a drumstick; chewing slowly she savored his mother's leftover fried chicken. Delicious. The grease from the chicken made her lips shine.

Daniel tramped down the urge to kiss them again.

They had managed to eat; minds elsewhere. Food did little to assuage the hunger. Not a word was said as they ate; both had much to contemplate. Emily knew what she wanted beyond this day; therefore, her mind was on the immediate, and the thing she wanted most was another lesson. She was two years behind.

Daniel was too busy making long term plans to notice Emily's take on that familiar glint. "Mother packed pie. Would you like some?"

Running her tongue over her lips thoughtfully, she replied, "We could; but then I never was much for pie," she said, grabbing the closest item. Emily stood then carried it to the edge of the cliff before spreading her arms wide and letting it drop. She'd watch it as it hit the sparkling waters below, raise her arms, spin and laugh; then she was back for more. It was quite the game. She laughed and dodged as Daniel tried to catch her. When the last of their dinner fell to its watery grave, she turned and found herself in his arms.

How did Daniel see her, she wondered? Did he see the woman before him or the child he had known for so long? When she looked into his eyes, they were blazing hot, there was no time to contemplate as his mouth came down in a fiercely passionate kiss, hugging her close all Emily could think was, no …no longer a child and then she couldn't think at all. Catching her breath, wondering what the next step should be, Emily asked, "still hungry?"

God hated a coward, God helped those who helped themselves. Wasn't that what she had been brought up to believe? Resigned to a specific course she slowly started pulling the ribbons at the front of her dress.

Open mouthed he watched as the shoulder sagged with each step she took back to the blanket. "I have been starving these two years past, with only my imagination for comfort. From your kisses, I can tell it is lacking. I wonder sir, are you man enough to teach me?" Shrugging, the loose material fell about her elbows.

Brat! Naive she may be innocent she was not. She knew exactly what she was doing. Not so much as chemise covered her bare chest. Clearing his throat, seemed to be becoming a habit, dropping to his knees, grasping her hand like a lifeline, he brought it to his lips. "You are so beautiful. So unbelievably beautiful." He stared at her for a moment, letting his desire show. "As much as I want you. This is not the way. Em, I love you, probably always have." He touched her breast. "Oh God, Em. Marry me?"

Emily could not breathe. For so long she'd waited to hear those words from him, she needed a moment to savor the sound of his voice, the desire in his eyes. For her. She nodded.

Pulling her forward into his arms, his kiss staking possession; claiming fierce passion, taught and learned, a promise for the future. Gathering the front of her gown his fingertips grazed the creamy swells he groaned closing his eyes. He was a damned fool. "Let's go," he said, between clenched teeth. "I believe I have a conversation with your father that cannot wait." Taking up the blanket and basket, he placed a proprietary arm around her.

Emily's head leaned against his shoulder as they walked down the hill. Teasing and laughing along the way, their journey didn't take long. Before the door, Emily placed a kiss on Daniel's lips. "I love you."

The talk with Emily's father took forever. Emily paced across the kitchen glancing down the hall to her father's study. "Em, sit." Her mother ordered placing a cup of tea on the table in front of her. "I don't know why you are worried; you know your father will say yes. Now stop fretting. It gives you wrinkles." Emily smiled at that; her mother worried more than anyone she ever knew yet even now in her late forties not one wrinkle dared show on her face.

"I'm not worried Papa will say no, I am worried he will torment Daniel until he flees taking his vows of love and marriage with him."

"You have so little faith in the young man then?" her mother asked, teasingly. "No, Mama. It's just that I do love him so. He has been back but a day, but I have waited a lifetime. What is taking them so long?" Emily's eyes glanced down the dark hall straining to hear. She heard nothing.

Her mother smiled knowingly as she set the table with cakes. Emily wondered if her mother's intuition was at work again. Sure, enough the door to the study opened. Soon after both men appeared in the kitchen, her father's arm about Daniel's shoulders. Comforting.

"Daughter. Is it true you wish to marry this scoundrel?" her father barked. Emily turned as red as a beat.

"Papa!" she yelled and buried her face in her hands. "Well daughter is this true? Do you wish to marry young Daniel? I told him that it could not be possible, not my girl. She wants a life of adventure. She wants to see the world. Told him I'd ask you if this is truly your wish. I personally think that if it is true the two of you should wait a year or two to make sure it is what you really want."

Angrily Emily was up out of her chair, she headed straight for her father.

Albert smiled at Daniel before taking a cautionary step back, laughing. As Emily pushed passed, Daniel snagged her about the waist, he too was laughing. Emily was too upset to see what they thought was so damned funny. She'd kill her father. Daniel yanked her back against his chest, her eyes spitting fire at her father. "Em, my little hellcat. He is joking. Calm down." Kissing her ear, he loosened his hold her breathing still erratic, Emily allowed him to usher her back to her seat.

Irene's eyes fired daggers at her husband. How dare he take it so far? Albert smiled and nodded toward the couple; her anger melted. Had she ever seen anyone control Emily when she was in a temper? Amazing. Sitting at the table Emily's head lay on Daniel's shoulder. Eyes closed breathing back to normal; all she said was, "When?"

His answer was a simple kiss on her forehead and, "Soon."

Emily stared at the dress she'd chosen to be married in. Daniel would be here soon. He arranged a meeting with Father Albright, to find when they could marry. Holding the dress in front of her Emily swayed back and forth watching her reflection in the mirror. Closing her eyes, she twirled when she reopened them, Daniel was standing by the door.

She went to him immediately enfolded into his arms he kissed her. "Mmmm. Again." She sighed. Dropping his head, Daniel did as she requested. Soon they were both moaning.

Chapter Eight

Moaning awakened Emma. Clearing her dream-fogged mind, she smiled. She was coming to love the visits from the girl. Emily's world allowed her a chance to know and feel love, to take what she was afraid of in the real world and see it in a new less terrifying light. At times she was a participant, but lately she'd found she could distance herself, stand back and watch as if seeing the scenes unfold in a movie. It gave her a sense of control.

Emma looked about the room. It was dark. What woke her? Then she heard it, another moan. Oh my God! She leaped out of bed, grabbing her robe she cinched it loosely. Dan! Running to his bed. Dan let out anguished cry. He was in pain. A lot of it. Placing a hand on his head she quickly noted he was not feverish, thank God. Hurrying to the kitchen where Emma found his pills, reading the label she quickly shook out twice the normal dosage. Opening the cupboard, she found the saltines, if she was giving him that much medication, she'd best see that he ate something first.

"Dan, I have some medicine for you. Come on wake up," Em continued calling softly, running her palm over his forehead pushing back his hair. She could see the pain twisting his face. Shaking his shoulders frantically, Dan finally opened his eyes.

He was in bed, Emma's spare room; it was coming back to him now, a vehicle had hit him. It was Emma, not Emily, standing over him. Grabbing his head, he closed his eyes. "My head fucking hurts!" he said.

"I know, darling. I brought some medication. Here let me help you sit up I want you to eat a bit." Reaching under him Emma used her shoulder to help him rise. With one hand she fluffed the pillows into a backrest. Leaning him back gently she handed him a couple of crackers. "Start with these." Dan ate the crackers and Emma handed him the water to wash them down with before handing him a couple more. Dan was looking better, still in pain, but coping. While he nibbled, Emma fluffed and cleaned until there was nothing left for her to take her distraught nerves out on.

"Sit down, Em." Dan tapped the blanket beside him. "I don't bite. Nibble occasionally, however I have had a few crackers earlier, so I dare say you'll be safe." He wiggled his brows then winced, making her giggle like a schoolgirl.

"Since you put it that way, how could I possibly refuse?" Sparing, joking, they were fast becoming a habit Emma would dread giving up.

Silence reigned for what seemed like an eternity, until Dan unable to take the stillness, asked Emma about her life. For an instant she froze color draining from her face. Dan waited. Wanting to understand. He hoped she would trust him, confide in him. Damn, he couldn't help without knowing. Laying a hand on her thigh; an offering friendship and support, nothing more, still she jumped as if she'd been scalded with boiling water. It was not the same sexual tension that gripped them the night before, nothing like the raging waves of a violent sea tossing ships to and fro. No, it was something else entirely. The look of stark terror embedded in her emerald eyes confirmed it.

Removing his hand immediately, Dan soothed. "Em, I am sorry I didn't mean to scare you. Are you okay?"

Emma looked away and tried to leave.

Dan wasn't having it. "No, look at me; don't try to tell me it was nothing. I saw the terror in your eyes. What frightens you, Babe? Surely you know I wouldn't hurt you. Isn't it about time you trusted someone? Level with me. Please."

Settling down on the bed again, she tried to smile. It looked more like a grimace still she braved on, shaking she fought her way back. So cold, she was so cold. When he posed the question, her mind didn't pick up on any of a hundred things she worked hard to overcome or accomplish. The haunted memories, memories she'd just as soon forget, crowded her mind. Why?

It couldn't have been his touch; no, she wouldn't believe his touch would affect her senses that way as well. It must be a lack of sleep. Though, Lord knows she was no stranger to sleepless nights, the only thing she wasn't used to; was, this intimacy. Sitting beside a man in her current state of undress. Foolish? Maybe. It did not inspire, at least in her, a feeling of calm. It did not induce thoughts of light-hearted conversation. Or maybe, somewhere in her subconscious she wanted to tell him those things. Rubbing her hands up and down her arms created a warm barrier; kept her fears at bay. Would he find her dirty? Disgusting? Swallowing hard to keep tears from pooling in her eyes she looked at Dan. No. He was strength. Confidence. Support. In that instant she realized she finally had someone to confide in. She could not have confided the whole to any of her family, not even Andre. Possibly he would have understood, tried to help. Yet it was impossible. Instead she told only what she could. And only to Andre.

Nightmares. So many she fought against. Her dreams aided her. Interrupting the nightmares. Emily had been her strength. How could she have been so blind? Emily had always seemed to be there, pulling her into a simpler world where she could relax if only for a short time. Emma had forgotten but was now remembering. Her dreams had been with her all along. Were they so frequent back then? Vivid? She would have to figure it out. Everyone dreamed, didn't they? She'd have to investigate it.

Right now, she had a person, a man of flesh and blood, looking at her with question, concern and something else in his eyes, she really didn't understand. If she were ever to move forward, she would have to let go of the past. She would have to trust someone. Why not Dan?

Dropping her gaze, she cleared her throat as she ordered her thoughts. A place to start, that wouldn't disgust him as much as plunging into the horror of that long-ago night, seeming to overshadow all else. She wanted to tell him before, but for different reasons. Then, she wanted to push him out of her life. Now she wasn't sure she could go on without him. She wasn't sure of anything at all.

Her views on safety had changed considerably. Emma felt protected with him. Foolish considering she'd known him a week, yet it seemed he'd been with her throughout a thousand lifetimes. She was going crazy. She would tell him. She must. He deserved to know. The question that haunted, was what he would do once he knew?

Dan looked at Emma; her color was better, since she'd decided to confide in him. Her eyes told all. Every changing expression enlightened him, line for line, the terror, indecision, resigned trust and acceptance. Then fear? Again? Although, not as pronounced. Uneasiness. Waiting tolerantly, Dan didn't press on even though his curiosity was unbearable. He tried letting her know all would be okay. Believe in me. Trust me. The dread receded but he could tell from the tension that lined her body it was still there. Without knowing what it was, he knew deep down, it was crucial to her peace of mind, to share it. "Em?" Dan waited, wondering. He'd wait however long it took for her mind to lay voice to her thoughts.

"I was never popular growing up. I liked to spend time with my family," she said, choking on the words; taking a moment she continued, "my dreams and my books. I always…well…I never fit in. Never felt as though I belonged; or in any case it had seemed that way to me."

"My family accepted me as I was, a bookworm, never pushing me to be more outgoing or social, in my dreams I was a little girl again, sort of." She frowned, her brow creasing in concentration straining for words that would not come. Emma could not figure out what possessed her to talk of Emily, when she'd said dreams, she meant the same sort of daydreams other little girls had. Didn't she?

"Anyway, like most girls, daydreams always took you to a happier more exciting place."

Dan didn't know why she'd opted not to speak of the little girl; she was hiding it from him. Why?

"In novels, I could venture out, enjoying the twists and turns without really risking any of myself. It was safe. I was safe. Nothing ventured – nothing lost."

Dan wondered if maybe he should correct her quote…the saying was 'nothing ventured – nothing gained' but he knew whatever happened gave her that outlook. As he listened, a deeper bond developed. Like a spider spinning a web each strand of their acquaintance overlapped, strengthened and reinforced. Together, it would make them whole. He debated asking her about her dreams; he too had been a dreamer. For him it was the lack of siblings, for her, the lack of friendship. Before he could voice the question, Emma continued.

"My brother Andre was in college, not far from my hometown. When I reached high school, I found for a lot of research the college library was better equipped."

Dan wondered if maybe it wasn't the safer place to go, she would not have to face anyone with whom she went to school, and her brother was there. Her one true-friend and possibly her hero too, if the single look of life that came to her eyes at the mention of his name meant anything at all.

"I'd drive to the college, a couple times a week, whenever I had an assignment to complete. Andre met me in the parking lot. He always said it wasn't safe to walk around campus alone. So, he'd meet me give me a hug and then arm in arm we'd walk to the library." She beamed, momentarily lost in the memories of her brother.

"I enjoyed those times. Andre was my favorite; mother and father said I should not hinder him so. Andre never thought of me as a hindrance, he would have said. There was only two years separating us, whereas I was five years older than the twins. We were always joking; forever laughing about this or that. The occasional fist fight broke out, which of course, I always won, not that he ever put up much of a fight."

Laughter escaped her so suddenly she started. All too soon, she sobered.

"At school things were different. I didn't fit in. Too pretty to be a nerd; too nerdy to be popular, after a while I no longer tried. Taking it as a confirmation of what I already knew…I didn't belong."

"As a family, we would go to football games; the rest of the time we did what we felt most comfortable. I guess in that sense we were just like any other family you may encounter."

Dan waited, watched, and listened. He could see Emma as a young girl, long blonde hair, green eyes that showed just the right mix of mischief and mirth. He could picture her taunting and wrestling her brother; sitting in the stands at a high school football game cheering. He easily saw her as a perfect pal, interested in many of the same things he was, and a body to temp any young man into doing what he didn't. What he could not see, however, and this bothered him immensely; he could not see his Emma as a loner.

It didn't fit. Had she hidden her passion behind a wall all those years? Maybe if she was a late bloomer, socially, that could be a reason. However, even the rarest of flowers bloom at some point. Emma had gone to college after high school, so by that time she should have fit in regardless. She's the type of person that should have attracted a lot of attention yet? Even when he met her a week ago…my God was it only a week? She tried to hold herself away, wearing that ice queen persona like a suit of armor. He saw through it, more than aware of her unleashed passion.

"I envy you." Immediately she stilled and stared at him. Shocked and bewildered. He continued, "I never had brothers or sisters. It was something I prayed for when I was younger." That said, Dan launched into a litany of questions. "What happened in high school? You said you never fit in, why? What about college? Did you fit in there? Did you have friends? I mean didn't you date at all or go out with a group of friends? Have a crush on some lucky boy? I cannot imagine all the males of your acquaintance being so blind."

Taking another sip of his water swallowing his pills he set the glass on the nightstand.

Looking back up, he noticed, once again Emma's appearance was ghostly. "Jesus, I'm sorry Emma, I…"

Before he could finish, she smiled anxiously and said, "It's alright. I've never told anyone this. I will try, I promise." Taking a deep shaky breath, she continued, "My first year of high school, reinforced my knowledge that I was not part of the in crowd and that was all right. You can't miss something you never had to begin with."

"By the second year, I knew mostly everyone's face, they knew me as well. Things hadn't changed. A boy transferred in that year. Travis MacPherson. Although for me it seemed love at first sight, I knew it would never be. He was out of my league. He made captain of the football team. Shortly after that he was dating Heather, the head cheerleader."

"I never spoke to him. Eventually pushed all thoughts of him and the crush I had, to the back of mind. Like a storybook romance, it was something that would never be. The final year of high school brought forth the prom. Never in a million years did I think I would go."

"Much to my surprise and a great amount of shock, Travis asked me to the prom. Things didn't go, as a date should. In fact, it was as far from a normal date as one could get. Something happened that night, which reinforced my belief that I was better, alone. That night, I never made it to the prom I; I was raped," Emma said in a whisper. She looked like death; her mind separated from her body no emotions, and only vacancy in her eyes.

He didn't interrupt; urging her to continue. She'd lost so much. So much more than he was aware of. How would it be like to be a young girl, happy to finally get her one wish and finding out that her dream was in truth a nightmare? If he could find this Travis now, he'd kill the bastard with his bare hands. She'd been sheltered socially for a woman of the nineties still she pulled through. She was strong; he'd give her that.

"In college I dated. Three times. None changed my mind about relationships. I knew I was better off with my studies. I buckled down; I graduated with top marks in every class. My family was proud. I was happy. After college I was offered the position here. I took it and here we are."

Emma focused on Dan sitting quietly letting the pills take his pain away. It would be good if he could get a little rest before the sun came up. They'd been talking for a while now, longer than she should have given his condition. Amazing, how easily she confided her inner most secrets; the great weight began to lift. "You should get some rest." As she smoothed back the hair from his brow, his eyes drooped.

"I want to hear more," he slurred.

"You will, right now you need rest. Shut your eyes."

His eyes slid shut.

Emma started to rise kissing him on the forehead.

"Stay," he whispered urgently. It took only a moment to make the decision, the bed was big enough, she would not hurt him, and she trusted him with her heart besides she thought finally he really wasn't in any shape to do anything.

Dan was not as far gone as Emma believed. Yes, he was a bastard, he admitted, but he wanted to hold her, and this was the only way he could ensure she would stay. Throughout her speech she seemed robotic. He wanted to feel her heartbeat. He smiled. "I am hurt; I need a nurse…and a friend. Stay."

Sighing, Emma stretched out beside him, at least he was below the covers; she wriggled about, keeping her distance, staying above the blankets, turning on her side she pillowed her head on his chest, she felt the rise and fall with every breath; ease surrounded her. Nestling deeper she gloried in the feeling, soon the steady sound of his heartbeat lulled her to sleep.

Chapter Nine

Releasing her from the kiss Daniel stepped back, but kept his hands on her shoulders until Emily's breathing returned to normal. Hand in hand, they turned toward their guests, smiling. Then placing a kiss on the underside of her wrist he raised their joined hands high into the air.

A roar went up as they piled out into the bright morning sun.

Standing at the bottom of the stairs Emily glowed. She was no longer Emily Claremore, young lady rapidly turning spinster waiting for the man she loved. Her eyes slanted toward her husband. So handsome. The one and only love of her life, she would protect him and love him. Always.

Daniel was thinking similar thoughts about his wife as they stood shaking hands and hugging everyone in line. Impatient, wanting to be away, he endured all. He had hit port over a month ago. Rekindled old friendships and fell in love. More than three weeks had gone by since he'd asked for Emily's hand. They had wanted to marry immediately, making the most of the time he had left before shipping out again. But there were rules, a special license had to be obtained and preparations to be made.

No one questioned the urgency of the wedding, not one bad word circulated. Although Em had said she didn't care one wit whether people talked about her, Daniel did. He didn't want people assuming the marriage was forced by a delicate condition or otherwise. Everything had turned out fine though. All who lived in the village knew Daniel would have to put out to sea soon. With the length of his last journey, it wasn't any wonder the couple sought to be wed immediately. Putting Emily's hand in the crook of his elbow they strolled to the picnic area behind the church. The ladies of the church auxiliary had done themselves proud yet again. They had created a veritable paradise.

A gorgeous sunny morning added to the magic of the moment as Daniel led his wife to a chair at the head table. Smiling down at her he placed a kiss on her forehead before sitting.

Throughout the feast there was much laughter. Afterwards, some of the men including Emily's father set a temporary stage as five men gathered; the first chords of a waltz played. Daniel took Emily in his arms twirling her about the makeshift dance floor. One dance then they would leave. Holding her closer than was proper they moved with a combined grace about the floor. His hand guiding her as they gazed into each other's eyes. The heat coursing through their veins was impossible to mask. All who looked upon them knew for certain it was a love match.

Daniel had fought to keep a rein on his manhood since the picnic. Every moment they spent together, had been charged with sexual energy; nevertheless, he would not have traded one precious moment. It gave him time to once again learn who Emily was. Her hopes and dreams for the future matched his. Why had he not seen it before? She was his other half and together they made a whole. Looking at his bride, she was smiling; his heart clenched when he realized how much he loved her. He would always love her, he vowed fiercely. Forever. When the music ended, the crowd cheered as they left the floor, making their excuses; they ran toward the awaiting carriage.

Helping her inside he followed, sitting across from her as the horses jerked forward. Small slits on either side of the drawn curtains allowed soft light into the carriage giving them the privacy they sought. Emily's face lit with excitement. Even in the darkened interior her complexion glowed as her eyes danced with mischief.

Daniel reached toward her and pulled her onto his lap. Not waiting for protest, he simply took what was now his due. Emily moaned beneath the brutal passion of his lips. He'd kissed her several times this past week every time he set her on fire. But this was an explosion. Daniel was startled when Emily returned his kiss with such fervor, growling deep in his throat his hand wound through her golden hair holding her to him, giving and taking air; the kiss took them to another world as liberated and untamed as the raging ocean.

His hand cupped her breast. God it had been almost a month since he'd seen those delicious globes bared before him in the afternoon sun. He longed to taste them to put them in his mouth and suckle until she screamed. Kneading her breast, the peaks hardened like pebbles beneath his touch inflaming him more.

They were to honeymoon aboard the Maiden. Over the past week their mothers had transformed it into a utopia. The carriage took them away from the village to the countryside before heading to the wharf, allowing time for final preparations. Daniel knew it would take an hour after their departure from the village; therefore, they would be driving for about two hours, to ensure the ship was readied and unoccupied. Solitude. He wanted to love her a hundred different ways before facing another human being. Maybe then he wouldn't have to fight so hard to conceal the bulge in his britches.

Undoing the top tie of the gown, Daniel pulled it beneath her breasts. Emily shuddered. He began teasing and tweaking each delectable nub. Leaning her back over the cushions he lifted his mouth and looked into her eyes. Such beautiful eyes, a deep green now but getting deeper as they filled with desire. He wondered briefly how deep they would turn when she was hit with the full force of excitement she'd yet to experience.

She returned his smile with a dazed one of her own. "The driver will hear you if you scream out. Shhh.." Daniel lowered his mouth licking, teasing her nipple with his tongue. When Emily arched, he took it into his mouth, sucking hungrily.

Emily nearly shot off the seat; flames of passion ignited; pooling below.. Emily shoved a knuckle in her mouth. Bit down. She couldn't possibly stop the moans escaping her, but she would not scream.

Watching Emily, Daniel played devil's advocate. Sucking harder, allowing the creamy globe out of his mouth only to bite down on the scrumptious nipple. Emily let loose a strangled scream. Twisting and turning she grabbed Daniel's hair pulling him from the nipple. Panting hard, Daniel allowed her this reprieve but all too soon his mouth left hers in search of the other. Emily needed more; she didn't know what; but before the night was done, she would find out. Pushing against Daniel's straining manhood; she was rewarded when an animalistic groan vibrated against her breast.

Releasing her, Daniel kissed a path upward stopping to pay homage to the sensitive collarbone area. Continuing his journey, he licked, kissed and nibbled at her neck until he finally reached her luscious lips. God, how he wanted her.

Emily felt Daniel's silk cravat cool and soft on her bare chest. Mind whirling, she soared. Putting her hand on the nape of his neck she kissed him back with all the knowledge she'd gained. The kiss deepened until both were filled with a heavenly but ruthlessly frustrated state. They battled each taking and taking until both were crazed. A faint breeze grazed Emily's legs as Daniel's hand upon her bare thigh, inched higher and higher. He was taking far too long. Emily wriggled, squirming, arching upward closer to that place screaming for attention. She wished she could force him to bring her to completion.

She was there, on the brink. She heard the others talk about glorious wedding nights, touching stars; she knew there was more. Beyond where he'd taken her. She wanted to shout; his questing tongue took that option from her. Plundering. Taking. A determined battle of wills. His. Hers. Theirs.

Finally, Daniel's hand reached its goal; his shrewd fingers probed her velvety mons. She was wet. So wet and ready he fought the inner beast screaming to take her. Here. Now. Tamping down the raging fire, resolute to ease Emily's suffering, he concentrated. The palm of his hand pressed hard against her moving in a circular motion. His finger slid up and down; soon Emily was lifting her hips in pursuit for something even more. She met his hand, stoking the fire to elevated proportions. Moaning and wreathing before him she was magnificence personified. Sliding his finger into her tight passage slowly he mimicked his tongue in and out. Using his thumb rolling her woman's bud back and forth waiting for her to loosen enough for an additional finger to slide into her.

Emily thought she would die. She burned with the heat of a thousand uncontrolled fires; the feel of his fingers inside her, where no man had accessed, was bliss. She'd anticipated this, so many times, not once had she come close to the reality. For a moment it seemed she'd reached a plateau. Breathes suspended in time, stopping. The biggest explosion she'd ever experienced rocked her body. She was lifting, soaring to where she didn't know; and didn't care if she ever came down.

Slowly the stars dissipated, and her breathing returned to normal. Daniel's lips left hers it was a loss she endured for soon in the future they would dance again. Her eyes opened and she gazed into her husband's black irises. How she loved the sound of that. Her husband...she could say over and over never tiring of it. Lifting her hand to his jaw she felt the power he barely restrained just below the surface. His teeth were clenched and in an instant, she knew what this endeavor cost him. Was still costing him. She loved him even more for the gift he'd given her.

Daniel would have liked to see her face when she climaxed for the first time. To hear her screams before, after and during the explosion an untold treasure. It would have been impossible though, not in this place. With the driver above to hear them, no, he could not allow it. He would not have his wife talked about amongst the villagers.

Sitting back Daniel pulled and tucked, an entranced Emily's gown from under her breasts placing a kiss on each globe he secured the gown before raising the curtain. "The coach will be stopping soon." Hopefully their timing was right; he didn't want people ogling his wife, whispering. Her hair escaped the pins. That at least could be fixed. Removing the rest of the pins, he ran his hands through the silken strands. Better.

Kissing the tip of her nose they waited for MacPhee to halt the team. Stepping out from the carriage Daniel held his hand to Emily. Placing an arm about her waist they walked down the wharf to the awaiting rowboat. Perkins and Roberts assisted the happy couple up the rope ladder to Maiden before rowing back to shore.

Emily pulled the satin nightgown over her head, delicate, whisper soft and completely see-through; she remembered seeing the fabric and knowing exactly for what it was meant. Smiling knowingly, her image stared back at her. Hurriedly she pulled on her robe. Pulling the brush through her wavy hair Emily dreamed, as she had a thousand times or more, she was in bed, his hands running over her body, staking his claim.

The cabin door opened softly, a smiling love- struck Daniel came up behind her. Taking the brush, he ran it through her long golden locks. Kissing the back of her head he set the brush aside. Hands on her shoulders, thumbs pressing gently massaging the base of her neck. Emily knew how she wanted this played out. She'd waited; planned, dreamed of the way it would be. She wasn't willing to alter her itinerary now.

"Go to bed, I'll be but a moment. Promise," Emily purred.

Sauntering over to the bed, he stopped, perfectly aligned with the mirror. Undoing his cravat, the soft silk slid from his neck. With a smile he sent it fluttering to the chair. He removed his coat, glancing at the mirror. Although he couldn't see, he knew Emily's eyes were affixed on his reflection. Taking delight in torturing her newfound desire, Daniel slowly undid the ties of his shirt one by one allowing it to gape open.

Emily watched the mirror through shuttered lashes; her mouth watered at the sight of the dark curly hair peeking through the opening. The slight detailing of muscles in his chest hidden behind the white fabric, tantalized. Trying to contain her impatience, waiting for him to peel off the offending garment, was harder than she imagined. Hurry. Daniel made no move to comply. *This is not the way it was supposed to be,* she thought.

Daniel knew he was getting to her. The small furrow of confusion lacing her brow spoke volumes. Allowing himself a small smile, his hands found the ties on his britches. Clearing his throat to cover a laugh he turned his back to the mirror as he sat. Removing his Hessians, shirt and buff-colored trousers, slowly he slid into bed. Tossing the blankets over his hips, trying to conceal his stiff manhood, he lay on his back folding his arms behind his head waiting for Emily to come to bed. Watching her expression was too much. Accidentally he chuckled.

Emily would have gladly killed him at that moment, had she not been reeling from the glimpse of his well-contoured back, she would have. So busy cataloguing every inch she barely got a peek at his buttocks before he disappeared beneath the covers. He was teasing her. What was she to do about it? Shrugging in resigned acceptance, gracefully she turned. Her dreams, all of them would be fulfilled. If not tonight, then in the nights to come; the chance to look upon her husband, drink her fill and learn every inch of his mouth-watering body; was her right.

Meeting Daniel's amused gaze, Emily leisurely unknotted her robe. Moving her shoulders in a sensuous dance, the material floated downward, pooling at her feet. The amusement in Daniel's eyes changed rapidly, replaced by heated desire. Taking note of the tension gripping his jaw, the gnashing of his teeth, his hands fisted twisting the covers fighting for control. Emily smiled. "Control is overrated, is it not?"

Daniel swallowed his eyes glued to Emily's nightgown. The garment was completely transparent revealing the dark areoles surrounding excitement-puckered nipples, the indentation of her waist he could span with his hands and the thatch of dark hair covering her mons; his mouth was dry, and his manhood throbbed. There was no longer a trace of amusement anywhere in his body. It thrummed with the incessant need to be inside her.

Emily sashayed to the bed, each sway of her hips, mesmerizing Daniel. The fabric lovingly whispered about her body; caressing her skin, taunting him. His eyes darkened as the beast within took over. This is what Emily had waited for. This is the Daniel she wanted to take her. Casually leaning over, harnessing her eagerness; to make her dream come true. Erotically caressing the covers, she met Daniel's heated gaze. Running her tongue over her dry lips she smiled.

His control shattered. Grabbing Emily about the waist, he held her tightly, covering his impassioned body. Seizing the back of her head he crushed her mouth to his. Forcing her lips open, with a primal growl, his tongue invaded her mouth.

Hand roaming the sheer gauze, feeling her heated body beneath, wasn't enough, rolling her under; Daniel tearing his mouth from hers. Rearing up, taking the material between his hands he ripped it from her body. He was out of control. He must tame the raging or risk hurting Emily. It was so damn hard. He breathed flinging the fabric across the room.

Knowing what was going through his mind, Emily fed the animal. He would not hold back from her. Not now, not ever. Her hands ran over his chiseled chest and the muscles jumped. Circling his nipples, with her fingertip, marveling when they puckered against her. Emily continued her exploration down his rib cage pressing into his hips before winding behind. She ran her fingertips over his buttocks, smiled when the muscles clenched; he was losing the battle. Splaying her hands, she brought her nails back around to grasp his manhood. He hissed. Emily squeezed gently. He roared.

His lips to her breast Daniel worked Emily's legs apart settling between them. Hips pressed against her in rhythm as he sucked her nipple passionately. Emily arched, screaming, spurring him on. He tortured; laved, nibbled, suckled soon Emily was writhing beneath him. Fingers parading through the curly black hair guarding her entrance, he found her ready for him.

Shoving a pillow under her hips, pulling her knees apart, his gaze roamed briefly before he plunged forward. Past the swollen slippery folds, into her tight passage, further through her maidenhead stopping deep within her womb. Daniel swallowed Emily's scream, his mouth taking her farther and farther from the pain. As the ache lessened, fire returned. Her passage eased. She was finally his. Her sheath adjusted welcoming him.

Sweat dripping from his brow, he prayed he could hold out for when he reached his peak; he wanted Emily right there along with him. Moving slowly in and out, Daniel watched her eyes fill with desire as her body responded, hips lifting to his. Long steady strokes tantalized sliding all the way out before entering once more. Her screams of delight filled him with a power he'd never experienced before. Increasing tempo, they sailed, he the conqueror and she the raging sea. Frantically they battled for higher ground. Moving with such blinding passion, the world around them could have crumbled.

Emily's spasms gripped him tighter, the friction of their hair, coming together then parting in sweet agony. The power was overwhelming. She was lifting into him, grinding her hips in a motion as natural as life itself. She felt the storm consuming her, pulling deeper into the depths of oblivion.

Clawing his back, eyes closed tightly, neck arched straining against the bedclothes, Daniel watched as she rode the wave of ecstasy relishing in her every expression as she climbed the crest. Crying out, the sound of his name echoed throughout the cabin. Her body trembled beneath his as her explosion triggered his. With a final plunge, he roared; spilling his seed into her womb.

Emily opened her eyes. Both were breathless. Smiling at each other in wonder as they waited for their breathing to relax. Daniel tried withdrawing from Emily, but she held on tight. Knowingly, he rolled over taking Emily with him; bodies joined. Kissing her hair, he watched her eyes close. As she drifted into a much-deserved slumber, Daniel closed his eyes, an hour, and then he'd wake her once more.

Chapter Ten

"Yes, Daniel. Please. Yes. Yes," she moaned, wiggling against him. What a lovely way to wake up. If only he would hurry. She needed him so badly. Shifting, rocking back and forth, side to side she tilted her head and brought her mouth in contact with the soft flesh of his neck; she laid a trail of kisses from his neck to his jaw. He groaned. He moved. She could feel him growing harder. Inside her...*inside her what the hell?* She came awake with a start.

Dan's arms tightened like steel bands around her as she made to lunge backward off the bed. Rolling her over onto her back, still joined, still buried deep inside, they stared at one another in shock. Dan watched her face intently puzzling out what the hell happened. Well it wasn't hard you idiot! You made love to Emma!

But how? Think damn it! She'd stayed snuggled protectively in his arms. No. Son of a bitch! She was above the covers. Well she's not anymore, his mind screamed. Genius! She had her robe on. Didn't she have anything on besides the damn robe? And where in the hell is that robe now?

Now she was beneath him his cock still deep inside her. What the hell had happened? He spied Emma's robe by the door, where he'd flung it the night before. No, no, no. This could not be happening. It wasn't possible was it?

Emma moved.

"Don't!" he grumbled in agony. She looked startled, embarrassed and confused. Fuck! Straightening out his arms so he was raised above her, "Em, sweetheart, I'm sorry please hold still or I will lose it. I don't want to scare you, but I can't...I won't leave you right now." He was as hard as a rock. He could feel her body caressing him...milking him, as she moved trying to find comfort and he knew if he didn't do something quick, they were both going to be insane with lust. He could tell by the look on her face, this intimacy was new to her. He had to be the one to lead them out of this predicament. And one hell of a predicament it was!

Breaking away, ending all contact, was out of the question. Not only would it leave them both wondering, wanting, the awkwardness would push her away. She'd build another damn shield to hide behind and then he would never have a chance. He couldn't allow that. This happened damn it! Was still happening and he'd make damn sure she knew it. Pain laced his ribs and head but neither were as severe as the ache in his loins.

Normally he would have run his fingers over her luscious body, but this slow rhythm was all he could manage. He was limited with his movements, at least until he healed. Then…nothing would stop him. His mind screamed, she was raped, an experience that had terrified her for many years, she didn't look terrified now. Her eyes were filling with desire getting darker and darker by the moment. She looked intrigued, contemplative and curious as she gazed into his eyes. Good. He'd use her passion.

Dan could feel her, hot and moist around him, as he stared into those green depths gauging her reaction; he began sliding in and out of her. Her skin pinkened as longing took hold. Smiling down silently beseeching her to acknowledge his love he pumped in and out persistently, kissing her repeatedly, "Let go, Em. Trust me." His mouth took possession of hers, his tongue moved in cadence with his cock. When Dan broke the kiss, Emma protested; the loss was quickly forgotten as Dan, viewing the look of wondrous delight etched on her face, took her to the next plateau. His lips on hers, Dan groaned into her mouth as a shattering climax engulfed them.

Heartbeats slowing, they came down from the physical and emotional high, giving her one last kiss he pulled out easing to her side. Crying, Emma snuggled closer. "I never knew," she said, as tears flowed onto Dan's chest. Holding her, he felt like crying himself. Never had he experienced anything of this magnitude. How could he of all people tell Emma this? She knew or at least he assumed she knew he'd had numerous sexual encounters. Would she believe him if he told her it had been spectacular for him as well?

Her cries exhausted her, as she vented years and years of pent up emotion. He soothed her with his hands and sweet nothings until she drifts off to sleep. Dan thought about all the possibilities that could have led to the position he found himself in when he awoke. Letting his mind drift back to the world in which he slumbered, he thought of Daniel and Emily, the love they shared and the life they would now lead. He felt great pride for over the years he'd looked upon Daniel as a younger version of himself. Perhaps even as a little brother? Dan smiled remembering how in love Daniel was. He too was in love.

Damn! No, it couldn't be. It wasn't possible. Dan's mind ran wild, his pulse thundered. A million questions popped into his head all of which he needed answers for. They will have to wait. Pulling Emma closer he forced questions to stop, he needed sleep; something told him he would require all his wits when they woke; not only for finding a solution; but he feared what Emma would do when reality sunk in.

The room was hot, the sun's rays penetrating through the blinds. Emma stirred. What had happened? Sliding from the bed and standing on stiff legs, she tried to put things into perspective. She was sore. Sore and sticky. It was an odd feeling, a new feeling. She needed a bath. Finding her robe, she slipped her limbs into the sleeves and knotted it. Oh God! What had she done?

Dan allowed her to go, not opening his eyes, giving her the privacy, she had found when she thought he was asleep. Sitting in bed he planned his next move. Marriage. Definitely. Not because he made love to her. He simply wasn't willing to let her go. Ever. Whether or not his dreams played a part, he'd found his soul mate. Relinquishing her now was not an option. He learned long ago that fate was fickle and if by chance she handed you a prize, you embraced it and didn't let go.

Emma had worked later than usual. Getting up late gave her a guilty conscience. Among other things. How many times had they made love? Once she was aware of, would she have been so sore after one time? It had been years, and yet? No. Why couldn't she remember? Forcing her mind back…Dan in pain, lying beside nestled in his arms. Their talk. The dream…Emily, married, so happy, so much in love. Then. "Oh No! No!"

Dan had been gone for the better part of the afternoon. After his shower, he kissed her deeply, leaving her knees weak, saying something about business. He would be back with supper, his treat. Emma worked frantically trying to dispel the thoughts, the good, the bad, and the ugly. Great, now she was a walking Clint Eastwood soundtrack.

Needing advice and having nowhere else to turn, she picked up the phone and dialed the office. Beatrice would gloat; she would endure it. She had to, for right now she needed a little guidance. Beatrice picked up on the first ring. "Emma, I am glad you called Hon; I was gonna stop by last night, but something came up. So. How are you treating the young stud?" *Like a mare in heat,* Emma thought.

"Beatrice, there's been some…ah, developments. No. Don't say it. I need to see you, can you come after work?"

"Sure, Hon. Everything okay?"

"Just peachy, all crisp sunshine and bloody roses! Couldn't be better! Just hurry."

"Em, you're sarcastic. Maybe I should come now?"

Emma looked at the clock, 4:30 p.m. Beatrice worked till five. Mentally she calculated road conditions; still she'd make it by 5:30 p.m. Dan would be gone till at least seven, that should give them enough time. With any luck, she could get her answers then get Beatrice out before she started gloating.

"No, Beatrice, leave at the regular time. I really am okay. Honest."

"I'll be there soon; I'll even bring you more files."

"Gee thanks."

Emma disconnected and started typing a denial letter. The client, Ricardo Santeras, wanted his marijuana released. The frickin' idiot, now awaiting trial for drug trafficking, didn't even deny he brought an illegal substance through Customs. Emma laughed. His lawyer, Samuel Burns, claimed it was medicinal and hereby requested its release. Three kilos. "Medicinal my ass," she snickered, "yeah sure and I'm the bloody queen of England."

It felt immensely satisfying to laugh at someone else's stupidity; she certainly couldn't laugh at her own. She groaned. Why the hell did her mind keep creeping back? Dropping her head in her hands she shook it despairingly trying to focus on her work.

"It was Em. What's wrong?"

"I don't know. She needs to talk to me after work."

Beatrice gave Dan a hardnosed look. Strumming her fingers on the desk she said, "You gonna tell me or do I have to wait to hear it from her?"

Dan shifted uneasily the repeated rata-tat-tat-rata-tat-tat of her buffed nails on the hard-cherry wood surface hit him like a jackhammer. He'd been in the office long enough for Beatrice to raise a questioning brow before the phone rang. What had Emma said?

"Okay. Something happened. But I don't think it warrants your anger. Maybe I screwed up." He ran his fingers through his hair. "I don't know. I need advice."

"Bloody amazing!" Beatrice said hitting the desktop astonishment coming across loud and clear.

"Damn it, Beatrice! Are you trying to give me a heart attack?" At Beatrice's raised brow, Dan was aware of his mistake. "Sorry. I shouldn't have snapped.."

Beatrice peered into a face of total desperation. "I cannot believe how much the two of you are alike. Even when you're talking, you come across with almost the exact words. It's eerie. Anyone who didn't know better would think you two practiced that technique. Oh well, just forget it. Maybe you had better tell me the all of it."

"I can't do that. No don't look at me like that. I'm trying to do the right thing here. I need you to help make Emma marry me."

"Marriage?"

Beatrice's shocked expression was not lost on Dan. Perhaps he'd better backtrack a little. How to do it, he wondered wearily. "I know this may seem sudden and all…but…I love her Beatrice. I must go back to Baltimore, straighten some things out. Porter, my business manager, is having some problems with rounding up enough cargo for the ship in dry dock. Emma said the paperwork releasing Reliant has been faxed to Baltimore."

Dan stopped momentarily adding timelines in his head.

"Anyway, it may take a couple of weeks, less if I can manage it; when I come back, I want to marry Emma." Dan paused allowing Beatrice to contemplate all he'd said, and all he hadn't.

"You move, fast don't you? But marriage? Are you sure? Well, it doesn't matter. Frankly I don't give a damn. I like you. Part of me was pulling for you two." Beatrice said with a shrug. "So, tell me, is Emma in accordance with your wishes? No of course not. That's why you're here. To enlist my help convincing her, did she say no or is she thinking about it?"

Dan's hands twisted and turned like a nervous six grader pulled in front of the principal for copying answers. "Yes," Dan said, as he cleared his throat. "Well, fact is, I haven't asked her. Yet. I left while she was working. Thing is…Damn it Beatrice! I'm scared as hell she'll say no."

"She can hardly say no; if you don't ask, now can she?" Beatrice chided.

"Funny…very funny Beatrice but this is serious. I am serious! It seems like I have been searching for her all my life. Corny I know; give a guy a break, will you? She can't turn me down. I need help. Will you help me do this right?"

Beatrice laughed.

"What? What the hell is the matter with you?" Dan asked as he glowered.

Beatrice couldn't help it *'little boy lost'* the very idea was outrageous; still that is what he looked like.

Disgusted at himself for even having the idea, Dan heaved himself off the desk.

Beatrice waved him back down.

"Sit. Give me a minute. Oh. There. Sorry. It's just that for a moment you looked so childlike. I couldn't resist. Now come here, before I leave, we'll figure out what to do."

Dan sat, tossing Beatrice a fat grin, he said, "I have a plan."

A little while later, Beatrice breezed cheerfully through the open door at Emma's and gave her a hug.

"What's that for?"

"For being you, aren't you lucky? Where's Dan?" Bea looked about knowingly.

"I don't know. He left this afternoon. Mr. Harding called; he dialed Porter, that's his business manager, then left. I assume he's busy. I'm expecting him back any time actually so can we forget the niceties and get down to business?"

Emma didn't mean to sound so insistent, but it had taken Beatrice longer than expected to arrive. She had kept watch on the clock and the door expecting Dan to intrude at any moment.

"All right, what's so urgent? Geez I swear you're a nervous wreck."

"Beatrice you remember those dreams I told you about. Well they've changed."

"What do you mean changed?"

"I mean the little girl, she's, and umm, she got married."

A frown creased Beatrice's brow, some of what Dan told her was starting to fall into place.

"Is that what has you so riled up? Jesus, Em, it's only a dream."

"Is it?" Emma questioned, as she paced back and forth across the carpet.

"Well, of course it is. If you're so anxious maybe you should look it up."

"I could, but…"

"But what?"

"I never thought it would lead to so much trouble." Emma said as she ran her palms over her forehead pushing back intruding thoughts.

"What kind of trouble, Emma? For God sakes you must be more specific. You're the one that said we don't have a whole lot of time here. One would think it would be better spent, talking rationally than beating around the Looney tree." Emma stopped pacing, and sighed. Taking a seat, she put her thoughts in order.

"I slept with Dan," she blurted.

Beatrice's facial expression never wavered; it was hard, but she managed it. Now what to say, she'd guessed after talking with Dan, but having it confirmed, well she was thunderstruck.

"Okay, so you slept with Dan, that's not the end of the world honey. It's the millennium. You're a grown woman. He cares about you; he's good looking probably a powerhouse in bed. What's the problem?"

As Emma thought back, she immediately turned red. Clearing her throat, "I wouldn't know, exactly. I am assuming the answer is yes, though the second time or maybe it was the third, the time I fully remember, he was more I don't know…subdued, gentle…" Emma's confusion was clearly written all over her face. Beatrice knew she mirrored her image. Tossing thoughts around she tried to catch up.

"What do you mean you wouldn't know? You don't remember the first time? Second time? Were you drunk?" she said, carefully.

"I know it doesn't make sense Beatrice that's why I called you here I need your direction. Can a person act out, I mean…unconsciously…and I guess maybe simultaneously…what is happening in a dream?"

Beatrice's stunned expression had Emma ready to back track. But damn it she needed answers, and Beatrice was the only person that could help her…besides maybe Emily, and that was laughable. Wasn't it? Talking to one's imagination. If it was an imagined occurrence that caused it…Oh bloody hell! Emma thought…*I'm nuts*!

Just when Emma was ready to start looking for a good psychiatrist, Beatrice slowly spoke. "I think maybe…Well, honestly, I don't really know. How about looking it up? I read in the paper last week or the week before, a doctor out of New York was hosting a dream workshop. If you contacted them, I'm sure you wouldn't have to leave your name,"

Emma's head shook violently.

"Okay so that's out, how about books? Don't look at me like that you asked. Now, as to the more pressing matter at hand; about Dan, do you love him?"

Emma was about to answer when the door opened, "Dinner's here! Who's hungry?" The door closed and Dan turned smiling casually. So much for clearing the confused mind, Emma thought.

Around the coffee table seemed the best spot for dinner. Dan and Beatrice sat beside each other on the sofa while Emma sat cross-legged on the floor. Dinner was filled with light conversation; if Dan thought it odd for Beatrice to be there he didn't say. Piling the last of the lemon chicken onto his plate, he regaled them with the story of his last voyage. Emma listened as she gathered the containers and headed for the kitchen, thank God Beatrice had stayed.

Still, soon she would be leaving. Then what? What can one say to a man you obviously accosted during the night? He was still recovering from injuries for Christ sakes. What was she? An animal? No better than Travis and his cronies? She wouldn't be surprised if he returned to his hotel. She'd be alone. Again. Swallowing the lump in her throat Emma scolded herself. It's your own fault you imbecile. For seven years, seven years damn it, you stayed away from men; now you let one close and look what happens. You molest him.

Fool!

Fool!

Fool!

While Emma berated herself in the kitchen, Beatrice filled Dan in on their conversation. She left nothing out. She didn't understand but Dan would.

Emma walked in, just in time to catch their conversation.

"You do? Well if you have any information, I am sure Emma would welcome it."

Groaning inwardly Emma took up her place on the floor, head down, picking imaginary lint off her slacks.

Dan winked at Beatrice. "Well as a matter of fact, I know quite a lot about dreams. I've seen professionals and have done a bit of research."

"Really?"

Emma's head snapped up so fast Dan feared she'd break her lovely neck. He gave a nod and continued. "For the longest time I was plagued with them, they were so intense, so drugging I felt threatened but now, I see them as a gift." He shrugged as though it were of little importance; as an afterthought he added, "Emma, was there something bothering you? I'd be happy to offer assistance."

Emma glared openly at Beatrice who let the look wash off her like water.

She was still for so long, Beatrice and Dan worried she'd clam up altogether. If she did it would be disastrous for their plans however to push Emma was like pushing an Arkansas mule. The harder you pushed the less it budged and kick you were liable to receive could be deadly.

"I have dreams; remember I told you about them? I never gave them a lot of thought. They were happy, except for a brief period in my life, and those were not the same. Those were nightmares eventually chased away by the others. Looking back, it may have been some sort of protection. If that makes sense?" Emma trailed off trying to find the words that would not make her look like a complete nutcase in front of the man she loved.

Loved? She did love him. She'd reached that conclusion before she called Beatrice. It was in fact the reason she called. She didn't know why or how it happened and in a short amount of time too. But it did. There was no other explanation that answered the question why? Why she hadn't shied from his kisses, his touch? Why she cared what he thought of her after learning of her rape? Why she stayed with him? Too many whys and only one answer. Only one thing could break down her defenses and past her fears…love.

Beatrice and Dan looked on as Emma sat quietly absentmindedly chewing her fingernails. Dan's eyes showed a hopeful gleam and Beatrice's answered back, a small shake of the head, a warning to proceed with caution. It was understood; Emma needed time. They both waited.

"When I was young, I dreamed of another little girl except, she wasn't of this time. I was her, in my dreams laughing, playing, and having fun with the other children, something I didn't succeed at when I was awake."

Emma knew she would have to go careful with the next part for Beatrice had never heard of her rape. She swallowed hard, finding the courage to state the facts.

"During my senior year." She clutched her dry throat. "When I…" Angry, frustrated and disgusted with herself she exhaled a jagged breath.

"Emma, it's okay, really love, Beatrice will understand." Beatrice stamped on Dan's foot. It took him a minute to realize what he'd called Emma.

Finding strength in Dan's simple words Emma continued stoically. "The dreams came stronger, after the rape." She swallowed again looking up tears shimming in her eyes and Dan wished he could comfort her.

"I had the most terrible nightmares after that night. I struggled with whom to confide. Andre knew there was something wrong. I couldn't even tell him all of what happened. He knew the basics. He was my hero. Always saving me. Only this time, there was nothing he could do. I think that was the worst part." She looked at Dan and he understood what she meant, by confessing to Andre, if only a little, she'd put a demon behind her. He hoped one day she would tell him all. Not that he wanted to hear the details, but because she needed in some small way to release them before she would ever really be free.

"But the dreams, the one with the little girl, they came stronger battling the nightmares until they lessened. When the nightmare left, for the longest time so did the dreams." Emma took a deep breath and gave them a wobbly smile.

"Until, the crash. Then they came back full force. It's funny, although I was so plastered most times when I fell into bed, so drunk I didn't remember leaving the bar or anything else that happened that day, I still remembered the dreams. Vividly. Why do you think that is?" Emma looked at Dan hoping he had the answer.

Beatrice excused herself making her way to the bathroom, her way blurred by the tears streaming down her face. My God, poor Emma! She'd been through so much more than Beatrice realized. Holding a hand over her chest momentarily trying to block out the pain caused from her short breaths, she managed to slow and deepen her breathing. Holding a cloth under the cold water before applying the cool moistness to her puffy eyes and tear stained cheeks, she held it there saying a silent prayer for the woman she loved like a little sister.

She had to get out of here; she'd done her part Dan would have to take over from there. She couldn't bear it. Not right now. The last thing Emma would want was to see her pity. Right this moment she couldn't stop it from showing. She had to leave. She needed time to collect herself. A full night of crying and cursing in her own apartment would allow her enough strength to face Emma in the morning, if she came in.

Stopping at the closet so as not to make eye contact, she said, "I have forgotten something, I have to go. I'll see you tomorrow. Thanks for dinner." Without waiting for a reply, she quickly ducked out the door.

Chapter Eleven

Sitting at her desk, Emma stared avidly at the words in front of her; the office was virtually back to normal, previous chaos having ended, now gave Emma time for her research. Aside from the few files that came in each day, there was nothing pressing. Pinching the bridge of her nose, she was trying to absorb all she read when Beatrice entered.

"Hey. Find anything?"

"I think so." She waved the book. "This one seems to have more info on the types of dreams I have been having. At least this one says such things are possible."

"It doesn't look very big," Beatrice said, as she eyed it critically.

"No, but does that matter if it gives me the information I need? It's an encyclopedia about dreams. Seems simple enough to understand as well. Not all that technical gobblily-gook you need a psychology degree to understand." Emma set the book down. "Did you need something or are you just checking up on me because Dan asked you to?"

Beatrice smiled back. "No, hon, I'm checking up because I asked me to. Is that okay with you?" Emma's big grin was her only answer.

"Dan should be back in a couple of days. Have you spoken to him?" Beatrice said, raising a questioning brow.

"You know very well I have Ms. Nosey," Emma said, with a laugh. "You're the one who transferred the damn call. Or are you getting senile in your old age?"

"I'm not much older than you," Beatrice chirped back. They both burst out laughing. When they finally composed themselves, Beatrice asked, "Okay, I'm for a bite. You want anything? Can't live on love alone. Or so I've been told."

"Sure."

"Well?" Beatrice said, tapping her foot against the carpet in phony irritation.

"Well what?" Emma quipped.

"Smart ass. Why did I miss you when you were away?" Beatrice hit herself on the forehead.

"'Cause I'm loveable?"

"Well loveable, if you wish to eat, you'll tell me what…no…don't say food. Name something specific."

Emma laughed. "Very well, spoilsport. Corned beef. Think you can manage that, should I write it down? Wouldn't want you forgetting, after all the walk could take oh, I don't know, at least a couple of minutes…then there is the amount of time you'll be spending standing in line…maybe I should write it down for you?"

Beatrice's pen whizzed past Emma ear. "Everyone's a comedian, just wait till Dan gets back; he'll put you in your place." And with a wink she was gone leaving Emma buckled over with laughter.

When Emma sobered enough to stand, she walked to the window gazing up at the sky. A magnificent sunny day, baby blue sky, big white puffy clouds. Tranquil. The days were so much shorter, and it was getting colder, but Emma had something warmer than the sun. For the first time in a very long time her heart felt light. Dan. He'd been gone eight days now. Business. Two weeks at most? She missed him. There was so much she discovered. So much to share; she valued his in site.

Emma hugged herself, sighing and twirling with unimpeded delight remembering their last night together. After Beatrice left, they continued talking, comparing. His parents; alive and well, lived in Dundalk. His childhood was happy, lots of friends but sadly no siblings; his business, was an offshoot of one his great-great-great-great grandfather had started. Everything. They parleyed about dreams, his and hers. There they ran into questions neither could leave unanswered. Deciding Emma would research the subject, they'd left the matter there.

After watching the sunrise while wrapped in each other's arms, they retired to the spare bedroom, Dan's room where they made love over and over. Exhausted, they fell asleep. Sated. It was glorious. Just the memory sent shivers through her.

Groaning, Emma strolled back to her desk. Six more days. It seemed like such a long time. Six days, then Dan would be back. She wondered what they were going to do then. Research their dreams of course but what of their relationship?

This was all so new to her. She hadn't the foggiest idea what to expect. So right now, she was trying to expect nothing at all, limiting any disappointment. It wasn't working. She found herself berating her wondering mind time and again. Focusing on things she could control.

She picked up the book and began reading, "According to this, there are hundreds, perhaps even thousands, of cases of shared dreams on record. Shared dreams are experienced the same night (perhaps at the same time) by two or more…"

Damn! He was a moron. He should have married her before coming back. If he had one-inkling it would take this long to accomplish something he normally could do in a day, he would have. He only hoped the conversation and the lovemaking they had would keep Emma from second guessing their relationship until he could get there in person. There had been one problem after another. Porter constantly assured him it would all come together. It bloody well better! And fast.

Everything but securing a load was accomplished. He'd seen his parents notifying them of his appending nuptials. Now all he had to do was ask his intended and pray to God she says yes. They hadn't batted an eyelash when he returned engaged to a woman they had never met. Being single at almost thirty-one with no prior prospects had helped considerably. His parents had urged him to marry flaunting daughters of friends, of course they would deny it if asked. They wanted grandchildren, before they were too old to spoil them his mother would say.

The Justice of the Peace was arranged for next Tuesday. Preparations for the use of the family cabin nestled along the banks of the Chesapeake, done. The perfect honeymoon spot, secluded, surrounded by nature. Emma would love it. There would be little traffic, no campers, fishermen or hikers to intrude on their special time together. Mrs. Wallace, a friend of his mother's would go and make sure all was tidied and aired before they got there.

Fall was upon them and with Thanksgiving fast approaching Dan wanted all the chaos out of the way, so they could spend a quiet weekend at home. Her apartment would do until they found a house; preferably in a quiet neighborhood, somewhere between Washington and Baltimore so commuting would not be a problem. On his income Emma didn't need to work but he knew deep down she wouldn't want to give it up. If they were both happy what should it matter?

He'd cleared his calendar; Porter would handle everything for the next couple months. He'd come back full time after the New Year. Porter had been with the company for ten years, taking over the reins when Dan was at sea. He would manage and if not, well, Washington was within driving distance if a phone call wouldn't suffice.

Beatrice managed, to secretly clear Emma's calendar until after Thanksgiving, just as planned. That meant he had to have the ship loaded and be back in Washington Monday at the latest. Come hell or high water he would get it done! Swearing aloud he picked up the phone. "It's O'Brien. What have you got for me?"

Emma was buried knee-deep in books. Sitting cross-legged in the middle of her living room, pencil tucked behind her ear and yellow post—it's in her left hand she marked each page before setting the book aside and grabbing another. She'd found, out of the fifty or so books she checked out of the library, ten that covered shared dreams, dream control and, although this seemed far-fetched even to her, pasts life encounters through sleep. She kept an open mind and considered everything. She had to.

Stretching, she spied the clock, eleven, time for bed. In the spare room, where she spent every night since Dan left, to be closer to him, she undressed and climbed into bed. The room was clean, bedding washed, except for the pillowcases which carried his scent. Hugging the pillow close she inhaled deeply, something uniquely him and just a hint of Old Spice, mmmm…Dan.

Her dad had used Old Spice. Not many wore it, but she loved the smell. It was comforting. Taking another deep breath, she drifted off to dreamland.

Standing at the rail, ocean spray on her face, the salty sea air attacked her senses. It made her feel alive. She loved it. They had put out three months ago. Every day she walked this rail while Daniel captained. He'd watch her out of the corner of his eye never losing track of her. It was the stipulation she relented to. "The men are foreigners. Drifters. If you are set on this course, my stubborn little wife," he said, chuckling her on the chin. "Then it's the cabin, or," he amended at her mutinous look. "Within my sight at all times."

Emily had had little choice, her father and mother stood silently in the background wanting nothing better than to be able to send her to her room for such foolish notions. A woman at sea.

She was no longer under their rule. She answered only to her husband. And she would. Providing he was within reason, of course. Being left behind was not an option, Daniel knew. Emily would eventually get what she wanted. Then he would not be there to protect her. She felt confident she would be setting sail on the Maiden providing she agreed to a few demands. Compromising wasn't a problem if it didn't interfere with the thrill of the adventure. Nothing he asked did, so they got along famously.

It had been four months since they married and if Emily had any complaints whatsoever, it would be not conceiving. She wanted to give Daniel a son. As she spied him at the wheel her heart constricted. He would so enjoy a son. Family was important to him; even now he threw everything he had into building a legacy. It was only natural for a man to want to bequeath something. Leaving his mark on the world for the generations to come.

Her complaint was a blessing in disguise for had she conceived there would have been no way to hide it from Daniel. Protector that he was he would have turned the Maiden around, full hold or no.

The sun moved westward; Daniel would soon relinquish the wheel to his first mate. Bidding farewell to the hypnotic picture before her, Emily headed for their cabin. Making eye contact with Daniel, she waved before continuing onward. Passing through a throng of off-duty men, Emily nodded politely. She didn't converse, another stipulation. Most of the crew treated her with respect except for one group of four men, emanating evil every time she passed. Just the thought of them left her feeling unclean.

Emily turned off the stairs facing the dark passageway. Even the sunny skies above decks did nothing to illuminate it. Lanterns hung from the walls every few feet but the light they cast barely allowed you to see your feet. A cold, eerie feeling washed over her. Someone was watching her. She looked around. She had sensed it before and was always careful. On guard. Abiding Daniel's wishes to the letter. To him, it seemed she was the dutiful wife; to her it was a simple matter of safety. Counteracting bad atmospheres.

Hurriedly she made her way to the captain's cabin. Lifting the latch, she entered butting her back against the door, breathing deeply. Gathering her wits, she secured the door before readying herself for dinner.

The captain's door clicked shut and the bolt slid into place. Klaus stepped out of the shadows into the hall below a lantern. The exhilaration that jolted his body and stirred his loins every time he scared the little filly was powerful. Guffawing evilly, he grabbed his crotch and squeezed. She would be his. Grinding his hand up and down his shaft, he sneered…one day soon.

Emma woke screaming, her pulse racing, sweat and tears stung her eyes; her hands shook. She fought to control the panic that seized her. Slowly she managed to get her terror under control. She was in the spare bedroom; all was fine. Talking to herself, calming herself, she relaxed. Shivering she grabbed one of Dan's T-shirts he left behind and threw it over her head. Still cold, she went for her robe before going to the kitchen. Tea. As she put the kettle on, she realized it wasn't a nightmare she had, for Emily was there. Emma walked into the living room gathering the book she was reading earlier, a piece of paper and a pencil she made her way back to the kitchen. Sitting she began to record her dream.

Hours ticked by. Endless scribbling, countless cups of tea and just as many trips to the bathroom later, Emma stood before the balcony doors watching the sunrise and re-reading her notes. What did it all mean? That man…Klaus…seemed looked like dingy dirty older version of Travis, but she was sure from the moment she seen him in the lamplight he meant trouble. Trouble, yes, but for whom? It was not her he was after. It had to be Emily. You're frickin' nuts she is only a dream!

Still, Emma couldn't shake the feelings transferred from Emily. They felt all too familiar. She'd fought her demons, yet they had bound her. Dan bless him, had set her free and damn it she was not about to feel that way again. If demons had taken over her special dream, she would fight them! Nothing was going to take away the happiness she discovered these past weeks. Nothing!

Suddenly, she needed to know more. Was he as dangerous there? Could he hurt her? No! She wouldn't allow it. She needed to find that book; there was a passage about transferring your thoughts back to your dream. Controlling it. Changing it. If she could figure out how, then she could warn Emily, have Daniel remove Klaus from the ship. Regardless of whether she was real, Emma was not prepared to stand by while another monster took hold. Setting down the papers, she headed for a shower. There was no way she could go back to sleep, not yet.

Her eyes burned and her head reeled, yet the need to compile more stats, note verified cases, to read and absorb everything was gnawing at her. The rumbling of her stomach grew louder interrupting her thoughts. She had been at it for hours, since three this morning. Rubbing the sand out of her eyes she hobbled into the kitchen on pins and needles. Emma took down the toaster and placed the whole-wheat bread into the slots. She'd eat then take a small break, possibly a nap.

Dan let himself into the apartment, thankfully the doorman knew who he was and didn't question his appearance at two in the morning. When he last spoke with Em, she'd been working hard, looking for answers that possibly didn't exist. Optimistic, she had found a couple leads and couldn't wait to show him. Setting his bag inside the door, he stopped. He was home. Hopefully tomorrow, with a little luck, Emma would say the word that would make it permanent.

Kicking off his sneakers and hanging his coat, Dan made his way to the living room and was immediately overwhelmed at the mountains of books strewn all over the floor, pages flipped open, little papers sticking out of them in various other spots. There was foolscap everywhere as well; pages and pages. What the hell? Shaking his head and side stepping the mess, he headed down the hall to Emma's room.

Quietly he tiptoed through the darkened interior to the bed. It was empty. His heart seized by panic, he cautioned himself to think. Turning, trying to keep from calling out or running through the apartment like a terrified child, he made his way into the kitchen. There was a plate in the sink, a cup...Where could she be? No sooner completing the thought, relief flooded his tired brain. His room.

Eyes adjusted to the dark, he spied her in the middle of the bed a pillow clasped tight against her chest. Love filled him. She was magnificent. Dan wanted to go to her to take her in his arms and make sweet love to her. God, how he had missed her. Pondering the idea for all of two minutes, he headed for the shower. He couldn't stand the smell of himself let alone subjecting her to it.

What a day he thought as he stood beneath the rushing water. He swore to Porter he'd get out of Baltimore today if he had to load the fucking ship himself. It was ten by the time the cargo was secured. Wanting to get the hell out of there, he left the paperwork on Porter's desk. Jumping into his truck, he stopped long enough to grab the suitcases he had packed previously and headed for Washington without looking back.

Wrapping a towel about his hips, Dan wondered into the bedroom. Emma was tossing and turning. He rushed to her side gently cajoling, attempting to bring her out of her dream. Dream? Hell, it was a nightmare! He'd never seen her this way before; he wouldn't care too again either. At wit's end he crawled into bed and pulled her onto his lap. Smoothing her sweat-drenched hair from her brow she finally opened her eyes.

Was she dreaming? Dan? Here? She flung her arms around his neck anchoring and hung on for dear life.

He held her tightly, until she was able to speak. Expecting her to tell him about her nightmare, he was worried when she launched into what she had learned from the books. All along he kept thinking there was something. It didn't matter, not right now. There were better ways to spend his first night home. Much better ways. He'd find out the whole of it…later.

Hungrily his lips claimed hers in mid-sentence the words quickly turning into a muffled moan of pleasure. Dan apt fingers shed her nightshirt. Rolling her onto her back, he came into her in one full smooth swift motion. Ecstasy. They moved together knowingly countering each other's movements. They were friends, lovers; adventurers, navigating the universe together. Conquering one undiscovered phenomenal plane after another.

Soaring higher and higher their breath jagged their bodies sweating, the dance as old as time transported them beyond the stars. In an explosion of the senses, somewhere between this world and the next, they found their release. No words were spoken. There was no need. Each knew, as they felt their internal nectars combining, that they had revealed yet another unexplained plateau.

Kissing her mouth softly, Dan rolled to his side taking her with him. Maybe someday, the need to stay joined after making love would lessen. Then again, Dan sighed contentedly, hopefully not. Lying there wrapped in each other's arms they both fell into a blissfully quiet sleep.

Chapter Twelve

Emma sat at her desk humming songs that whirled willy-nilly around in her head. She was so utterly, gloriously happy. The rain splashed against her window; soon, if the weatherman was right, it would turn to snow; nothing would dim the sun that shone in her heart. Nothing.

Work had slowed, whether it was in anticipation of the coming holidays or not she didn't know. Had it ever been this slow in years past? Did she care? Emma worked casually on the last remaining file in her bin.

Emma remembered Beatrice bringing it in. "That's it so far. I guess those bimbos at the end of the hall finally learned to handle their fair share."

Emma had smiled at Beatrice. If Beatrice noticed anything different about Emma, she didn't say. Emma was grateful. She didn't want to share Dan right now. His being back in town was her little secret, one in which she could hold close, wrapping around her heart until she was ready to share it.

What Emma didn't know, was that her little secret was now standing in the outer office going over a host of last-minute wedding details with Beatrice. After a hug and a peck on the cheek, he turned toward Emma's door.

The sound of the door clicking closed had Emma looking up. "Couldn't stay away?" Emma said, fluttering her eyelashes before bursting into laughter at her own foolishness.

Her laughter hit him like brandy, smooth and warming, and he was becoming addicted. Hell, who was he kidding; he'd been addicted from the first. Good thing he would soon be able quench his thirst more often.

With that, he put his scattered wits together to perform the task he'd come here to do. The wedding was a go for tomorrow morning. Every detail had been worked out…well almost. The final detail the he was about to cinch, this very second, was the bride.

His earlier conversation with Beatrice had him worried; she almost had a heart attack when she found out he had not asked Emma. "You're a procrastinator of the worst sort. It would serve you right if she said no! For your sake I hope she'll be able to control her temper."

Dan's silence had Emma's heart plummeting as her mind conjured up her new worse nightmare.

Seeing her face pale Dan spurred into action. Walking around the desk, he grabbed her chair and slid it backward, kneeling he took her hands in his. He watched a look of stunned confusion skitter across her face. "Ah, Babe, don't look so worried." Bringing her hands to his lips he kissed them. "Em, I noticed the first time I saw you; you were the one. I wanted you. Needed you. You are the other half of me. My light. My air. There is so much more…" looking into her eyes seeing the tears of happiness, as they made her eyes glow like the finest emeralds, was all the courage he needed to complete the sentence "Em? Marry me?"

Still kneeling, breath held, Dan's eyes shone with love hope and yes…uncertainty. Emma's heart constricted in a strangled whisper she managed to get out an, "I love you."

Taking out the engagement ring, purchased almost two weeks ago, Dan took it from its velvety satin lined home. Kissing the emerald, an emerald not a diamond; diamonds were the norm of course, but Emma deserved more than the norm. The emerald's green twinkle was the perfect match to the light that shone in his fiancé's gorgeous eyes, as he placed it on her finger.

A perfect fit. Rising, Dan's lips met Emma's as she flung herself off the chair and onto his lap right there on the office floor. Holding her, her buttocks pressed up tightly against his groin he hardened immediately. All thoughts of what he left unsaid disappeared.

"Well? Do we have a bride for tomorrow?" Beatrice's happy voice shouted over the intercom.

Emma stiffened.

Dan groaned. Coming to his senses immediately he remembered what Emma's closeness and her kisses had made him forget. Emma's expression showed her confusion. And yes, damn it a little teensy bit…well maybe more than a teensy bit of annoyance, he stood and pounded the intercom. "Yes, Beatrice…she said yes." Shutting off the intercom, Dan sat back down in Emma's chair pulling her tense little delectable body up onto his lap. Wrapping his arms about her leaning his head on her breast he sat silently awaiting the explosion he knew was coming. He was not disappointed.

As the words he didn't decline soaked in, she trembled with rage. Surprisingly she was containing it. What that meant, Dan had no idea, but he wasn't foolish enough to think he had gotten away with it.

Maybe, she'd misunderstood. Not wanting to jump to conclusions. Emma waited patiently for Dan to correct Beatrice's obviously premature statement. Silence stretched. Holding her as if to protect a child or anyone else, from said child while it threw a temper tantrum, only managed to stoke her ire.

Eyes spitting sparks of green fire met his. "What…Did…" Her voice vibrated with contained fury. Low and husky, Dan knew she was pissed. Squirming and wriggling Dan tightened his grip. He wasn't about to let go. If he kept her pressed against his heart, where she could feel the beat, then maybe he'd have a chance.

"Love. Please. I know you're angry; I was heavy-handed and took you for granted. I went ahead without your consent, without your opinion." Dan tried his damnedest to let his feelings show in his eyes as he looked at her. "Em, I'm sorry. In my defense, I figured if every detail were worked out, fate wouldn't allow you to say no. You see Em? I did it because I was worried, I would lose you."

The fire abated, he was slowly getting through, just a little more groveling and she would give in. Not that all would be forgiven, he'd pay dearly for his indiscretion at some point, he was sure, but he'd cross that bridge when he came to it. Preferably after, they had both clearly and before witnesses, said I do.

"Em, I am sorry, please believe me. I'll make it up to you. I promise. It will be fantastic. Beatrice assisted me with the arrangements. She even contacted the powers that be and requested time off. Our honeymoon will be at my parents' cabin. You'll love it. Oh, Em, I am sorry. Will you forgive a damned presumptuous fool and marry me tomorrow …?"

Emma had already forgiven him, but something had to be done to ensure he'd not ride roughshod over her in the future. She was not so naive as to believe he was truly sorry, he wasn't. Well, maybe a little sorry, for getting caught. It was nice though, all the hogwash he threw in to try and make it look like he was groveling. She fought hard not to smile; his handsome face pulled long like a bloodhound with big sorry-filled eyes; she'd have loved to see him slobbering at the mouth but then again that might be a tad too much. And

Beatrice, damn her hide, conspired right along with him. She'd deal with Beatrice later you could bet on it.

Emma watched the big white puffy snowflakes drifting freely past the window, floating to the ground. They were a symbol of what Dan had done for her. He came into her life, making her face the past allowing her to float freely, happily. It was only fitting the wedding be amidst the white backdrop of winter. She loved Dan with all her heart, but this was not the eighteenth century, for Christ sakes.

Men and women discussed things as a unit, not I rule – she obeys. As he sat spewing all he was and wasn't, Emma interrupted while tapping her fingers. "Pig headed, arrogant, egotistical, overbearing," she said, watching in amusement as Dan fought to control his own rapidly rising temper.

"All right! Enough! Just say you'll marry me tomorrow and I'll spend every day of our lives together kissing your lovely feet and licking your scrumptious toes." He waggled his brows.

That little move succeeded more than she would ever let him know. Fighting to contain a pre-mature smile or even God forbid a giggle she responded in a lowered almost sensual voice. "Fine. That's all I needed to hear. For now."

"Does this mean you'll marry me tomorrow?" Dan asked hopefully.

"I will," Emma whispered.

Not wanting to risk her saying more or chancing she'd change her mind, his lips descended on hers, showing her with his lips exactly how much he worshipped her.

Beatrice burst into the office to find them, lips locked, tongues dancing and hands roaming. Nothing outside their little bubble existed. Well, Beatrice thought satisfyingly, it's about bloody time! "Now break it up there's work to do, or is Em going to appear stark naked in front of the JP?" Taking pleasure in rocking their world, Beatrice cleared her throat, smiling.

"Dan out! Emma and I have lots to do before tomorrow." With a gleam of mischief, she added, "As I have been forced at my young age to play mom to your bride, it's my duty to maintain proprieties. So, Emma will be spending the night with me. We will meet you downtown at ten tomorrow now beat it!" She looked at Dan tapping her foot.

Dan looked like he wanted to argue as Emma's twinkling eyes met Beatrice's. She fought hard to contain the laughter bubbling to the surface.

Beatrice's idea though it was the first time she had heard it was a marvelous piece of genius and just the punishment Dan needed for his highhandedness.

Sitting in front of the vanity, patiently waiting for Beatrice to finish her hair, Emma couldn't remember a time she'd ever been this beautiful. Luckily, they found the perfect dress yesterday. An emerald gown, softest, lightest velvet she'd ever seen, simply cut a low heart shaped v-bodice, made her eyes glow enhancing her body in a way she couldn't help but feel amazing. It was a little old fashioned, most would walk right past; and they had, which had attributed to the bargain basement price tag. The color made her creamy skin look mouth-watering. Dan would go crazy, Emma thought with a satisfied smile.

How much longer? Emma had never spent so much time on her hair. She kept it long and a simple tie always sufficed. But Beatrice had other ideas. Sighing, Emma let her mind wander, a speed of sound journey through all that had happened. The loss of her family was painful. It always would be. However, her dreams and Dan, made it tolerable. Quickly she thanked Emily for giving her the courage to free her heart.

Her stint with the bottle wasn't one of her more brilliant ideas; though the bar tender had befriended her and in a way, kept her sane. She had grown quite fond of him all things considered. Was he worried about her absence? They should stop by before they left for their honeymoon, let him know she was fine and no longer needed the table. Dan was her tequila, an endless supply of courage, without the hangover. Still, she craved the drink. Staying away was hard. Submersing herself in her job would have weaned her back eventually, hopefully; nevertheless, the loneliness she faced would have remained.

Beatrice was still transforming Emma; she noticed she saw a glimpse of Emily as she gazed in the mirror. Where she and Dan connected through more than their dreams? It was so hard the grasp.

"All done," Beatrice said, as she squeezed her shoulders. "We better get going before the groom comes to haul you off forcefully."

Emma nodded still stunned at the reflection in the mirror.

"You look lovely, your parents would have been so proud." Kissing Emma on the cheek, Beatrice pulled her into a standing position and gently shoved her toward the door.

Dan was pacing. "Where the hell were they!" he growled. Dan looked at his watch, damn. It was ten already; they were supposed to be inside this very minute. Shoulders tense, stress lines showing on his face, he continued pacing rolling his shoulders. If she missed this appointment. Dan finished the thought as a pair of very well-formed slender arms slid around him from behind. Finally. He let out a shaky relieved breath twisting about in Emma's arms hugging her fiercely before guiding her silently into the chambers. Leaving Beatrice to follow behind.

The pace of the ceremony would have made a New Yorker proud; the balding, portly little man stood in a three-piece nondescript grey suit rattling off the words that would make them man and wife. Neither complained about the speed in which the Justice of the Peace had them in and out of the office. They were lucky he'd waited. Arm in arm they emerged from the courthouse smiling. Beatrice ushered them to her car in the parking lot across the street.

Three hours later, Emma sat in the back beside Dan, wondering if Beatrice had lost it when at last she pulled the car into an empty parking lot. Now what in the hell was she doing? She remained quiet as Beatrice played with the buttons on the front seat then pulled down the visor and preened herself in the mirror. Still silence.

Since leaving the courthouse, they had made a quick stop at the apartment before Beatrice took them all over Washington, acting as their personal tour guide. Now they were parked in an empty lot adjacent to one of the finest restaurants in Washington and Emma's stomach was growling.

"Alright. I can't stand it. Somebody talk! I'm hungry and as a bride I should be entitled to a little input so let's get going. I need food and this place doesn't open until seven. I'll have you know I'm not waiting."

"Okay, chill. Dan, do something about your bride will you?" Beatrice chirped, with a sassy smile.

Dan kissed Emma's head before opening the door. She stared at him standing there, arm stretched out. Now what? If they thought, she was going to walk a good ten blocks because she was hungry, they had another thing coming. She watched the catty grin spread across his face and could do nothing but place her hand in his.

Beatrice led the way, while Dan watched his wife from the corner of his eye. She was stunning. He hadn't taken the time to tell her so until after she'd put her name next to his on the marriage certificate. Had she once looked down at his mid-section, even once, she would have known her effect on him immediately.

Beatrice walked to the front door, of Le' Chablis and tapped twice on the door. It was opened immediately.

"Miss Beatrice! Madam you are lovelier every day," he said, kissing both her cheeks.

"Thank you Pierre. You are more the silver-tongued devil every time I see you," she said, tapping him on the shoulder.

Emma looked at Dan; he lifted his brow as if to say I haven't the foggiest idea, then she turned to Beatrice with the silent question in her eyes.

"Emma, Dan, meet Pierre a good friend and the owner of Le' Chablis. In honor of our friendship, he opened a little early so that we may have a private little party."

Pierre kissed Emma's hand and shook Dan's hand before offering his arm to Beatrice leading the party to an elegantly set table, next to the kitchen.

Dan couldn't believe Beatrice pulled it off. However, she did it, he owed her. Even now as they sat sipping champagne the chef prepared Steak Diane, flames jumped from the portable table and the smell of heated brandy permeated the air. It magically enchanted atmosphere.

Chapter Thirteen

"It is going to be a very long drive," Emma declared, quietly as she and Dan left Fred's pub. She would have given anything to stay at the apartment tonight instead of driving to the cabin; all day long she had wanted to throw him down and jump his bones. She groaned inwardly as Dan's hand caressed her lower back as they walked to the car.

Fred had made toast after toast not allowing them to leave. Staying true to what Dan called his Radar persona; Fred swore he knew marriage was in the cards all along. It was only a matter of time he stated. "Only a matter of time, seen that, weeks ago."

Leaving the city lights behind, Emma sighed. The quiet solitude of the Chesapeake Bay would be welcoming, too bad they couldn't transport there.

"Try and get some sleep, Sweetheart. I want you rested when we get home. Here put your head on my shoulder and close your eyes. You'll have a good hour and a half, a little longer, depending on traffic." His lips lingered on her forehead before his attention turned back to the road.

She should sleep. They had stayed up until the wee hours, talking and watching movies. An old-fashioned slumber party or so Beatrice had said. Emma had never had one and by the time her sisters were old enough; she had already left St. Charles. Staying up hadn't bothered Emma, as it was, she barely closed her eyes before Beatrice announced it was time to get ready.

It was great spending time with Beatrice away from the office. They had been close, right from the first, but not completely open with each other.

She remembered Beatrice coming into her office on the first day. "Tea, not coffee. Settles the nerves. Anything else you just holler. Okay? Now be a good girl, drink your tea and get to work; we have a rep to maintain in this office."

Emma had laughed. 'Good girl'. She was twenty-two and couldn't remember being bad, but she no longer fit the girl mold.

Snuggling deeper on Dan's shoulder Emma closed her eyes and told her body to relax. She had been practicing a technique called lucid dreaming. All the books so far, commented on how relaxation before sleep, was the key to interaction with dreams.

Taking confidence in the fact that it was dark, and Dan wouldn't notice Emma practiced the pot shaped breathing she read about. Distending her abdomen, as much as her dress allowed, hopefully it would be enough, she breathed in. Imagining it was pure energy. Then exhaled, allowing the energy to travel throughout her body. Over and over she repeated the procedure until a heaviness overtook her brain, her body.

Slowly she drifted to sleep.

Eyes. Eyes everywhere. Watching her. Emily wanted to scream. Never had she feared going anywhere. Doing anything. She often roamed the village and cliffs with no concern for what might be about. Yet here in the middle of the ocean confined to a ship where the only fears should be weather and pirates, Emily, for the first time in her life was really frightened.

For days she had stayed in the cabin unless Daniel or Decker came to escort her above. No longer was it safe to walk the companionway alone. She liked Decker, a name he acquired years ago, because he was so small when he first boarded. The captain wouldn't allow him to do anything but swab the decks, or so Daniel said. Decker was fifteen now and had been aboard Maiden for the past five years. He was dark skinned with deep chocolate brown eyes. He had grown into a strapping young man, big, brawny and as gentle as a lamb. Moreover, he could be trusted and right now there were too few Emily could trust.

It started shortly after they set sail. Various times, she could feel eyes on her. It would not bother nearly as much if she knew whom those eyes belonged to, but she never spotted the person, only felt their eerie gaze. She shuddered.

A knock sounded on the cabin door. Emily knew it was past time for Daniel to come; her heart raced before she realized it had to be Decker. Taking a calming breath, she walked confidently to the door slid back the bolt and pulled it open.

Odd. No one stood on the other side. She probed the hall. No one. Frowning, she was about to take a step into the corridor to see if Decker hadn't waited, when she was filled with doubt. Trying to shake the unnatural feeling, Emily straightened her shoulders. Her feet wouldn't move. It was like they were nailed to the floor. There was a flutter of movement in the dim light, she called out; no answer came.

Decker would have answered.

Slamming the door Emily threw the bolt in place. Her sides heaved. Her fists clenched and unclenched as she paced the small room, growing smaller by the minute, like a caged tiger.

What was she experiencing? Who was trying to scare her? Why? She knew everyone aboard Maiden. The most recently acquired crewmember, Johnson, was picked up during the last voyage. All would have sailed with Daniel for at least a year.

She was being foolish. Who here would want to harm her? No one. This uneasiness these tricks of the mind had to be brought on by the fact that this was her first adventure. Swallowing her uncertainties and stiffening her spine Emily headed for the door. It was ridiculous to be trapped in her cabin like a frightened child. Her imagination was running amuck. On that note she opened the door, stepped into the companionway and without looking back made her way above decks.

Had Emily turned she'd have seen Klaus stepping out of a darkened crevice down the hall. He liked the spot. He could see the captain's cabin real clear. It had become a daily vigil for him to watch the misses. Yes, he snickered to himself he was quite proud of not being seen when he watched her, oh but he could feel her. She was scared. He loved that. It was by far the best part.

As he passed the lantern Klaus came to a dead stop. Whipping around he stared at…at what? Klaus was certain there was something there. It was not a person of that he was sure, more of a flicker of light, then it was gone. Muttering about bad ale and the like, he stepped out once more heading for the deck above. It would be time to start his shift soon.

Emma saw Klaus in the lantern-light. He stopped, turned, looking straight at her. He looked more evil, if that was possible, but she saw him clearly. A shudder ran through her. Travis. So like Travis. She must warn Emily. Emma sat up, not yet fully awake, she screamed Emily's name. Screaming did little good; the dream had left her. Gone, and she had done nothing to warn Emily of the danger. She must find a way. She had to.

Dan hit the brakes as the car skidded to a halt by the edge of the road, they were almost at the cabin, but he was not about to let his wife's torment last one more second. By the time he jammed the car in park, Emma had calmed herself, still, her breathing came in quick raspy spurts, she was deathly white he noticed, as he flicked on the interior light, and so very quiet. Reaching across the seat he clutched her ice-cold hand against his heart, rubbing softly forcing warmth into it.

Emma fought to put her dream in perspective. Mentally cataloguing the events. She couldn't forget. She couldn't. Emily needed her. Dan's heartbeat beneath her palm. It reassured her. Her breathing slowed; her mind cleared leaving crystal clear images. Emma knew her husband was waiting for an explanation, but she couldn't. Not now. She squeezed his hand letting him know she was okay. Simultaneously, she pleaded with her eyes. She needed time.

Dan cursed knowing he'd get nothing more from her right now, he switched off the cargo light, and pulled the car back out onto the road. They sat in a pre-ordained, if not comfortable, companionable silence. Dan glanced in her direction. It was so bloody dark he couldn't judge what she was feeling. Reassured by the soft rhythmic sound of her breathing he drove on.

Pulling onto a small gravel road, the car came to a stop in front of a small cabin. The moonlight provided enough light for a quick assessment.

The lawn was low indicating it had been mowed recently. Flowerbeds encircled the cabin, but it was too dark to tell what types. Emma figured this late in the year, there may not be many to see.

A large covered verandah spanned the front, almost as large as the cabin itself, a swing beneath a large picture window, a place where lovers could sit watching the sunset and stargazing. Peaceful and picturesque were the words that came to mind. Dan had been right, she loved the place already and she hadn't even made it through the front door.

Dan watched Emma survey the landscape. This place had always been special to him. Even now he came here to escape, when he was not at sea. He never relaxed in the city; here he basked in the serenity, a piece of heaven in a hectic world. It would be a delightful place to bring their children in the years to come.

Inside the cabin, a wood fire burned warmly in the hearth giving off the most rustic, soothing, aroma. As much as she would like to have looked around, Emma knew what she must do. Sitting on the couch before the fire she removed her journal from her purse and began recording her dream. Dan, bless his heart, said not a word but turned to start unloading the car.

Dan stared at his wife, her head bent nibbling on the end of her pen, brought thoughts and feelings spiraling throughout his body. Damn he wanted her.

Tramping down his urges, Dan made his way to her, they needed to talk. He had to know why Emma had been frightened. And she was frightened.

There was something she was not telling him. The last time, this time, it was all connected. Yelling out Emily's name, her voice filled with terror, and yet Dan couldn't remember dreaming of Emily in danger.

Gently he took the journal from her hands and placed it on the rustic coffee table he and his father had made together when he was nine or ten. Scars, showing its age and use, marred the brown surface.

"Emma, something's wrong. I've known for a while. Waited. I need you to tell me, Em."

Emma looked into the loving eyes of her husband. He was her strength. If anyone could help her it was him.

"Do you remember the conversation we had before you left for Baltimore?" she hedged.

"About the dreams? Sure. But you always took pleasure in yours. You said they gave you strength. But Jesus, Em, the night I came home, and tonight was a far cry from peaceful. You were tossing and turning like a psycho was after you, and tonight was the same. You were terrified. Something has changed and I want to know what."

Emma tried looking away not yet ready to say her thought aloud. Dan wouldn't allow it; his hand grasped her chin gently but firmly. "Your dreams, Em. Tell me," he demanded, softly hoping he wasn't pushing too hard yet but knowing he must.

Emma shook her head. "You first," she said, stubbornly.

Sighing Dan nodded. "Yes, I've dreamt. As far back as I can remember." His eyes took on a glazed look as his mind traveled back in time. "They used to bother me, never terrify me. It was sort of like watching a series on TV. Though I didn't dream every night the characters were the same. A boy, I guess you could say he was the main character, he reminded me of me, looks, likes, dislikes. I was part of him; I felt what he felt, thought what he thought. Interacted as one."

"Professionals said my dreams were subconsciously recreated complete with family because of my longing for siblings. I never could understand why, if that was the case, I had not created a world of this time. The boy, Daniel, was a ship's captain like me so in a way I thought they had to be right. Still I

143

couldn't stop it and the worst part was going to be each night only to awake exhausted, almost like I'd been fighting the experience."

"But you're not tired anymore. Are you?" Emma couldn't stop herself from asking.

"No," Dan said, smiling.

"What?"

"It was simple, really. Shamus."

Emma lifted her brow in question. Dan chuckled and patted her hand.

"The old sea dog told me I was lucky to be given two lifetimes, it is not every day son, a person has the chance to correct past mistakes, or practice before he makes new ones'," Dan drawled.

"I thought about what he said, and he was right. The best part, the advice didn't cost me a dime," he said, with a wink.

Emma took her time processing everything Dan said. She had hoped he could provide a link ever since that night. She blushed as she recalled their first night together. Still to have him confirm it, all she could do was stare.

"Emma?" Dan said his worry evident.

Giving her head a shake Emma offered him a smile. "Daniel? That is what you said?"

"Yes, Daniel was the name of the kid in my dreams." Dan's mind started following the direction that Emma's led. "You can't mean, Emma it's impossible for two people to have the same dream."

Emma shook her head. "No, Dan, it's possible, I have it marked in one of the books. I'll show you tomorrow. The important thing is, that 'shared dreams' can and do exist. A researcher, Herbert Green-something-or-other, discovered cases where people have had the same dream at the same time on the same night. Only…" Emma took on a perplexed look. "Only, they usually occur with people who have known each other a while. That's why I didn't mention it before; it didn't seem possible we just met."

Dan was astounded, could it be possible. Evidently it could, but Emma was correct in the fact that they had not known each other long. Yet, the feeling the first time he met her was one of remembrance. "Em? Do you think the first night we made love something like that happened? In my dreams that night, oh damn. It is all so hazy now. I could have sworn Daniel got married. Those bloody painkillers I took. I don't know. It's fuzzy."

Emma started pacing excitedly, she felt like jumping up and down, laughing and twirling. Suddenly she stopped staring straight at Dan giving him a megawatt smile.

"That's exactly what I think! I'm not crazy!" She said gladly.

"I had a hard time remembering my dreams until recently. I started recording them in this journal." She grabbed the book off the table and flipped it open to the first page. "See here?" She pointed, sitting down. "Emily, that's the girl from my dreams, she married Daniel."

Dan took the book from her trembling hands and examined her words for himself. Even seeing it in print, it was still so un-fucking-believable; he had to read it again. Setting the book back down he gave Emma a cocky grin. "I would say that that Herbert fellow would be rather interested to hear about us." Throwing his arm around Emma he pulled her close, laughing.

Gazing into each other's eyes their laughter died immediately being replaced with a heated charge so strong it threatened to overwhelm them. Their lips met in brutally enflamed fervor adding fuel to the already raging inferno. Hands roamed as lips caressed and tongues fought a hungry duel. Too many clothes, Emma thought burning hotter with each passing moment.

Dan felt much the same way. He ached with the desire to be inside her. Nevertheless, he couldn't take her here in the middle of the living room on their wedding night. This night had to be extraordinary. Something she would remember forever. In the past, when he'd made love to her he had been controlled, gentle, so he wouldn't alarm her. He didn't want to trigger bad memories. He remembered the terror in her scream. No, he would never want to frighten her like that. To hear it, feel it…was bad enough. He'd never forgive himself if he were the cause.

Dan tempered the kiss each movement becoming softer. Their hearts still hammering he pulled his lips from hers. Emma looked at him stunned. It gave him a sense of power that he could affect a woman this way. And she him. Smiling tenderly, he ran his thumb over her swollen lip. Standing, arms under her, he hoisted her in the air, spinning once and kissing her hard; she squealed when he ran toward the bedroom down the hall.

Chapter Fourteen

Kicking the door closed, Dan lowered Emma to her feet. She was still laughing and giggling about his methods of persuasion, when he whirled her around in front of him. Leisurely he embarked on unfastening the small hidden clasps of her gown. With each one he opened he placed a kiss on her back. Soon Emma couldn't laugh, hell she couldn't even think, as the little twinges rippled through her with every touch of his mouth.

Emma sought to hold him, stroke him, kiss him return and his caresses, Dan, however, held her firmly in place torturing each newly exposed inch of her soft skin with his mouth. As the last hook slid from the eyelet, his hands roamed under the soft material over her ribs burning her flesh with each pass, driving her insane. Every movement ravished her senses trailing fire to her already hardened nipples. Gown gaping at the neck; she could see her breasts move and her nipples harden as Dan worked his magic.

Her muscles grew limp as the steadily increasing desire flooded her brain. Her head drooped forward exposing the expanse of her swan-like neck; Dan's lips skimmed the column of her throat his tongue tasting her heated flesh. Dispersing a hot moist breath over her already heated flesh rewarded him with a shudder; her nipples hardening to the point of pain. He rubbed his thumb over the tight pebbles arousing her to a higher pitch as he nipped at the base of her neck.

Her legs trembled beneath ready to give way, Dan scooped her up; depositing her on the bed before him. Emma moaned protesting the loss of contact. "Hush love, I'm not leaving." Dan gave a smile as understanding reached Emma. For all her limited experience, she understood.

Standing over her, he peeled the gown from her heated flesh. A rush of cool air surrounded her body as he slowly tugged the garment down. Watching through shuttered lashes was erotic. She lay before him like a feast waiting to be consumed. Unsure she could speak the words even if they had come to her, she reached her arms toward her husband pleading with him.

146

Slowly he began removing his clothes. One by one each article landed on the floor. Emma was having a hard time containing her anticipation. She was drinking in the sight of him, completely naked, for what seemed like the first time. Eyes open wide she stared at him with ill contained fascination. Dan almost laughed. Almost. Had his body not been in such a state of evident arousal he very well could have. However, having waited for what seemed a lifetime for this night, laughter was not in the realm of his capabilities. Forcing a smile, he lay alongside Emma leaning his head on his elbow as his fingers trailed, reheating her naked flesh.

"You are so beautiful. The body it is a treasure to behold…yours. Mine. One should never be embarrassed by that gift." Sliding his hand along her throat he cupped the nape of her neck, kissing her lips he began once again to stoke the embers. Sighing softly into his mouth she gave up all hope of thought, content to simply feel.

Her embarrassment gone; her senses soared as the expert caress of Dan's fingertips followed the curve of one breast. Wandering fingers traced, teased, flirted increasing the powerful longing growing inside her. She shifted murmuring the sound trapped between their lips.

He understood what she needed. For knowing fingers traced again, and again, their touch growing more determined. Her flesh grew heated. She arched like a kitten asking for more.

He cupped her soft mound. Sensations poured through her, melting, spreading like molten lava throughout. His wicked fingers constricted, kneading. Nerves she didn't know she possessed came alive beneath his touch as he transferred his attentions from one breast to the next. Eyes closed, she followed mindlessly as he led her from one sensual plateau to the next. Their mouths remained fused a drugging stimulation of a slow deep kiss. She was lost to the fire building within her as he teased her to tightness evoking a much deeper ache.

It was an amazing discovery that anything sexual could feel this good. Not the torment and pain that Travis and the others had caused. Or the sweet simplicity, for that is how she thought of it now, Dan's first intimate introduction had caused. This was different. So much deeper, satisfying. A complete awakening. She was becoming addicted.

Dan broke the kiss; his lips skating along her jaw line to the fragile basin beneath her ear. He didn't have to think to know what she wanted; it was as natural as breathing. Although he was at breaking point with need, he savored every delight her body offered him. They had all night. Come hell or high water he would make it last.

Emma's superficial breaths stirred the hair on his brow, stroking his skin with vines of persuasion. Taking his lips lower, gliding the length of her throat he found her pulse rapidly under her fine skin. Her small fingers were clenched in the course hair of his chest driving him on as he listened to the pounding of her heart, beating like a distant Indian drum. He thought of the heated and swollen peaks that filled his hands, finding the taut nipples, he tweaked and then slowly squeezed them until she gasped.

His lips blazed a trail across her collarbone and down over the curve of her breast. Feeling her quiver, he didn't pause but licked. Moaning, she arched into his open mouth as he sucked the pebble curling his tongue around it. She sobbed and Dan was nearly undone. She radiated in the pure pleasure of his lovemaking and if he had any doubts before about her innocence it was now confirmed. She hadn't been with anyone since her rape.

Holding her steady he devoured showing her the pleasures that awaited her. This moment would be forever etched in his mind. Knowing that it was he and only he that would teach her the darker delights. Soon she would know only gratification; eventually she would forget the pain.

Emma watched as Dan feasted on her, running her hands through his hair tugging and pulling him closer.

Catching her gaze Dan suckled harder until her fingers sprang free of his hair clutching the sheet beside her, Emma bowed off the bed, Dan took even more of her into his mouth sucking and nipping until he had her panting shattering before his eyes. Bringing his head back to hers he covered her mouth savagely claiming what she offered.

Hands were everywhere. Finding it hard to breathe, she fought for air, but Dan's questing fingers traveled lower and lower finding the hair below, parting her his fingers caressed her nub, Emma relaxed, taking the air she needed from him. Immediately she opened to him becoming soft and pliant. Inviting.

Hands blindly grasping his chest, his shoulders driving forward surveying the landscape before her. Emma struggled for more. His hair was course where her finger touched his chest, yet his skin was smooth and totally at odds with power he contained within his well-sculpted muscles. Her nails biting into his back sent Dan's brain into a tailspin.

Fingers roamed within, torturing her slippery folds, inserting a finger into her softness; her hips reacted with a natural thrust against him. Matching the rhythm of his plunging tongue heat built within her until she had to break free to breathe. Dan took the opportunity to slide back; on his knees he pressed her thighs apart settling between them.

Emma felt him leave her; mind so clouded with sensual mist she could hardly react let-a-lone speak. Raising her hands, she waited. Dan didn't come back; instead he placed his mouth upon her navel; sucking and laving moving downward, tantalizing her senses. His hot breath trailed lower and lower driving her insane, his lips closed over her, shooting her body off the bed. Grabbing her hips and holding tightly against his mouth Dan listened with pleasure as Emma screamed his name. Over and over bolts of lightning shot through her.

She yelled for him to stop and then not to stop as the emotions whirled out of control. He was pulling her down into a sexual whirlpool then tossing her back up to be carried on the wave of erotic enchantment. Boneless and unable to do anything but be led Emma let him feast. His hungry tongue lapped in and out tasting her. Nibbling her sensitive nub, he stoked the fires that touched her very core, until with a massive quake, her nectars flowed freely into his waiting mouth.

To Dan, he had never tasted anything better; she was sweet like honey and so very hot. He drank until he quenched his immediate thirst then took her mouth with his tongue.

Emma tasted herself on his lips; never had she imagined the exhilarating feeling of control the act could give her. After having all control wretched from her grasp, by this simple act Dan had given it back to her. Shared it with her.

He could wait no longer, he ached with the need to be inside her. His cock probed for her entrance; finding what it sought, he plunged in. There was no need to go slow. Coming to a stop at the entrance to her womb he bent her legs back driving deeper than ever. Her sheath closed about him caressing him as he moved within her. She was his; totally his and her body welcomed him.

An unyielding echo fed the hurricane raging inside them. A starving undeniable tide of need combined with an already frantic blaze of desire clashed creating a powerful storm. Soaring, unrestrained and unrestricted their powers came together…erupting. A tempest swirling them uncontrollably to an Eden where lovers meet.

Cries could be heard about the cabin as they found their release. Gasping for air, the two sweaty entities slowly returned to earth, exhausted but sated. Holding each other tight they rode out the rest of the little tremors together. Combined bodies locked en masse.

Dan noticed as his breathing slowed that Emma still trembled beneath him. Rising, he cursed himself. He'd been anything but gentle. So, filled with need he hadn't thought, just took. And gloried in it. Obviously, even though Emma appeared to be right there with him, she had been scared. Rightfully so, it had been a potent experience.

Disgusted he had made her cry; Dan placed his hands under her exhausted body placing her on his lap. "Don't cry love. I'm sorry. I didn't mean to frighten you. I should have been gentler. Forgive me."

That comment sent Emma's head whipping upward. Placing a fingertip on his mouth she shook her head swallowing. "You didn't scare me. You didn't hurt me. What you did do my love was show me how truly wonderous, this," her hand waved over them, "this could be. Don't change. I could never be frightened of you. Ever."

"But you're crying?" Dan whispered, softly running his hands over her face taking away the tears.

"Because you great oaf, I'm happy. I have everything I could ever need right here." She tapped him on the chest, before snuggling into his arms. She was warmed clear to her toes surrounded by his love.

Closing her eyes, she quietly thanked the little girl who throughout life has shown her the path that led to this moment. She was convinced of it now, Emily was the reason they had found each other. Closing her eyes, she fell into a dreamless sleep.

Feeling her body relax Dan relished the pressure of her breasts pushing into his chest with each intake of air. She slept. He knew her so well, yet there were certain aspects he was certain he'd never understand in a million years. And that was okay for he had no intention of leaving her for at least that. With Emma wrapped protectively in his arms, he closed his eyes, feeling like he was experiencing this night for a second time.

Chapter Fifteen

Sitting on the floor reviewing all the passages Emma had marked. Dan watched and listened; a contented smile playing about his lips. When Emma deigned to look up, he'd wink, and she'd blush. He felt like a teenager.

They stayed abed the previous day. Only getting up occasionally for food, which they fed each other in bed. It was an experience they would replay for years to come. Their lovemaking was endless. Glorious. Sating. She discovered many things about the male body she would never have known. Her train of thought had her tripping over her words and blushing fiercely. Her concentration gone for the moment, a steady condition of late, Emma set the book aside and made her way to the kitchen with Dan's chuckle in the background. He had known what she had been thinking and she felt like a kid caught with her hand in the cookie jar.

Still laughing, Dan looked up from the floor as Emma smacked a plate down on the coffee table and glared at him. Dan's arm lashed out snatching her about the waist and hauling her onto his lap, kissing her soundly. When he felt her body ease, relieved of tension, he backed off staring into her dazed expression. Now, they could eat, he thought with a smile.

"Back to work slacker," Dan said, swallowing the last of his sandwich.

Emma grabbed the *Encyclopedia of Dreams* and held it up. "I had a lot of problems finding books with content easy enough to understand. Finally, I discovered this one. It's in layman's terms, not all that medical terminology you need an interpreter for."

"So, what did you find?" Dan asked patiently, running his hand up and down her spine.

"Well not only did this book provide me with some of the information I sought but it also had an excellent reference section." Emma motioned to the remaining nine books scattered about the floor.

"At first I didn't know what to look for. I scanned the pages looking for something, anything that sounded familiar. When I came to this," she held the book open to page thirty-three so he could see the words. "This man Herbert Greenhouse, I told you about him the other night. Anyway, he did a study on shared dreams. That at least told me that some of what I experienced had been proven."

She blushed profusely and Dan knew what she was thinking. Taking pleasure in seeing his former ice queen blush like a schoolgirl he urged her on. "So, what made you think you had shared dreams?" Emma read the passage about a shared dream happening on the same night and at the same time by two or more people, before she realized what Dan was doing. Closing the book, she promptly did what any good wife would do, and hit him with it.

Dan fell over backward laughing. Gathering his wife in his arms they rolled about the cluttered room in a mock battle until she duly surrendered. Smattering kisses all over her, Dan soon had Emma feeling giddier than ever. Seizing his roaming, tickling fingers, she bit them before reprimanding him. Reaching for her book, she shook it at him. At this rate it would take months to get through the information.

Clearing her throat to cover a laugh, Emma continued, "This," she picked up a book entitled *The New World of Dreams*, "is the book Herbert wrote. It goes into some of the different case studies, although those cases revolve around people, who even if they lived far apart, knew each other. So, although my dreams meshed with yours, I couldn't relate. We hadn't met. Yet the dreams were something we've both experienced for a very long time."

"Have you found anything that would indicate why the dreams seem to be running in sequence?" Dan asked, his mind back on track. Emma remained silent a moment, consulting her notes. "No, not really. I did find however, a couple of different quotes that led me to believe it could happen," she said, hedging. "Even if I could find no current documentation. I didn't exactly have time to go back to the library." Emma gave Dan a look that told him exactly why she did not have time; he had the good sense to look a little shamefaced.

"Sorry, love. We can go to the library as soon as we get back to the city. Okay? Now tell me, what were the quotes?"

"You're forgiven. For now." Smiling, Emma scanned the annotations. "Ah, here it is, research has proved that dreams are interfaces with alternate realities. I assumed that if they were interfaces with other realities then it would be possible to somehow have a link whereby, we could view their lives in the same way that one watches a movie or reads a book. What do you think?"

"I think you may have something my brainy wife, but it would be nice to have more information on it."

"Yes, wouldn't it," Emma said, strumming her fingernails; he was still in the doghouse for their hasty departure. His wife could hold a grudge. He would do well to keep that in mind. "Was there more, you said you had 'found a couple quotes'?"

"Oh. Yes, lucidity. *Lucidity Dreaming* by Stephen Laberge suggests dreamed events can be timed in two ways. 'Regular occurrences taking place in the same time span that they would in real life', like having a cup of coffee or driving to the office. The other, 'longer ones, spanning time, are spliced together by the brain in the same manner filmed scenes are spliced to make a movie'."

"I have not figured out if this is what is truly happening to us, or if it is even possible for this type of thing to occur night after night. There's something we're missing, but without having a library close by…"

"Yes?"

"The only way to see if they are correct is to try lucid dreaming," Emma said quietly.

Dan looked pensive; he didn't like the idea of fooling with the mind. That was one of the things that first worried him about his dreams. Yet when the professionals advised him to try these methods, he ran faster than melted butter. Now Emma was asking him to do the same thing. Was it wise to fool with the mind? Well, the answer didn't matter, he loved her, and this was truly bothering her. The choice was made.

"Alright let's go over the info on Lucid Dreaming again before supper, then Em, I want us to put the books away for a while. It can't be good for the mind to keep cramming like we have been doing. Do you agree?"

Emma rewarded him with a smile that would light MCI Center during a blackout. Knowing from previous conversations how much Dan hated this sort of thing, she was shown full force how much he loved her. "Thank you," she uttered, reaching for her book on Lucid Dreams, quickly brushing her lips against his along the way.

Sitting on the front porch swing, Emma's head resting on his shoulder, an Afghan warded off the autumn chill. Kissing Emma's forehead while she slept Dan thought about all the hard work she had done. She had done a hell of a job wading through all the crap and making sense out of it. She was intelligent.

The moon and stars did nothing to dim the mesmerizing effects of mystical northern lights as they danced overhead. Emma had been exhausted. After supper they went exploring, he showed her his favorite haunts not leaving anything out. He needed her to know everything about him. It was a compulsion.

Gazing at the heavens, Dan gave thanks for this precious gift. Even after such a short span of time, she was as important to him as oxygen. If anything should happen to her. Hugging her close, he sat letting her body's essence flow through him. She was peace; with her he was truly home.

Emma could see Emily; she was walking along the railing, staring out over the ocean. Summer? How could one tell staring at the ocean, she did not know, but to her it seemed summer? There was no one around her; that made Emma nervous. Scanning the ship, she looked for Decker. He was nowhere. Daniel, she noticed, stood behind the ship's wheel, eyes straying occasionally to his wife.

Emily looked so young, why couldn't Emma remember her age? Had she ever known her age? Emma tried to fit Emily's likeness to her own in order to determine an approximant age, but it was difficult, seeing her wool skirt and petticoats, the attire made it hard to establish. Sighing forced her concentration back on track, there were more pressing matters. As a separate entity she should be able to reach out to Emily in some way. Concentrating, Emma placed a hand in front of her face. Nothing, ghost-like. Great. If can't see myself then how in the hell can I expect her to?

Well if she were a ghost maybe she'd best play the part. Calling Emily's name over and over, she hoped the girl would turn around. Her hopes were dashed for instead of Emily turning around she began to fade. Finding something within the dream to hold onto, she turned toward the sea, watching the water ripple as the ship moved ahead of its wake.

The ripples faded, like driving through a fog, then brightened in contrast. Holding onto the sight like a lifeline, Emma's gaze remained fixed in that spot. Soon the waters cleared. She had managed to maintain lucidity. Moving like a celestial being, away from the ship's rail Emma went in search of Emily. Where had the damn girl gone? Floating about the deck Emma searched. Emily was nowhere.

Hovering toward the hatch she decided to go below, maybe Emily went to the cabin. The hatch was closed. How in the hell could she open it when she couldn't see her hands? After a moment Emma scolded herself, you silly twit, she thought angrily, it's a dream, damn it you control it. Now open the bloody door. Fighting with herself was giving Emma a headache but she was too close to give up now. She had to find Emily.

Below, the corridor was dim; Emma made her way to the Captain's cabin. Opening the door would scare the bejesus out of Emily. What to do? Shrugging she stepped up to the door. Well it worked for Casper hadn't it? As she was about to walk through the door, a shiver skittered down her spine. Something or someone was close. Eyeing the hall Emma saw Klaus duck into his regular hiding space. Creep. He was so much like Travis it was uncanny. She must warn Emily.

With that she breathed deep and stepped through. Shuddering at the odd sensation Emma stopped. Emily sat at the table, her head in hands, the weight of the world on her shoulders.

Being separated from Emily, Emma couldn't tell what she was feeling, but she knew instinctively, it was bad. What happened to the laughing carefree girl? She needed to know. Relaxing Emma allowed herself to become one with Emily. The girl shivered on contact almost as though she knew someone was with her. Her breath hitched before she relaxed.

Emily was worried; she kept telling herself it was all in her mind. Who would want to torment her is such a way? It had been months since they left port. Constantly throughout that time, someone stalked her. It was frightening beyond anything she'd ever known. Ten months. Each day feeling the eyes upon her. She was so jittery it was getting harder and harder to keep the truth from Daniel.

Then there was the voice, telling her to heed her feelings. She was not a coward. Had never been a coward and she was not about to let some foolish nightmare haunt her. That's what she kept telling herself, but she didn't believe it. Not for a moment. Was it any wonder with how nervous she'd been, she hadn't conceived? Would she fail at that as well?

"Tell him. Tell Daniel." Words replayed in Emily's mind. She let out a bitter laugh. Yeah right. Tell him what? That his wife of less than one year is crazy? She chased him, longed for him, planned and schemed until she had him; now she was ready for bedlam. "Daniel, honey, I love you, but I am sorry I belong in a sanitarium." Feeling worse for her pouting Emily angrily started pacing about the room.

Emma had to reach her; it was harder than she realized it would be when she re-entered Emily's mind. Being a part of someone else took away her ability to think and act as a single unit. Emily's thoughts and fears threatened to over-ride what she came to do. Weeding through the marshland of Emily's thoughts, Emma fought them aside.

"Listen to me." Emma words were transferred to Emily. "Someone's watching you. It's true. Beware. Tell Daniel." Emily's head shook back and forth at the thought of troubling Daniel over a matter she was well capable of taking care of. "No. You'll need help. Daniel must get him off the ship."

Emily was confused. Thoughts were flying about in her head uncontrollably. Get whom off the ship? Who was watching her?

"Emily, you do know. It's Kla…"

"No! No damn you no!"

"Emma love wake up it's getting cold out here we should go inside. Sorry I startled you. I wouldn't have woken you, but you had a death-grip on the blanket. Shhh. Let's go inside." Emma couldn't help the tears of frustration streaming down her cheeks.

Dan had a feeling something more, than him waking her, had her upset. But what? Christ, it was too much. Now her dreams even had her crying. Once they got back to the city, he'd seek professional help.

Carrying his wife, he gently lay her down on the bed. Emma was awake but still crying. Going into the bathroom Dan took a little round pill out of the bottle he'd brought from the apartment. Hopefully it would help her sleep more peacefully. Emma had changed and her golden hair now fanned outwards on the pillowcase. If it wasn't for the tear streaks marring her complexion. Dan would have wondered if it was all in his head. It wasn't. Handing her the little blue pill he placed a glass of water in her hand.

"A sleeping pill, I don't want it. I can't stand them. That's why there was some left," Emma said, shaking her head.

"Please Em. You need some sleep." The last was said with a smile and a wiggle of his dark brows. Emma's mood shifted a smile tugging at her lips. Opening her hand, she took the pill washing it down with a sip of water before placing the glass on the nightstand.

"That's my girl," Dan said, moments later climbing into bed and settling Emma in the crook of his arm. "Let's get some sleep." Kissing her forehead in a paternal gesture that threatened to bring Emma's tears back, he switched off the light, soon succumbing to sleep. Even with the sleeping pill slowly hazing her mind Emma was not quite ready to give up the fight. She had reached Emily tonight. She'd done it. Moreover, she remembered every detail clearly.

She should have jotted it in her journal? Would she remember come morning? Going to the living room was out of the question, her whole body was numbing. Yawning she closed her heavily lidded eyes and fell into a deep sleep.

At the helm, sun descending on the western horizon, Daniel marveled at the sight that never ceased to amaze. The sea was calm, the trip relatively uneventful. They had made some profitable purchases; the remaining space would be filled from the ports on their way back.

Emily had surprised him, taking to ship life with the ease of a born sailor. She adhered to his rules never being alone never out of sight. She spent an enormous amount of time in the cabin. She would come above only to return after an hour or so in the sun. Her creamy skin had deepened, still creamy and oh so soft, but golden; the shade making her hair lighter, more vibrant.

She seemed distracted, depressed. Daniel assumed it was due to not conceiving, he had to make her realize that although he wanted children, it was not essential. They were young, she ten and eight, he twenty and three; they had nothing but time to make their dreams come true.

Had she conceived; they would have already turned back. This wedding trip was more than most. They had a lot of time to discover one another in bed and out. Heat jolted to his groin. She had always been an outgoing personality, even though he had not been interested in her romantically, she drew him, like so many others, with her sunshine. Now, she was as addictive as the sea. In the bedroom she fulfilled his fantasies and more. He never dreamed of having a wife so uninhibited. Shifting couldn't ease the tightness below, sighing he motioned to his first mate and gladly relinquished the wheel.

Donavan smiled knowingly. Daniel's lust had not faded with marriage of that he was certain. If anything, it had grown. Served the young buck right, Donavan thought with a chuckle.

Daniel stopped in the companionway; from nowhere, Klaus appeared in the hall. "You. What are you doing down here? It is not your shift."

Klaus looked at his Captain forcing the snarl off his face, "Right ye are Capt'n, was just seeing on somet'ing for Donavan, I's headed back up top now I am."

"Right. Carry on then. Be warned, I find you shirkin' your duties and I'll leave you at the next port without qualm."

Klaus nodded, the only outward sign he'd heard. Watching him scramble up the stairs to the hatch, Daniel shrugged. Good crewmembers were hard to find. Klaus joined them on his last journey off the coast. Like so many others signing on late in life, one wondered what had forced them to take up life on the sea.

Emily turned at the sound of the door. Oh dear, she had bolted the door when she came in. Daniel would want to know why. Thinking of something to tell him, she walked to door unfastening the bolt.

"Sorry, I didn't mean to lock you out. I was however contemplating a sponge bath. Care to join me?"

Daniel immediately forgot the question strumming through his mind grabbed his wife pulling her hard against his chest and kissed her soundly. Emily's knees buckled and Daniel anchored her against him. His arousal pressed through her skirt and petty coats; she glowed, knowing the power she wielded. Breaking the kiss Daniel initiated, Emily raised a questioning brow. In answer Daniel threw his wife over his shoulder and headed for bed, with Emily giggling all the way.

Hours later, Emily lay in her husband's arms completely sated. Her head rested on his chest while her fingers traced patterns around his nipple. She loved him so very much. How could she tell him? She couldn't. Putting bad thoughts from her mind, she kissed his tight nipple. Daniel's hand was smoothing Emily's hair, when he thought of the locked door. If she were worried about someone coming upon her while she was having her bath wouldn't she have come into the bedroom and locked that door instead? Something wasn't right with her story.

Emily noticed the frown creasing Daniel's brow; she hoped he was not contemplating the locked door. She was sure she'd put his mind at ease, among other things, she reflected with a satisfied smile.

"Should I ask what has put that lovely smile on my wife's adorable face?" Running his finger over her curving lips, he smiled his hand gripped the nape of her neck steeling for another drugging kiss. Stopping just before their lips touched, "I love you so. You'd tell me if there was something wrong?" Without giving her time to answer his mouth closed over hers.

His hand kneading the tender flesh of her breast, he had paid homage to those glorious globes again and again. Still it wasn't enough. Increasing the intensity of the kiss, he ran a finger around her sensitive aureole; the nipple hardened. Experienced fingers teased and tweaked; his lips traveled her jaw line to the pulse thumping erratically in her neck. Taking his time, he kissed every inch before his mouth reached its destination and closed about the nub sucking it into his hot hungry mouth.

Emily's mind raced throwing back her head she arched up forcing him to take more of her. Never, would she get enough. When his hand found her mons time for thought was at and end. She could only feel. Fingers gently parting the folds to her woman's center he found her clitoris. Squeezing it in the manner as his mouth squeezed her nipple, Emily cried out, "Yes, Daniel, oh my God yes!"

Trembling with the force of the building excitement it did not take long after Daniel's finger entered her for body to convulse. He knew her orgasm was near, he moved quickly. Wanting to be inside her feeling the force of the waves, he parted her thighs and plunged in, burying his sword to the hilt in her warm sheath. Putting his hungry mouth back to work on her already inflamed nipple he sucked hard then gently bit as he pushed himself even further.

Rocking back and forth he fed the storm's power until with a burst of raging passion Emily shuddered, exploding around him. Pushing her legs farther apart he came out only to take a final deep thrust in. With a growl he let loose his seed into her womb. In a sweaty heap they lay joined, falling into and exhausted sleep.

The sun was pouring through the cabin window when Emma woke. Dan was asleep beside her. She was hot and sticky, though she could not figure out why. If Dan had made love to her surely, she would remember? Chalking it up to the sleeping pill, she rose from bed.

Dan hadn't stirred while Emma was in the shower. She dressed quietly and made her way to the kitchen for a much-needed cup of coffee. She still felt fuzzy. She'd taken only one pill. It didn't seem possible they weren't that strong. Maybe it was like Dan said…she'd had a hectic couple of weeks. Her body needed a break.

Switching on the pot Emma's mind replayed her dream the previous night. She remembered bits and pieces but was unsure how long she'd retain them. Getting her journal, she immediately recounted her dream. Klaus's face flitted across her consciousness. She gave an involuntary shiver as she allowed her mind, for the first time in a very long time, to drift back.

Chapter Sixteen

St. Charles, Seven years ago

It was a glorious sunny day. Emma sat under Goliath, a huge oak tree, outside the school. Over the past three years this oak had been her safeguard against the school masses. Most hung out in the cafeteria or closer to the smoking areas just left of the south exit. As soon as the bell rang, Emma grabbed her lunch and books and headed for the tree.

Leaning against it she studied for an hour until her Chemistry test. She'd written her English exam this morning and was confident she would once again achieve honors. That was one thing to be said for the lack of a social life, there was never a lack of study time.

She should have been used to it by now. Meeting and maintaining friends had never been her strong suit. Andre, her brother, had always been her best friend. They were two years apart, and when he started college, Emma coped well beside the old oak. She drove to the college often, seeing Andre and using the library.

He'd meet her and sign her in under his student pass. After a couple hours with him and the books she headed back home. It was a good thing her parents had given her a car for her birthday. Although she had yet to turn eighteen, it came in handy. Driving her to the college two or three times a week had been an incentive for them.

Emma's two younger sisters, the twins Chrissie and Mandy, had already proven their social skills would not lead them to find seclusion away from the norm. They were ten, so much younger than her and Andre they seemed more like nieces then sisters. Shortly after she'd turned two, her mother went back to work, wanting a career, or so she thought. It lasted almost seven years, until she became pregnant with the twins.

Now her mother was like Martha Stewart. Always there, cooking cleaning being the ideal homemaker, with no more longing to return to work. If Emma had been a normal teenager, that would have been a problem. As it stood, she really had nothing of consequence to keep from her mother's prying curiosity. Emma worried about what life could be like for her sisters once they reached their teens.

Glancing at her watch, she noticed it was time to make her way to the lab. Gathering her books, she began walking back to the school. Passing through the smoking room, out of her way, but a daily ritual non-the-less, head down so as not to be noticed, Emma walked quickly without appearing to be running and listened. She heard the familiar laugh…It was Travis MacPherson, a hunk who she had fell in love with, when he first transferred in.

It didn't take him long to make captain of the Ogres football team making him totally unreachable as far as Emma was concerned. Not that he would have ever been reachable. She never dated, never had a boyfriend. Part of it could have been that her head was either in the books or the clouds, but either way Emma hadn't felt comfortable with the idea. Her mother said she'd know when she was ready.

Besides, the captain always dated the head cheerleader, and that was Heather Clement, a tall, beautiful brunette. He really couldn't do much better. Staying true to the rules of propriety among jocks, they had been going steady for a year and a half. Rumor had it they were going to get hitched after high school. Some wondered why they were not going to college, but most were smart enough to know Travis had gotten Heather pregnant.

Thoughts rolled through her head and before long she'd made her way to the lab, walking in she found her desk waiting for the tests to be passed around.

"Put your pens down, time's up. You may set your papers on my desk on your way out. Thank you, I hope you have a great summer. Remember should you have any questions, those of you who will be following with Chemistry in college, please feel free to drop by the school at any time. I will always be here to help a former student." The bell rang ending Mrs. Harrison's speech.

Getting up Emma set her paper on the teacher's desk before exiting the classroom.

In the parking lot, Travis flagged her car down, as she was about to leave. Coming over to the driver's side of her car, he smiled making him even more gorgeous. Emma was dumbfounded; he'd spoken to her off and on over the past two years, but always away from school and always alone. Looking about, Emma noticed some of the other football cronies hanging about and wondered why Travis would be coming to her out in the open like this.

"Hi, where you headed?" He leaned into the window. Closely.

Emma cleared her throat. "Did you need something? I'm in a hurry." Emma seen what looked like anger cross Travis face before he covered it with a come-hither smile.

"To the college? Again? You spend an awful lot of time there," he said, nonchalantly.

"Yes…well, it does have a better library than most. I still have some more exams to study for. You?"

"I have a few more too," he said and shrugged nonchalantly. Which he didn't of course, if rumors were true, he would be married. "I guess you heard Heather can't make it to the prom?"

Emma was puzzled, why would she care, even if she did know? Nothing was making sense and she could feel the eyes of the others on her little yellow Geo. She wanted to get going.

"Travis, I really do have to leave. I am sorry about Heather. I hope you enjoy yourself at the prom anyway. There are sure to be others there without dates."

"That's what I was wondering about."

"What, I am sorry you're losing me."

"Well, it wouldn't do for the captain of the football team to show up without a date. I'd like you to come with me."

"Sorry Travis I don't date; you'll have to find yourself another girl." The statement was out of Emma's mouth before she'd even processed it. Travis the love of her life was asking her to the prom. She was a fool. A complete and utter imbecile, why in the hell had she said no? Travis's face fell. The look was so out of place on his handsome face, Emma almost started laughing.

Putting his hands into the pockets, he looked down at the ground. "Come on Em, I thought we were friends. I don't want to have to go alone and there is no one else I can ask. You know Heather, she will have a bird if I ask anyone else." Emma knew exactly what he'd meant by the last comment. Heather would get upset if he asked one of the other girls because they were popular. Every one of them at some point in time had designs on Travis. As for the nerd crowd well, that would look too obvious. Emma at least was pretty, she knew that much, but as far as Heather was concerned Emma didn't stand a chance with Travis and that thought angered her.

Sitting on the swing in the back-yard tracing letters in the sand with the toe of her shoe, Emma could not believe she'd agreed to go. She never went out. Never. She hadn't bothered going to the college, calling Andre as soon as she got home then locked herself in her room until supper.

After cleaning up she came outside. The twins were at a sleep over and her mother was driving them. Her father wasn't home. All was quiet except her peace of mind. Kicking at the dirt, lost in thought, she hadn't heard her mother return.

"Want to talk about it?" She pulled at the grass in the lawn.

"Oh, Mom, I don't know, thank you, but..." her mom's head snapped up trapping Emma's forlorn gaze.

"Listen here, young lady, I may be old, but I was a teenager once. Give me a shot you may be surprised. I'm smarter than I look." That caused Emma to laugh. It felt good like being released from imprisonment.

"Okay, Mother, you win. But I reserve the right to determine your intellect level," Emma chirped giggling.

Her mother looked at her, love and mischief in her eyes. "All right smarty-pants. Go on and tell me but remember in order to judge you have to be smarter than the subject." With a big grin and a wink her mother sat silently waiting for her to speak.

"I was asked to the prom." Emma relayed everything that happened and all her anxieties about her answer before she finally fell silent. Her mother took her time contemplating what to say, Emma hopped off the swing nervously. "Forget it. It was silly; I'll just tell him I reconsidered."

"Emma, hold up."

Emma stopped and turned.

"Come back here, sit and listen. If you really don't want to go, fine, call him but remember this; you only have one prom, do you really want to throw away the opportunity? Travis may not be your boyfriend; maybe it's better that way. He will stay beside you, his friendship, if he is indeed a friend, will guide and protect you. Do you trust him?"

"I think I do; I just don't know him well enough to be sure. I do like him. I have liked him for a very long time. He was always out of my reach, if you know what I mean?"

"You have always held yourself back. I realize it has been hard for you, but if you like this boy, then go. There will be chaperones there. If it gets ugly you can call me, I'll come and get you. Okay?"

Emma thought, what her mother said made sense. She may never have a chance like this again. If she went maybe it would give her confidence a boost, a trial run before college. Emma nodded.

"We'll go into town tomorrow and buy a dress. Prom night's a week after your birthday, if we can't find something special enough, we will order it. Don't worry all will be fine. You'll see."

That decided, Emma's mother sauntered back into the house, Emma following close behind. She was still apprehensive but at least she'd made a choice.

Emma couldn't believe prom night arrived and she hadn't backed out. Sitting in the living room waiting for Travis to arrive her father looked at her with pride. "You're gorgeous darling. Your date will be outshined."

"Thanks Dad, but it's not a date. I am just the stand in for Heather," Emma said, without remorse.

"Maybe he'll take one look and say Heather who?"

Emma thought of the reason behind which Travis was to get married; shaking her head in a silent no she let her father's statement lie. There was no point in telling her parents why there would never be anything more than friendship between her and Travis.

The doorbell rang, Emma jumped up to answer the door. Her mother waved her back down. Her father answered the door. Emma groaned inwardly. A few minutes later her father stood in the living room beside a very handsome Travis. He was wearing a tux with tails, and deep purple cummerbund. Emma swallowed a nervous lump as Travis walked to her.

Her palms were sweating. It was a good thing the dress her mother obligingly picked out was old fashioned complete with the long white gloves, otherwise Emma would have looked around for something to wipe her hands on before she touched him.

Taking her hand, Travis felt triumph surged. Emma was even more magnificent than he'd imagined. She'd caught his eye when he started at St. Benedicts, but she'd always looked down on everyone at school, probably because of the college guy she was dating. I don't date. Her words came rushing back to him. The simple truth was she thought she was too good for the guys in high school.

Her dress was old fashioned, burgundy; the tight cut low neckline pushed her breast up. Travis felt the tightening in his crotch. He'd been looking forward to this for a long time. Careful planning had made it come about; nevertheless, before this night was through, he'd show her just what she's been missing.

"You look fantastic," Travis said, without any hint as to what was going on in his head. "Shall we go?" Emma nodded. Saying good night to her mother and father and headed for the door.

Travis pulled his jeep into the drive. "You don't mind, do you?" he said, referring to his letterman jacket. "The others will have theirs, and besides it will keep you warm later. You're a sport Em, why don't you come in; see how the other half lives," he said, with a chuckle.

Emma peered at the dark house; something didn't feel right.

Seeing the doubt on Emma's face, Travis added, "Don't worry. Mom and Dad are home; they've probably hit the sack. Come on, don't be chicken."

"All right," Emma said, hesitantly. Slowly she followed Travis into the house. "Stay close, I'll turn a light on once we get to my room, so it won't wake my parents." Grabbing her hand, he pulled her up the staircase. Emma shuddered hoping he wouldn't notice and call her a chicken again.

Inside his room the door slammed shut. Emma jumped. "Travis what's…" before she finished the lights were on. Travis stood in front of her sneering. Beside him stood three others from the football team, Buba, Jay Jacobson and Roger Horvath, Emma looked at them then back to Travis. "Travis?" her panic made it came out as more of a squeak. His sneer turned into a grim smile, which matched the faces of everyone in the room.

Emma's darted for the door but before she could get any further, Bubba, the biggest of the lot, the biggest in the whole damn school for that matter, grabbed her about the waist and held tight. Kicking and fighting for all she was worth Emma still could not break the hold he had on her.

"I'll scream you son of a bitch, let me go!"

The back of Travis's hand smacked against her mouth; her head snapped back into Bubba's wall of a chest. Emma could taste the blood pooling in her mouth. Her jaw hurt and her teeth ached she kept kicking but she couldn't get away.

"Go ahead, you little slut! Scream. No one will hear you. There's no one here but us."

"Your parents," Emma said, hoping but knowing they weren't home. Travis spotted the realization in her eyes.

"That's right Emma they've been gone for fucking week already. They won't be back for at least another. Bubbadamn it...take her to the bed. Hold her down. She's going to end up connecting with one of us yet."

Emma felt herself being hauled backward toward the bed. She wasn't going to make it easy for them. She'd fight and when she got her chance she'd get away. She just had to wait. Closing her mouth against all she wanted to yell at the bastards, she continued twisting and turning trying to break Buba's hold.

She felt the mattress beneath her, Bubbagrabbed her wrists pulling her arms above her head he placed them under his knees securing her. Travis and the others towered over her at the end of the bed. Emma kicked out with all her might but laughing Travis dodged her foot. Soon Jay and Roger had her ankles effectively pinning her to the bed.

Having nothing left with which to fight, Emma lay panting trying to catch her breath, trying to think. Travis's finger ran over the tops of her breasts just under the neckline of her gown, she tried to squirm away. He laughed; taking his hand he pulled the neckline down below her breasts baring them for all to see. "You bastard!" Emma spat.

"Now, Emma how can you say such a thing. I have parents," Travis chirped, and the others laughed.

"You know what I mean. Now let me go, you prick!" Emma yelled.

"Tsk, Tsk, Tsk, I know you want it, almost as much as I do. Lay back, relax we'll show you what you're missing with those college guys."

"I don't know what you're talking about, you creep, I don't want this, and I have never wanted this!"

"I've seen you Emma. Followed you. I saw you in his arms, hugging him."

"Who? Damn you, you don't know what the fuck you're talking about, I haven't been with anyone!" Emma said, frantically trying to make sense of everything. Travis's fingers ran over her nipple. She felt repulsed, how could she have ever liked this guy? Twisting her nipple painfully Travis said, "Your lying Emma, we all saw you. You're a three-time-a-week slut. You like this don't you?" Squeezing her painfully again.

"No, no…Travis listen you've got it …" Emma said trying to block out the pain and keep the tears of frustration from falling down her face. "The guy I meet, I don't know what you saw, but you're wrong. I go there to study. The only guy I meet is my brother. That's how I get into the library. I use his student pass."

Travis snorted in disbelief. The others remained quiet.

Reaching into his pocket of his suit pants, Travis retrieved a knife. Waving it, he pressed a button and with a click a long silver blade sprung forth. Shaking her head back and forth screaming anything she could think of to stall him. Grabbing the hem of her new gown, he poked the knife through the fabric. Hearing the rip Emma stilled. He'd torn it up to the waistline. Running the cold blade over her flat stomach, he inserted the knife under her pantyhose. God was he going to cut her? She was almost relieved when she heard the knife cut through the nylon and not her skin. She didn't want to die. Everything else she could cope with.

His hands were on her poking and prodding, he wasn't gentle, but Emma would not give him the satisfaction of crying out. Biting her tongue, she looked away. Forcing her mind away from the events that were taking place. Capturing her chin in his hand he forced her to look at him, to see him. Fighting against the repulsion she was feeling she glowered with all the hate in her.

He stood there stroking his cock, talking to her telling how much she would enjoy it, how she wanted it. Jay and Roger pulled her legs farther apart and before Emma could scream Travis came into her. She felt like she'd been broken in two. Her mind fogged. "God damn!" She heard one of them say in shock, "she is a fuckin' virgin…you said she was a slut Travis, you said she deserved this. Travis damn you! What the fuck have you done?"

Travis stilled for a moment inside Emma before he began trusting back and forth harder and harder, Emma did cry out this time, she couldn't help it. She was so sore it felt like her insides were on fire. "Shut up, you asshole!" Travis grunted between thrusts. "I have done nothing, the bitch begged for this. You know it as well as I do. You can't back out now. It's done. The plan remains as it was before. We all have a go, that way no one squeals. Got it!"

Emma heard the words but could not comprehend their meaning. She was being called away. She saw a little girl smiling as she played on a swing. She saw the sun and heard the ocean waves. "You enjoy this don't you, yes, I knew you would." It was Travis his face inches from hers…he was kneeling beside her…How could that be? Emma still felt ripped apart though her mind couldn't grasp how Travis could be in both places at the same time.

"Travis she's bleedin' real bad man. Maybe I should stop?"

"Bubba, for fuck sakes…just finish already!"

"Your name, child?" Emma opened her eyes, blinking against the bright lights. She was so sore. "What happened?" She didn't realize she'd spoken out until she received an answer. "We were hoping you could tell us." There was a long pause before the voice continued. "Dear, I'm Rita, your nurse. Do you know who you are? Can you tell me your name?"

"Emily Claremore. I am Emily Claremore." Emma didn't know why she responded like she did. "Where am I?" The nurse picked up her hand, she flinched, and the nurse immediately released it. "You're at Mercy General, Emily, an EMT found you in the parking lot." Emma didn't say anything everything that was running through her mind couldn't be voiced, not to her, not to anyone. Upper most in her mind was what time it was and how she could get home without anyone knowing what happened to her.

The Mercy General was in La Plata that much she knew from her visits to Andre. She couldn't call him though. He would want to know what happened to her. No one could ever know. She remembered the threat Travis had made about her little sisters and she didn't doubt for a minute that he would make good.

"What time is it?" she asked at last. "A little after one. If you are up to it there are some officers from LPPD here to see you. The doctor called them shortly after you were brought in and he'd seen that you had been raped, but he wouldn't allow them in until you were awake."

Emma sat up only to be gently pushed back onto the pillows. "No, it's okay you're fine, or at least you will be. The doctors gave you a few stitches and prescribed a pill to ward off pregnancy." My God she'd never even thought of being pregnant how stupid of her. She had to think. No police. Leave. Then figure out what to do.

Managing to elude the police, she left the hospital in her hospital gown. She found a phone. Calling home, she told her mom that she was staying at a friend's place for the next week. A week would buy her the time she needed for her face to heal. She didn't want to make the next call but there was no longer a choice. She couldn't go home, and she didn't have anywhere else to go. Quickly she dialed Andre's number before she had second thoughts.

Chapter Seventeen

Dan awoke, to find Emma's place empty and cold. What time had she gotten up? Getting up he showered and dressed. Now, he stood at the end of the hall watching his wife at the table in the kitchen. Her head was bowed, chin resting in the palm of her hand; deep in thought. Too deep in thought. Shaking his head, he walked up behind her and gently placed a kiss on the back of her neck.

"Good morning. Are you hungry?" she asked, as though nothing was wrong.

"A little but I can wait. Right now, I want to hold and kiss my lovely wife." He returned. Taking her hands, he pulled her up out of the chair kissing her soundly before sitting and pulling her down into his lap. "Now, that's the way to start the day, better than Maxwell House," he stated, with a smile.

"I have never before had the chance to experience a true good morning kiss with an actual husband, so I am afraid to pass judgment. I may just need further collaboration with said specimen," Emma said.

"Specimen. Am I?" Dan returned kissing her again this one much more intense that the last. When at last he released her, it took her a moment before she could remember her own name. Leaning back into Dan's protective hold she gathered her scattered wits. God; how she loved him. He was everything good. He was her strength, her courage and protector. She felt safe in his arms. He would help her. "Dan?"

"Yes, my love." He kissed her head. Emma swallowed trying to find the bravado to go on. "Something is wrong with Emily." She waited to see if he would reply. When he didn't, she continued. "In my dreams, I feel her fear, someone's stalking her Dan. I know it. I have been trying the lucid dreaming techniques, and last night before you awoke me, I reached her."

Dan was silent. Even though the dreams came to him as well he still found it hard to believe all this stuff about lucid dreaming. Contacting someone in a dream. Was it possible? Dan didn't know anything for sure, but if his wife needed him to believe, he'd believe. "How do you know?" he said, at last.

Emma thought for a moment choosing her words carefully. Dan knew about the rape she'd suffered but he did not know the details.

"After I turned eighteen, the night of my senior prom. The rape. The man in my dreams, the one who's watching Emily, this is going to sound crazy, but Dan he is like him. I've felt his intentions. I swear it is just like Travis!"

Emma's pulse had sped up and she was panting as though she'd run a mile, so this is what has been scaring her. Placing his hands on the back of her neck, she was so full of tension he began massaging. Slow easy movements, willing her muscles to relax.

"Are you sure? I mean, of course you're sure, but Emma could this entity in a…oh hell this is hard. Could another thing from a dream harm another thing in that same dream? And if it could and I do mean if, then what bearing could that possibly have on the real world?"

"I don't know. All I know for sure is that this guy is after her. This girl, imaginary or not, has come to mean a great deal to me over the years; maybe it's a manifestation because she was there for me," Emma said, remembering clearly the night she was attacked. Emily had pulled her away from the pain. "I have to be there for her. I was unable to help myself back then, but I am stronger now. Maybe my subconscious is throwing this into the mix so I will finally have the chance to avenge what happened."

Emma clutched her temples. "What is it? What's a matter?" Dan asked, concern overshadowing all else for the moment. When she did not answer him, he turned her in his lap so he could see her face, only with her head bent it was unclear. With his knuckles, he lifted her chin, he could see the pain etched in her face. The lines of tension under her eyes, his worry, made him snap. "Emma, damn it!" he said, flinching but did not answer him.

"Sweetheart I am sorry. You've got me so bloody worried; at least tell me you're okay?" Her face cleared leaving no trace of the pain she had been in, yet he hadn't imagined it. He couldn't have.

Emma came back; saw the look of worry on Dan's face. She didn't know how to explain what happened just now.

Her mind just left.

It had happened before, but usually what she sensed made her relax. Not this time. This time she felt…what did she feel? Hurt? Not hurt feeling but hurt physically or was it the fear of being hurt physically? How could she begin to explain that to Dan?

"I'm okay, really. Just a bit of a headache but your magic fingers have done the trick. It's gone. I'm fine now. Thank you." With that she placed a kiss upon his lips. "How about brunch? It's almost noon. I for one am starving. Must be all that extracurricular activity we've been doing lately." Rising quickly before he could see her blush she headed for the fridge.

Dan let her go, analyzing. She was hiding something or else she never would have resorted to sexual innuendos. She was still too innocent for that as her blush proved. They'd go fishing today he decided; get her out of the house and away from those damn books, memories, dreams and severe emotions, at least for a day. It would give her, them, time to recoup. Hopefully a little fun was all she needed. A day completely worry-free.

After lunch Emma packed sandwiches into a hamper while Dan went to hunt down the fishing rods. Deed accomplished; he entered the kitchen to find the hamper sitting closed on the table; there was no sign of his wife. "Emma?" he called. She emerged in the hall a bounce in her step and a smile on her face.

"I didn't know how long we would be, I wanted to make sure we had some more clothing with us in case it got colder." She held up a couple of sweaters and a blanket. "That's my brainy wife, always thinking," he teased. It had been a relatively warm November thus far, but you never knew, anything could happen. The wind off the water would cast a chill in the air once the sun went down. Taking hand and hamper, Dan led her out the door.

Outside the sun streamed down on them. The splash of vitamin D renewed the vigor in his wife's step. Eyes clear and sparkling, mind unencumbered. He wanted to see her this way forever. Longer if possible. Following behind, Dan playfully slapped her bottom as she slowed to step over a fallen tree. Not one to be out gunned, Emma quickly stuck out her foot as Dan arms fully loaded, blankets hamper, and rods couldn't see. For a second Dan lay flat; then the race was on. Supplies forgotten, he raced down the path gaining on Emma, who was laughing and screaming zigzagging all the way.

Entering a small clearing by the river, Dan leapt tackling his wife to the ground. Her screech was piercing as he tickled, and she squirmed.

"Now, see here giggle-puss," he growled. "I hope you know our lunch and everything else is back by that tree, assuming some hungry critter doesn't get it before I do."

Standing, laughing he mumbled something about women knowing their places. Emma doubled over with laughter and writhed about on the soft grass.

She was still trying to get a hold of herself when her husband came back, supplies in hand. "Worry wart," she exclaimed.

Dan shook his head, his wife of not even a week had him acting like a schoolboy, and he loved it. The best part was seeing her turn into a giddy schoolgirl. It was like one of those Master Card commercials where they're always stating a price for everything. Well this was undeniably priceless.

Dan lay next to his sleeping wife. She had done well with her extracurricular activities tonight he reflected. Her inhibitions were now overruled by her curiosity. That was just fine with him. He liked having her curious. Very, very much he thought with a smile.

Fishing proved fun; Emma was a natural. Throwing back what they no longer needed, they headed back. Emma enjoyed a hot bath while he prepared supper. Dan laughed. She'd catch them, she'd eat them, but…she'd never, ever clean them…cooking was negotiable. Dan grinned wolfishly; he would find more interesting things to negotiate.

How long would this freedom last? Sighing, his thoughts turned inward. He could not get Emma to leave the books alone. She showed him documentation on lucidity and dream control till his control threatened to snap. What could he do? There had to be a way to get past this. It was eating her up inside.

Overtaxing his mind to point that he could no longer think, he settled down deep into the mattress and immediately fell asleep.

Daniel was standing at the rail with Emily, a small quarter-moon shone in the night sky as Dan looked on. His arm about her shoulders they stood watching the water ripple from the ship's passage.

I wish Emma could see this, Dan thought. I'll have to take her sometime. It would not be the same as it was here, now, for the ships of today did not have the ambiance they did back in Daniel's day. Sighing with contentment he pondered Emma and what she'd told him earlier in the day.

Someone was after Emily. Could it be true? Lucid Dream? Dream control? Talking and acting out in one's dream? It all seemed so implausible. Feeling a little foolish Dan decided he would give it a try. What would it hurt? It is not like anyone would ever know. Okay, mind made up he stood there for a moment…how?

Dan noticed a movement in the shadows, it was a man, he could tell from the build. Then giving his head a shake in way of a reprimand, idiot he thought, of course it's a man. In this era women didn't frequent ships like this one. He was floating toward the movement. He had to get a better look. Why would a crewmember stand back in the shadows like that? He was up to no good that was for sure.

Could that be the one Emma mentioned? The man who seemed to terrify her. He wasn't large, but he was gruff looking. Yet back then all sailors were gruff looking; it came with the territory. Even with the slice of moon, it was dark making it hard to tell, dark hair…mussed, unshaven nothing unusual there. Though there was something about him Dan didn't like.

Emma never told him what her rapist looked like and he could only imagine her fear. His mind kept going back to thought. What he wouldn't give to bash the cocksucker's head in. Just the fact Emma had told him a man aboard ship made her relive the terror of her rape was enough of an incentive. Not knowing what came over him he snatched the guy by the shirt collar and let fly with a right hook. The guy staggered back and fell knocking over a barrel.

The commotion drew the attention of Captain Daniel who came running to investigate. Spotting Klaus laid out flat over the barrel, he searched the area. Seeing nothing he grabbed the sailor by the collar.

"You bastard, there is no drinking on my ship! You're off at the next port!"

"Donavan! Donavan, get over here now damn it!"

Donavan arrived in short order, "Yes Captain?"

"Take him, lock him in the hold. He has obviously been drinking. I want him off my ship at the next port."

"Aye, aye Capt'n," Donavan answered, taking Klaus by the arms, he escorted him toward the hold.

"I'm sorry Darling. Would you like to stay up a while longer or go below?" Daniel said, taking his wife in his arms. She was shivering. Kissing her cheek, he muttered, "You're cold. Let's go below. I'll warm you up." He wiggled his brows at her. Emily didn't giggle or say a word but obediently followed him to their cabin.

Dan came out of his hiding spot, though why he was hiding he hadn't a clue. No one had seen him not even that guy, 'Klaus' that's what Daniel called him. Well if he was Emily's tormentor then Emma had nothing more to fear. He'd solved the problem. Klaus would be put off the ship at the next stop.

"Dan. Dan…" someone, no not someone…he knew that voice. "What the hell?" Dan said, out loud snapping himself from his dream; he could have sworn that was Emma's voice. Sitting up in bed, Emma staring down at him. What the hell just happened? Trying to shake off the lingering effects of his dream, Dan said, "Emma? What's a matter? It's still dark. Did you have a nightmare?" Rubbing the sleep out of his eyes he waited for Emma to reply.

"Oh, Dan you did it!"

"Did what? What are you talking about, Love?"

"Dan you got Daniel to get Klaus off the ship."

"How the hell did you know that?" Dan barked then winced as he realized how he must sound. Before he could apologize, Emma threw her arms about his neck and tackled him down to the mattress. "Oh, you silly man you. How do you think I knew?" Then she dropped her lips to his, kissing him with such joyous passion, Dan was immediately swept into the wave.

Twining his hand in her long golden hair he pulled her close, drinking all that she gave. Running his tongue over her lips, she opened giving him access to the sweetness inside. Tongues danced, hands roamed, and pulses soared as the wave of ecstasy rose higher and higher. Dan's roaming hands found the bottom of Emma's nightshirt pulling it up he raised her momentarily so he could get the blasted contraption off her. He really had to talk to her about wearing such things to bed. A nuisance, that's what they were.

Pulling her back down on top of him, his mouth claimed hers once more while he positioned her legs on either side of him. Sitting there straddling him, his manhood hard between her thighs, Emma marveled in the power this position allotted her.

He let her set her own pace. Emma loved it. It gave her a sense of power, control. She'd always believed when it came to sex, no matter what the books said, the women relinquished all control to the man. Dan had never been meaning or hurtful with that control, but when she was on the bottom and he on top, he usually had her mind so far gone that she couldn't have possibly been in control.

Slowly at first then picking up speed, Emma rode her husband. Sitting up she notice he filled her even more and when she leaned back her world tilted. She felt herself whirling out of control, but this time it was different. She couldn't say how, it just was. Dan's hands on her hips urged her on as the tremors started throughout her body; he helped her complete the ride. Faster and faster the world blurred asher heart was beat wildly.

With the final plateau reached and a shattering orgasm just around the bend, Dan gripped her hips, arching his back he held her there as she convulsed around him. With a roar he followed. Emma fell forward collapsing on top of him. For the rest of the night they slept. Neither moved. Neither dreamt.

When the pink light of dawn flooded into the bedroom, Dan quickly and quietly wriggled from his wife clutches long enough to place another blanket over the window blocking out the light. There, that should ensure a few more hours with his sleeping beauty. This need he felt to be close to her. It was amazing. She'd always had the ability to draw him to her, even when she didn't know what she was doing.

He looked down at her sleeping form. He would be content simply to have her in his arms. To hold her; knowing that she loved him and only him. He returned to his side of the bed moments later gathering his wife into the crook of his arms he drifted back to sleep.

Chapter Eighteen

It was almost time to go home. Back to Washington, to her...not their apartment, at least until they find a nice house to live in. Emma walked around the outside of the cabin; survey all that could be done before they closed it up for winter. No one would be back to this little haven until next year.

There was an older retired couple, who lived not far away. They came here often to mow the lawn or ready the cabin when Dan's parents were coming up for a while. The Middleton's were the ones who readied the cabin for their honeymoon.

Emma thought back to the lit fire and food stores that were waiting for them. She had to make sure that she got something special for them both in the way of a thank you. Kneeling beside one of the flowerbeds, Emma sighed; it would have been lovely to see this place in all its glory in spring or even summer. There certainly wasn't much left here in the fall, she would have to see a gardener back in the city and find out what could be planted so that they would be able to enjoy fresh blooms right into winter.

She started yanking at the thistles and other paraphernalia that had lodged itself between the rose bushes. She wondered what color the roses were. Would Dan know? No matter, she would see for herself next year.

Their time here had been a peaceful since the night Dan attacked Klaus on the ship. There had been no more problems; at least she thought there were no more problems. However, since she'd not had any dreams recently, she could not be sure. Still, she did not feel the tension she'd felt before; and that, had to be a good sign.

She'd learned so much about Dan, and his life. She'd always felt a connection, as though she'd known him, and maybe the dream contributed to that, yet she did not know what his life was like or had been like outside of those dreams.

He was a lonely child, something he'd mentioned before but it had slipped her mind. His mother and father had ten acres outside of Dundalk. From the sounds of things, they had been there for a very long time. The house had been passed down to his folks through generations. Though how many to be exact she hadn't a clue.

That would be one of Emma's next projects, curious as ever needing mysteries to solve, she'd investigate Dan's family tree. Sitting back on her heels stretching out the crick in her lower back, she swallowed. To be honest, she felt this need to examine Dan's family tree because she no longer had one. The pain was still there whenever she thought of her family but with each passing day it lessened.

Removing her glove, she wiped a lone tear that ran down her cheek. Keep busy she told herself. Find things to do and you will be fine. Putting the glove back on she continued removing the weeds. At least she hoped they were weeds, she really needed to get a book about this stuff.

The thought brought a chuckle to her. She could see herself next year, with Dan's mother walking about the yard stopping in front of the beds and her asking, 'I wonder what became of my prize-winning azaleas?' Another chuckle escaped her as she invisioned her husband trying to explain that his bride threw them out thinking they were weeds.

Dan heard Emma laughing, the sound drawing him from the shed out back that he was readying for winter. Coming around the corner of the cabin, watched his wife kneeling and laughing before the flowerbeds. She looked young and carefree. He was glad the dreams had seemed to stop.

Emma had not told him of any, but he found her easy to read and if she'd been lying to him through omission he would have known. He watched as Emma sobered and began once again to finish the job she'd started. Dan had found her a pair of work gloves, but the things were so large on her small hands that they flopped back and forth like a clown.

Dan approached Emma, she smiled up at him causing the all too familiar ache below. Sitting beside her on the lawn, Dan looked into her eyes; they were still sparkling with mirth. "What's so funny? I heard you laughing clear through to the shed."

Emma vibrated with the effort to contain her giggles long enough to tell Dan what was so funny. "Nothing, really. I was just thinking about my lack of knowledge concerning flowers. I do hope I don't throw away anything that's not a weed." Somehow Dan knew there had to be more to the story, but he didn't think it was serious enough to press the issue.

"We leave in three days. Are you ready?"

"It's strange, I miss the city, in its own special way it was a safe-haven to me, but this place," She looked around emphasizing the point with a wave of her floppy gloved hand. "This place has given me a peace of mind that I had never found in Washington. I love it here."

Dan leaned forward kissing her reddened lips. Emma reached up cuddling his face in her hands pulling him closer as the kiss continued. When at last it came to an end, Dan pulled away. Emma immediately burst into another fit of giggles. Dan looked puzzled. "I'm glad I make you happy," he paused "but was I really that funny?"

"Oh…oh my…no…no…really it's not that," Emma said gasping. "It's…it's, oh hell…" Emma removed the glove and reached for Dan's face trying to remove some of the dirt there. "There's no help for it," she said, laughing. "You'll have to go inside and wash. You're blacker than the ace of spades." Realizing what was so funny, Dan laughed.

Grabbing a hand full of black dirt overturned by Emma weeding, Dan smeared it in Emma's face. Then the fight was on, by the time to two overzealous counterfeit teenagers finished their battle, they were black from head to toe. Picking Emma up Dan did the only thing any good husband would do. He headed to the bath.

Sitting before the fire that night, Emma clasped in Dan's arms, they stared at the fire each relaxing in silence. Emma tensed momentarily; Dan wouldn't have known at all if his arms had not been around her. They continued sitting but every time the fire flickered or snapped Emma tensed again. Dan tried massaging her neck still nothing worked.

Emma realizing, she had to get away from Dan before he noticed something was not as it should be. She made her excuses and headed for the bedroom. She needed a little time away to try and figure out what was happening.

Feeling uneasy she paced the bedroom floor. They had been sitting in front of the fire; she should not have been cold. Yet she was. A deep-seated cold deep within, the portent that something bad is about to happen. She thought briefly about Emily. No, nothing could be wrong there. Dan had seen to it that Klaus was eliminated if indeed he was the problem and Emma felt sure that he had been. He was no longer aboard the ship; therefore, he should be of no threat to Emily.

Stopping in front of the window, Emma looked out into the dark night. Another shiver of fear ran through her. This was crazy, the dreams had not come in a week or there about and everyone that was important to her was right here. The only family she had to be concerned about was Dan. Unless…no nothing could be wrong there could it? Emma glanced at the clock. Ten. Going to the phone she called Beatrice.

"Hello?"

"Beatrice it's me, Emma. Is everything all right?"

"Why, yes dear. What's wrong? You sound worried. Everything's all right with you and Dan? How's the honeymoon? Can't wait till you get back here and tell me all about it. How's the dream research going?" Emma let Beatrice drone on and on, the sound of her voice calming her. When Beatrice's questions and catalogue of events came to an end, Emma said, "No Beatrice, all is fine here. Just had a funny feeling something was happening there, figured I would call and check up on you. But you're all right so I guess I am worrying for nothing. We will be home in a couple of days I'll give you another call then and fill you in about the dreams. Okay? Yes, sure thing Beatrice. Bye."

Emma put the phone back in the cradle. Breathing a sigh of relief, she headed back out into the living room to see what was keeping Dan. He sat before the same fire; he hadn't moved. "Dan?" He looked up but hadn't said a word. "Dan, what's wrong? Why haven't you come to bed?"

"Em, you'd tell me if there was something wrong, wouldn't you?"

Emma had a sense of déjà vu about these words, like she'd heard them before but could not remember where or when. The feeling gave her another icy chill. "Definately. When there is something wrong, I will let you know. Right now, I think I am just over tired or maybe I caught a chill outside when I finished the work in the flowerbeds. Either way I am fine right now. Okay? Please don't worry."

Sighing Dan got up from the fire, checking the screen in front of the grate, making sure all would be fine until it burned itself out; he turned and walked to Emma. Taking her by the hand they headed for bed.

It was a sunny morning; the air was crisp but that was to be expected for November. Emma sat on her knees before the flowerbeds. She'd promised herself she would clean the beds, as a surprise for Dan, trying to give him back something of his happy childhood memories. She had only two days left before

180

they headed back to the city so while Dan slept, she would do what she could. Her knowledge of flowers was limited she only hoped she did not pick any of Dan's mother precious flowers.

The pair of old gloves, they were floppy, but they suited the purpose nicely making sure that her hands stayed clean and any thistles didn't poke her. The sky started to darken. Emma looked up and silently hoped that she would be able to get everything done before the rain hit.

Lowering her head, she began picking the weeds. The ground seemed to be soft beneath her. As a matter of fact, it seemed like it was too soft. She began sinking. She moved over, setting the pad under her knees she started working again. The sky was blackening, so dark.

Why was it so dark?

Emma was sinking, sinking again, only this time she couldn't move quickly enough. The earth had swallowed the pad. Emma tried to stand. Tried to move. She couldn't. Her leg was stuck. As she struggled to get her leg free, the other one became embedded in the soft earth. It was hot, wet; something wasn't right. Sinking. Sinking rapidly; she fought with the earth to free herself. The more she fought the quicker she sank.

Her head was almost under now; she was frantic…screaming…she called for Dan…he was in the shed.

"Dan!" she took in a mouthful of dirt. Spitting it out and called again. "Dan! Dan!" More dirt—it was coming into her mouth again, running in like thick liquid. She spit, and tried calling again. She began coughing uncontrollably. It was so dark. Please she prayed. Just then everything went black. She was floating, no not floating. What is happening Emma thought wildly? Where the hell was Dan?

Emma did not know how much time had passed, but she felt something cool, soft and moist pressed to her face. Dan heard Emma struggling; she was hot to the touch. He ran to the bathroom for a cool cloth, coming to the bed he placed the cloth gently over her face and began to smooth away the sweat. Calling to her softly while patting her cheeks. Finally he managed to get her to open her eyes.

"Darling. Sweetheart come on now open your eyes. That's right. Good girl. How do you feel? You're running a temperature. Are you better now?" Emma's mouth felt dirty and her throat was sore and raw. She was coming back to her surroundings. Seeing the bedroom he mind registered that she was in the cabin. Slowly she was able to let go of the nightmare, that had held her in its grasp.

"Dan?" Her voice was croaky as though she had laryngitis. She cleared it and tried again. "Dan, I think I'm okay. Just c-c-cold, r-r-really c-c-cold. M-m-more covers." she stuttered.

Setting the cloth aside Dan went to the linen closet, and grabbed another quilt. Placing it over Emma, he tucked it under her chin. Seeing her eyes close and some of the shaking dissipate, Dan climbed back in under the covers and held his wife, keeping her warm.

Sitting in the car the following afternoon, Dan was worried. He had insisted that they head back to Washington a day early. He wanted to be close to the doctors should Emma need one. Although once she awoke in the morning, she seemed fine. There had been no sign of illness, but she seemed a little too happy, so Dan had insisted they head for home. If he didn't know better, he would say that Emma was in denial that anything had occurred last night. But he knew her well enough to realize that quite the opposite was occurring. She may seem happy on the outside but inside that gorgeous head of hers; her mind was racing. Something happened last night to make her body react the way it had. If she was not sick, then he'd only one conclusion to draw. A dream…no, not a dream and nightmare.

What could it have been about? Even when she was worried for Emily, she'd not reacted this way. She'd been terrified to be sure, but this was different. Could she be pregnant? It was possible. He'd read in several places that if one is pregnant then their dreams could become more intense. It was a fear…but something still didn't seem right. Hopefully when they got home, she would be better.

Emma sat quietly throughout most of the trip. She did not want to go back just yet. If she went back, maybe what had induced the dream would not follow. She'd tried everything she could think of to make Dan feel that she was okay. That she did not need to leave their little haven any sooner than originally planned, but it was all for not. He packed the car and closed the cabin for winter.

Trying to analyze her dream Emma mentally ran through all the possibilities, still she came up empty handed. She was tired; maybe if she got a little sleep, she would be more prepared to tackle this once they were home. Sliding over to Dan's side of the car Emma lay her head on his shoulder and closed her eyes. Dan gave Emma a quick kiss on the forehead, taking a hand off the wheel and placing it about her shoulders, he pulled her close.

Saying hello to the doorman, Dan walked past, Emma was in his arms still asleep. He'd not seen any sense in waking her up. Taking the elevator from the parking garage and then to the apartment meant he didn't really have to carry her all that far. All their stuff could be unpacked tomorrow. They had time, neither had to go back to work until after Thanksgiving.

The more Dan thought about the quiet Thanksgiving at home in the apartment the more he wondered if maybe his mother and father would have something planned for the weekend as well. It really wasn't all that long of drive to Dundalk and maybe meeting his parents and getting to know them would make Emma feel more at ease. She could also take them on as surrogates if she felt the need, he knew they would be ecstatic with the idea.

They were a little upset that he'd not brought her out to meet them before the wedding but under the circumstances, that of which the bride hadn't been aware there would be a wedding, would have been a little hard to explain. Maybe he would talk with her tomorrow about going there.

Letting themselves into the apartment, he headed for the bedroom and set Emma down on the bed. He would make himself a cup of coffee before he retired for the night. Settling down on the couch with his coffee, Dan brought the cup to his lips. Inhaling deeply the relaxing scent; when a cry rang throughout the apartment.

Spilling the coffee all over himself, swearing, he heard the sound again realizing it was Emma yelling for help. "Jesus Christ!" he swore, aloud on a dead run to the bedroom.

Coming into the bedroom he spotted his wife on the bed instead of being on top of the covers she'd somehow managed to work her way down under them and they were up around her head literally choking her. She was turning blue. "What the hell?" Dan said, as he ran to the bed pulling the covers from her grasp and massaging her throat to get it working again.

"Emma, come on Emma wake up. It's just a nightmare. Emma, damn you open your eyes!"

Emma blinked. "What happened?" she asked confused.

"You were choking yourself with the God damn blankets you had them around your throat." Pulling her into his arms and rocking her as if she were a small child Dan sat weaving back and forth on the bed.

Emma's small frame started convulsing in his arms. He held on tighter trying to keep her warm, trying so damn hard to protect her from something she didn't know, and he couldn't see. He could hear her teeth chattering and although she seemed to be getting warmer to the touch it would be a long time yet before her body warmed and her mind numbed. He wished she would tell him know what was bothering her. Did she even know? Had she seen something, felt something?

Smoothing the hair back from her face he kissed her cheeks, and closed eyelids. Tomorrow he would sit her down and go through those fucking books one more time. There had to be a reason why this was happening. He knew enough about dreams to know that each mystery they presented had to be solved for the haunting images to go away.

Soon Emma's breathing changed, became less labored, less nasally. He knew that she was sleeping. Would the nightmares remain at bay, that he did not know? He needed to be prepared. Pulling a cover over them, but not bothering to get undressed Dan closed his eyes and allowed himself to sleep holding tight to Emma.

Chapter Nineteen

They had spent the better part of the day engrossed in their books. Dan had given Emma little choice in the matter. When she awoke that morning, he had breakfast made for her and told her to eat while he ran a bath. Later she found Dan in the living room, all their things had been brought up from the car. Her books were spread throughout the room.

"Where's your journal?" Dan asked, seeing Emma staring at the mess about the room.

"It's…uh…it's in my handbag," Emma said, wondering what was going through her husband's mind. He hated those books with a passion. It wasn't so much the books as the fact of what they represented. Their dreams. Giving her head a shake trying to gain some control over her wits, she said, "Dan what are you doing? Why do you need my journal?"

"We are going to get to the bottom of this, and as much as I hate the thought of this whole thing Emma these books seemed to have offered us the information we needed to set things to rights the last time. Maybe they will again."

Emma said no more and immediately went in search of her handbag, and her journal. Once found, she sat on the couch and tried to record what it was that happened in her two previous dreams. It was hard. There wasn't really anything to record. Images, flashbacks only a few…but feeling there were plenty of those. Conferring with Dan, she decided to just write anything that popped into her head when she thought of the dreams.

Around supper, Dan called for pizza and the research continued non-stop for the remainder of the night. They really did not have much to go on; Dan was racking his head against the wall. Leaving Emma to look through the books he re-read her journal. Looking at everything again, most of it did not pertain to this latest endeavor. But the latest entries were the ones in which Emma had written today. In one continuous line on the page, feelings. no story line, no people, only feelings were written.

Darkness, cold all over, holding me, pulling me, going under, suffocating, fighting, swallowing, choking, heat, moistness…the line went on and on. "Emma, darling, this doesn't make any sense. Can't you remember anything else?"

"What do you mean, I wrote everything I felt."

"Yes, you did, but you wrote nothing else. Your feelings seemed to overshadow everything else. Come here a moment." Emma walked over to Dan. He pulled her down into his lap. Leaning her back against his chest he slowly began to massage her temples. "Close your eyes. Yes, that's right." He kept massaging in a slow easy rhythm.

"Relax, think back…what were you doing when you felt the darkness?"

Emma didn't think, she was beyond natural thought, so relaxed she only answered the question without delay. "Gardening. I was weeding the flowerbeds."

Dan thought about that, nothing sinister with the flowerbeds, he'd to go deeper. "What happened when you felt cold?"

"So cold, the sun was covered, it was dark," Emma said, her teeth beginning to chatter.

"No, sweetheart it's neither cold nor dark here, you must not chatter so. It's all right I will keep you warm. I promise. Good girl. Now tell me about what was pulling you under?"

"The ground."

"The ground? Emma what ground? Where are you?" Dan said, still massaging her temples.

"The ground in front of the flowers. I was on the pad you gave me. The ground moved. I moved the pad to a different spot, but when I settled back down the pad went into the earth. Then my leg sunk down. I was worried I fought to stand. I couldn't. I called you. You didn't come. It was choking me!"

"It's okay Emma I got to you in time. You're safe now. Tell me who was choking you."

"The ground, Dan it was the ground it had pulled me under completely. My head was covered. I couldn't breathe."

Dan pushed Emma up abruptly. She turned to see his face alit with knowledge. "What, you know something. What is it?" Dan smiled. "I have not solved it Emma, but I believe I have a lead. Quicksand. Pass me that book again." Emma handed over the encyclopedia of dreams. "Quicksand?"

"Yes, quicksand, what you described ground pulling you under, there is only one type of ground that could do that. Quicksand. Now where in the hell did, I see…? Aha! Here it is."

Emma looked to the section in the book that Dan held open. She was about to read over his shoulder when he started reading out loud. "A destructive aspect of the unconscious mind. Being pulled down by quicksand symbolizes losing one's emotional footing and being consumed or overwhelmed by emotions, fears and anxieties. Such dreams are common during times of stress and upheaval. Other meaning: A shifting unpredictable and potentially dangerous emotional landscape."

"You mean I am crazy?" Emma asked, hurt at the thought. Seeing the look on her face Dan reached and placed a kiss on her lips answering.

"No, sweetheart you're not crazy. Don't you see? Maybe this has something to do with Emily. You were always so closely connected maybe it's her that is going crazy."

Emma looked at him disbelieving. "Dan, that's even more ridiculous. Emily isn't me. She's a dream for God sakes."

"You didn't look at her like that when that Klaus fellow was after her." Dan raised an arrogant brow. Damn the man, he was right, but that was different, wasn't it? "I don't know? It just seems…" she let the statement hang there. They both knew what it seemed like, but neither was willing to admit that Emma was losing her mind. "It is our only lead Emma, and we are going to see what we can find out."

Emma heard the finality in Dan's voice, with a slight nod of her head she reached for another book. Dan watched his wife, as she scanned the pages of the books before her. There had to be answers in one of them. He refused to think that she might be crazy, yet it was getting late, and getting run down from lack of sleep was something neither one of them needed. With that decision made, Dan took the book from Emma, marking her spot so they could find it in the morning; he pulled her up "Let's go to bed."

It was dark; there wasn't even enough light coming from the crescent moon for Emma to be able to see what was chasing her. On instinct, she ran. Down one path then the other. She did not care if she was going in circles, she only cared about staying one step ahead of the thing that was behind her.

She could hear the clop of his feet…feet. She had to remember that. She couldn't hear feet unless it was a person wearing shoes. What was it she was running on? Cobblestones? That's weird. Emma kept running. She felt pains in her chest. Each breath hurting more than the last.

Emma knew she had to catch a glimpse of the person chasing her. She could not leave this dream world until there was some sort of clue as to what was happening to her. Finding a crevice opening in the wall, she squeezed inside. Her heart was pounding so loud she prayed he could not hear her as he drew close.

She could hear him. Feel him. His shoes or boots sounded like drums as with each step he came closer and closer to her hiding spot. His breathing did not sound labored at least not nearly as much as hers, yet she could tell he was getting closer. She held her breath waiting for him to pass by.

She waited and waited; the sound stopped. Where did he go? Allowing herself to breathe once more, she peeked out of her hiding spot. She was shaking with the terror of being discovered yet she could not cower behind this wall forever. She must see his face. Edging out little by little she looked up and down the empty alleyway. Nothing.

There was no one there. That's odd Emma thought, if he were gone then wouldn't the dream be over? Shouldn't she be awake? Slowly walking down the alley, looking for a way out, Emma heard her name being called. She knew that voice. It did not belong to someone she liked sending chills through her. Her steps sped up as she listened to the haunting sound of her name coming from somewhere behind.

Soon she heard the familiar sound of his footfalls as his shoes hit the cobblestones. Not again. Jesus, how much more could she take. Taking off on a dead run Emma tried to find a haven. How the hell had he gotten by her? He would have to pass by the crevice in order to be behind her now. Emma ran faster than she ever had before, eyes darting from side to side hoping to find another hiding spot where she may catch her breath.

"Emma…E-m-m-a…I'm going to get you…stop now!" The haunting words were repeated over and over. Emma would never forget the sound of that voice nor the words as they echoed through the air. She was becoming frantic; he was closing in. She had to get away.

Her foot hit a raise in the cobblestones, falling to her knees on the cold ground; Emma could not make herself get up. She was tired, her legs were sore, and she could run no more. Holding her side trying to stop the pain that jolted through her, Emma felt great despair. She'd only felt this helpless once in her life. Travis…Son of a bitch. Those ugly self-assured sneers that she heard come from his mouth that night so many years before.

"There you are, Bitch!" Emma knew he was behind her. Lifting her head, she peered over her shoulder. It wasn't Travis, at least she didn't think it was, he. He looked different. Older. No, not older exactly…oh shit…Klaus! She tried to make sense of something…anything, yet nothing that had happened made sense.

He could see her; how could he see her? Emma was still trying to figure this out when Klaus grabbed her smashing her face into the ground. Screaming out Emma grabbed her nose. It was bleeding. She felt the blood flow, she felt the moist stickiness pooling in her hands as she held them up in front of her face.

She refused to answer him, if he was anything like Travis, he would relish hearing her scream, she wouldn't do that either. No, she would remain silent, maybe he would get upset enough that he would tell her what he wanted. Here in the dream world at least she was protected. He could hurt her; true but whatever he did would not be carried over into the real world. She would find out what he wanted and then she would think of a way to fight back. Never again would a man use her and abuse her as Travis did.

"I've been looking for you, bitch; I'm not done with you. When I am finished with you, I am going to get that husband of yours too. He never should have put me off the Maiden and to drop me here in this hellhole. I am so glad you stopped by, frankly I have been waiting for you, I wanted to take you on the ship but there was never a chance. You were scared though. Weren't cha? I could feel your fear."

Twisting his fingers into her hair he pulled her up off the ground. "Answer me, bitch!" he screeched. Emma stared straight into his eyes. They were evil. He was evil. When she did not answer, Klaus slapped her hard against the face with his other hand. Emma's head snapped back, before she could stop herself, she cried out in pain.

"Emma, honey wake up, oh my God, Emma what happened your nose, it's bleeding. Let me get a cloth." Dan took off in a flash; soon he was back tipping her head forward and holding an ice pack to her face. He switched on the lamp and watched as Emma's blooded crusted hands held the pack to her nose.

"It's stopped now I think. Let me go wash it off then I will come back and change the sheets," Emma said, easing herself out of the bed. Dan watched her leave. He wondered if she had nose bleeds normally. He had known a boy once, who had nose bleeds every night; his parents took him to the doctor to have it cauterized. Emma came back, her face and hands free of blood; in her hands she held some pillowcases and sheets.

Dan got up to help strip the bed and re-make it. The night was almost over when they both laid their heads down once more. "Do you have nose bleeds very often?" Dan asked.

"No, not often."

Dan seemed okay with that comment as he reached over her to shut off the lamp. Lying back down on his pillow he yawned and promptly went back to sleep leaving Emma with her thoughts.

Running through everything in her mind Emma wanted to make sure that she could remember the details for the morning. She was glad Dan had not realized she'd been dreaming and that her nosebleed was somehow connected. She hadn't thought that what happened in the dream state could be brought over into the real world. Apparently, she thought wryly…it could. She only hoped that the slap in which Klaus gave her would not cause a bruise. Then she would not have to share this with Dan. She didn't think he would take it well at all.

The question was what did Klaus want with her? Dan did get him kicked off the ship. Could he know? Did he see Dan? Was this Travis all over again? Maybe she was getting the images confused. Something still didn't ring true. She wished Emily would contact her somehow, letting her know that she was okay.

Sighing, Emma looked toward the window. Dan had been asleep for over an hour and Emma's contemplating had gotten her nowhere. She would have to consult the books. Hopefully she could find something in there that would help her wade through this mess to find an answer. She had no false illusions that the dreams would stop. No, they would continue until she solved the puzzle. Solve it she would, and if Travis contacted her again for some reason then she would not run. She would somehow find her wits and stand her ground. One way or another she would get to the truth.

Chapter Twenty

It was late in the afternoon before Emma got a chance to do some research. Dan had been in the apartment all morning and they had looked through the books tackling the problem of her quicksand nightmares. She'd purposely delayed writing any information in her journal in case he looked in there. Instead she'd taken sheets of paper with her into the washroom, and while she bathed, she recorded what she could remember.

Placing the sheets in the dresser drawer where she could get them later, she went into the living room to confer with Dan and the books. Dan had coffee ready for them. They had managed to get quite a bit done but still he was no further in solving the mystery of what might be troubling Emma enough that she was having this type of dream. They did however find some references to other books that might be of help to them.

Beatrice called about eleven o'clock that morning. She wanted to leave Emma a message to call her upon her return. To her surprise Emma answered the phone right away. She explained that they had come back earlier than planned. Beatrice talked at length about what was going on in the office. All was basically fine; the others were handling her workload so there would not be any surprises when she returned…the last was said with a laugh that Emma echoed happily.

"No," she said, I have had my share of surprises. The last surprise I married, and I really don't think I can handle more than one. Hearing the last, Dan's head shot up. "More than one what?" he asked with a smile. Emma waved her hand at him to tell him to be quiet. He laughed.

It was decided before Beatrice hung up the phone that she would stop by after work. Saying goodbye Emma hung up. Dan left shortly thereafter. The fridge had not been stocked so he was on the way to the grocery store and would make sure that he stopped at the library to check out any other books that may be of some help. No sooner had the door closed behind him and Emma flew to the bedroom to get her notes.

Reading what she'd jotted down earlier, she tried to pick out any important symbols like Dan had done before. He was really a lot better than her and before long she gave up. There seemed to be nothing that she could interpret from Travis or Klaus or what had happened.

Running her fingers through her hair she could not help but notice that her scalp where Klaus had yanked her hair still hurt. Dreams weren't supposed to hurt. Yet she felt everything, luckily, she did not have a bruise from the smack he'd given her. Touching her fingers to her cheek she imagined the imprint that his hand should have left behind. Damn I wish I could figure this out.

She heard the keys jingle in the lock; that didn't take long, she thought. Knowing she would not have enough time to run back to the bedroom and stash her notes she tucked them under the end of the couch, pasted a smile on her face. Dan as he came into the room arms fully loaded. "I have more in the car." He set down the bundles and turned, "I have to go back out and get it."

Emma started to put away the food when she heard him leave the apartment again, she headed for the couch, got her notes and took them to the bedroom. Opening the drawer, she placed the notes inside and quickly closed it again. She did not notice in her haste to get back to the kitchen that the pages were sticking out of the corner.

Beatrice showed up a couple of hours later. Dan had been going through the new books he'd checked out and Emma was in the kitchen making Fettuccini Alfredo. Beatrice came over, said a quick hello and promptly went into the living room to sit down beside Dan to wait for supper. A few minutes later Emma hollered, and they all proceeded to the kitchen.

After supper, Beatrice sobered. "Okay tell me. I know you were on your honeymoon and all, but I do imagine you had some time to research these dreams of yours?" That was Beatrice direct and to the point, unless of course it was to her advantage not to. Emma and Dan looked at one another wondering how much to tell her. "Just spill it!" Beatrice said impatiently.

"Emma had managed to find out quite a bit of information before I even came back to Washington. We did find something intriguing though. After discussing it, it appears… well it appears that our dreams are or at least were linked."

"Oh my, that is interesting," Beatrice said. "Emma never did tell me much, only that she was looking for information concerning her dreams. I know her dreams were about a young girl. Are you trying to tell me you had the same ones?"

"Well not quite, my dreams were of a young man, the very same young man that her Emily married." Emma could tell by the look on Beatrice's face that she was ready to call the National Enquirer. "Beatrice, let me remind you this is to stay between us."

Beatrice looked affronted. "Of course dear. I am not a gossip." Emma didn't know what to say. Beatrice could chat up a storm with the best of them.

They spent the next couple of hours filling Beatrice in on everything they had discovered about their dreams and what they had been practicing with lucid dreaming. She left shortly after that, without hearing any of the latest developments. Until they knew for sure what was happening there was no point in confiding in her.

They retired to bed shortly and made love until dreams were the furthest things from their minds. Or so they thought. Snuggled in spoonlike fashion in the middle of the bed, both slept.

He was after her; she could hear his heavy footfalls as they hit the cobblestones beneath her. Running, Emma had to get away, no not Emma. Emma could tell she was disorientated, but why panting and gasping for air, Emma stopped and tried to focus on one point in order to bring herself back in control of her dream.

Looking about frantically she spotted what she thought was an alley. Staying where she was listening to the steps coming closer and closer, she knew she couldn't move until she was in control. She had to get her bearings. There was some piece of the puzzle she was missing. But what? Making her mind endure the sound that was threatening her wellbeing she focused on a brick in the alley.

The fog that surrounded her as well as her brain seemed to lift as she stared at the one brick she'd picked as a focal point. There, this was much better. Emma, feeling more in control, slowed her breathing. This she could handle. She looked around; she'd not noticed in her flight that the footsteps were different. There was more than one. She'd assumed Klaus was chasing her but now she wasn't so sure that was what was happening at all.

Control it Emma, she told herself. I need light. She concentrated on that simple fact. Her head was hurting after a few minutes but eventually she was able to see a lantern a little further in the alley. It had not been there before;

she was happy that she'd managed in some small way to manipulate the dream. Yeah, she said to herself as she started walking, maybe next time I'll put the damn thing where I need it.

Walking toward the light she kept her trained for the sound of shoes hitting the roadway. By the time she'd reached the light, it had started to flicker, shit, she berated herself you didn't put oil in the dang thing. Realizing how stupid she sounded and burst out laughing. Just then the light died. Total darkness ruled once more. Grabbing her temples and pressing, she concentrated on light, I need light and soon the lantern was back.

The people were upon her; she could hear them talking, they didn't sound scary she thought, but they did sound familiar. When they got closer Emma saw it was Daniel and Emily. That shocked her, for this was the same alley she'd encountered in her last dream. Just to make sure Emma went in search of the crevice that she had hidden in before.

She found it, stepping inside she watched as Daniel and Emily passed by talking about this special birthday trip. It was Emily eighteenth birthday and Daniel had decided it would be a good time for them to go ashore. They appeared so happy as they strolled arm in arm. This isn't so bad, Emma thought as she stepped back into the alley. At least now she knew Emily was safe.

The alley started to fade as a thick mist fell over the dream. Emma opened her eyes and smiled remembering the glimpse of Emily with her beloved. It still did not look like Emily was pregnant that could be a possibility.

Rolling over Emma put her arms around Dan; she looked down into his face, she couldn't see if of course. It was the middle of the night and the room was dark, but she knew it would be there all the same. Too bad he's asleep she thought, if he wasn't, she could turn on the light…at that moment the lamp switched on Emma stared down in terror at Klaus.

Before she had a chance to jump off the bed, he grabbed her hard rolling her beneath him. "I'm gonna get her ye know. There is nothing you can do to stop me." With that he was gone, and Emma sat bolt up in bed wide-awake. Dan had not heard her; still asleep beside her Emma slowed her rapidly beating heart. Then she remembered Klaus's words. He was after Emily.

She had to go back there, she had to warn Emily. Quietly getting out of bed Emma went into the bathroom looking through the medicine cabinet and found the bottle of Ambien the doctor had given her months ago. How many to take? She wanted to remain asleep until she found Emily, but she didn't want to overdose. How many she, thought hysterically. Dumping five into the palm of her hand she downed them immediately. She didn't want to take the chance of Dan waking so she decided against the water. Walking back to bed she lay down. Slowing her breathing and practicing the techniques she'd read about soon she was floating off to sleep. She hoped it would be enough.

When Dan woke up, Emma was still sleeping. She'd gotten out of bed in the middle of the night. He assumed she had a bad night so he got dressed and decided he would do a bit of reading until she awoke. By ten o'clock she hadn't stirred even though he had been in to check on her a couple of times, but she seemed totally out of it.

Walking into the bathroom, he noticed the medicine cabinet open. He wondered briefly about it, then closed the door and left. There were some errands he could do, so leaving a note behind on the table for Emma he left the apartment.

Emma stood trying to find a point of reference. She could see nothing through all the fog. Tapping her foot against the ground she listened for a sound that would tell her what she was walking on. She'd expected it to be cobblestone, yet that echoing ting didn't follow the fall of her foot. Dropping down on one knee, Emma used her fingers to feel what was beneath her.

The ground was covered with soft moist grass. Where the hell was she? Standing up she carefully began walking. She'd know idea which way to go, why was there all this damn fog? Disorientated as far as direction or where she was headed Emma continued walking. She saw what seemed to be a break in the dense fog, a small ray of light shone through. Turning, she headed toward the ray of light.

As she got closer the light seemed to move farther and farther away. It was eerie this feeling of nothingness. There was no sound at all. She found herself straining to hear her footfalls. She felt claustrophobic surrounded in all the heavy wetness. Still she kept her course, walking in the direction of the light.

Emma felt uneasy and didn't know why. Slowing her footsteps, shuffling her feet as she went along she made sure there was ground under them. Coming to a clearing in the fog, Emma was glad her instincts had not fled. There, before her was a drop-off into the sea. Shaking her head, she opened and closed her eyes. She could not believe the sight before her. An iceberg? What would an iceberg be doing here?

Remembering that somewhere in one of the books she read, it said that things out of the ordinary are quite often signs. What kind of sign? That was the question. She didn't have reference material with her, and her brain seemed hazy, probably an after effect of the pills she'd taken. Thinking momentarily of Dan she hoped she would be awake before him in the morning.

Pulling her eyes away from the sight before her she looked around. There was nothing. No people, no town or village of any kind yet down at the bottom of the cliff there appeared to be a ship. She looked behind her, in that direction there was still nothing but dense fog. No point in going back, she thought, I would never be able to see anything in that direction any way.

Cautiously, Emma took the path, appearing out of nowhere, down to the ship anchored below. The walk seemed to take forever.

The path twisting and turning. Grass covered and wet, Emma could feel the moisture through her clothes. Although cold, she continued. Gazing around periodically to make sure she could still see the ship.

Reaching the bottom Emma was exhausted, only determination kept her going. The closer she got to the ship, the more it looked deserted. Raising out of the mist it resembled a ghost more than anything else, but it was still there and that gave her hope. When she reached the dock, she saw a long gangplank leading from the wharf to the ship.

Emma took the gangplank; it was slippery causing her to fall a couple of times before reaching the deck. Stepping onto the ship, Emma began to have second thoughts. The place was silent, no sign of a crewmember, and no remnants of a cargo that it could have been holding. Closer inspection showed cobwebs clinging to the ship. This could not be the right way, Emma thought. Turning to leave the ship, Emma placed one foot on the gangplank, when all of the sudden it gave way disappearing into the ocean below.

Jumping back, she managed to grab the side of the ship and pull herself up before she too ended in the cold murkiness. Lying on the deck trying to catch her breath, Emma heard noises. Men walked about checking the mast and readying the ship for sailing. No one appeared to see her, which was just fine by Emma. Not being seen gave her an advantage should the environment turn hostile.

Dan didn't know what to do; Emma was still sleeping when he walked into the apartment that afternoon. He shook her and shook her but was unable to wake her at all. What the hell? She didn't appear to be running a fever of any kind, as a matter of fact aside from being a little wet from the warm day and being buried under the covers for so long, she was perfectly fine. Only she wasn't waking up.

Dan's mind floated back to earlier that morning, when he came into the bathroom and found the medicine cabinet open. Getting up he went back to the bathroom and pulled the door wide. Aspirin, Tylenol, razors and personal products lined the shelves. Behind, Dan spotted the prescription bottle. Grabbing it, he turned it back and forth in his palm while he tried to figure it out.

Emma hated these things. He knew that from before. Would she? What else would make her sleep that long? She hadn't seemed distraught when she woke up last night. Dan turned the bottle so she could see the label. Thirty pills. She had been given them a few months ago. How many had she taken back then. With her dislike for the things he would say not too many.

Popping open the lid, he spilled the tiny white pills into his palm. One by one he counted as he placed them back inside the bottle. "Holy Hell!" he said out loud when he'd put the last in the bottle. Fifteen, that's all there were, plus the one he'd given her; that made sixteen. If she'd taken the meds for a week when she first got them, maybe twenty-three. He needed to call Beatrice and see if he could find out when she started going out after the crash, fuck that still left seven unaccounted for.

Dan took the bottle with him to the living room; grabbing the phone book he searched for the name of the doctor. He couldn't find the name anywhere. Looking at the label again, the pharmacy's number was listed. He picked up the phone and immediately dialed the number.

"Value Pharmacy, how may I help you?"

Dan was glad he didn't receive one of those automated machines. "This is Dan O'Brien; my wife had a prescription filled there a while back and I cannot find the doctor's phone number in the book. I was hoping you could tell me the name or number to the clinic?"

Dan waited for a response; he could hear the voice of the pharmacist in the background probably talking to a client at the counter.

"What is the doctor's name sir?"

"What…oh I am sorry, I thought you were still talking to the person in the background. The doctor…his name is Dr. Corpian; I think that's how you say it." Dan listened while the pharmacist spelled out the name to be sure it was

197

the right one, when Dan agreed the pharmacist gave him the contact number for the doctor and disconnected.

Dan picked up the phone, listened for the dial tone and began punching in the numbers.

"Midwest Medical Center, can I help you?"

"Yes, I was wondering if you could give me some information about Ambien," Dan said.

"I may be able to help you what is it you need to know?"

"I was wondering what the overdose rate would be, and if an overdose should occur what has to be done to counteract it."

"Well give me a second while I look it up, all right?" Dan listened to some awful elevator music while the receptionist went to look up the information he needed. She came back a few moments later, "Ambien is a sedative, prescribed for sleep disorders. Let's see. It is prescribed in different doses; what was the dose your doctor gave you?"

"5 mg," Dan replied.

"Okay then, maximum dose is two-three tablets per day. As far as an overdose, there are a couple different scenarios, which are you most interested in hearing?"

"Just give me the whole scoop, there are others in the house I will store them safely out of the way, but you never know I'd like to be prepared," Dan said.

"Okay, well if a child should get their hands on them, bring them to the nearest emergency. Bring the prescription with you for the doctor on call. If another adult should get a hold of them there are some medical conditions that one must be aware of…" Dan cut her off telling that no one in the house had any serious medical conditions.

"All right then, if you should succeed maximum dosage by one or two tablets, not a lot will happen to an adult. It will cause sleep and there may be some breathing complications upon awaking, if this happens, see your doctor immediately. As for the other, if you are in a depressed enough state that you overdose by taking a bottle of…"

"That's okay, ma'am you have answered my questions thank you." Dan hung up the phone. How many pills had Emma taken? Not enough for suicide of that he was sure. Not only would she not commit suicide, she would have had to take close to the whole bottle for that to occur, she didn't so that leaves only one conclusion. Those damn dreams! She had forced herself under for some reason, but what? She'd not mention anything other than the quicksand dreams. He had nothing to go on. Damn it, what if she was in trouble?

Dan decided he'd better call Beatrice. He'd have her come here after work and fill her in on the situation. If he went under to bring her out of that dream he wanted someone here to watch them. The thought of taking those little pills turned his stomach, but there really was no other way.

Chapter Twenty-One

Emma, flitted about the ship, it was quite intriguing watching the people work. No one had seen her of course; she hadn't really expected it. The mist still hovered, surrounding the ship. One could barely see the water let alone anything on the horizon.

"Land ho, Capt'n," came the call from the crow's nest.

The man had to have smelled it, Emma thought, because there was no way in hell, he could have seen it. Men scurried about the ship pulling in this sail or that one; Emma had a hard time understanding the orders that flowed from the Captain's mouth. It was truly a sight to behold.

She heard the anchor being lowered and wondered how far offshore they were? If they had been able to dock, then the gangplank would have been lowered wouldn't it? Emma really wished she knew more about ships. The Captain was the first to disembark. Stepping into a smaller boat Emma saw it being lowered into what she assumed was the water below.

Not willing to be left behind she floated closely behind the Captain. When the boat had hit the water there was a splash and then some of the other men came over the side on rope ladders lowering themselves into the boat. Grabbing their oars, they began rowing for shore. Having no dock, the boat came into a beach and the men jumped over the side and began hauling it up onto dry land.

This is where she would leave them Emma assumed. They would go their way and she would get back to the business of locating Emily. She thought about the alley way where Klaus had chased her. It was in the town, she thought as she scanned the area, there did not seem to be any sort of civilization about. She listened carefully to the Captain as he spoke to his crew about the cargo and how to unload it and where.

Emma had not heard him mention the name of a town although he'd motioned to bring the cargo. The men nodded and headed back out to the anchored ship. The Captain began walking through the trees; Emma followed.

She could hear his boot crunch the leaves and twigs on the path. The moon was bright and offered a fair amount of light even amidst the treelined path..

Staying close beside him not wanting to lose her way, Emma almost ran through him when he stopped abruptly. Turning he searched the area, shrugging, he stepped out again. Emma sighed in relief; she really didn't want to be seen. The less people who knew of her whereabouts the better, at least until she had found Emily.

She was thinking about how she would break the news to Emily, when she found her, that is. Hello, I am…am what? This was not going to be easy, any of it. She would cross that bridge when she came to it though; right now, she had a gigantic headache, probably from extending her stay. How long had she been out? Putting the pain behind her she continued, pain or no, she was here for the duration.

Emma heard a growling behind her. Thinking that whatever it was, it was after the Captain; she watched him closely to see what he would do. The growl came again, the Captain continued walking like it was nothing out of the ordinary. Well maybe for him it wasn't the ordinary, but Emma wasn't of his inclination. What was it? A wolf? She did not know for sure but just the thought sent shivers down her spine.

Emma turned behind her; she could see a set of yellow eyes just beyond the trees. She heard the telltale growl and knew for certain it was a wolf, why wasn't the Captain worried? Emma looked back to where the Captain had been in front of her. He was gone. Damn! Where the hell had he gone? She looked about trying to find him. The growl was coming closer and closer. He couldn't possibly have seen her…could he?

Emma's question was answered immediately when she was knocked to the ground by the vicious snarling beast. Putting her hands in front of her face as she'd seen on Discovery Channel, Emma quickly tried to find a way out of her current predicament. Screaming out in pain, Emma felt his teeth sink into her arm, his hot, wet saliva wetting her sleeve as he bit and pulled at her tender flesh.

Feeling around on the ground with her other hand she found a rock; bringing it up hard against the side of his head, Emma heard his whine as his teeth left her skin. Watching him slink away, afraid to take her eyes off him, Emma grabbed her arm pressing it tight against her. It was bleeding. Removing her shirt, from her pants, she ripped a piece from the bottom and wrapped it securely around the wound. Wasn't the best, but it would have to do.

Dan heard Emma cry out, he ran to the bedroom. Sitting down beside her, he took the arm she'd cradled against her chest. For some reason there were scratches on her arm, some of them were deep. They were bleeding. Retrieving the antiseptic and a bandage from the bathroom he cleaned the marks and wrapped them. Where the hell was Beatrice? She would be off work by now. She should be here at any rate; what time is it he wondered?

Opening the drawer in the nightstand, looking for a watch or anything that would give him the time, without leaving Emma; he found the papers shoved in. Plain lined paper with Emma's handwriting on them. Dan was going to put them back, and then reconsidered. Now was not the time to respect her privacy, not if there were a chance her notes could tell him something.

"Damn her hide," Dan said, if she were not in so much trouble already, he'd skin her alive. Why in the hell didn't she tell him? Dan sat staring down at the notes. The details of Klaus's attack, then it dawned on him, her nosebleed, she'd been hit. It somehow carried over into the real world. How? He looked back down at her arm. Running his thumb over the bandage, Dan drooped his weary head, "Oh, Emma," he said quietly. "Why?"

Beatrice had been pounding on the door; when she got no answer, she used her key and let herself in. It was a good thing she hadn't given the key back to Emma when they returned home. Closing the door behind her, Beatrice walked past the empty kitchen and living room down the hall. At the door to Emma's room she paused.

Dan sat there at the side of Emma's bed, some paper squished firmly in his hand, and if she wasn't mistaken, he was crying. "Dan?" she said, softly. "Is everything all right? Is it Emma? Why is she still sleeping at this time of day?"

Dan looked up. Sure enough there were tears in his eyes. Beatrice's heart thudded wildly, running to the bed she grabbed Emma's wrist feeling for a pulse, when she felt it beat beneath her fingers she let out a breath that had been caught in her throat.

"My God Dan, what is the matter, the look on your face and Emma laying here so quiet, for God sakes you nearly gave me a heart attack!" Beatrice yelled.

"Sorry, Beatrice I didn't mean to worry you. I'm just frustrated I guess." Wiping the tears from his eyes he continued, "Why don't we go into the living room for a bit I will fill you in there, okay?"

Beatrice followed Dan out of the room, sitting down on the couch her hands clutched together in her lap she waited for him to gain control enough to talk. "We didn't tell you everything Beatrice, about the dreams I mean." Dan said.

"Oh?" Beatrice raised an inquiring brow.

"No actually there has been some more, it all started about three days ago," he began. Soon he had told her everything. She was shocked to say the least, but she never once said anything about either one of them being ready for the looney-bin.

"So, let me get this right. You two have been fooling around with your dreams, experimenting? Isn't that kind of dangerous, I mean my God Dan…" she let the rest of the statement lay there, but they both knew what she was getting at.

"Actually Beatrice, I don't think it's dangerous; I mean they have been working with dreams for a long time now, but…Damn it Bea, nothing I have read competes with this."

"The other day she woke up in the middle of the night, she had a nosebleed, there was blood all over her hands and her face. I thought nothing of it at the time because let's face it; people have nosebleeds every day. Then today I found this." Dan handed Beatrice Emma's notes on her last dream, about Klaus hitting her and the blood in her hands etc.

"Now wait a minute …you cannot jump to conclusions, maybe she started to have a nosebleed and that was how her body told her. But portraying it as being hit in her dream, I think that is much more likely, don't you?"

"Yes, under normal circumstances I would believe you, but now, she has been out since sometime last night, I have no idea when the sedatives will wear off, but this afternoon she screamed out like she was being attacked, when I ran to the bedroom I discovered her clutching her arm. It was scratched. I bandaged it but I could not help thinking that something or someone did this to her in her dream."

"Okay, Dan so what do you want to do? Should we take her to the hospital?" Beatrice asked.

"No, I don't want her to go in there. They will call it attempted suicide and lock her up in some damn psych ward. She's not crazy! I won't have her going through that." Dan got up pacing the room. "Look, I called the doctor. As near as I can figure she only took six or seven pills. That is not enough for a true overdose, just enough to make her sleep a long time. So, I am not worried on that score."

Beatrice's eyes followed Dan back and forth across the room. "So, what am I doing here then?"

Dan stopped and looked directly at Beatrice. "I asked you to come because I am going to try putting myself under."

Beatrice looked like she was about to argue, but Dan held up a hand stalling her. "Look, it's the only way I can think of. If I can find her there, then I have a chance of bringing her back out of her dream state in one piece. She has it in her head that this Klaus fellow is out to rape Emily, she's feels she has to try and warn her."

"I have to have someone here in case anything goes wrong with either one of us. There are bandages and stuff like that in the bathroom, but more importantly, I want you to monitor our heart rates; if something goes amiss you can call for an ambulance. Only as a last resort Beatrice, do you understand? Will you do it? Will you help me?"

Beatrice said nothing for the longest time. Dan feared she was going to deny him, but she wouldn't do that he argued,. she loved Emma just as much as he did.

"All right, I'll do it. Let me call into HR that way they can get a temp for tomorrow morning." Beatrice grabbed the phone and made the necessary call while Dan got everything readied in the bedroom.

Clearing the nightstand of anything unimportant gave him enough room to lay out bandages, clothes, thermometer and other paraphernalia that Beatrice may need throughout the night. Going back into the living room he grabbed the book on dream control and began sifting through the pages as quickly as he could, refreshing his memory with all he may need to know.

Beatrice followed him into the bedroom looking around she asked Dan if he could bring a chair in from the kitchen. He brought in the computer chair instead knowing it would be a little more comfortable for her long vigil. All right, that's everything he noted silently. He could do this. He would go in and bring his Emma back. "Beatrice," he said, "you know all about temperatures and heart rates, don't you?"

"Actually, Dan I don't have a clue." Beatrice didn't think it was important to let him know that she has vast amounts of information on unconscious victims though. It would only worry him. Dan seemed to be thinking for a moment, "In that case, don't worry unless our temperature goes past 103, and as for the heart rate, I don't know but we have nothing to measure that with anyway. Just do the best you can. I am sure you will know when and if you need to call someone."

Dan went into the bathroom and took some of the meds. Bringing back the bottle, he handed it to Beatrice telling her he how many he'd taken and how many he suspected Emma had taken.

She may have to tell the paramedics. Lying down on his side of the bed, Dan took deep calming breaths allowing the pills to take effect and send him the dreamland.

Beatrice sat quietly not daring to make a sound in case it bothered Dan as he drifted off. Seeing his eyes close she remained silent for a good ten minutes until she heard a definite altering to his breathing. Picking up the book Dan had earlier she began to read. She'd gone through several chapters, what she'd read confirmed all she'd heard from Dan and Emma. Providing this information was accurate, all should be fine.

Standing up bending over Emma, Beatrice felt her forehead she was not hot. She checked her pulse it was slow, maybe too slow, but considering she took sleeping pills it was probably how it was supposed to be. She wished for a moment she had access to all the fancy equipment they had at the institution. Everything always showed on the screen, simple and easy to read and understand. Leaving the room to get a cup of coffee Beatrice thought about the strangeness of the situation, no one would ever believe it. Coming back a little while later with a decanter of coffee, Beatrice sat down to read more while she maintained her watch.

Dan was being pulled down; it was not a scary feeling so he allowed the heaviness to ascend upon him; praying he would know what to do once he encountered the dream state. Mists closed in around him, blanketing him making him feel like an infant in its mother's arms. He felt safe. He could smell the salty sea air, and like always even in real life it relaxed him. Falling…he was falling crossing over through time and space and still he felt at peace.

Wondering if he would ever encounter something below him, Dan continued his journey downward. Emma, he thought, I must find Emma. Repeating the words over and over, just like it had said in the book. If you wanted to remember something in the dream world, you had to keep that thought upper most in your mind while you descended.

He could feel himself falling faster and faster, he was beginning to worry, no longer did he feel in control. He didn't know if it was an effect of the drugs he'd taken or not, but his mind for the moment couldn't stay with one complete thought. Images careening wildly through his brain; he was thankful at least that Emma was in most of them; her image provided a much-needed patronage for his wayward mind.

Beatrice sat by watching and reading, she noticed Dan's fists as they gripped the covers. He had not cried, and nothing seemed to be amiss, but Beatrice felt a moment of uneasiness as she loosened the death grip he had on the blankets. Taking his hand in hers she smoothed it out. Comforting him from she knew not what, she tried to ease his tension. It would certainly not do them any good if he freaked out.

Through Dan's mind flashed images, Emma laughing, Emma the ice queen, Emma the little girl who had fallen and sprained her ankle…no that wasn't Emma. It couldn't be Emma. She had never hurt herself like that.

His mind sent images back and forth. Some were of times in the real world. Some were of times so long-ago. Dan had a hard time trying to figuring out where they all fit.

The scenes were starting to slow; Dan felt a contact to the outside world, whatever it was it slowed the speed of his fall, allowing him to think. Making plans as he waited for the fog to lift. Settling down on the ground Dan knew the main journey was at an end. Now all he'd to do was find Emma. Lying there on the cold hard dirt Dan tried to open his eyes, he couldn't. They seemed stuck, almost glued in place. Placing his fingers over them he rubbed the lids getting them to ease. He was so tired he so very tired…his hand dropped back to his side and all went black.

Dan had been under for some time but aside from his bout with the covers all seemed well. Bea checked on Emma who seemed to be perspiring at a rapid rate. Taking the cloth Dan set out she journeyed to the bathroom to wet it with warm water. Coming back, he gently bathed Emma's head. Taking the thermometer out of the package, Beatrice placed it between her closed lips.

Waiting for a minute she pulled it out, no fever that was good. Although what was making her sweat so?

Emma was walking; her arm hurt like hell. It was burning and she held it cradled close to her. Walking, she'd been walking for so long now, still she'd not found the Captain. The wolf had not come back, thank God, still she was sweating, and she hoped he did not have rabies. The moon was still high; strange. She would have thought it would have been put to bed long ago, being replaced by the sun.

She heard not a sound since the Captain left her behind, yet she remained on the same path he set out on, hoping that it would eventually lead to a town. There she would hopefully be able to find a clean bandage and wash out the wound before it became infected. There was a breeze, the air was clean and cool, it felt so nice against her heated body.

Beatrice put the cloth back on the nightstand and went back to her seat. It was only seven o'clock, it seemed a lot later than that. Sipping her coffee, she began reading again. Dan started tossing and turning, Beatrice ran to him hoping to get him under control before he hurt Emma or himself. Smoothing the hair away from his brow, in a motherly gesture she kissed his forehead. He began to quiet as she murmured to him in a calming voice.

This is going to be a long night, she thought once Dan was quieted. She prayed she would not fall asleep. That would be all they needed, for her to fall asleep and stop monitoring them, it could lead to total disaster. With that, she went back to her book; no, she would not fall asleep. She would stay awake and protect them.

All remained quiet for several hours. Beatrice was worried; she liked it when they moved or moaned for then she felt as though she was part of what was happening. What she wouldn't give for a TV right about now. She would love to be able to stay tuned for the next episode in the Dan and Emma saga. At least then she would feel like she was doing something to help.

She'd finished reading the book; it really was quite interesting. If she understood correctly what she'd been reading, that meant, Dan would be able to contact Emma through a lucid dream state and maintain control of the situation, as needed. She'd read about some doctor's wife, a Dr. Rhine, she believed, at any rate the doctor's wife had been on a train back home. Realizing she had not contacted her husband telling him what time she would be in. Coming in late at night to a train station in the middle of a big city is not wise unless you have someone there waiting for you. Unable to call she resorted to a method of ESP, whereby she'd said over and over that the train would be at the station at 2 a.m. Not knowing for sure if it would work, she repeated it over and over throughout the journey. At the same time, at home in bed, her husband was dreaming, he kept hearing something telling him to be at the train station at two in the morning, waking up disturbed he called the station to see if there would be a train in at that hour. Upon finding out that the train was due in from St. Louis; he knew he had received a subconscious message from his wife. He went and met the train when it came in and sure enough, she was on it.

There were many other reported cases of ESP through dreams, she assumed that was one of the methods Dan was going to try to use to locate Emma. Hopefully the drugs would not hinder him in anyway. In everything she'd read, not once did it mention enforced sleep. What would the side effects be, she wondered?

Deciding it best to clear her mind and only think of one problem at a time, Bea checked on her charges before going back into the living room to find another book. If she kept reading maybe she would discover more about what to do when they both woke up. If they both woke up. Stop that you old hen. You're making matters worse; it will be a long enough night without you auditioning for the nut house too.

Muttering to herself, she sifted through the books, taking a couple she returned to the bedroom. Settling down in her chair she opened the first book. She noticed right away all the yellow stickies Emma had used to mark the pages of interest. She would read those first and if need be then she would read the rest of the books if she still did not understand what was going on.

Finding the section Emma had marked about shared dreams, on the little piece of paper Emma had marked both hers and Dan's names with a big question mark. From what Dan and Emma had told Beatrice when they got back, there was no longer any question as to whether these two unlikely people shared the same dreams. Obviously, they did. But why?

Reading further she noticed that all the cases documented knew the person they shared the dream with. Yet Dan and Emma had not known each other at all. Maybe the people who didn't know each other weren't documented because no one ever knew. What were the odds of two people…shrugging Beatrice turned to the next section in the book?

Past life experiences. This seemed a little far-fetched to Beatrice. There has been about as much controversy over past lives as there had been over alien abduction. Could it be? Beatrice looked back at Emma's notations, it simply said 'Emma-Emily, Dan-Daniel', that's odd. The names are so similar too. Beatrice pondered the idea a little while; she was about to believe just about anything at this point. Maybe when Dan or Emma came out of it, they would be able to give her more information to go on.

At the back of one of the books there were a list of symbols and their meanings, Beatrice found some that had even related to her. Interesting, she never would have thought that dreams had any hidden meanings. She had to solve the current crisis. But then maybe she would see if there was a way to contact her love through dreams. Oh, how she would love to speak with him again.

"If there was a will, there was a way," her mother had said.

Beatrice grabbed Emma's note, the one Dan had shown her earlier. Reading what was written there she found what she thought could be symbols. Reaching into the drawer she found a pen, turned the page over and started writing out some of the symbols. She spent the next several hours looking them up in the book and jotting down their meanings. All the while in the back of her mind, she kept hashing over the possibilities of communicating with Dexter. If what Dan and Emma were doing worked, if they succeeded then the possibilities were endless. That gave her huge amounts of hope and started the adrenalin flowing.

Chapter Twenty-Two

Emma's arm hurt like hell. She'd been walking forever, no sign of anything. She'd heard what she thought was her name being called out but that was ridiculous who would be calling her name here? Putting one foot in front of the other Emma continued walking. That's odd, she thought. The ground seemed so hard now. Before it was just like a path in the forest, soft and moist, now though, it was different. "Damn, I wish I could see," she said aloud.

Stopping, she knelt. She could feel the smooth, damp surface. Using her fingers as a guide she allowed her fingers to roam. She found what she thought were a series of rocks. She was so bloody tired it took a little while for her awareness to kick in. Cobblestones. Yes! Feeling her vigor return, she stood and continued walking; now she could see a lantern up ahead.

Briefly she wondered why it had taken her so long to reach her destination. It seemed strange, though everything right now seemed strange. Maybe it was because she had taken those pills? It had been necessary. She was not sorry for it. Now to find Emily and Daniel and warn them to be on the lookout for Klaus. She figured that she should try to alter her clothing so that if they could see her, she would appear to be from their time at least.

As for explaining who she was to them, she really did not know. Maybe luck would with her and she could simply say that she was a friend. She was sure it would all fall into place when the time came. Emma could hear the distant sounds of laughter; it was a welcoming sound. She couldn't wait to get inside somewhere and dry off.

Her arm needed to be tended to as well. Focusing on the light up ahead so her course would remain true, Emma walked a little faster. Being so close, she could almost feel the warmth that had eluded her. Thankful for the bit of fever that her wound had given her on her long journey, there was at least something to be said for bad luck.

Standing outside, Emma looked up at the sign that hung precariously over the door, chuckling to herself about the name, the Boar and Hound; this should be a good place. She wondered how it would stack up against Fred's little pub back home. From the sounds of things, it was filled to the brim but a quick look down the street told her it was probably the only tavern for miles.

Looking up she tried to judge whether this place would have rooms above, like she'd read about in the romance novels set long ago. She could hear the robust laughter of men relieving stress from a hard day's work, probably not honest work she reflected. Swallowing, she stiffened her spine. This was her dream damn it, and if she wanted, she could be the worst of the lot. She hoped.

Well at least it was warm inside; she might even be able to find something clean enough to tend to her arm. As she walked through the door into the darkened smelly room, she wasn't all that sure. All was silent as she walked over to the bar. The bar tender, a gruff looking chap in a dirty apron, looked her up and down.

Emma could feel the eyes of everyone else boring into her back. She asked the bartender for a room and shuffled her feet nervously waiting for his reply. "Ain't got any rooms. T'is, here's a bar miss, seems to me, you're a might lost. Less you'd come for a job, now there be a lot I could do with the likes of someone as fine as you, yes sirry." His eerie, open-mouthed grin showed blackened, crooked teeth.

His breath was overwhelming. Tamping down her nausea, she offered him a small but sickly smile. "No, sir, that's all right, I'm not in need of any work. Maybe you would be so kind as to get me some of the cleaner rags?." Emma lifted her arm slightly.

The man assessed her wound. "And just what might ye be payin' with? Can't be throwin' away good rags on the likes of you."

Emma reached in her pocket, she didn't even know what type of currency they had in this time, hoping that with her being in control of her dream she would have something of substance in there and not just lint. She didn't have to worry though for a man came up behind her. "I be payin' for the littl' lady." His voice sounded familiar, but Emma knew she would have to turn around in order to view is his face to be sure.

Oh my God, she thought silently, could it be? Yes, it was, if her dreams were accurate. Coughing to hide her astonishment, Emma muttered a quick thank you. The man dropped some coin on the counter, looked like gold to Emma, but what the hell did she know? The creepy bar tender went through a little door at the back of the bar, presumable the kitchens, and returned a short while later with some terribly grayed rags. They looked like they would make the wound worse; Emma's distaste must have showed in her face, for he snorted, "Not good enough for the likes of you is it?"

"They're fine," the man said. Grabbing hold of Emma's arm, he pulled to the back of the tavern and pushed her down onto an old wooden bench. "Where's the Captain?" he demanded.

Emma just stared at him, what could she say? She had no idea where the Captain was. Yet if she was Emily, and clearly Donavan thought she was, she should know where her own husband was. What to do? She thought frantically.

"Well, where on earth do you think he is?" Emma said, her tone haughty.

"Well the last time I be speakin' wit' him, he was a takin' you back to the ship. Leastwise til' tomorrow when he was goin' ta bring ye back in ta town for yer birthday. Now I know he'd not let ye walk about this late at night without him so's how's about you tell me why ye left the ship," Donavan said.

"I left the bloody ship, because I couldn't sleep. I did not intend to come into town, but I was chased by a wolf, this is where I ended up," Emma said, waving her arm in front of his face as if he were some sort of moron. Donavan caught it; bringing it to his face for a closer inspection he removed the ripped shirt and tossed it on the table. It was covered in dried blood, but Emma thought sickly, the table looked like it had seen worse. Much worse.

"Hold still!" Donavan shouted, as he poked and prodded at the teeth marks. Grabbing the bottle on the table he up ended it pouring some burning concoction all over Emma's arm. She tried to pull her arm back, and Donavan rewarded her with a look that said he'd like to smack her.

Well too damn bad, Emma thought in a huff. She felt woozy as he tied one of the rags around her arm. Fighting against throwing up she held her breath. Bad move. Donavan went to pull her out of her seat, but her legs buckled; she heard him saying something about heading back to the ship just before all went black. Donavan picked her up and threw her over his shoulder, she would have some explaining to do when he got her back.

Emma bounced unconsciously against his back like a sack of wheat as he left the Boar and Hound, heading down the street. Damn woman; he swore silently; it was a long walk to where the ship had been anchored. Longer with her on his back. He supposed he could take one of the carts the smugglers left in the alley when they stopped in for a pint. That would be asking for trouble; he'd just as soon go without.

The Captain had to anchor well away from the wharf. He didn't want to be mistaken for a smuggler should any patrol ships spot them. There whole cargo could be confiscated and they could not let that happen. Turning toward the trees, Donavan found the worn path leading him away from town and around the seedy docks. Little miss could have been killed had she ventured there; "bloody women," he muttered out loud. Only good for one thing I say, just one thing.

Dan was cold, his bones felt like icicles. Propping himself up on his elbows he raised his head and looked around. The whole place was shrouded in a heavy mist. Where the hell was he? Forcing his numb legs to carry him, he stood. Rubbing his hands together to get the circulation working again he looked around.

He saw a shipped in the harbor below, but nothing else appeared on the rocky shoal. No sign of a town. Nothing. The ship looked like a 19th century merchantman, safe enough, he hoped as he started the long trek down to the seaside. He'd find out if anyone had seen a woman fitting Emma's description.

Reaching the seaside didn't take very long at all and soon Dan found a swarthy looking fellow mending the hull. She seemed to have taken a hit. As he stood back and surveyed the ship, he could see the guns. He was in awe. He never before, accept maybe in his dreams had ventured or close enough to investigate the grandness of a ship, any ship, from this time.

Waving to the man working at the bow of the ship, Dan walked over like he'd been on the docks all his life. "Ye wouldn't by any chance have seen a young lady hereabouts? She is not that big, blonde hair and green eyes. She's my sister, we were separated a while back."

The man pulled at his gray beard, "Naw can't say as I have, we just put into port after a run in with the damn patrol, you'd think one could tell a smuggler from a merchantman. There's town, not much of one, but you may be able to find her there. Separated you say? Not such a nice place for a little lady, but you'd be better off trying there anyways."

"No, sir it certainly isn't, I am sure you can understand my worry," Dan said.

"Yes, I do," the older man replied, "but like I told ye before the best place to ask around would be the town." The man waved a weathered hand toward the direction of the trees. "Just stay to the path and ye'll get there. Hard to see from here, it is. But she be there just the same."

Dan thanked the man and headed for the path. The forest was dense, it wasn't any wonder he had not noticed the town. In his time there would be skyscrapers and the like, monuments one could spot for miles but here there was nothing of the sort. Walking along, it did not take Dan long before he noticed the telltale signs of civilization. The sun was high in the sky making the town look even dirtier than what he'd originally guessed it would be.

The man back at the ship didn't seem to think it was the best place in the world, as a matter of fact he gave Dan the impression he would just as soon be gone from these shores. Dan passed by some old wood buildings, their idea of stores. The ground now was covered with pebbles instead of dirt. Prehistoric infrastructure Dan thought as he stopped to look around.

There was an eerie feeling to this place, but Dan could not tell if it was because of the era in which his dream was from or if maybe something more sinister was at foot. Dan spotted a tavern just up the road; the sign overhead read 'Boar and Hound', well that should be as good a place as any to start. Walking to the door, he reached for the handle. It was locked, probably had not opened for the day yet. Banging on the door, Dan listened for any signs of life. Nothing.

Turning he headed to what looked like the general store; there were barrels set outside the entrance, he assumed they would have some sort of goods there. Walking into the store, he looked around, Christ this is something out of Little House on the Prairie he thought, well not definitely the right era but old just the same.

There was a pudgy little woman behind the counter. Harriet Olsen, Dan thought chuckling to himself. "And what be ye doin' on this fine day Captain?" The woman asked. No not Harriet Olsen he reflected there was far too much old English in her speech to be her. She called him Captain, Dan thought about it for a moment and realized that maybe she'd confused him with Daniel.

"I came in to see if maybe my wife had come in. Have you seen her?"

"Not since yesterday My Lord, when ye both came in looking at the fabric ye did, but ye already knows that."

Dan hadn't known that, but he did now. Taking the information and tucking it away for future use, he nodded while turning to leave the store.

"Ye want me to say yer lookin' for her My Lord?"

Dan stopped and looked back at the elderly Mrs. Olsen; he could not stop thinking of her as such no matter how she sounded.

"Yes, that would be great. Thank you."

With that Dan walked out into the bright sunshine. So, they thought he was Daniel, well aside from being a little older there was a resemblance. That did him little good when he did not know where Daniel or Emily was at this moment. He had no doubt that if he found them, eventually he would find Emma. She was like a missile homing in or her target. She would not stop until she'd connected.

Dan walked down the street back to the Boar and Hound; maybe someone would be up now. The town really wasn't all that bad, maybe it housed smugglers and the like, maybe it could be rough but during the day, everyone seemed friendly enough. Various people had waved to him, well Daniel most likely, but it gave him a chance to see them in a different light. Had they known he was a stranger then it is all too possible that that environment would have been a hostile one.

Deciding to go around back this time he found the door and banged on it. After about the third bang, Dan heard her someone yelling on the other side.

"Hold on, hold on I's a comin'!"

It was a gruff voice and when the man opened the door Dan seen why. He looked like he'd been run over by a Mack truck. His hair stood on end his nose was bashed into his face, a sign of a bar owner in these rough and tumble times. Someone must have connected well with this guy's face.

"What ye be doin' here this time o' day Capt'n? You know better than to wake me at such a cursed hour! What ye be wantin'?" Running a weathered hand through his hair, the old man paused for a moment. "This here wouldn't be about yer bride now would it? I's only had a littl' fun with the wee gal. Nothin' more than that, then your man Donavan took her back to yer ship. Threw her over his shoulder he did. Done tuckered out she was. She couldn't even stand no more. No one touched her I swear." His eyes fell to Dan's side.

Dan looked to see what the man had his eye on and there, hanging at his side was a saber. At least he thought it was a saber. Though he couldn't say for sure what its actual name was. How the hell had that got there?

Putting what he hoped was a sneer on his face Dan looked at the man. "You better hope no one touched her, when she came back to the ship, she was unconscious she has not woken yet." Dan prayed that she was all right. He knew Donavan. He was a good man and if he thought Emma was Emily, he would protect her with his life. Then when she awoke, he would tan her hide. Dan felt a surge of respect for the man. Emma needed a good spanking.

That had some merit. Here, in this time, he could not be faulted for taking her over his lap. Chuckling at the thought he turned from the bar owner, he would let the old man get back to sleep.

He was hungry; he'd seen a restaurant a while back he'd go there and get some grub. Grub is probably what it would be, but at least one could not get food poisoning from a dream…could they?

Walking into the restaurant, he was surprised by the cleanliness of the place. The tables and chairs were nothing to sneeze at, just rough old planking for tables and benches they were scored with knives and the like, yet they were washed and all in all, the little place smelled clean and well cared for. A little old lady, plumper than the one in the mercantile, came waddling over to his table. Betty Crocker or the Pillsbury Dough Boy he couldn't be sure which, maybe a mixture of both. Both he thought, looking into her rounded, dimpled smiling face.

"Why, Capt'n where's yer lovely wife this fine morn'?" Taking a cloth from her apron she started to wipe the already clean table in front of him.

"She's back at the ship, we may be back later this eve, but right now I could use some sustenance I am as hungry as a horse."

"Why, yes Capt'n a growing lad such as yerself, newly married and all I'm sure ye need lots of sustenance. Let old Mags get ye somethin' from the back," she said, winking. Turning she quickly headed back to the kitchen.

She walked quite quickly for someone of her stature Dan thought, maybe she was a little embarrassed but what was said. Daniel, even though he was a sea Capt'n was of higher peerage than most of the local folk in this village. He would try to set her at ease when she brought his food back to him. As he waited for her to return, he looked around, noting the small seascape paintings on the wall, they were very well done. He wondered who had the talent for such paintings in this small town.

The curtains that covered the window were bright and cheery. He assumed 'Betty Crocker' made them, to liven the place up a little. Let's just hope her cooking ranks up there with the namesakes he'd assigned her. If the smells coming from the kitchen were any indication there would be no problem on that score either. Soon the little woman came out of the back, hands laden with so many dishes Dan wondered if she were feeding an army.

"Here ye be young man." She set dishes of venison stew, potatoes, roast beef pie and fresh baked buns before him. "I thought ye might be hankerin' for a thirst of fine ale, so's I brought ye some, if'n ye want somewhat else ye just let old Mags know."

Good God, he thought as he surveyed the bounty before him, what else could he possibly want? He didn't think he'd be able to get all this down. Smiling up at her, he said jokingly, "Thanks Mags, care to join me?"

Wiping her hands on her apron, Mags shook her head no, "Gots meself too much to do as it is, sides you be needing all this yerself; losing weight since the last time you were in. Got to take care of yerself. Ye children won't be wantin' a frail papa."

"Don't worry Mags, children are not here yet, and I am not as frail as you may think," Dan said, with a wink. "Thanks again."

The meal was delicious, as mouthwatering as the smells were; he had to admit he'd been more than a little worried. Now, after having the first bite almost melt in his mouth, he was trying to figure out ways to take Mags back with him. Emma would love this. Where in the hell was, she? What in the hell was going to happen when Donavan realized...oh hell he probably already knew it wasn't Emily; the barkeep said he carried her off last night.

What the hell was she going to say to them to explain her sudden appearance and her close resemblance to Emily? He'd not thought of what he would say to Daniel either, he had hoped he would just be able to find Emma and get out without being seen, that was not to be. So, while he ate, he thought of different possibilities that could somehow be believable to a 19th century couple, which knew nothing of dreams.

Chapter Twenty-Three

"Who do you think she is?" Emily asked her husband.

"I don't know my love, but she sure does look like you." Daniel could not fault Donavan for thinking it was his wife, that he had seen in the tavern last night. It didn't matter right now that the girl was not Emily; she needed to be taken care of. He'd tended to the wound in her arm himself. It was filthy, he hoped he'd managed to clean it well enough that an infection would not set in. Donavan had told him a wolf had bitten her. That was her reason for ending up at the Boar and Hound. Still that place at night is no place for a woman.

"When will she wake up do you think?" Emily asked, impatiently tapping her foot against the floor.

"I don't know Emily, my love, but she is not hot to the touch, so she should be coming around soon." No sooner had the words come out of Daniel's mouth, they heard Emma stir and open her eyes.

"Emily? I have been looking all over for you," she blurted.

"But I don't even know you," Emily said. "Why would you be looking for me?" Emma realized her mistake, but she'd been so relieved in finally finding Emily that she'd forgotten to use the story she'd made up. Time to improvise she thought. "No that's right you do not know me, but I was on the path to town when a man came by, I jumped back into the trees so that he would not see me."

"He was mumbling something about finding the Captain's wife and giving her what was due. I was worried; it did not sound as though it boded well for the Captain's wife whoever that may be." Emma paused to see if there was some sign that her story was being taken as truth. Emily stood beside her husband and both were looking at her, but she couldn't tell what they were thinking. Throwing caution to the wind she continued.

"I was searching for a Captain trying to find out which one had a wife with him, when I was attacked by a wolf. I made my way to the tavern in town, when your man, I am sorry I do not believe he gave me his name, mistook me for you and brought me here," Emma said, shrugging. "As for how I knew your name, that's easy I heard your husband call you by name before I opened my eyes." There they couldn't dispute that, Emma hoped.

Emily walked over and sat down on a chair beside the bed. "It really is remarkable, don't you think?"

Emma did not have to ask her to what she referred because her gaze bore into every contour of Emma's face.

"Yes, quite." Emma said.

Turning toward Daniel Emma asked, "Do you know of any other Captains that have their wives here?"

Daniel took his time thinking about all the people he met the day before. None of the smugglers would have brought their and he'd met only one other Captain since they had docked. Emily and he were invited to supper aboard their ship while it was taking on repairs. There was no sign of a wife.

"No, I am the only Captain within miles that has his wife aboard, I fear. Tell me about this man," he said, sitting on the arm of the chair beside his wife.

"I'm sorry, I cannot tell you much about him aside from what he said that is. It was dark so I could barely see what he looked like, but I remember he was large, he had dark hair and a really gruff voice that carried a hint of a Scottish accent."

Emma could not give a better description or tell them Klaus's name in case they wondered how she knew so much, being come upon in the woods like that. Hopefully the information that she was able to give them would lead their minds in the right direction. If not, she would think of something else when the time came.

"Well, who do you think could be?" Emily said, to Daniel.

"I don't really know love, there was only one man that could have fit that description, but we dropped him off in a port hundreds of miles from here. It just couldn't be Klaus. Could it?" The last part, Daniel hadn't meant to say out loud.

Emma could tell by the way he immediately clammed up and his face turned as hard as granite. Well at least it worked, his mind was moving in the right direction.

Kissing his wife on the forehead Daniel said, "Why don't you two visit, Emily has not seen many women her age since we left port. It's been almost a

219

year and all she has seen is rough seamen. I think it would be nice, since you're not going anywhere for a while, that she has someone like you to talk to." His sentence completed he headed for the door.

This young lady could keep his wife out of trouble here on the ship while he went into town to see if anyone knew the whereabouts of Klaus. It was possible that the bastard could have landed himself another position; ships were always looking for able-bodied men, no matter what they had done before as long as they could man the gunners or mend the sails, they had a job.

He couldn't have arrived much before them. That left only a couple of possibilities, Captain McLeod's ship. Dan couldn't remember from which port that ship hailed, he would have to check it out. Then there were the smugglers. He wished he had a little help where they were concerned; smugglers were always a rough bunch.

Donavan was at the helm when Daniel reached topside. Taking a quick look around to make sure all was as it should be; Daniel strolled over. "The young miss awakes, Capt'n?" he asked. Daniel nodded, looking out over the sea, deep in thought. Donavan wondered what had his Captain so worried. All was okay when he left him after the briefing before sunup. Clearing his throat as to catch Daniel's attention, Donavan waited for him to say what was on his mind.

"Did you see Klaus about during your sojourn into town?"

With a shocked look, Donavan replied, "Klaus?"

Daniel nodded again. "Apparently he has been spotted on this isle and he is out to get Emily, or so the young lady has said."

Now that Donavan knew the heart of what was troubling the master. He wished he could tell him exactly where that Scotsman was. But truth be told, he didn't know. He'd not seen nor heard of him while he was in town.

It was possible that he could have been in the tavern, Donavan had not been there long when he saw what he thought was the master's wife come into the crowded room. If Klaus was here and if he was after the Captain's wife then likely, if he was smart, he would remain hidden until he made his move but smart wasn't exactly the word, he'd use to describe the Scotsman. Big, dumb and mean, was more like it.

"What ye be wantin' to do Capt'n?" Donavan asked. Daniel shook his head, "I guess maybe we should go into town. Soon the Boar and Hound will be busting at the seams with thirsty men, and if he is anywhere, he will be there. I have not known him to leave the drink alone for too long." The seaman nodded whether it was his Scottish blood or just his own powerful thirst Klaus always had a pint in hand.

Daniel motioned over a helmsman, the ship was relatively empty being anchored just offshore, the men had been given leave to find whores and drink before continuing their way. As a Captain, there was one thing he knew for sure. Men needed to blow off steam every so often to keep them from acting up and endangering the lives of all on board. One of the men, each relieved by another each morn', was the only crewmember on board aside from Donavan or himself.

"Donavan and I have to go into town; I can't say when we will be back. The women should remain in the cabin. Just keep watch out for anything suspicious."

The helmsman looked baffled, "Suspicious Capt'n?"

Daniel exhaled noisily, "Yes Decker, suspicious. Klaus may be close; he is none too happy I dropped him in that last port. Just watch and keep the women safe. Can you do that? We will return as soon as we can." Daniel looked at the boy. He was a good lad. He knew he would protect Emily with his life, but he also feared that when it came down to it, he would be no match for Klaus.

They would hurry back, and all would be well. He didn't think the gruff seaman would have the balls to come aboard the Maiden. Stepping inside the boat with Donavan, Decker lowered them into the water. The men rowed in silence each lost in their own thoughts until they reached the shore. Stepping out they pulled the boat over the land and concealed it in the trees not far away. If Klaus did spot the ship, he'd have a hard time finding a way out to her. Daniel and Donavan headed toward the path leading to town, with any luck they could discover what they needed to know and make it back to the ship before nightfall.

Daniel and Donavan walked through town going into one shop or another asking questions, waiting for The Boar and Hound to open its doors for the day. They had come up with nothing so far. Frustrated they walked toward the pub.

"Capt'n it won't be very busy just yet, can we stop at Mags, I could use a bite my gullet is complaining' something fierce." Daniel nodded and together they ducked into a doorway on the right. The place was empty as per usual once the bar opened. They sat down at a nearby table.

Mags came out smiled then stopped dead in her tracks. "Ye cleaned up all yer dinner Capt'n why are ye back?" Donavan and Daniel looked at one another. "Are ye batty woman? We only just got here and ye have not fed us one scrap yet." Donavan said.

Mags patted her head as if the knock some sense in. "I's sorry truly I am but I know what I saw, and you came in just before the Boar and Hound opened. I fed you venison stew, potatoes and roast beef pie, don't ye remember?"

"Mags I don't know what to say old girl, but Donavan and I just got into town a little while ago and this is the first time we've been in here. Could you be a sweet thing and get us some grub before we parish?" Mags took one last look at Daniel and headed into the back to get him another meal. Men, she thought, they're always eatin' and sleepin' I'd have thought the captain was different. She was not batty. Angrily she loaded up several platters and took them out to the table.

Dan was sitting in the corner of the dingy little tavern. It was loud and noisy and more than a little rough; fights were breaking out almost every other second. Several times he'd jumped to avoid a body being slammed back into his table. He'd not seen any sign of Donavan or Daniel, but he'd seen one familiar face but, in the darkness, he could not be sure whether it was the bastard or just a trick of the atmosphere.

The barkeep said he would motion to him when Daniel arrived in case through the entire ruckus Dan managed to miss him. "He doesn't stay long, he doesn't, not with his new wife awaiting back at the ship," the barkeep told him. Dan didn't care if he stayed long or not, he wanted to get out of this hellhole as soon as possible but he did not want to take the chance on missing him altogether. This was his one shot.

Already he'd started having headaches and sure indication that he'd stayed way too long within this dream. He was worried that he would be snatched from the dream-plane back into reality before he managed to get a hold of his wife. How did Emma manage to stay so long, he wondered? She was smaller than he so in all likelihood the barbiturates would remain in her system for a longer period of time, but taking so many, one would think, that it would have left her knocked out much longer than he was when he first crossed over.

She'd been doing this longer then him though. She'd been practicing, he would bet his ships on it, probably before he came back from Baltimore. She hadn't said, but it was in what she didn't say that told him the truth. "Oh, Emma my love, where the hell are you? I could beat you right now if I could find you," he said, slamming his fist down on the table.

He heard another thud of the door opening and closing, through the smoke and the filth it was hard to see who had come through.

Soon the barkeep came up to the table with a pint in his hand. "He's here, Capt'n, over yonder by the bar. Though how it is that you ain't him I'll never know, sure as shittin' I never seen the like," the barkeep said, wiping the table with a dirty rag, he set the pint of rotgut in front of him.

Dan waited for him to leave, took a sip of the awful stuff. I wonder if this is what horse piss tastes like, he thought. After several minutes he got up drink in hand and walked to the bar. Standing beside Daniel, Dan said, "Bar keep a drink for the Capt'n if you please."

The barkeep nodded, went into the back, and came out a moment later with a bottle of brandy. Oh hell! He's been poisoning me with this shit, and he has good brandy in the back.

Setting the glass in front on Daniel, the man smiled. "Found yer wife did ye lad?" Turning to Dan he winked.

Daniel followed the barkeeps gaze; his jaw fell open as he stared into his very image. "Donavan?" he said to somewhere behind him.

Donavan could not answer; his mouth too, was open wide and almost touching the floor. Daniel sent a well-placed elbow into his man's ribs, satisfied when he heard the air catch in Donavan's throat.

Dan smiled, "Well Capt'n isn't it customary where you come from to thank a fellow Captain for a drink once it has been offered and given?".

Daniel nodded robotically and Dan burst out laughing.

"Holly Hades! Capt'n," Donavan stuttered. "He even sounds like you." Donavan was still staring. Not even blinking as Dan's laugh once again rang throughout the tavern.

Daniel nodded. "Yes, yes, it is. Thank you."

Dan clasped Daniel on the shoulder. "I have heard much about you young Daniel. I am, well that's not important right now, what is important is that I have finally got to meet one of the youngest, most successful Captains in these parts. Your headed back home I presume?"

"Yes, my wife and me. Normally we do not make this port, but it is my wife's birthday today, so we docked a couple of days ago intending to spend her special day here."

"And did you?" Dan asked, taking a sip of his ale. "No, I am afraid something else came up and my wife has had to remain on the ship, I dare say we shall venture out tomorrow before we hoist anchor. And you?"

"My wife is with me as well, we don't get to travel together as much as we like, but when I have an easy haul, I like to bring her with me. I'm afraid she is aboard the Dancer, sleeping." Dan hoped that no one knew of a ship named Dancer at least until he got the hell out of here. Then he didn't care what they did or didn't know.

Daniel nodded. "Maybe we can get together tomorrow; my wife would like the extra company. I am sure she would look on it as one of the best birthday presents, she could get."

Dan understood what it might feel like to have no one to talk to, women sailing was not the norm for this time. Although Emily had Daniel, he could also see that it would be a lonely life for her as well.

"It's hard for the women, not having someone to talk to, she must be quite lonely," Dan said.

"She was, but we have had an unexpected visitor,"

"Unexpected you say?" Dan took another sip of the horrid concoction he held in his hand.

"Yes, Donavan," Daniel motioned to the man standing on the other side of him, "he found the little thing last night, he did, as a matter of fact thought she was Emily and hauled her ass back to the ship." Daniel burst out laughing remembering the sight of Donavan completely worn out with a woman slung over his shoulders. His mind flashed back to the night before.

Panting from the long-burdened walk back to the ship; his man had come into the cabin the door slamming open and bellowed for the Captain to come. Daniel had thrown on his robe and come out of the sleep quarters to find Donavan standing there with a woman.

"Yer bloody wife, Capt'n," he said, in such a tone that told Daniel he should take better care of what was his.

Daniel simply called for Emily.

"She's right bloody here. I found her at the Boar and Hound, how the hell did she sneak out past ye?" Donavan said, irritated.

Emily's timing was impeccable as she came out of the bedroom. "What's a matter love?" she asked Daniel.

Daniel couldn't answer as he ran to take the load from a weaving Donavan. "Sit down old man; you must be more tuckered than you thought," Daniel said, taking his burden from him. Turning he strode into the bedroom and placed her on the bed. "Light the lamp love."

Emily came into the room, walking to the nightstand; she lifted the lampshade and lit the wick. Placing the shade back down she turned just in time to see the look of awe on her husband's face. "My God she looks just like me!" Emily exclaimed.

Daniel nodded; looking back and forth between the girl on the bed and his wife. "I think she is a little older but not enough for her appearance to differ considerably," Daniel said.

"Whatever is the matter with her?" Emily asked.

"I don't know, I'll ask Donavan what he knows. She doesn't appear to have a fever or anything maybe she was just exhausted."

Donavan came into the room. "It's not just me then? I've not lost my stuffin'? I could have sworn it was ye mistress."

Emily looked at the big man standing there wringing his hands like a naughty child. "It's all right Donavan, we both see the resemblance, it is most unnatural. What do you know of her?"

"Not much mistress. Just that she came into the bar, I thought it best to get her away from the barkeep. She told me she'd been bitten by a wolf. Had bloody rags on her arm. I looked at it and rewrapped it quick-like. I did not want to dally and brought her here straight away." Daniel reached for the woman's arm. The bandage was not the best. He looked back at the seaman..

"I's sorry sir truly I is but the mistress, well I guess she's not the mistress, any how I did not want to be in the tavern overlong, so I wrapped it with what the barkeep supplied us."

"It's okay, now that she is here, I will get some more wrappings and Daniel can use some of his fine brandy to clean the wound. She'll be all right you'll see." Emily walked into the main cabin returning shortly she handed the bottle of brandy and ripped clothes to Daniel.

"My shirts?" he said, wincing.

"Well of course love ye did not expect me to use my new petticoats did ye?" Emily winked to show she was teasing.

Daniel had the wound unwrapped and was wiping it with a wet cloth that Donavan had found somewhere. Taking the bottle of brandy, he slowly poured it over the teeth marks. The wiping the excess away with a cloth, he took the new acquired makeshift bandages and wrapped the woman's arm. Tying it off he sat back and surveyed his shirt, he had always liked that shirt.

"Get some sleep old man; I'll need you on deck in a few hours. I'll go up now, you can watch her?" He pointed to the sleeping figure on the bed.

Nodding Emily pulled up a chair. It had been hours before their guest awoke and when she did, she'd told them about the danger. Donavan had recovered better than expected and although Daniel and Emily had gotten over the appearance of the young woman, he'd been set off guard once more with what she said about Klaus.

"Is there a problem Captain?" Daniel heard the voice of the other Captain and it brought him back to the present.

"Sorry, woolgathering, I guess. There have been some mighty strange happenings lately," Daniel said, shaking his head.

Lifting his glass he saluted Dan and took a long swallow. "What has this old scallywag been feedin' you?" The barkeep took Dan's drink from him and replaced it with a glass of the same brandy he'd fetched for Daniel.

Dan took a sip Mmmm…smooth as a baby's behind. He took another healthy sip.

Daniel smiled knowing exactly what he meant. There was nothing as good as a finely aged brandy. "So, what about it then?" Daniel asked.

"About?"

"Yes, how about you and your misses coming to the Maiden tonight? We will have a bit of a birthday celebration for my wife there."

Daniel looked at Donavan; he shook his head indicating that he'd not spotted Klaus. He would stay behind until closing time and see if the Scotsman showed up. Daniel and Dan both downed the remainder of their drinks; setting the glasses back down on the counter Dan followed Daniel out of the pub into the night. "It's not my regular stop, thought it would be all right Emily's birthday and all. Town is okay during the day but at night it's crawling with smugglers and wreckers. The smugglers aren't a bad lot if you mind your business but the wreckers; well they are a different matter entirely."

Dan knew what smugglers were but wreckers, he wasn't sure he'd heard the term before. But how does one ask about something that seems to be commonplace in these times without sounding like a complete fool, so Dan kept silent as he walked beside Daniel down the path. "Oh, I forgot where are you anchored? We can collect your wife if it is not too far. If it is though, I suppose Decker could always row around to her if you think she'll come back with him. He's a darky. Some women can fear the unknown, and unless you have traveled near Oran and the like I don't suppose she has seen one."

Dan didn't really hear anything past 'collect your wife' now what the hell was he supposed to say? He opted for a partial truth. Shrugging, he said, "My wife is missing I'm afraid. It is why I came into town. I needed to look for her. I have my men out scouring the land. She took ill on the last voyage, fever and the like, thought she was okay when we came into port but last night she took to wondering while I was helping the men. No one had seen her leave. I have been worried sick ever since."

Daniel looked at him in disbelief. "You lied to me. Why?"

"I didn't know if you were friend or foe, the barkeep said that a woman left with a man the night before, with his description, I was sure it was my Emma, so I stayed hoping you'd return and when you did," the barkeep pointed you out. "You did tell me your wife was on the ship talking to someone. I figured if I could get to your ship make sure it was her and she was alright then I'd tell you all of it then."

"I see, I guess I'd do the same if it were me." Daniel said, satisfied. "Shall we hurry then? You must be eager to see if it is her."

Dan nodded realizing that Daniel couldn't see him in the dark "Yes, let's." Clasping him on the shoulder as he'd done back in the bar the two walked in companionable silence the remainder of the way.

Chapter Twenty-Four

Emma enjoyed talking to Emily. She'd never have thought it were possible but here she was. There was so much she didn't get to see in her dreams. So many gaps. However, without letting on she'd managed, to get Emily to divulge much of what she wanted to learn.

They had a lot of similarities but many differences as well. They both had loving parents. Emily's were alive, and she missed them greatly. Emma's of course were dead; it seemed like forever ago. Emma told her as much of the truth as she dared. As to the rest, she filled in with this or that from books she had read. Being a bookworm payed off.

They talked for hours; a boy named Decker came in and served them some lunch. It was delicious even though the salted meat rations, Emma had never tasted anything like it before. It was a lighter fare as the crew including the cook were on shore leave, until they headed home.

Emma never asked where home was; questions like that would lead to the same back and Emma did not know enough about 19th century geography. She wasn't even sure they called it United Kingdom then. She found herself wishing she'd read more of the boring history books instead of side stepping those courses for one she found much more interesting.

After lunch, Emily showed Emma some of the pieces she'd been working on. She wasn't pregnant yet, but Emma could tell that she hoped to be soon. Her work was amazing, small minute stitches, bead work and the little designs that one put on clothing, that for the life of her, she could not remember the name of at that moment. Some of her creations could easily bring hundreds of dollars apiece back home maybe even more.

She'd made dresses for herself, petticoats, pantaloons, scarves, and shirts for Daniel, blankets, comforters and numerous baby things. It may seem commonplace in this era but back home a woman was lucky if she could cook well enough not to starve to death. Thinking of her own cooking she shuddered.

Emily noticed, "I've tired you out. You should rest." Taking the things from Emma's lap, Emily took them back to the trunk and began putting them away.

"You'll stay?" Emma said.

Emily looked as though she would decline but gave in and nodded.

Emma allowed herself to close her eyes soon she was fast asleep.

Emily sat down in the chair with her embroidery she was making herself a gown. Looking at the figure upon the bed, Emily decided in that moment that when she was finished with this, she would give it to Emma.

She worked for hours. Setting down the dress she walked out to the corridor. Decker should be up on deck; maybe he would know how long Daniel would be. This was her birthday and although she understood why Daniel had to go, he did promise her a day in town. She meant to see that he didn't forget that. Walking over the where Decker sat tending the sails. "When will the Captain be back?"

"Oh, mistress," Decker said, dropping the material in order to stand. Seeing what he was about to do, Emily quickly flagged him back down. He looked torn. It was not any easy decision to make does one conform to protocol and stand in the presence of a lady or does one take an order from a lady to remain seated. Holding in a chuckle Emily thought, Donavan has obviously not taught the young man everything.

"Don't argue with me Decker. There isn't a soul on this ship to see whether you are standing or not, and you do have work to do…do you not?" Emily pointed to the torn sail.

"Yes, mistress," Decker said, sitting back down.

"Good. Now about the Captain?"

Decker looked up; he shook his head. "No sign of him as yet mistress, don't rightly know when he be back, didn't say nothing only that he'd be back as soon as he could and that I was supposed to look out for ya."

Emily nodded, she'd heard the recital before, and she didn't like it any better now. If Daniel thought, she was going to miss her last chance for shopping before putting out he was seriously mistaken. Heading back to the cabin Emily thought of a way to get around the watchdog stationed above. Come hell or high water she'd find a way. Once back in the cabin she went in to check on Emma.

Emma was already partially out of bed. "Where were you? Did I sleep that long?" she said, looking a little lost.

"I'm sorry. You were sleeping so soundly I thought it would be alright if I went up top to speak with Decker. It looks like my husband will not make it back until much later. How are you with adventure?" she asked with a raised brow.

"I love adventures," Emma said, before her sleep fagged brain had a chance to weigh the repercussions.

"Fabulous!" Emily exclaimed and before Emma knew what-was-what, Emily had tossed her the gown she'd been working on. "Put this on. We are about the same size but if it does not fit, we can always alter it before we set out."

Holding the dress Emma ran her fingers over the soft velvet. "Set Out?"

"Why yes, it's my birthday don't you know, and Daniel promised I could go shopping in town on our last day in port. Well today is the last day. I have a pouch of money if that's what you're worried about," Emily said, like it was all settled.

"No, I am not worried about money, but do you think we should be going into town without a man for protection. Donavan said the town was a rough one."

"That's only at night. We will be back here before it gets too late. I just want to look around and maybe purchase a few things that I don't actually have to sew myself."

Emma could see that this was important to her, and after all, it was broad daylight, who'd trouble them in the middle of the day? Decision made she donned the petticoats and dress. It was a perfect fit; Emily did not have to do any adjustments at all.

"We're all set then," Emily said, heading for the door. "Wait here one moment; there is something I have to take care of before we leave. I don't want you ascending the ladder alone. I won't be long." Emily walked out, the door closing firmly behind her.

Emma wondered what had to be taken care of. She seemed like she was in such an all-fire hurry before. Sitting down behind Daniel's desk, Emma was amazed how much it was like her own.

She was running her fingers over the cool mahogany when Emily breezed through the door a little while later.

"All set," Emily said, thinking of Decker. He would be upset to be sure, but he'd get over it. Just think of it as another lesson Decker, she thought with a smile, one you aren't likely to get from Donavan.

Emma looked at the cunning look on Emily's face but did not mention it. Instead, she followed her companion in crime out the door.

Up top, Emily ushered Emma quickly to the last remaining boat. Unhooking the pulley, she and Emma climbed in together and managed to lower the heavy boat into the water. Each picking up and oar they began to row inland. It was funny Decker didn't come to help lower the boat. He could have even rowed them ashore then returned to the ship. They could easily catch a ride back with Daniel.

When they hit land, Emily took the bottom of her gown and petticoats lifted and tucked them into her sash. Emma did the same then they both stepped out into the shallow water to pull the boat the rest of the way in. Laughing at what they must look like and of course the thrill of adventures taken safely in the light of day, they started heading arm in arm toward town.

The journey had not taken them all that long; a few hours had gone by quickly with the non-stop chatter and comradery. They had quickly become the best of friends. Sisters. Walking over the cobblestones through one store and then the other, they shopped till they dropped. Stopping for tea in a little restaurant, the owner, Mags, was a very nice lady. She'd made fresh pastries supplied with their tea and they devoured them with relish. Shopping, talking and laughing was all that seemed on the agenda for today. Nothing sinister lurked as the hours ticked away.

Thinking back, Emma pondered what the lady had said when they first came in. Emily had shrugged it off as though it was nothing, but Emma wasn't so sure.

"My, my," Mags said, coming to the table. "If'n that don't beat all. Now I have the pleasure of seeing ye. Thought when the Capt'n came in here twice before, you'd not be comin'. Who this be? Yer sister?"

Emily had introduced Emma as a close friend of the family, making up something about them always looking alike.

Mags nodded sayin', "Yer husband don't have a look-a-like, does he?"

Emily shook her head.

"Me didn't thinks so, he came in again because he wanted more cookin'."

Emily laughed. Daniel coming into a place twice did not necessarily sound odd. Mags left the table, but Emma still wondered at the words the old woman had used.

Daniel coming in twice. Something didn't sit right. Emma knew for a fact that he did have a look-a-like. Dan. But would Dan be here? That was unlikely too, wasn't it? He hated lucid dreaming, why would he attempt to do something he hated? Emma was worried that maybe she'd been out longer than just the night. She'd thought it once before and shrugged it off, but what if Dan did awake before her what would he do?

Many people had come and gone out of the little diner while they sat sipping tea and talking. Not noticing how late it was, they sat there going through their purchases real and imagined.

Mags came over a little while after the place had cleared out. "Ye be headin' back to the ship mistresses? Maybe I can find ye and escort."

Emma shook her head. "That won't be necessary, Mags but thank you anyway."

Grabbing their parcels, the girls joined arms and went outside. Emma jumped when the door closed behind them. "God Emily!" she yelled. "What time is it? Oh my God it must be late? It's getting dark out."

Emily looked at Emma's worried face. "It's alright there will be a full moon tonight to guide us should we need it. We won't though, stop worrying you'll see. We will be back at the ship before you know it."

Emma wasn't so sure; she looked back toward the closed door, "Maybe we…"

Emily didn't let her finish the sentence. She pulled her along down the street.

Parcels and packages in hand it would take them a little longer than usual to make it back to the ship, but if they got to the path then all should be well. All Emma's dreams happened on the cobblestones not on the dirt. Picking up her pace Emma hurried for the path almost dragging Emily along. Now that they had made up their minds to go it alone it was best they got to where they were going before their situation could change.

Emily wondered what was wrong with Emma. For a girl who seemed to like adventure as much as she, well, she was acting peculiar. They had almost made it to the path when Emily stopped. "Wait!"

Emma came to a stop and looked at Emily. "What's wrong?" Emma asked.

"I saw Daniel, let's go back and he can escort us back to the ship."

"Daniel?"

Emma looked around but could not see anything. "Are you sure?"

Emily nodded breaking free of Emma's hold she turned back toward town. She walked quickly past one alley then the next stopping to scan the area as she passed by.

Emma was hard pressed to keep up. She was a quick little thing, one more item to put on the difference's column. Emma was almost running to keep up. Finally, she yelled out for Emily to stop. Emily did. Turning around, she looked at Emma, query in her eyes. "I cannot keep up in these," she held up the bottom of her skirt and pointed her toes to Emily.

A look of understanding came over Emily's face. "I'm sorry; they can be quite something if you are not use to them."

Emma dropped her skirt and began walking toward Emily. "I cannot see them anywhere maybe you were mistaken about seeing them. They are probably back at the ship right now and wondering where we are. Let's go back," Emma pleaded.

Shrugging Emily agreed if it wasn't them she'd seen, then they very well could be back at the ship and if they had found Decker locked below, they would be even more irate.

Linking her arm in Emma's once more, they made their way back to the path. The further they got into the trees, the darker it became. The moon shone brightly but the trees secluded them from much of it's light. It made walking slow. At this rate it would take them forever to get back to Maiden. If there was a hotel in town Emma would have suggested they stay there. But she knew from previous experience that there was no such thing here. They continued along in silence, which also added to the lengthiness of the journey.

In the trees a man stood watching as the two women passed. An evil sneer marred his face, as he thought of his good fortune. Time to round up the troops,. They would be on this road for some time yet. There was plenty of time to get them before they reached the ship. The more they walked on their own, the less he and his comrades would have to carry them. Backing away from the path, he headed back through the trees to his destination.

Emma shivered; something wasn't right. She could not see anything amiss, but portent told her that there was danger about. If they could only move a little faster, then they could make it to the ship, and safety. Decker was there and if need be there were weapons and places to hide. She'd never used any sort of weapon, but drastic situations called for drastic measure. However, if they could not get to the ship then what sort of chance did they have? None. "Do you have a weapon?"

Emily stopped dead in her tracks straining to see Emma's face. "Whatever do you mean?" she asked.

"A weapon, a knife or some such thing that if the need should arise, we can use to protect ourselves?"

Emily shook her head. "You worry overmuch, for someone who likes adventure." Emma didn't know what to say, she liked adventure, yes, those adventures found safely between the covers of a book.

"I do but is there anything wrong with being cautious?"

Emily lapsed silent for a moment. "No, suppose not. Yes, I do have a small dagger my pa gave me years ago. I always keep it in a leather sheath strapped to my leg. Now come on, we are wasting time. If we keep walking, we will be on the shore before you know it."

Emma felt a little better as she resumed her march. If Emily had a weapon, even a small one meant they might have a chance.

"Come you lazy blokes! They be passed the shelter soon and I for one am not about to board the Maiden if'n I don't have to." The three men stared at their crazed leader. "The Capt'n will make us pay but good should he find out what we've done," one of the men said.

"That may be, but he won't find out will he. There will be no witnesses. The trail is the perfect place to get them."

The others looked back and forth between them. Klaus may have been ousted from the ship, but they still had their positions. "Ye said there be two of them. Where'd this other come from? It is true that we've not been aboard since we got into port but there was only one Capt'n's wife when we left."

"Not wife ye stupid oaf! Another that looks like the Capt'n's wife but isn't, they be the same but different. I followed them today, they never seen me, but I see them, they looked so much alike they could be sisters. They seem to have developed a friendship, how that is I don't know, but it works to our advantage cause now there is more to share."

The men stared at their leader. Could it be possible Klaus had finally lost it? The same but different indeed.

Plan in place and ready to be carried out the men left their refuge in the woods heading for the trail ahead. They would catch the women there. Then they'd see for themselves how much this other woman looked like Mistress Emily. They had all been craving her for so long; the addition of another person had just about turned them off their course. Almost. They were men after all.

Just like opium when one gets a taste all they want is more. Emily had been the forbidden to them. A treasure they had been forced to look upon. Her beauty tormented them. Knowing they could not touch her. Have her. Made them mad with want. Each passing day of the long journey they planned for this very moment. Sure, things had changed with Klaus being thrown off the ship but now that they were all together again, with a small adjustment in the plan they could go after and soon have what they so craved.

Chapter Twenty-Five

Emma's senses burned; her nerves stretched beyond measure. Looking about her anxiously she cursed the darkness that covered the danger. Hearing a rustle in the bushes she grabbed Emily by the arm and started to run head long down the path.

"Slow down." Emily yelled as her packages dropped from her hand. "I cannot keep this up, not to mention one of us will get hurt on a branch or the like."

Emma ceased her hysterical running long enough for Emily to retrieve the fallen packages. "I heard something. We must be on our way!"

Having just finished picking up the packages, she looked at Emma, barely seeing the outline of her face, but she knew from the tone in her voice that she was scared. "What's the matter?" Emily asked.

What could Emma say, there was nothing short of the truth, now believe it or not it was time for Emily to realize what danger lurked about. Daniel may not have wanted her to know, but this had gone way too far. Emma could not protect the girl if the girl was not willing to help just a little.

"Emily, there is a man after you. Klaus. He was aboard Maiden a while back. Emily he was after you even when he was aboard the ship. Don't you remember someone was watching you? It made you uncomfortable. Right? Well, it was him. He found out you are in port and he means to follow through with his plans!" Emily didn't move. She just stood there as if she was in a trance.

Emma grabbed hold of her arm tugging her toward the beach.

"But how? How could you possibly know this? I just met you. How could you know?" Emily said, stumbling along in Emma's wake.

Emma didn't know how to answer her questions, so she opted for silence instead.

Emily pulled back on her hand "You are a sorceress; a witch. How else could you know!" she screeched, frantically fighting Emma's hold. Oh, dear this has gone from bad to worse, Emma thought. Now she thinks I am the danger.

"No, Emily, I am not a witch, I promise you that. Remember when I first woke up on the ship? Well, do you remember what I told Daniel? I did not tell him all of it. I was with Klaus, on the very same ship that brought him to port. I heard him detail out his plans and when we docked, I went in search of you. I am only here to keep you safe. Please believe me. I am not a witch! Now come! We must hurry!" Emma did not know if Emily believed her tale or not, frankly she didn't give a damn.

Pulling on her hand, Emily followed in silent contemplation. They had just spotted what appeared to be an opening in the trees up ahead, when out of nowhere four shadows broke through. They were big and they were fast, and Emma and Emily had no chance to react before something was thrown over their heads taking away what little light, they previously had. The packages fell back to the ground as the women were thrown over the shoulders of their abductors.

It was hard to breathe in the sack; Emma tried to stop her panic enough to get a full lungful of air. Her ribs ached as her body bounced up and down. As the men moved quickly the girls were bashed against their brawny shoulders. Each step knocked more of the precious air from their lungs, Emma did not know for certain how Emily was faring, but she would lay odds that the girl was in a panic and therefore using up more the stuffy air available in the sack.

If the journey was going to be a long one it was possible, she would lose consciousness before they arrived at their destination. Fighting to keep her wits about her, knowing she would need all she possessed once the miscreants reached their destination. She strained to hear little things, anything that may give her some indication as to which way, they were headed, away or toward the sea. If she could hear the it, then when she and Emily escaped, and they would escape, they would have some idea as to which way to run. Mostly all sounds were drowned out except for the crunch of her captor's feet as they hit the fallen leaves beneath.

Daniel observed immediately something was wrong when he reached the shore. There in plain sight was the shadow of one of his boats. Running for the trees, where he had hidden their boat from detection, he ripped away the debris throwing it every which way.

Trying to still Daniel's mad fit, his companion asked, "What in the world are you doing? There is a perfectly good boat right there on the beach."

Daniel did not cease until he'd uncovered the other boat completely. "That should not be. There should be only one boat on this shoreline. One. This is it right here!"

Dan could not see what the big panic was over having a second boat on shore. He glanced out toward the water. He could not see the ship through the ink-black of night. The moon provided very little help on that score; a boat could easily hide in the blackness. Daniel, tense, ready for anything that might be lurking about in the gloom, eyes scanning the area, senses honed.

Dan could still see nothing, as he silently followed Daniel's lead. Walking back to the boat, they launched heading for the Maiden. Once docked, they climbed the ladder. Where the hell was Decker, Daniel thought, angrily.

Dan followed behind Daniel searching the ship, his sword at the ready in case he encountered any intruders. They searched the deck, all seemed calm, nothing had been touched, and yet Daniel was still like a raging bull. "Hold up just a minute. Don't you think it is about time you told me what is going on? I mean likely if something is awry, I should be made aware of it to, my wife is possibly on this ship too."

"The crew has shore leave. All but one was in town until we ship out tomorrow. I cannot find the one I left here to protect the women."

Dan looked back at the shore. "You think he pulled out?"

Daniel shook his head and said, "He is not that way, he would have stayed here as ordered, forfeited his life if needs be to protect this ship or his mistress."

Now Dan was beginning to see what was bothering Daniel. If the man was not the type to up and leave where on earth was he?

Daniel headed for the companionway. Opening the hatch, he stepped into complete darkness. Not taking the time to light a lamp he went quickly to his cabin door and flung it wide. Nothing. Turning he ran into Dan who had just found his way to the cabin. "Stay here. I know this ship you don't." With that he was gone.

Dan made his way to the desk. Fumbling around he managed to find some matches to light a lantern. He waited, seated in Daniel's chair thinking of outcomes to a problem he had no solutions for. Thirty minutes later Daniel came back to the cabin, followed by a browbeaten youngster. Dan knew immediately, it was Decker. "What happened?"

Decker's eyes grew wide at the sound of a man's voice so familiar to him. He looked from one Captain to the other "Shir, there be two?"

Daniel laid a comforting hand on Decker's shoulder, the last thing he needed was for the boy to pass out. "It's alright, he is a fellow Captain, but he is not me, as you can see, I am right here." Decker nodded. "Now seat down and tell us both what happened. Who locked you in storage?"

Decker looked as though he would like to make something up, telling the Captain that it was his sweet little wife who had tricked him then locked him below would not earn him any points. After a moment's hesitation, he blurted, "It was the mistress, sir."

"Emily? Damn her hide!" Daniel fired questions at Decker finding out that Emily had done the little deed without much effort on her part at all.

Dan liked the fact that there was another man who had problems controlling a strong-willed wife. He could have laughed if the whole issue had not been so serious. It was. The women had apparently left the ship, using the boat they had just returned in, sometime after lunch. There is no way they shouldn't be back her by now. Unless.

The three of them headed back to shore anxiety causing silently but escalating fury. All were in accordance that when they finally found their errant women, providing they were okay of course, they'd kill them. Jumping out of the boat hauling it inland, they lit the two lanterns they had brought from the ship. Checking for prints along the shore seemed an impossible task, so knowing the women were headed into town, and would eventually return, they headed for the break in the trees.

It was slow going with each man spread out using his feet to brush aside leaves and twigs looking for any sign that might lead them in the right direction. Swinging the lamps back and forth this was and that, was slow going. Hoping they would find some sign as to where the women left the trail, if they were indeed taken from the path. If they found nothing then hopefully, they would find their ladies safely tucked away at Mags, for they were sure to have stopped by there.

About thirty minutes up the trail, the three men stopped and stared. There on the ground were four wrapped packages. Dan handed his lantern to Decker as he bent to retrieve one from the fallen leaves. It was a simple square package wrapped in brown paper and tied with a string, yet the sight was menacing for it meant that the women had not left the path by choice.

Daniel ran his finger through his hair, "It's theirs. It must be no one else would be coming down this trail with packages. Decker let's check the bushes, whoever took them must have left a trail of some kind. It may not be easy to find, but it has to be here."

Dan dropped the package and started searching as well. In the obscure light, the job was tedious. Looking at every branch, determining whether it had been broken by nature or by man. Many places had been trampled as animals darted off the trail, one was decidedly different; there were more broken branches and leaves almost like someone had piled them there. Looking at Daniel, Dan knew they thought the same thing. Emily and Emma would not have gone quietly; therefore, they would have had to be carried. If they were carried, then there would have to be two men for that alone. There was at least a third who had spent some time here covering their tracks.

Pulling the leaves and twigs away from the opening, you could tell once it was done that a large man had walked through. The cavity would have been easy to spot in the daylight. So, whoever took them were confident that they would either be out of the way by the time the sun came up or they would have finished what they had set out to do. Neither option was one they wanted to explore.

The night creatures sounded as each member of their party reasoned and concluded that, "There must be at least three."

"They must have nabbed them here. Taking off in that direction."

"What is it that they're a wantin' with the women? Why take 'em, Capt'n, why?"

Daniel felt icy fingers run along his spine as he contemplated what Decker had said.

Dan noticed the brief tremor that ran through the other man's body. So quick had he not been watching him closely he never would have seen it. "You bastard! I knew there was something you were not telling me back there. Jesus Christ!"

Taking an enraged step toward Daniel, Dan came face to face with Decker. "Tell me damn it! I deserve the truth. Now! Damn you, and tell your little watch dog to back off. I want to see your face." Daniel placed his hand on Decker's arm moving him out of the way.

"It's all right, Decker. I don't know much. The woman you claimed was your wife was found at the Boar and Hound last night by Donavan, given her looks, he thought she was Emily."

"She was passed out by the time he arrived at the ship. When she awoke, she seemed to know Emily, called her by name. Said she'd overheard a conversation where a man said he was going to get my wife. The man she described was a man I had thrown off my ship for drinking on shift."

"Klaus!" It came out before Dan could stop it.

Daniel and Decker both looked at him.

The word was uttered softly but in the dead of night they heard. Shit!

"How do you know Klaus?"

Dan was expecting the question but still did not have a plausible answer. Dan raised his shoulders. "I can't explain how I know. I just do. You must trust me. I am one of the good guys." He was getting nowhere fast as both men stared their expressions telling him, what he said was not good convincing enough by far.

"Oh, hell you two. We can stand here all night, or we can go and get the women before something terrible happens. What is it going to be? Are coming with me or not?" Dan stepped through the break in the trees; before he set his foot on the other side Daniel had his sleeve, whipping around ready for a fight.

Daniel nodded to Decker, "Let him go ahead he's better at trackin' than the two of us."

Decker took the lead, hunched over directing the small halo of light closer to the ground. At this rate, they'd better hope the villains did not go far, for it would take forever to find them. Impatience growing by leaps and bounds they followed Decker. The only sound, was that of the animals as they scattered when they got too close or the occasional hoot of an owl that had found his dinner. The calm made the time drag on as carefully they each placed one foot in front of the other.

Emma slowly came to her senses. She still could not see realizing her kidnappers must have left the sacks over them. Striving to hear something, she lay quietly not daring to move until she could make sure she was not being watched. Minutes ticked by. She wiggled. They had not bound her; reaching down she groped for the opening at the bottom of the sack but it was tightly bound. The immoral brutes must have secured it somehow.

Rolling on to her back she moved her fingers, hands then arms trying to get some circulation back into them. Surely if anyone was about, they would have called out by now. Feeling a little safer for what she was about to do, Emma called softly "Emily? Emily…" Finally, there was a faint moan. If Emma could verify which direction the sound came then she would know how to get to her. She continued calling urging her to keep making some noise however hushed.

Thinking it safer to search from her current position Emma began rolling about pursuing Emily's whimpers. It was so hard to keep her sense of direction when she could not see and hadn't the balance to stand. Many times, she'd rolled into nothing at all, other times she progressed no farther than what she assumed was a wall. Praying her luck did not run out before she'd located Emily; she kept calling and rolling toward the any sound she received back.

Her fortitude paid off as she rolled into something soft and heard the roof that came with expelled air. "Emily, my God are you okay?" When she got no reply, she repeated her words once more.

"Yes, I'm fine, I think. I must have fainted. They were bouncing me and I could not get enough air."

"They did the same with me. I think we are alone. They have not bound our hands and feet, but the sacks seem to have been tied with something. I can't seem to find the knot. I don't know if we will be able to get them off, but we have to try."

Emma ran her hand down the crease in her legs. Wedging her fingers between them she extended her reach past her knees. Hoping she'd found the bottom she pointed her fingers upward.

Success. But she still couldn't feel a rope, her damn fingers were still so numb she doubted she would have the coordination to untie a knot if she found one. Having no hope of finding the ties on her own sack she decided if she could get close enough to Emily then maybe Emily could feel for the rope that held them. Telling Emily what to do, together they focused their minds on finding anything that felt like rope. Her fingers were falling asleep again and her back was killing her from being in such and awkward position for so long, yet she would not give up.

"Jackpot, now hold still."

"Jack--- what?"

"Nothing. I've found the end, now hold still and pray I was a good Girl Scout."

"Girl--- what? I haven't a clue what you're talking about. Did you hit your head?"

Emma sighed. "No, I did not hit my head. Just forget what I said and hold still. I just about have it." Emily did as she was told and before long Emma had the knot freed. "All right, you're undone. Try to take the bloody thing off then you can set me free as well." Falling back against the wall she brought her fingers back under the sack. Kneading them she waited patiently for Emily to come to her rescue.

"Oh, that's better. It is still dark, but I am starting to feel a little better."

"I would like to know if anyone is about. We've made a lot of noise already. We should try not to make more until we get safely away from this place. Let's find a corner; from there we can start feeling the walls to see where a door is." One hand on the wall and the other in Emily's grasp Emma made her way down the wall feeling for a corner. "All right here it is. Now you go that way," she said, placing Emily's hand back on the wall. "I'll go this way. Keep going until we meet again. If you find something quietly let me know."

They set out in their perspective directions feeling for some break in the barrier. It was slow going, not wanting to miss anything they each laid one hand next to the other before moving it and continuing. So much time had passed Emma was worried the scoundrels would be back at any instant. If Klaus had intended to rape them, which she was certain was his plan, then why leave them here for too long. He wouldn't of course, which meant they most likely left shortly before Emma came to. She'd guessed that it took her about fifteen minutes to locate Emily and another fifteen to get them both free. It seemed a lot longer but that was the way disasters were.

Soon they met back at the opposite corner. "You didn't call out."

She could hear Emily breathing, "I did not find anything, and you did not call out either."

"I did not find anything either. We must have missed it. You keep going redo my section while I go over yours." Setting out on their hunt once more knowing if they found no exit, they would have to wait for their captors to return.

"That's it then. We must be buried." Emily thought about the general area the town was situated in. "It could be an old mine. Sometimes they are under ground."

Emma could feel hope rising. "Mine or not there still has to be an opening somewhere and if we are below ground then it stands to reason the door is above us. Reach up can you feel the roof?" Raising hands high above her head Emma could just manage to put her palms on the ceiling. "Do you feel it?"

"Yes, but how can we find a door like this?" Emma only knew they had to keep trying. Giving up was not an option. "The room is not that big. The door would not be by the wall, one would think it would be somewhere close the middle." Emma tried to calculate the possibilities in her head. She had woken against the wall but… "I have an idea. Stay here." Emma made her way back to the other corner. Stretching out, leaving her fingers so that they stayed in touched the crook, her body flat her arm extended back in Emily's direction.

Telling Emily to do the same she waited restlessly. "Okay, I've done what you asked now what?"

Emma felt deflated; she was hoping that their fingers would touch giving them some indication as to the width of the room.

"Stay there, I am going to come to you." Emma sidestepped in Emily's direction within in two strides she'd made it close enough that their hands touched. Okay about three feet. That wasn't bad. If she went back one step and turned having Emily do the same, they should be able to follow in a straight line to the other end of the cell.

Emily did as Emma asked and soon the women's patience and intelligence were rewarded as, they found a crack. Stopping, each traced the crack with their fingers. It was a square possibly three feet by three feet. "A trap door." Emily's words came out in wonder.

"Yes, let's each take a step closer together then push up. We will see if we can move it." The door moved upward but they were not tall enough to make it flip out of its bed.

"Get on my shoulders." Emma prayed she had the strength to lift Emily that high. "We aren't going to have much time. I do not know how long I can hold you, if I manage to stand up, you might not have a lot of head room. Be ready, push as hard as you can."

Emily climbed on. Emma stood. She had been right; she was not able to hold her for very long. Thankfully it was long enough, Emily used all her strength and with one great heave the door flipped back landing with a resounding crash that echoed about the room.

Emma collapsed, Emily landed on top of her. Catching her wind, she stood once more. "I'll give you a leg up then you can find something to help me get through. We've got to hurry. That crash could have been heard by anyone."

Emily landed on her stomach on the floor above. It was lighter here; shards of moonlight came through the cracks in the old run-down cabin. Still there was nothing she could use to help Emma up. "Emma, can you get back to the ropes? If you can find them, toss the end up, there is nothing here that I can see."

There was a little light coming through the hole in the roof so it made it easier for Emma to find the ropes. Coming back, she tossed one end up. Emily clasped it tightly. Sitting on the floor bracing her feet against the other side of the opening. The makeshift ladder was enough for Emma to climb up.

Muscles sore, they struggled to stand. Making their way quickly to the door, they dashed into the moonlit night heading away from the cabin. Neither knowing which direction to take nor how much time remained Emma and Emily only worried about getting themselves safely away from their jail. Walking as quickly as feasible they headed for the shelter of the trees and the shadows.

Heads down concentrating on seeing the trail neither heard the approaching footsteps.

"Well, well. What do have h're? Looks like our littl' guests didna want ta wait for the celebration. And here we's planned such a fun time for ye."

Emma grabbed Emily. Turning, they tried to run on stiff legs away from the two men before them. They had not made it more than a couple of steps when two more men blocked their escape.

Dragging them kicking and screaming back to the cabin, they were simultaneously thrown on the floor in a heap, where, gasping for breath, they stared up at their guards. Emma was already planning, as she moved away from Emily she reached up under her skirts, her actions hidden by her body, she pleaded with her eyes not wanting Emily to give their movements away. She soon felt what she sought. Undoing the strings that secured the small dagger in it sheath, she slid her hand back keeping it hidden from view. As she moved into a sitting position, she slowly inserted the dagger under her own sash.

The lanterns lit. Providing them with a good look at their captors. Klaus's tallish-bulky figure, scraggily filthy brown hair that if clean should have been light brown but as it was looked almost black. The growth of hair on his face was scattered unevenly giving him the appearance of the demon he was. His blackened and missing teeth showed as he stood grinning maliciously, hands on his hip's feet spread wide and the stench emanating from him, was sickening.

The others weren't much better big, brawny, and stupid looking. Emma figured she stood a chance if Klaus was the smartest of the lot. One of the men was very large, and if they relied on strength alone, they would never get by him. He stood in front of the doorway a little ways back from the group, hands over his chest as though surveying what he saw and not liking it one bit. He must know what Klaus intended. If he did not like it then why was he here?

She may be way off base, but Emma did not think so. Reading people was her job. She was good at it. Being able to determine what a client was feeling had enabled her to go about the problem at an angle in which the solution would be satisfactorily reached. She had other concerns for now. She'd find a way to use that one when they were free of the more threatening ones.

Three of them, evil sneers upon their ugly faces, advanced to where they were huddled in the corner. By unspoken vows, neither showed the fear that coursed through their petite frames. Emma knew from experience people like these received more thrill from seeing the fear, causing the fear, than the actual act itself. Emily had not said a word, Emma knew she was scared. Yet she did not show it. She sat glaring up at the men even as they stooped grabbing them viciously about the shoulders and hauling them into a standing position. Backs pushed against the wall they had little hope of moving. Yet.

"Stand back ye bastards they be mine first! That little bitch had been askin' for it since she boarded the Maiden and now I's gonna give her what she's been missin' with that husband of hers." Standing to the side the men held on tight as Klaus advanced toward Emily. Twisting her breast in his hands he waited for the sound of terror that never failed to inflate his loins. What he got instead was as much of a surprise to Emma as it had been to him. Emily puckered her lips sending a goodly amount of spit into Klaus's repulsive face.

Emma was hard pressed not to laugh. Klaus did not remove the spatter from his face as he lift a huge hand and bringing it down hard over Emily's left cheek. Tears welled up in her eyes, but she refused to release them. Emma knew her bravado could not possibly last forever she had to draw Klaus's attention away from Emily allowing the girl time to compose herself.

Emma's leg struck out, even held down by her skirts she managed to connect with his shin, but it was enough as he stepped in front of her. Seizing her chin between his fingers squeezing tightly as he stared down into her eyes. Returning look for intense look, she shook the other man's hand off her shoulder. Reaching out she placed her hands on either side of his ribcage.

"Now that's more like it." Klaus gave a quick look of disgust to Emily. "See m'dear she knows a real man. Don't ye?"

Giving her an open-mouthed grin that made her stomach curdle like sour milk his lips descended on her with brute force. Keeping her stomach in place she pulled him forward closer to her, as fast as lightning her leg came up. Klaus let out a foul oath as he tumbled forward sliding down her to the floor holding his crotch. Emma silently thanked Andre for his lessons in self-defense.

Giving a nod to Emily, they turned sideways landing the otherwise occupied men with the same blow. Neither was close enough to make good contact and although the blow was enough to be felt neither man dropped like their leader. Stepping over Klaus they headed for the door. The big guy smiled at them but said not a word as he reached for the latch on the door.

Just as he turned to allow the women free Emma saw a silver streak, yelling she was not quick enough as the blade of the stiletto sliced through his side literally pinning him to the door. Emily bent over vomiting. Emma tried to help but it was hard to take her eyes off the only savior they had in this mess. "I'm so sorry." Was all she got out before the big man's eyes closed; he slumped his dead weight pulling the big knife through his body until he lay effectively blocking their escape route.

Emma turned to Emily then. Helping the girl stand she took the bottom of her skirt and cleaned her mouth before walking away from the mess. Standing in the corner they considered their next move. They weren't given long. Klaus was up and hobbling over to them rage distorting his features. He was followed by his two dogs that didn't look any happier than he was. At least, Emma thought, they should be sore enough they won't think of rape for a while. What would they do to them in the meantime? Surely, they would make them pay. She hoped they both had the strength to survive what they would dish out.

Tied in chairs, butted up against the wall, their heads drooping as they gathered what little remaining power they had. It had been a long night. Their bodies, stiff with disuse and their wrists sore from being tied so tightly behind their back. Dawn was breaking, light was streaming into the cabin. Yet Emma could barely open her eyes. They had paid for what they had done. Several times she echoed Emily's pain filled screams as they were struck one blow after another. Whenever they would succumb to the peace of unconsciousness, water was tossed upon them. Still drenched and achingly cold they sat, waiting for the next round of punches.

"We're runnin' outta time! Shouldn't we be takin' them? Surely someone 'll come lookin' for 'em," one of them said.

"The fight should be outta em now. Untie em and we'll have a bit of fun 'efore its time to make a run." It was hard to be thankful as the ropes were removed allowing circulation to flow. Dragging them out of the chairs they laid them on the floor. "We do em both together?" There was no comment coming back so Emma assumed their time had run out.

She heard the rip of the fabric the roaring sounds of men disrobing. She'd lost. She was weak. Once more she was at the mercy of some bastard. Only this time she was not alone. She'd dragged an innocent girl along with her. She'd only made matters worse by fighting. It would have been better had she played the whore. Maybe then she could have saved Emily from this fate. God help her she was still a coward. Her heart constricted but her pain ebbed into a blissful numbness as she accepted her destiny.

Chapter Twenty-Six

The light was a godsend in one way at least. The men were now able to see more than a few feet in front of them. It made their progress much quicker. Decker was the first to spot the cabin in the distance. It was the first sign of any place that looked like it might hold what they had been searching for. It was run-down. Most likely it had been abandoned for years. Secluded, it offered everything a villain could want when he was up to no good.

Quickening their paces, the hurriedly made their way noiselessly to the door of the cabin. Listening for sounds from within, it didn't take long until they heard the men discussing the fates of their captives. It was a fate neither Dan nor Daniel was ready to accept. Assessing the situation, it became clear the only way in was through the door. Hopefully surprise would be on their side.

Decker and Dan stood on either side of the door waiting for Daniel to land the kick that would send it flying. That was the plan. Then they'd converge on the sons-a-bitches before they had a chance to react. Daniel's leg came up, landing a well-placed blow to the middle of the door. It moved but did not open. The noise would have alerted the men inside, their only hope was to get past what was barricading the door before the men inside turned on their prisoners.

All three merged into one force pushing against the door. Feeling the door move and hearing something sliding on the floor pushing harder the barrier was finally out of the way. Charging through the door their fears released. Coming to a stop both men cried out in horror. The faces of their wives were battered and bloody, their skirts had been torn beyond repair. They were filthy, rumpled and soaked. However, that was not what had these powerfully built men in such a fret. No; it was the shiny silver blades held tightly at their throats, that worried them, most of all.

"Let em go Klaus, your fights with me."

Klaus smiled. "There ye go again thinkin' it's all just about you. It was never about ye. Never. I've wanted her and now I've got her so's ye best be gettin' back from the door unless you want to see her die."

Both men took a step back. Wishing they could see into their wife's eyes, they stood in front of the door backing no further, but quickly weighing their options. Daniel was first to come up with an idea.

"The law of the land says if you want something that belongs to someone else, there must be a duel, spoils going to the victor."

Klaus hated the young Captain. He never could stand taking orders and when those orders came from a boy instead of a man it only served to antagonize him more. What he wouldn't give to see the little son of snake lickin' his boots. Handing Emily off to the man next to him he came at Daniel like a raging bull the impact throwing them both out the door.

Emma looked up, seeing Dan was like digesting all the power in the universe. The man's grip had loosened somewhat as he struggled to see Klaus taking on the Captain. A great deal would depend on the outcome of that fight. He was not as dumb as Emma had originally mistaken him for. Not quite, she thought as she bent her arm bringing it back as hard as she could into his mid-section.

Dan made his move as soon as he seen what she was about to do and by the time the man's lungs filled with air once more, he had him. Wrestling the knife away from him he gave him a hard blow the temple. He went down quickly. Dan pulled Emma close feeling her; so glad she was all right. Looking up he noticed the other man had pulled Emily back and was heading out the door. Emma tried to break free of Dan's hold. She had to get Emily free. Dan simply shook his head knowing that somewhere just beyond the exit Decker lurked.

"She'll be okay."

Emma heard the words at the same time she seen a hand come down on the back of the scoundrel's neck. Hanging on to the man's shirt Decker waited for Emily to get out of the way before letting go. The man fell to the floor. Emma went to Emily, wrapping her arms around her, she held her close. They had survived. Emma was not the hero, but they had survived.

Leading both women back to the chair Decker tended their cuts and bruises as best he could while Dan ran to help Daniel.

He was in time to see Klaus's fist fall knocking Daniel to another world. Younger of the two he really stood no chance against Klaus. He fought well but he fought like a gentleman. Dan feared he couldn't do much better but jumped in full force hoping that Klaus was at least tired enough he could compete. He could fight when he had to, but in his time; he hadn't had to very often.

Putting Klaus in a chokehold was damn near impossible but Dan was doing the best he could. If his bloody neck weren't so large it would have worked instead it reacted like a red flag in front of an already enraged bull. Klaus stood lifting Dan off the ground. Fist coming over his shoulder met with Dan's eye forcing him to lose what precarious hold he had. Klaus spun around faster than someone of his size had a right to move, or so Dan thought.

Ducking he evaded the fist coming at him. Dodging the blows giving him time to think he let Klaus swing punch after punch. He'd be all right if he could stay out of arms reach. With any luck Klaus would tire then Dan would get his chance. Anger built in him as he thought of those fists coming down on Emma and Emily. These thoughts although bringing anger to his body clouded his mind. He had to let it go.

Decker cleaned the women as best as he could. There was a little water left in a bucket on the floor. Smelling the water, he wrinkled up his nose. It was not the cleanest, but it would have to do until they got away from this place. He wanted desperately to go out and help but knew that he could not justify his leaving the Captn's' woman and her friend. Turning to Emily, finished with Emma, Decker began gently cleaning her face.

Klaus caught Dan by the throat. Squeezing he could feel himself go as the world before his eyes blurred. No! His mind screamed. No! This cannot be happening it's a fuckin' dream! Dream. Yes, that's what it was. Then why couldn't he call upon himself for more power? He couldn't clear his mind fighting for air as he was. He drifted, threading his fingers through Klaus's hair, maintaining a delicate hold on the dream world by focusing on Klaus's ugly mug then pushed all other thoughts from his mind.

Emma came out of the cabin; a knife she had found tucked in the folds of her skirt. It was not the dagger, a little bigger more cumbersome and harder to hide but it was sharp and if it was needed, she would find a way to use it. Daniel was on the ground apparently unconscious. Dan was nowhere in sight. Klaus stood staring at his hands as though they held the answer to some secret

251

question only he knew. Scanning the area for her husband. Where was he? He had not taken off, he wouldn't. What had the bastard done with him? Emma carefully removed the knife, as she silently moved behind Klaus.

Turning Klaus struck out the blow did not connect as well as it could have but it did connect well enough to send her and the dagger flying in opposite directions. Emma lay on the ground before him staring as he grabbed his head. He was in pain that was plain to see yet Emma could see no sign of the cause. Buckled over he started to straighten. Emma could swear she seen Dan's face within his. His image was there only for a moment before Klaus's features took over once more.

Snatching her dress, he raised her high off the ground. Emma was looking down into his eyes. He looked as though he'd gone insane. His eyes glowed, almost black, as his gaze burned through her. Then a hint of blue, the pure blue of the sea, they were Dan's eyes she thought before his hold on her released and she rushed toward the earth.

On his knees Klaus rocked back and forth holding his head. Emma swiftly found her little dagger; it was not the greatest weapon. She looked toward Daniel; his knife lay in the dirt beside him. Bigger was not always better, one had to be able to control what one was wielding she uttered as she bent down to retrieve the dagger. Klaus was on his feet again, coming at her. His great weight slammed into her knocking her to the ground.

"Damn you! Use that thing. I can't hold him!" It was Dan's voice.

She heard Dan's voice; still she could not see him. Looking up she stared into the sapphire blue eyes that surely belonged to her husband. "I love you." She thrust the dagger upward embedding it into Klaus's black heart. He writhed for a moment, then squirmed and turned over on his back with a long sigh as the life hissed out of him. Daniel kicked Klaus's body off her. Helping her up off the ground Emma fused herself to him sobbing.

"Hush now, dear; it's all right, shhh…Hush now," Beatrice said, as she cradled Emma in her arms. "It's all right now, Em; I've got you. You're safe now. Come on dry the eyes. Calm yourself down and tell me what happened."

Emma shuddered trying to control her running away sobs. Beatrice's hand was so soothing against her back. She felt like a little girl again. Being comforted by a parent; only she was not a child, all be it acting like one she thought criticizing herself, and Beatrice was not her parent, though probably the closest thing she had right now. Emma lifted her head off Beatrice's shoulder "I'm okay now really. Where's Dan?"

"He's asleep, dear. He's been beside you all night." Emma looked down at her sleeping husband. "I don't understand why you are here. What time is it? Why is Dan sleeping while you are here?"

Beatrice moved back to the chair. "Dan called and asked me to come by and watch over you both. He told me about the dreams Emma. Really you should have told me. We were both worried sick when we discovered the pills you took. How many of the bloody things did you cram down your throat anyway? You have been out, near as I can figure for close to 24 hours."

Emma rubbed the remaining wetness from her cheeks. "Why is Dan sleeping though? He came to me in my dreams. I think I hurt him. Why isn't he awake?"

Stretching over she placed a hand on his forehead. He laid spread out completely clothed. Calm and peaceful he did not move. Scared Emma touched her hand to his heart. "He's okay you know. At least I believe he is. Time will tell. He's only been out for eight hours. Let's see how he is after twelve. I don't think it will take him as long to come around as it did for you."

"What do you mean?" Emma pinned Beatrice with a glare.

"Well, I mean just what I said. Dan took the same medication you did. Now wipe that look off your face it's not like I told him to do it. As a matter of fact, my dear had you not run head long into this mess scaring the daylights out of that young man there. I venture to say none of this would have happened."

Emma knew she was right. But she really thought she could have the entire problem handled and be back here before he woke up. Twenty-four hours. Dan must have been going crazy.

Beatrice left the room quietly. Getting a pot of coffee under way she sat at the table waiting for it to finish. She was so tired. She'd fallen asleep for a little while only to be startled awake by Emma thrashing around in the bed. Her body jumped like she'd been going through convulsions. Beatrice had been ready to call the ambulance when the convulsions stopped. She stayed with her hand on Emma's forehead judging her temperature when her nose gave way to a stream of blood. She'd held her nose, covered it with a cloth, and done everything she could possibly think of to get the flow dammed. After about fifteen minutes it had slowed to a trickle, before finally stopping. Bathing her face and tossing the bloodied rags in the laundry she went back to her seat. It wasn't long after that Emma awoke, sobbing.

Coffee finished, she brought everything into the bedroom. Emma was on the floor kneeling on Dan's side of the bed her head resting on his heart. "Whatever are you doing Emma?" Setting the tray down on the nightstand Beatrice handed Emma a cup of coffee. "I can feel him breathe better from here. If I can hear his heart, it reassures me."

Once a long time ago, she'd known a love like that. She still did, thinking of Dexter, only it was different now. Different yet still there. It was a love that would last forever. It would grow stronger over the rough times only to soar over the great ones. It is the kind of thing that only comes once in a lifetime.

Beatrice had never lost hope after Dexter's accident; she could never leave him or allow him to leave her. He was still in there somewhere, still there, still…still…still. Her heart would always belong to him. While others took comfort from their so-called normal relationships Beatrice took comfort from the memories. Found solace in her dreams. Memories she'd shared with no one. She never would. They were hers and hers alone, at least until the time came that she could in truth be with her love once more.

"You look tired. I'll call if I need you. Why don't you grab a few hours' sleep in my room?"

Beatrice nodded, the only sign she'd heard anything.

Shortly after she left the room, Emma brought her chair to Dan's side of the bed. Holding his hand, as she'd done in the hospital, she spoke to him. Calling to his unconscious, urging him home.

Dan could hear singing; it was the sound of angels. Following the sound, he floated above his body looking down at the body lying face down in the dirt. This was it then. He was dead. He could not remember what happened. Had no recollection of the pain that had caused his demise. The angels sounded lovely. He was tired. They offered him a quiet solitude where he could finally rest.

The journey was arduous, but the rewards would be beyond measure. The light shone bright in his eyes as he followed the angel's song. Closer and closer the light came. It was almost blinding in its intensity. The words pouring from the angel were becoming clearer, the haze was lifting as he realized he was close to the end of his trek. So nice; sing some more.

Emma had run out of things to say just before the sun came up. She let the light pour through the blinds hoping Dan would feel its heat and come home. There were not many songs she knew but when there were no more words, she blended various verses together in some semblance of a song. She'd just started on another verse of you are my sunshine, it seemed fitting in the morning light, when Dan's eyelashes fluttered.

She stopped singing, only to hear his voice softly slurred with sleep "So nice; sing some more." She smiled.

It was a good thing he was out of it. She really was a terrible singer. Picking up where she left off, she belted out the remainder of the song.

Dan opened his eyes and murmured, "I knew an angel was calling."

"Hardly an angel. You had me worried sick. Beatrice is sleeping. How are you feeling?"

Trying to assess her rapid-fire questions Dan propped himself up on his elbows, "You look like an angel to me. I wonder what the penalty would be for killing an angel."

Emma smiled. "Many, many years in purgatory I would imagine."

Pulling her close he kissed her soundly.

"What was that for?"

"I figured if I couldn't kill the angel, I should at least take pleasure where I can." Wiggling his brows, Emma laughed.

Snuggling close, Emma tried to think of something to say about what had happened. Finally, by silent mutual consent they let the matter rest. Neither understood completely what had transpired nor why. It was a mystery better left unsolved. For now.

Storming into the room a couple of hours later, Beatrice looked at the two lovebirds in annoyance. "How long has he been awake?"

Emma looked at Beatrice. She was really upset. "Just for an hour or so. What has you in such a huff this morning? Oh my God! You're late for work. I should have woken you I'm sorry."

"No, I'm not late for work. I took today off because of your little stunt. Of course, you wouldn't know that, because you were among the comatose at the time. And I'm not in a huff!"

Dan's body could no longer contain his laughter and soon Emma was laughing right along with him.

"What's so funny? Have you taken more drugs?" Stamping her foot arms crossed over her chair Beatrice waited for an answer.

"Sorry…Beatrice…Oh my…Just give me a minute." Emma said between fits of laughter.

It was Dan who got himself under control first. "Thanks for standing by. You truly are a treasure."

Beatrice blushed with the compliment. "Well just get yourselves out of bed and come into the kitchen. I have breakfast started. You need to eat. Then you need to talk."

It was an order; both Emma and Dan knew it as they watched her leave the bedroom once more.

Dan sat down at the table. "Smells delicious."

Emma walked over to Beatrice and kissed her cheek, "Thank you."

The words were simple but whispered as they were they held a wealth of emotion. Beatrice fought the tears that threatened to undo her. Wiping her eyes as though to remove a particle of dust she set a plate of pancakes on the table where the delicious meal together.

Placing the dishes in the sink Beatrice handed Emma another plate, "I read those books of yours last night. They are very interesting. Have you read them all?" The plate hovered above the soapy water only a second before being submerged with the rest of the dishes.

"Yes. Why don't we go into the living room with Dan for a while and let the rest soak?"

"Sure, I'll be a quick minute." Beatrice went to the bedroom and retrieved Emma's notes from the night before. She'd made some good references to the symbols she'd written. Coming into the living room whatever Dan and Emma had been saying was cut short by her arrival. Beatrice knew they would rather talk of anything else but she didn't let that sway her. Soon she would have all the details of their dream, or at least what they could remember.

"Emma, I found more information to go with the note you made. The one Dan showed me."

Emma looked at Dan in confusion.

"It was the one that you avoided showing me. The one you buried in the nightstand so I wouldn't see it. It was also the one that led me to believe you had gone into the dream world unnaturally."

Emma turned back to Beatrice not wanting to cross that bridge yet.

"I had a lot of time to think last night. That sinking ground, it could have been quicksand, and so I looked it up under the dream symbols. I found that quicksand represents an unpredictable shift in the emotional landscape, one that could be potentially dangerous.

Dan's expression said they already determined that one. But when he looked as though he would speak, Beatrice cut him off.

No, don't interrupt I'm not finished. The man in your dreams, well I had a harder time with that one, the way you wrote about him reminded me of the monster stories from when I was a kid, so I looked up monsters. There were quite a few explanations but there was one general one; the need to confront something, either past terrors or repressed emotions. Those fit in with what you told me about your dream. There are symbols, I jotted down while you two were relaying your stories. Care to hear them?"

Emma and Dan both nodded. "All right then, a ship; is a means of transportation across unconscious waters. The iceberg; a place where the unconscious and conscious minds meet, a signal of sorts, you spotted the iceberg, then the ship was that correct?"

Emma nodded and Beatrice continued.

"The mist; that simply conveys confusion. Given how you both went under I am surprised that's all you encountered. It could have been much worse. Where was I…oh yeah? The jaws; something overwhelming enough it threatens to consume. The wolf; devouring forces, representing the principal of evil, craftiness and fierceness and lastly, the wound, is a symbol of unresolved emotions or fears, so you see they're all linked."

"But what about Dan he never encountered those things."

Beatrice shook her head. "He wouldn't, his only fear was for you. He may have had a foggy mind, but he was not being warned of a danger for him there was no danger."

"How can you say that I stabbed him?"

"No dear, you stabbed that Klaus fellow. Dan was merely the altar where you found the wisdom to do what must be done. Did you know a sacrifice such as Dan made is also a sign? It is. It symbolizes letting go; through sacrifice comes change and new beginnings. This book is amazing! Just Fabulous. Look Dan your angel, it wasn't Emma, oh sorry dear that didn't come out right. An Angel is used to guide or inform. Isn't this wonderful?"

Dan and Emma stared at the woman they thought they knew. One night without sleep, a few books and she'd become an addict.

It was funny how she took to the whole thing. Here they had been so worried about telling her everything for fear she would think them crazy. Here it was not even twenty-four hours after the incident had occurred, one where most would have checked them both into the looney bin, and she was now some kind of expert. She really seemed to enjoy being hooked, so what was the possible harm in giving a lonely woman a hobby?

They spent the rest of the day lounging about and partaking in idle chatter and watching TV. Just after the final supper dishes were done Bea left for home. They had decided to meet again after Thanksgiving and go house hunting; Beatrice had more than deserved the right to accompany them. To Emma she'd passed over the line of just being a close friend. To her, Beatrice was and older sister, a fine substitute for the family she no longer had on this earth.

So much had seemed to happen in such a short time, they all had the feeling of being long-time acquaintances, days had turned into weeks; weeks into months; months into years and years into decades. It was a bond they shared now. Not just Dan and her but Bea as well. It was a bond that would last forever.

Dan and Emma had watched a movie before heading to bed. They made love for hours. Recent near-death experiences seemed to add fuel to an already raging inferno of passion. Not that either of them would care to come that close again. She did hope the dreams continued, just not in such a dramatic fashion. It was one more thing they could share. Even without it though, they'd always have the fire, the passion and the love. They always would. Emma vowed quietly, throughout all time.

Epilogue

Thanksgiving One Year Later, Dundalk, MD

Dan's mother had put on a family dinner so they had driven there the night before so that they could lend a hand. His mother would not allow Emma to do anything except sit and talk. "Tell me about yourself." She had asked in a manner that brooked no refusal

They talked and talked, Emma knew right away that she would get along with them. They were a little older than her parents had been, and they were so welcoming.

Dan's mother was a small woman, dark hair and blue eyes, not as startling as her husband's but captivating just the same. The resemblance came when she was introduced to Dan's dad. He was an older copy of Dan himself. Emma joked with him that maybe she should have been introduced to his father before deciding to marry him, that she would have known what she was in for.

Dan answered back with a smack across her bottom. Where the hell he ever picked up such a thing she would never know, secretly she enjoyed that fun form of discipline not that she would ever be dumb enough to tell him that. He already had too much to Lord over her should the need arise. They had been married for over a year now, and the love that they shared still grew with each passing day.

The dreams they use to share, were now a rarity. All seemed to be right with both worlds. The last time she'd dreamt of Emily, she'd just given birth to a healthy baby boy. Emma ran a comforting hand over her stomach. "Soon little one." She was pretty sure that the dream she had was telling her she was about to have a baby boy as well. They opted for not knowing, deciding that a little surprise now and again did wonders for the soul.

His parents were the doting grandparents, Emma could already tell they were going to spoil Dan junior rotten. That was okay by her. Life was too short not to have a few spoils. She laughed thinking of the spoils she'd received from

Dan when she first told him she was going to have a baby. He left the house, returning hours later with toys and toys some for the baby and some for her too. They had laughed and made love, right there on the floor, toys all around them.

They had bought a little three-bedroom rancher just outside of Washington. They both fell in love with the simplicity of the place and the surrounding area. The house was white; the previous owners had planted flowers everywhere. They did not know what they were until all started blooming at the beginning of summer. The scents would waft throughout the house with just the slightest breeze from outside.

Dan didn't Captain the ships anymore unless he absolutely had to. Porter handled everything at the office conferring with Dan over the phone. The house had a spare room, which served as a home office. Emma was on maternity leave right now, but she fully intended to go back to work after a year at home. Dan figured that would give them enough time to iron out any bugs with the arrangement. He'd taken more of the office type duties which up til' now he seemed to shun. Porter assisted tremendously with the transformation, and Dan was doing quite well now. Only he was worried.

"Honey, come and help me," Dan called, from the base of the stairs.

"What do you need love?" Emma called back.

"Come now and you'll find out." Dan said holding his hand out to lure her to him. Emma heaved herself up out of the chair, she really would be glad when this child decided to make his appearance into this world. He was a week late already and Emma was tired of being tired. Walking to the stairs she stared up at the great number of steps that lay before her.

"Oh, don't be a wimp," Dan teased. Taking her hand in his he led her up the fight of stairs. Instead of going to their room, which is where she'd assumed, they were headed, Dan reached up and opened a trap door. Pulling down the ladder from inside Dan handed Emma up the rungs, following close behind her in case she should slip.

"The attic?" Emma said, already knowing it was but couldn't fathom why he would want to come up here.

"Yes, the attic, but you already guessed that didn't you my smart wife," Dan said, with a raise of his brow.

"Smart ass," she answered back softening the insult with a peck on his cheek.

"I meant why?"

"That my dear is the surprise." Dan said sitting down on an old crate, he pats the top, motioning for Emma to sit. "I had a chance to talk to my father this morning. He said there might be some things in here for the baby. Among other things."

Emma looked at him "What other things?"

"Well as I have told you before, O'Brien's have lived in this house long before my family did. Everything from generations had been stored up here. Dad and Mom have never thrown anything out even though they had no interest in what might be up here."

"So, being as how I have free time on my hands, working at home, I thought maybe I would do some research into our family tree? That way if our son or daughter wishes to know where his or her roots are, then we have something to show them." Dan cradled Emma's stomach with the palm of his hand. He loved this child so much and it wasn't even here yet. He was about to remove his hand when he felt Emma's muscles tense, a sure sign that the baby was about to move. They waited silently and sure enough, it kicked. "That little thing must be part mule," Dan said. "I can't believe how hard he can kick."

It was Emma's turn to raise a brow. "He?" Dan looked at her slyly and shrugged. Reaching for the first box, he never answered Emma's question, as he lifted the lid and began removing the contents from inside. Emma watched as he exclaimed over this or that. Most weren't too old, most likely something of his mother's or father's.

Picking up one thing or another Dan modeled for Emma, soon she was laughing so hard she had to make her way back down the long stairs to find a bathroom. Relieving herself she came back up into the attic to find Dan in a dark corner staring down at something. His hands were shaking.

"Dan what's wrong?" Emma demanded, concern shadowing all else. She ran to the corner almost tripping over the things strewn all over the attic floor. "Dan?" Emma said, placing a comforting hand on his shoulder. "Whatever is the matter?" Kneeling beside him Emma took a book from his hand. It was old, leather bound in the dark reaches of the attic it was all she could make out. Taking the book, she walked closer to the trap door.

"Don't bother," Dan said hypnotically.

Emma looked over at him. "What?"

"I said don't bother I know what it is."

Emma shook her head and said, "How could you possibly know it was too dark over there to read anything or see any markings."

Dan got up and walked to her, taking the book from her grasp, saying, "You gave it to me. Years ago. I remember you gave it to me on my first journey after you had our son. It was a present from you."

Emma stared not knowing what the heck he was talking about. "Dan, your scaring me, I don't understand. Can't you let me see it?"

Dan was apprehensive but he nodded removing the fog from his head, he opened the book. Running a loving finger over the inscription he read, "Captain's Log." Handing the book back to Emma he continued without seeing the words as Emma followed along in astonishment.

"The year of our Lord 1803,

Cornwall, England.

Property of

Captain Daniel O'Brien of 'The Maiden'

'Wherever you are my love, my heart will always be with you.

Throughout all time we are forever linked'

Forever yours, Emily Claremore O'Brien."

By the time Dan had finished reciting the inscription Emma was crying, her mind flashed back to a small cottage. She could hear the waves crashing against the rocks echoing in from the cliffs. She dipped the pen into the inkwell, wrote the words that would stay with Daniel throughout all time whenever he was away from home.

"Throughout all time we are forever linked," Emma said, grabbing Dan and hugging him close.

"Throughout all time," he replied, kissing the top of her head.

END